The King's City

The Demon War Chronicles Book 3

Nina D'Aleo

First published by Momentum in 2016
This edition published in 2016 by Momentum
Pan Macmillan Australia Pty Ltd
1 Market Street, Sydney 2000

A CIP record for this book is available at the National Library of Australia

The King's City: The Demon War Chronicles 3

EPUB format: 9781760302641
Mobi format: 9781760302658
Print on Demand format: 9781760302719

Cover design by Raewyn Brack
Edited by Vanessa Lanaway
Proofread by Lauren Choplin

Macmillan Digital Australia: www.macmillandigital.com.au

To report a typographical error, please visit momentumbooks.com.au/contact/

Visit www.momentumbooks.com.au to read more about all our books and to buy books online. You will also find features, author interviews and news of any author events.

For Dad.

I look into the life after this and I see the kingdom of my soul. Though darkness blinds, though my enemies surround me, I feel no fear. I will never die. My footsteps echo into eternity, where I will stand with honor, forever more.

Parthian Song of the Brave

PART 1

Chapter 1
Saeed

HYDRIA

ADRIA SEA

The ugly son of a family in disgrace stood at the bow of the ship. The besieged vessel pitched and rolled, thrown upon the mercy of an unforgiving sea. A howling wind drowned out the crewmen's screams. Hardened pirates, saltwater in their veins, lost their legs and cried to the skies, begging for salvation, as malformed shapes rose from the black depths and clawed their way aboard.

No stars shone above. The gods had turned their eyes away. They had no stomach for the ways of demons and men.

Saeed slid a hollow bone from his pocket. He pushed a marn leaf inside and lit it with a spark from his finger's click. Light flared across a misshapen face. Torrents of rain and seawater blasted Saeed from every angle, but his cloak hung dry. He held his position even as the waters threatened to capsize the vessel, and furious winds shredded the sail from end to end and brought the mast crashing down to the deck, just inches from his back.

The boat rose up high on the peak of one mountainous wave and Saeed gazed across the Adria Sea toward a distant outcroft of land – a land not one crew member of this doomed vessel would ever reach.

The Northern Halos.

He kept his eyes fixed on the land as the ship roared down the other side of the wave. In the distance, he could see the waters crashing into jagged rocks at the base of a cliff, where a cluster of boulders formed a walkway to the entrance of a cavern. In the tempestuous darkness, the cliffs looked to Saeed like a fallen giant, the cavern its mouth, open in final prayer, fists still clenched in defiance of a death sure to be his. *We shall never die.* That cavern, Saeed mused, would be a perfect place to construct a harbor. All the waters of the Adria, and seas beyond, naturally ran to this point and the cave alone had space enough for an entire seacity. He could see, even from this distance, that its tunnels traveled deep beneath the cliffs. Yet not even a simple jetty waited to welcome the ocean-weary mariner. On this side of Hydria no such thing existed. Northerners didn't sail. They didn't even swim in these waters they called *Mĕthmalay* – deathbringer. Who would have predicted simple plains dwellers could be so accidentally wise?

Wet footsteps crossed the deck behind him. All manner of demonic growling and teeth gnashing sounded from the shadows. Saeed inhaled deeply from his pipe, smoke curling from his mouth as he savored the mint flavor of the marn. In this scent he returned home, if only for a moment in time. Within the simple smell hid such complexity, and such deception, for home was now a mirage, existing only in the wild desires of his heart. And reality was creeping up behind him, patiently waiting to tear out his throat.

Without haste, Saeed turned, his eyes sweeping across the masses of sea demons crowding the deck below. One side of his mouth twitched up in a mockery of a smile. His eyes flared, glowing green in the pitch dark. The dread monsters of *Mĕthmalay* gave a united gurgling gasp of fear and cleared the decks so quickly they may as well have been fleeting ghosts of a forgotten nightmare. The waves calmed to flat. The wind halted in its tracks. The rain dried. Even the heavy clouds drew back from Saeed, revealing a full moon, king of the sky, and his legion of warrior stars shining in brilliance over the ravaged vessel, now empty of souls in this silent night. And in the silence, true terror took hold of Saeed's heart because he saw it for what it was – the calm before the end. He could sense the ratha demons coming for them.

He looked down at his feet where the child lay wrapped in a blanket, peaceful in potion-induced sleep, and he found himself entranced by the sight. There he stood, a Parthian foot soldier, but this child was Draigar royalty. An eternity of mighty battles raged in this babe's blood. Yet right now, this future warrior looked no more than a small curly-haired child, with a tear-stained face and thin, fragile arms wrapped around a tiny silver-black foal. Both of them had seen too much, way too much for small souls to bear. That their fate now rested with him was, to Saeed, the bitterest of ironies. A sharpness stabbed through his forehead and he scrunched his eyes shut against it. Through the pain he saw to the past, to a time before the Draigar had come to his land, the Farnorthern Halos.

"*Allanta-deseyever,*" Saeed said and the words hurt him inside. He had never spoken his own language so loud, only in faint whispers behind doors closed and bolted. Before the Draigar, the Parthians had lived and died on the Farnorthern Halos, the only warriors standing between the whole of Hydria, Farnorth and North, and the everliving demon masses that kept rising from the hellands of Woulghast and the Pits of Utara. Only the strength and skill of the Parthians had held back these hideous miscreations. So many wars his people had won. So many apocalypses they had diverted, pushed away, squashed down. And then, but once, they had failed. Their mortality had betrayed them. They had fallen. Lost. And a demon invasion had savaged their world. Hydria had seemed to face its final end. And then the Draigar had appeared, as angels from the beyond, to force the demon masses back to the hellands. And since that time, and for all time in history, the Draigar had been revered and the Parthians mocked. The Lost Battle had been centuries upon centuries before his day and even so, Saeed had grown up with Parthian warriors all around him who continued to fight for the cause, but who had lost their hearts and pride, lost their trust in each other and themselves. To be Parthian no longer meant anything honorable. All it meant was that they were second class to the Draigar commanders, their lords and kings. If they were lucky, they made the draft to become foot soldiers – disposable battle-fodder – and if they didn't, they were drudgery servants, field tenders, beggars, thieves and whores.

In knowing this, he could understand why his eldest brother, Amad, had thrown down the sword of their father and abandoned the cause to hunt his own hedonistic desires. Why fight and die without honor? Without honor there was nothing. Break your bones and spill your blood for what? For who? For people to make jokes and sing songs of Parthian cowards soiling themselves and running in fear? *That* had never happened. They had never fled. Despite every dishonor spat their way, to this day the Parthian guardians had continued to fight the hard fight, staring not just death but damnation in its hideous face day after day, and yet they were *cowards*? Saeed found his hands clenched into shaking fists at his sides. He forced air through his lungs and calmed himself until he was again stone.

Time was treacherous in its repetition and it had eventually turned on the Draigar as well. He had been yet a boy when the ratha demons had broken up out of the earth, too many, too strong even for the Draigar. The demons had surged a bloody path through the Farnorth and across the ocean to the Northern Halos. There the ratha king, Mordan-Grieg, had tricked the four rulers of the Barbarian Plains into signing an unknowing pact. It had delayed the destruction of their lands, all the while dooming them to a much worse fate. They had been but momentarily spared while the Farnorth continued to writhe and burn. As a final desperate act, the Draigar had called upon the Omarians, a fierce but volatile race, who had come through their portals and tipped the battle back in the Draigar's favor. Mordan-Grieg and his ratha demons were defeated and sent back to the Pits. For repayment the Omarian king had demanded that the young Draigar princess, Oren Harvey Darro, be wed to his son, the Prince Lecivion, and they had taken her back to their realm, leaving Oren's younger sister, Oriana, as heir. Hydria had exhaled in relief, and settled back for the continuation of existence – until seven days ago, when the ratha had returned. The oracles had cried out the truth: Oren had disgraced her vows and left the prince and he was taking his vengeance on their whole world by releasing the demons to exact their revenge. Saeed gave a strangled laugh – they were all dead. All his people and all the Draigar, equals at last, in the grave, and he was the only one left – he and Harlow Harvey Darro, only child to Queen Oriana and heir to the Draigar throne.

A terrible weariness pressed down on Saeed and he lowered his head. Amidst the shaking, the rattling, the shrieks and squeals of the devastated vessel, a floorboard creaked. Saeed's attention snapped in the direction of the sound. It could have belonged to this ruined symphony, but it did not. He knew. The ratha were already there. His time was up.

Saeed forced himself to breathe deeply, steeling himself for the fight ahead. Again he stared out across the dark sea, focusing on the cliffs growing ever closer before him. Atop the cliffs he saw a castle taking shape from the night mist. Surely here the child would find mercy among the women – the Draigars made such pretty children, both boys and girls, and this child was particularly endearing – unlike Saeed when he was a boy. When he was just an infant his mother had told him that she could never love him. He was too ugly, too slow. She'd wanted to leave him to die after birth, but his brothers had stolen him away and cared for him. They hadn't seen his deformities, they'd just seen their brother, a fifth son who his father said was so disappointing that he may as well have been a girl. They were all dead now; only this disappointing, ugly son remained to redeem the honor of his family and his entire people in the final hour.

Saeed seized the sleeping child and the tiny horse and lowered them into the rowboat suspended off the side of the ship. He touched the boat and whispered the words of protection that would keep them safe for as long as he lived. Then he started winding the crank, lowering them toward the sea. When they were low enough, he cut them free and watched the boat float away. He saw the silver-black foal was stirring, nudging the child to wake also, and his grandfather's words came to him unbidden – *the rider does not choose the horse, the horse chooses the rider.* The old man had lost his mind and drifted into a time when Parthians had been allowed to ride, back in the time of honor. In his memories Saeed saw the old man shambling around the house, dancing – in his foggy state he'd thought himself a magnificent dancer, he'd thought himself fifty years younger, he'd thought himself a king. What blissful fantasies he'd lived in those last years while everyone else mourned his death even as he yet breathed.

Saeed saw the rowboat reach a peak and the child sit up just as it vanished again. He saw forms of soldiers on the walls of the cliff-top castle, and beyond them on a hill, he spotted the silhouette of a horse and rider – one man with five guards. One man with a presence so distinct and far-reaching that he could never be mistaken for any other. Apollo, king of Corinthia. Saeed's brow furrowed. That the Corinthian king stood here, far from his royal city, at this very moment, brought question to his mind of how and why. Was Apollo aware of the fate of the Farnorth?

From the corner of his eye, Saeed caught sight of a ratha demon leaping from the side of the ship and into the ocean below, making fast for the drifting rowboat. With a yell, he launched himself after it. As he flew, he drew his sword, blessed by the fires of Utara during his initiation pilgrimage. He slashed it down, cutting the ratha's horns from its head, robbing it of its immortality. The second strike took its head, but not before it raised its lava-formed sword and drove it deeply into his chest. He hit the water dying and struggled to stay afloat as his blood turned the waves red. With seawater blurring his vision, he caught a last glimpse of the little boat vanishing over the crest of a wave. With that sight, he felt a strong surge of regret for all the words he'd left unspoken, all the things he'd left undone – *too quick – it's all gone too quick*. He gasped, fighting the end, staring into the sky above. Before his eyes, the darkness turned to light and he saw his brothers there, beckoning to him, calling him into the afterlife, and he saw pride in their faces, because even though he had not lived long and he had not lived well, he had done everything he was meant to – he had done what he was born to do. With his final breath he whispered his name for judgment before the gods and heard the words echoing into eternity – *Saeed Akeem Arafat Melchoir*. His sword slipped from his grasp and sank silently through the waters into the depths of the ocean below.

Chapter 2
Eli

AQUAIS

SCORPIA (LIBERTYTOWN)

It had been so long since he'd bathed and shaved that he'd actually grown a beard, something Eli had previously believed was, for him, a physical impossibility. In the ruggedly-masculine-body-hair-department, he had always failed. There'd even been several humiliating incidents involving stick-on moustaches and chemically-enhanced follicle growth gone wrong. Having to be rescued from his own horribly overgrown pubic hair had not been a great experience, to say the least, and had been forever relegated into the "let us never speak of this again" basket. Yet here he was – bearded! Unless of course it wasn't facial hair at all, but some kind of fuzzy mold that had sprouted as a result of his recent lack of attendance to personal hygiene. Eli glanced into the rear-vision mirror of his transflyer and studied the beard with suspicion. It was just patchy and tragic enough to be authentic. He stared at his reflection. Squinting back was a thin and wilted looking imp-breed with bleary, bloodshot eyes and ink imprinted across his forehead from where he'd fallen asleep on his papers the night before. Bed sleep was a luxury he couldn't afford these days – so were clean underwear and any peace of mind whatsoever. A sadistic serial killer was loose in Scorpia, and the longer it took them to catch him, the more people would suffer and die. As an Oscuri Tracker, this pressure had always been part of Eli's work and life, which were inextricably blended at all times – except now it wasn't his only worry. There was also that tiny issue of the Indemeus X, the invincible demon god picking off worlds one by one and slowly but relentlessly dragging the entire universe down into the half-life misery of his hell realm.

In the past several months the planets Bandos, Eumaios, Eradanis and Meteor had completely vanished from the skies, entire worlds gone, as though they never were, and Eli suspected many others that weren't visible from Aquais had been taken as well. And they already knew the Arequium Mors were inside Aquais, or at least in Kullra Fornax, the frozen mazeland of tunnels beneath the above lands. Upon their sudden and violent arrival from this secret underworld, the survivors Saint Croy, Darius DeCavisi and a ship full of the race known as Dray, led by Shah-Jahan RaAhura, had given a full account of the invasion of their city, Nÿr-Corum, and its fast and horrendous demise. Their reports were consistent with what the other trackers had seen in Omar Montanya: the Arequium Mors were a type of spectral-breed with the ability to incite violence in others, and they seemed to be gaining sustenance from ripping the faces off the dead and placing them over their own, like a mask.

The thought made Eli's spine tingle. He'd run extensive remote-scans searching for any underground survivors in Nÿr-Corum, but had located no sign, and with the risk of returning to the city in person too great, they'd had to conclude that everyone in Nÿr-Corum was dead. Yet there hadn't been any Arequium sightings or attacks in Scorpia or, according to Eli's monitoring devices, any unnatural darkening of their suns, both signs of imminent destruction. It was a mystery to Eli why the Indemeus X was taking so long to move on them, but he was sure, with worlds falling all around them, that whatever time they had left was running out.

Now king of Scorpia, Jude had set up a whole new branch of the reinstated and renamed Aquaian Armed Forces to deal exclusively with the threat, hundreds of thousands of soldiers and scientists working day and night to uncover more information on the Indemeus X and find a way to stop him, but as Diega had said – 'Good luck with that.' Eli knew Jude was coming from a place of strategy, the more people working on the issue, the better their chances of finding an actual solution, but in all this time the entire branch had come up with nothing tangible. The trackers were the only ones to have actually encountered the Indemeus X and, so far, the only ones to have dug up any real information on him, and that was all thanks to Ev'r, who had literally dug it up, in the Matadori Desert.

Eli's eyes crept back to the small wooden case sitting on the passenger seat beside him, within which the sum total of their research was locked. It was a very small case, and on it sat an even smaller and extremely irate otter, who was eyeballing him with such fury her whiskers were trembling. Eli jolted as her face came into focus. He'd reneged on his promise to take Nelly to the water park and she was supremely unimpressed. He'd been doing far too much reneging lately.

"I know, girl, I know," he spoke to her. "I'm sorry, but I just need to do this one thing, just this one last thing and then we'll go straight after, okay?"

He gave her a reassuring smile and Nelly launched herself at his neck, teeth bared. He caught her out of midair and held her against him.

"I'm sorry," he said, stroking her back. "I'm so sorry." The first sorry was for her and the second was whispered to Azalea Rian Belle, a fairy-breed who had been found in Moris-Isles, murdered, her wings severed and stolen. She was the latest of thirty-seven victims, all discovered in the same condition, dead from a single stab wound to the heart, wings removed. Eli had autopsied all thirty-seven victims himself. All had been murdered somewhere else, wiped completely clean and then dumped, and even Silho, using her skills, had been unable to find any leads on the killer. When she'd accessed the walls, all she could see was haze. That meant that so far they really only knew three things about the killer – they were using magics to conceal themselves, they were targeting the winged population, and they only seemed to kill when it was storming. And as a person with wings, still suffering post-traumatic flashbacks from previous clashes with dark witches, this made Eli inexpressibly uncomfortable. The media had dubbed the killer the "Wing Ripper". Which really didn't help anything at all.

A bright light shone into Eli's eyes and he flinched, seeing the flight-deck controlman waving him through with the exaggerated enthusiasm of someone who has been waving for some time. Eli gave him an apologetic nod, tucked Nelly into his pocket and started up the transflyer's engines. The *Stardust*, his newest craft, burst to life. It was a conservative model in comparison to designs conceived during the wartime deregulation, but now Jude had reintroduced the skyway laws, and although Eli enjoyed some leniency, a perk of being friends with the king, he'd still had to rein himself back significantly. That said, the *Stardust* could clock speeds faster than any fighterflyer and was supremely strong, with the added modification of turning into a submarine once submerged in water. The *Gypsy Rose* he'd given to Ev'r and Ismail. The sky laws lost jurisdiction outside the city walls, and the pair had spent most of their time in the Matadori since Eli had brought Ev'r back.

The *Stardust* lifted into the air and Eli edged her toward the drop spot, as the controlman directed him through the heavy Alpha Building traffic. The trackers had priority take-off and Eli was glad of it today – Headquarters and the whole of Libertytown, the military base taking up most of Level 3, formerly known as Sejon, were packed. It reminded him of something the commander had said – Jude was bringing in so many recruits and contractors, but what if the killer was among them? The commander had recommended against mass enlistment, suggesting instead a slower and more rigorous recruitment process, but Jude had chosen not to consider this suggestion. No huge shock there. The animosity between the two men had only grown more savage with time. The commander wasn't a person to let anything go, and Jude … well, Eli got the feeling he would fire the commander on the spot if not for the massive outcry it would cause. Most people were still terrified of Copernicus Kane, but none could deny his skills. Jude was demanding daily updates on their investigation, but the commander had ordered them to filter through only minimal information, just enough to keep him off their backs. Copernicus had no confidence in Jude's leadership ability. Being stuck between two friends who had once been so close, but were now so bitterly angry with each other, was a prickly position to be, but all things considered, it was the least of Eli's worries.

Eli brought the *Stardust* to a pause at the edge of the drop spot and looked out across Libertytown, stretching from the Alpha Building into the horizon, where the rising suns had exploded into a pink blaze that flooded across the entire sky. A multitude of transflyers and larger crafts traversed the scene, heading to and from and across the military base in never-ending glowing lines. Eli took in a slow, deep breath, staring in wonderment. No matter how many times he saw the suns rising or setting over Scorpia, the beauty took him by surprise every single time. Sitting at a desk behind a closed door all day and night, it was all too easy to forget the vastness of the city, the way the lights shimmered at dawn and dusk and filled him with such awe and hope. As he watched, the Gentry Bridge, which connected the two halves of Libertytown, started to glow, neon blue and pink that reflected in the waters of the Refined River. The infantry building, which had been constructed to look like a wolf, loomed, a black shadow beyond the bridge. Much closer to the Alpha Building, the long spires of the Triple Towers reached high into the sky, and between the two was the carefully planned city of military buildings and residences, all centered around the General's Dome, where the Commander in Chief of the entire armed forces resided. His name was High Commander Sven Lightenhousen and he'd been appointed by Jude even though so many people had called for the commander to be given the position. There were rumors that Lightenhousen had been given preferential treatment over Copernicus because he was Ar Antarian nobility, like Jude, but Eli knew the truth. He'd been given the position because he wasn't Copernicus Kane – in fact, he was as far from it as a person could get. He was by the book, he was to the letter, predictable, agreeable, high born, high bred, highly polished, and practiced in saying the right thing at the right time and shaking the right hands when it mattered. He could fake-smile convincingly and he'd never seen the color of his own blood.

Eli watched as dark clouds rolled in from the west, and heard the rumbled warning of an approaching storm. The city was heading into monsoon season. It was hoped this year-cycle there would be more water rain and less acid storms and fire hail than the previous year, but something about the snarl of the sky made Eli doubt it. Previously, he'd quite enjoyed a good storm, but now they sent fear shivering through him. The so-called Wing Ripper didn't strike during every storm, but it had never killed without there being one – so far.

The controlman directing Eli in waved both his light wands up and down, clearing him to go. Eli gave him a quick head tip and revved the engines. He shot out into open air, dipping into a flight stream and punching the acceleration up to match the flow. He burnt across the darkening sky, past the Triple Towers and over the infantry's wolf, swerving into another stream that was exiting the level. The flight pace slowed, the skyway clogged by the sheer volume of outgoing military flyers. Jude had ordered that watches be set up in every suburb in every level, outside of the gang-controlled areas, including the majority of the underside levels, to protect everyone from the killer regardless of wealth or status. The magnitude of the operation was mind-boggling, and it also made for extremely slow flying. Impatience wasn't usually one of Eli's vices, but this morning he felt time flying faster than he was, and he needed to gain back the advantage.

"Siren time," he murmured to Nelly. He flicked a switch on his control board and the *Stardust* let out a wail of sound that only tracker crafts were permitted to emit. Everyone ahead of him dodged to one side or the other to clear the way. As he flew past he caught glimpses of anxious faces peering through transflyer windows. He knew what they were all thinking – another victim. Either that or the end of the world.

Eli left Libertytown and sped down the back wall entering into the level below. He avoided the heavy traffic, keeping low, skimming just above the tops of the buildings. It was illegal to fly off the skyways like this, but with his tracker siren blasting, no one was arguing with him – in fact, he caught sight of people in surrounding high-rises waving him on. A tingling shot of courage surged through him, followed immediately by a spiraling squelch of fear. He sighed, rejoining the skyway where it entered the connection tunnel. Once he merged into the tunnel, he switched off his siren and kicked the *Stardust* up to hyper-speed, rocketing down over 500 levels in a matter of minutes, until he cut out of the pipeway into a suburb known as Blueblack. It was an underside red-light district full of multi-leveled grindhouses, transflyer chop-shops and tiny hole-in-the-wall eateries which apparently served all kinds of mouthwatering delicacies to those who didn't mind a side of robbery, death or gratuitous pornography with their meal. Eli flicked up his lights to high beam and slowed again, peering through the neon-lit gloom.

"Windscreen wipers," he murmured as he turned the switch.

As part of the underside, Blueblack never saw the sunslight or the rain, but minute cracks in the level's roof meant that water from the submerged level above, Adliden, was constantly drizzling down on the buildings and streets below. Faux rain, Diega called it. It spattered and drummed on the *Stardust*, interspersed with larger bumps as gigantic balloons drifted into Eli's path. The previous week had been the Sleagh Maith Balloon Festival and afterward many of the huge floating creations had been cut loose to waft between the buildings, through the mist and holo-screen billboards. To Eli, the gradually deflating balloons looked like depressed creatures from a lost time. He spotted a dragon shape to his left and did a double-take, thinking for a moment that it was Savoy, the firebird dragon who Silho and the others had brought back from Omar Montanya. They'd named her that because every time the creature snorted, it sounded like a gruff resounding *sah-voy*. She was currently in the largest enclosure they had in the Scorpia Zoological Park, closed off from public viewing and being pampered by a legion of zoologists and mythologists combined. But the times Eli had gone with Silho to see Savoy, the dragon had seemed restless, and as Silho had said, even the largest enclosure didn't seem anywhere near large enough. Only the open sky would cool the firebird's heat, but how could they release her knowing she was the last of her kind in a possibly inhospitable environment? She might not find enough food, or the right type of food, or she might just decide *they* were the right type of food and raze the city. There were too many risks to entertain the thought of releasing her just yet. Eli dipped low under a pedestrian bridge that joined two upper-class grindhouses. The outer structures of both buildings were constructed entirely of glass, and in every space, a girl was standing or dancing or whatever else, like items for sale in a shop window. Eli even noticed a drive-thru on the side of one building, where people could order 'take-away' girls. There was a line-up of flyers waiting to give their order to a machine. The sight turned Eli's stomach. He wasn't a prude by a long stretch, but – *seriously?* – was that what these lives had been reduced to? Take-out?

He navigated the *Stardust* through a hologram sign and came out above Spinifex Square at the center of Blueblack. The locals had converted what had once been a fly track for illegally modified crafts into a cluster of stylish nightclubs and bars surrounding an ice-skating rink. The place was always packed with partiers attempting to skate in their inebriated or drugged-up states. As he passed over it, he saw a bunch of young, rowdy fairy-breeds skating nude for some reason. One belly-flopped onto the ice and Eli flinched. He'd be feeling that later.

The *Stardust* suddenly rocked and shuddered as two high-powered transflyers shot past on either side of it, locked in a drag race, ignoring the terrible flying conditions. They roared along Dewinter Avenue, shaking the windows of the high-fashion stores lining the street. Eli clicked his tongue at them and murmured, "*Lai-Lai.* Youngsters." He couldn't help but grin.

"Must be getting old," he said to Nelly.

Just the act of smiling helped to loosen the stress knots in his belly, and he flew down Dewinter feeling slightly more optimistic. He gazed into the exclusive stores as he passed. The first time he'd discovered this hidden pocket of labels in Blueblack, he'd thought it was extremely strange for such big fashion houses to be selling down here in the underside, but then it had clicked. Someone in an office somewhere in the levels above had discovered what the gangsters had known for centuries: that there were massive amounts of money to be made in criminal activity, and criminals liked to spend said money on all the things they wanted but didn't really need, like enormously overpriced gloves, belts, bags and shoes. The truth was, getting dirty money was never a serious challenge – the problems lay in keeping it, growing it and not getting caught or killed in the process, especially with the massive increase in military presence everywhere. Eli flew past the Gulliver and Guilermo fashion store and passed a military checkpoint positioned on its 360-degree rotating roof. The Guardians there flashed a beam across the serial number on the *Stardust*, checking he was legitimate, then waved to him as his stats came up on their system. He flashed his lights in greeting, and his com buzzed. Eli glanced down at the caller ID and saw the name *Jude*. His stomach re-knotted itself doubly tight and he answered, trying not to give his reluctance away.

"Eli," Jude's voice came through, sounding weary and irritated. Now that he was the king, he no longer wore his tinted glasses and he didn't try to mask his upper-level accent. It was heavier than ever, and heavier still when he was angry. "Can you please tell me why Kane is not responding to direct requests from High Commander Lightenhousen?"

Eli grimaced. The Commander and Jude were like two people sitting across the table from each other refusing to talk, and he had become their go-between. It reminded him of his grandparents.

"I'm not sure," Eli said, trying to keep his own frustration from surfacing, "but you know him. He does things his own way and always has."

"Well that needs to change," Jude said, repeating something he'd been saying incessantly since he was crowned.

Eli sighed deeply and when Jude spoke again, his tone had softened. "Look, I'm sorry, Eli, I shouldn't be dragging you into the middle of this."

The way he sounded now was the way Eli had always known him, and it reminded him of how long it had been since they'd seen each other in person, months maybe. He didn't want to admit it to himself but they were drifting further and further apart in a way he'd never thought they would. They'd been through so much together.

"But he's a problem," Jude continued, his words tightening up. "And he's becoming increasingly disruptive and recalcitrant. He's creating discord in the AAF on purpose, when now, more than ever, we need to be united."

"He hasn't changed. He's the same he's always been," Eli said, feeling immediately defensive. "And if you're looking for support to discharge the commander then you will – *won't* – get it from me."

"I see," Jude replied after a loaded pause. "It's very clear where your loyalty lies. I know he's instructed you not to give me any information, but I must say that I thought better of you. I thought you were beyond such manipulations."

"He's never said not to tell you things," Eli lied. The commander had in fact sent him written instructions explicitly stating that he should not tell Jude anything.

"I know for a fact that he has, and I fully expected it of him, but I never thought I'd see the day that you'd lie to me, Eli. End."

Jude hung up, leaving Eli with a very solid lump in his throat and tears blurring his vision. He blinked them back so he wouldn't crash into one of the malls as he crossed the level's main shopping district. Having someone else disappointed in him was difficult, but he was disappointed in himself too, and that was a whole new level of torment. Jude had been there for him so many times, with his encouraging words and gentle-hearted friendship. They'd saved each other's lives, and now it had come to this. He had lied to Jude, but what choice did he have?

He wiped a tear from his cheek and blew out, trying to steady himself. His com buzzed again and, assuming it was Jude, he said, "Answer ... Jude, I'm really sorry, but you know I'm not going to support criticism of the commander. It doesn't mean I don't care about you. I wish things could just go back to the way they were."

The silence from the other end made him look down to check the ID – *The Boss*. Eli flinched, wishing he could unsay what he'd just said, but it was impossible, so he settled with a squeaky and awkward, "Hey boss, how's things?"

A hologram flickered up on the passenger side of the windscreen, Copernicus, Diega and Silho flying in the *Ory-6*, staring at him with an array of expressions. Silho glanced down, uncomfortable. Diega's nostrils were flaring and colors flashing, while the commander looked stormy, but controlled as always. The three of them had been going over the Azalea Rian Belle crime scene again, searching for any details they may have possibly missed. Eli had left the commander a message telling him he was flying to the *Manticore*.

Copernicus was the first to break the silence.

"He's pressuring you again, is he?" His voice was a sharp, hard sword, but his eyes cut deeper. There really was no option but the truth when it came to Copernicus Kane.

"He thinks I'm lying to him, about the information veto, which I am, so it's hard to feel too wounded," he said, even though he did.

"You understand why I've put this request on you," the commander said.

"Of course," Eli said immediately. Copernicus wasn't trying to be petty, there was a serious risk of information getting into the wrong hands and causing more deaths, a risk that Jude was refusing to acknowledge.

"Jude knows why as well," Diega said. "He's just being a trutting gadfly."

"He's angry," Eli said quietly.

Diega snorted. "Please. He needs to get over it and move on."

"It is what it is." The commander stepped in, turning the conversation back to business. "You've just dropped off the grid, you must be nearing the *Manticore*."

"Yes boss," Eli replied. "The facility is up ahead."

As he spoke he flew across the border of Blueblack and into what had been the slums of Seth. The AAF had recommissioned the entire zone, which took up most of the rest of the level, flattened everything and stuck up a gigantic wall to contain the military's worst kept secret, the *Scorpian Manticore*, and all the Nÿr-Corum survivors.

"Why are you going to the *Manticore*?" Diega asked him. "Have you found something?"

He hated to squash the hope in her voice but had to say, "No, I'm just clutching at straws really. I'm going to ask Shah-Jahan to take another look at the map pieces." He glanced over at the wooden case on the passenger seat. "Just in case, but you know what he's like. I was hoping you'd meet me there. I feel like you're the only person he takes seriously, boss."

To say the captain of the *Scorpian Manticore* was a complicated man was the understatement of the year-cycle – of the era, actually.

"Understood," Copernicus said. "We've just left the Isles, we'll be there shortly. Go inside the compound and we'll meet you there. And make sure you're armed. It's storming in the upper levels."

"Storms and wings – bad combination," Eli gulped. "I hear you."

"End," Copernicus said, and the hologram fuzzed out.

With the facility guard tower looming almost directly in front of him, Eli didn't have long to stew. Instead, he flew up beside the tower and stopped midair. He lowered the *Stardust*'s window and hot air tainted with the vapors of fuel gusted into the flyer. A familiar face popped out from the tower window.

Mo Modalias, a former Transflyers and Traffics unit guardian, was now part of the Manticore Watch. He grinned at Eli. "Eli, buddy! What's happening my friend?" He held out his hands, ten of them, anyway, he had a few, being a human-breed of centipede blood.

Eli slapped down one row of hands and said, "Just the usual, Mo-Mo."

Mo peered closer at him and said, "You actually don't look so flash, my friend. Girlfriend dump you?"

"I know, and no," Eli replied. "You have to first convince someone to be your girlfriend before she can dump you."

He heard someone pointedly clearing their throat from the backseat of his transflyer and only just managed to suppress his startle reflex. He knew who it was without turning around, the only person who was faster than him and always smelt like strawberries. She must have slipped in at Headquarters while he was lost in thought.

Mo-Mo gave a bark of laughter, then scanned the *Stardust*'s serial code. "You've got clearance, you're good to go." He held out one hand and Eli tapped it again.

"Thanks, Mo-Mo."

"Anytime, buddy, anytime!"

Eli revved the craft's engine as the heavy compound gate trundled aside. He flew through and heard it booming shut behind him. The *Stardust* glided down to the visitor's parking lot and he landed, shutting off the engines before turning to look in the backseat. Diamond LeSwer sat there wearing a pink tutu and clutching an absurdly enormous bag of candy. It looked like she'd stolen it from a gargantuan-breed, it was bigger than she was. Diamond peeked around the bag.

"I know someone who wants to be your girlfriend," she said, making suggestions with her eyebrows.

Eli stifled his first reaction of exacerbated laughter. If a person was to look up "persistent" in the Urigin dictionary they would find a hologram of Diamond's face, all glitter, blond curls and jiggling eyebrows. Mr Nimbles, her slinky minx, clawed around one side of the bag to hiss at Nelly, who was giving her the evil eye from Eli's pocket.

"Here. I brought this for you," Diamond muttered around a gobstopper and tipped the bag toward him, showering him in an overflow of sweets. Eli tried to fend off the downpour, only managing to push the bag upright when he was already chest high in candy.

"Diamond!" he panted. Half-drowned in edible love hearts was not the way he wanted the rest of the team to find him.

The little imp-breed girl gave her cheeky grin and said, "Yes, Eli Anklebiter, I will marry you. I thought you'd never ask."

Eli tried to get angry at her, but failed. All he could do was marvel at her skill – how had she smuggled not just herself but this mountain of candy past Headquarters security, past his transflyer security and onto his craft without him knowing, then sat there so silently that he heard and sensed nothing?

She really was one of a kind. She threw him a fizzing popper and he snatched it out of midair. He couldn't help himself, manic playfulness was in the imp-breed genetic make-up, and as a cross-bred Glee and Greer, there was no one who understood him as well as Diamond LeSwer. She made perfect sense on every level, except the level where he was supposed to be in love with her, because he just wasn't, that light hadn't turned on, even though at times he wished it would.

"How's the investigation, anything new?" she asked, shoving the candy sack off her lap and onto the seat beside her.

"You know I can't tell you anything," Eli said, unbuckling his restraints.

"Of course you can!" she said, speaking in their mother tongue. "I won't tell anyone, I promise."

Eli laughed out loud. In general, imp-breeds were incapable of keeping secrets – it was just not a concept they understood. Even he struggled at times, despite so much behavioral reconditioning and having lived away from his kind for all this time.

"I could help you!" she insisted.

"I know, Diamond, trust me I know. I wish you were part of the team, but unfortunately Commander Kane didn't recruit you."

"Commander Grumpy Pants," Diamond muttered. "So serious. What did I do that was so wrong?"

"Really, Diamond? You really don't know?" Eli said, giving her a look. She stared back, completely innocent.

"Alright – so let's see, what did you do to the commander?" Eli said, pausing for effect. "You glitter-bombed him, hugged him, you licked his face, you snatched the papers from his hands and threw them into the air squealing *'weeee'*, while wedgying him so hard you *ripped the band off his underpants*, then you stripped naked while singing 'Hey Mary'. Did I mention naked? Is there anything I forgot? Oh yes, you shot him – in the butt – with a dart gun that made him fart uncontrollably for an entire week. *One whole week*."

Eli stared at her with what he hoped was his severest sternest expression. Diamond's face took on a pensive look for half a second, then she burst out snorting with laughter.

"You said 'butt' and 'whole'," she sniggered.

Eli sighed deeply. Diamond had been so overawed by meeting *the* Copernicus Kane that she'd lost all control. And in the face of her serious misbehavior, even though the commander had clearly seen her brilliance, he'd had to reject Eli's bid to bring her on board. That conversation, where they'd had to basically shout to be heard above the thunder of Copernicus' unremitting farts, was not one Eli would soon forget. And even despite *all* of that, the boss had still left them with one ray of hope – if Diamond attended therapy, if she learned some control techniques, he would reassess her. That was way way WAY more than he would have offered anyone else.

"Did you go to your sessions yesterday?" Eli asked her.

"Yes of course!" she lied, and Eli shook his head. As a tracker, she could be so many things, do so much good, but she just wasn't motivated and he couldn't understand why. Maybe it was too late for her to change, maybe she didn't really want to, after all the tortures of her therapy when she was growing up. Maybe he was just trying to force her into what he wanted her to be, maybe she was actually fine the way she was. Who was he to judge her anyway?

"I have to go in," Eli told her. "And you have to stay here inside the craft. Diamond, I'm serious, the city is in lockdown for a reason, there's a killer out there and he's targeting us, winged people, and —"

Diamond leaned back in her seat and placed a foot over his mouth, muffling him. He took her foot and lowered it.

"Diamond this is serious, people are dying," he told her.

She gazed at him with her wide, innocent eyes and said, "I'm safe as long as I'm with you, my lover."

"I wish that was true," he said. "The safe bit, I mean. Just stay here."

She started singing something about a pink porcupine, so he grabbed the case off the passenger seat and jumped out of the transflyer amid a deluge of candy. He locked the *Stardust* down and armed all the shields, but he knew if Diamond decided to go wandering about there was nothing he could do to stop her. She was too brilliant, kooky brilliant, curious brilliant, cheeky brilliant. Brilliant, brilliant, brilliant.

Eli sighed again and glanced back at the gigantic gate closed behind them. Hopefully that would at least be enough to keep her inside the compound. With the faux rain dampening his jacket, he clutched the case and made a run for the doorway of the enormous hangar that took up most of the compound space.

A long line of Watchers guarded the door. As he neared them he started to slide out his tracker badge, but one of them called out, "No need, Specialist Investigator Anklebiter."

They hauled the doors open wide and then saluted him, leaving Eli feeling confused and slightly dumbfounded. This was a whole new level of respect that he'd never been shown.

"Must be the beard," he murmured. Either that or someone was playing a trick on him and he was about to be pelted with stinkwater bombs. He peeked upward with trepidation, but there was no one there, just the soldiers ahead of him. He attempted to walk in a distinguished way, which for some reason developed into a limp, and when he was close enough he said, "Thanks and continue guarding and that kind of thing," then he dashed past them into the hangar. Before the doors closed he looked back to the *Stardust* and saw Diamond still sitting inside the craft, smiling to herself, a smile that said she was already plotting the next trick she'd play on him, or more likely a whole bag of them.

Chapter 3
Ev'r

AQUAIS

MATADORI DESERT (THREEGULLS)

Dawn broke the long dark of night, shooting golden lights across the graying sky, making harmless forms of menacing shadows and fleeting thoughts of monstrous fears.

Who would have thought? Who would have even dared to suggest to Ev'r Keets that this vile parched sty, this faithless badland of atrocities, treacheries and incestuous sands, this baptism into malevolence, this spiral into madness, this Matadori Desert could look so ... beautiful?

The desert sands glistened, still waters beneath the new day suns, rising vast and blue. Fast tracking clouds chased time across the sky and beneath them a flock of birds flew high. They were just tatty corpse birds on their way to feast on the overnight dead, but at their height, they looked somehow majestic. Angelic, even.

Ev'r shook the thought out of her head and said, "I'm losing my edge."

From beside her Ismail murmured, "Beautiful, isn't she." He nodded to the Matadori beyond.

"*She* is a rabid toad, spewing blood, pus and poison," Ev'r muttered. It was crazy to feel jealous of a man calling a desert beautiful. But then, she'd always been crazy when it came to this man.

Ismail snorted and slipped an arm around her waist.

"Watching the sunsrise, it's supposed to be romantic."

"That's the sunsset," Ev'r told him. "No one finds the sunsrise romantic. Except lunatics."

"I don't know," Ismail said, his breath warm on her face. "I think it's romantic."

"As I said," Ev'r replied, and Ismail gave a low chuckle and tightened his grip on her. He turned her toward him and kissed her face, tiny spikes of his stubble scratching her skin.

"I blame you," she said, lifting a hand to stroke his face.

"What's new?" he replied and pulled her closer to kiss her lips.

She closed her eyes and in the darkness of her mind she saw the truth. This was all a dream, the sweetest of nightmares, and he was about to vanish, to turn to sand and slip between her fingers and fly away. How many people got this? How many people got to see their loved one again, back from the dead – to hold them, feel their warmth, hear them breathing, see their smile, laugh with them, cry with them, say all the things that could never be said – *I love you. I'm sorry. You mean everything to me.* No one got this. Because it was impossible. So it couldn't be real.

Ev'r opened her eyes and Ismail was still there, looking down at her. The dawn light erased his scars and lines, forgiving the hard year-cycles and pain, and making his dark eyes glow and shimmer.

"Right now you look like you did when we met," she said.

He smiled, an expression he'd had to relearn. He leaned down and rested his forehead against hers, whispering, "Zara."

Ev'r let the word roll over her. She didn't argue with his conviction, but Zara really wasn't who he was holding. The question was, if the scullion girl Zingara Ohavor died in the Lava Diavol Mountains beside her soulmate's grave and Ev'r Keets, outlawed treasure hunter, perished in the tunnels beneath the Galleria Majora, lost to the poison of the Ravien – who stood here now? Who was this person who looked like her, spoke like her, wore her scars, bore her madness, but wasn't her, because she was dead twice over and this person was most definitely alive. She could taste the tobacco on her tongue, feel the strength of the arms wrapped around her, hear the thuds of the robotic heart inside Ismail's chest – solid muscle, fragrant sweat – feel the cool desert wind stirring the sand beneath their boots and hear the distant rumble of an acid storm. All these things felt so real, but Ev'r knew the mind played tricks, hers more than most, so all this could still be a dream. Only one thing made her sure that it was real, that she still lived despite the odds, to spite the odds. It was a particular pain. A dull, throbbing ache low down in her belly along with the hot blood trickling between her thighs. If she was fantasizing or dreaming, *this* wouldn't be part of it. No woman would include this sanguinary curse in their dreams. It was foul and obnoxious, turning up at the least convenient moment, but then again, was it ever convenient for the insides of your body to rip out and bleed down your legs?

Ismail caught the scent of the blood and his eyes shifted downward. He made a start at mentioning it but Ev'r shook her head. Perhaps it was the homicidal glint in her eye or the apparently romantic sunrise, but he decided against venturing into that grisly conversation and instead kissed her again. Wise move.

She enjoyed the touch of his lips, silencing the doubt in her mind as it whispered again. She was here. He was here. This was real, impossibility defeated. And they owed an unpayable debt to one short, overeager and unstoppable soldier. The thought of Eli Anklebiter gave her the unwanted warm and fuzzies, but it also reminded her why they were standing on the dunes just outside of Threegulls, a town that reeked of savaged innocence, lost dreams and abandoned hope, but more than anything, of rotten fish. Shanty towns like this reminded her of her home town, and that was never a good thing.

There was no doubt something terrible lay ahead. Aside from the vanishing planets, premonitionists all over the city were taking themselves and their families out in droves, all marking their death scenes with the X of the Indemeus X. No one was seeing any way out of the horror that was coming for them. Ev'r and Ismail had agreed not to look too far into the future. They both believed it could be changed, but not if they were too paralyzed by fear to act.

The new so-called King of Scorpia, Kane's former lapdog Jude, had locked up all the remaining foreseers he could identify, most of them scullions, to save them from themselves. But who was going to save them from the Indemeus X? Apparently, a guy called Shah-Jahan – some cave dweller who'd recently crawled out of a deep hole, wearing an overcomplicated loin cloth and claiming that an old woman had told him he was the savior of the universe. Call her cynical, but Ev'r had heard that one before. The O'Tenery Asylum had been full of self-professed saviors.

Even so, she had agreed to help, but only because it was Snacksize asking. She'd told him at the start, they'd find as many of the map pieces as they could, but then they were out. They were gone. She and Ismail together, just the two of them, over the boundary wall and into the Brine. It sounded like further insanity, but she'd seen things as a Ravien that made her think it was their one chance to survive – but only if they separated from the trackers and made their own way. The odds of saving the whole world as Snacksize was trying to do were nonexistent, but the odds of saving just her and Ismail ... maybe.

Ismail had become snagged on the thought of leaving Silho. He had a strong need to right the wrongs of the past, but he still understood they had to go. He was just hoping they could convince Silho to come with them. Fat chance. She belonged to Kane. And even though everyone could see Silho still wasn't in control of her skills, and she was a hazard to herself and everyone around her, he shielded her. Ev'r guessed she wasn't the only one losing her edge.

Ev'r pulled back from Ismail. He wrinkled up his nose, looking even more wolf than he usually did, and said, "This place trutting stinks."

"Let's get this done and get out," Ev'r said in agreement. "Last one."

Ismail cast his gaze down across the sleeping village and said, "Looks pretty quiet. Maybe we could just go in and out, stealth."

"Where's the fun in that?" Ev'r muttered, then added, "There's always a pack of worshippers at the Mother, and lookouts at the four points." She indicated to where the hunched figures sat on the shanty rooftops. "They'll raise the alarm and surround us. We could take them out stealth, but the body count will hit high thirties for sure."

Ismail considered her words and shook his head. "As low as possible. Like we said."

"You said," Ev'r responded. "I made no promises."

Ismail gave half a smile and teased, "Just do as I say, woman."

"Dreaming, you're dreaming, my friend," Ev'r shot back.

"Feels like it," he responded, his eyes serious again, moving across her face. She couldn't read minds like he could, but she knew what he was thinking, the same thing she had been thinking a few minutes earlier, and pretty much constantly. This had to be a dream. She resisted the urge to grab hold of him just to prove to herself yet again that he was real.

Instead, Ev'r crouched down and opened her bag, examining her stash of potions and weapons. Old habits died hard. She selected a nuclear grenade and raised her eyes to Ismail. He shook his head.

"You'll wake every Skither from here to Tracy."

She sighed and put it back, picking out a charge grenade instead.

"That's more like it." He held out his hand.

Ev'r clutched the device to herself.

"Come on, let me do it," Ismail said.

"You did it last time," she reminded him. "Besides, I'm better at this than you."

He gave a growling laugh as Ev'r entered the sequence and pitched the grenade out into the barren sands on the outskirts of Threegulls.

One second, two, three, and then an eruption shook the ground so violently that the dune where they stood half collapsed beneath them and Ismail had to touch the ground to steady himself. They exchanged a glance, even the charge had been too much. But it was too late now. The town woke angry like an anthill. Unclothed, bleary-eyed scullions shoved out of their tents and shambled into the makeshift streets. Ev'r and Ismail watched them as they flocked toward the detonation spot. She could hear the robotic twinge of the voices calling out to each other. Blue-ten addicts, even the kids. She noted the lookouts heading off as well.

"That's it, abandon your posts and run toward the explosion," Ev'r muttered. "Shouldn't natural selection have taken out these gadflies by now?"

"They're scullions like us," Ismail said softly. "We don't die off so easy."

"They're scullions," Ev'r agreed, "but they're not like us."

"We won't have long to get back up and out," Ismail said. "Maybe you should —"

"If you're going to say, maybe I should wait somewhere safe while you go down and get it, then you're pissing in the wind, my friend." Ev'r raised her eyes to his and he replied, "Actually, I was going to say maybe you should go down and get it while I wait somewhere safe."

Ev'r stifled a laugh. She did things like that these days. Laugh.

Ismail gave his savage grin.

Ev'r stood up, pulled her hood over her head and started down the dune, her boots sinking deeply into the sand.

Chapter 4
Ramses

HYDRIA

CORINTHIA (CORINTH CITY)

The grinning, the uncontrollable humming, his all-encompassing contentedness with life – it all directed Ramses to one conclusion: he was not entirely sober. Indeed, he had seen the line of inebriation ahead of him, where agreeably tiddly became utterly slaughtered, and he had run staggering toward it. And why not? Happy was happy, was it not? And as he stood now, tilting slightly to the left, smoking a fine cigar, with beautiful tits and asses as far as the blurred eye could see, he could say, without reserve, that he felt happy. But to keep modest, as that was important, he would say to whomever should ask that he felt not too bad today, thank you kindly for asking.

A harp strummed soft and soothing somewhere out of sight and the madam of the harem house bowed low to Ramses, extending her arms out graciously – *all that I possess is yours.* Her scent was desert rose and she seemed to float beneath her silk and lace and flowing dark hair, but her eyes were sharp as they darted to her girls, standing by the wall. They hurried forward, bearing trays of the exotic, dark chocolates from Aghamore, fruits from Berevo, and liquors made from the sap of black and red woods from the foothill towns of Underwood and Finnanbar. Rich, sweet tangs lingered in the air, but Ramses waved everything away. He wasn't there to eat or get drunk – drunker, to keep things honest.

He dropped a royal coin into the madam's hand and she bent to kiss his feet before rising and clapping, summoning all the girls in the interium to come forward, to join those already on the beds and lounges below them in the recessed central landing. Bearers fanned Ramses with huge feather kioms, following his every step as he approached the top of the stairs. He paused there, unbuckling his cintus and dropping his subs. The women gasped at the sight of his naked body. They stopped pleasuring themselves and each other to gaze at him instead. Their exaggeration made him grin. Make no mistake, his body was magnificent, a shrine to the might of Corinthia, but it wasn't enough to induce shock or fainting. When he stood shoulder to shoulder with the other sworn Companions, his muscles were no harder than theirs, his manhood no bigger, no more impressive, even though, on numerous occasions, he had claimed just the opposite.

One of the girls sat up and beckoned Ramses to come down the stairs to them. He obliged, but gave her a half-warning look. As the saying went, harem girls got away with what even the gods would not dare, gesturing to a Companion was an offense. But this girl's body was perfect and her mouth so hot and deep when it closed around his cock that all thoughts of law left his mind, and all he could do was shut his eyes and hold back the groans as the rest of the women crowded around him, kissing and touching his body. One, even bolder than the first, took the cigar from his hand, gripped his shoulder and raised herself on the tips of her toes, trying to taste his mouth, but he turned his face away. Not even in this lust and wine drunken state would he forget himself to that extent. They couldn't have his love, just his body.

Time lost meaning in the best sort of way until a chill breeze crept along his skin, bringing Ramses back to focus with a start. He gazed across the interium to an open door, where coolness beckoned him from his feverish heat. He started untangling himself from the women, pushing through them to the other side of the room. With much purchased dramatics, the girls called out for him to stay, to return, to remember them, but in truth, they were, each of them, already lost to the fog of memories of flesh and hips and lips and tongues, a lifetime of endless nights with nameless women. What could be sweeter?

Ramses reached the far steps and motioned the kiom bearers away from him as he passed through the doorway onto an expansive balcony overlooking the old quarter of the city. The magnitude of the palace Ironeye rose up behind it, great towers and turrets reaching far into the twilit sky, rivaling the distant mountain ranges of Kirith-Jerom. A soft veil of early night had settled over the royal city, but the Mascald heat remained long after the light gave to dark. Sweat steamed on Ramses' skin and the coolness he'd sought moments ago seemed only a dream.

He walked to the railing and looked out over Corinth City. True to their time, the streets of the old quarter were narrow and paved with cobblestones. The buildings, crumbling in places, were held together by moss and creeping vines, their wrought iron balconies overflowing with flowers, pink, orange, violet and blue.

A hot wind gusted over Ramses, sweeping up from the Barbarian Plains, beyond the city walls, which stretched across Corinthia to the borders of Theselon. The wind carried scents of scorched rock and grilling meats – steel, smoke, sweat – horse and man mingling together, and beneath that a note of sweet fruits ripening: mangoes, peaches and grapes. Normally the old side was quieter, most of the entertainment, that which didn't require discretion, and all the sports taking place in the central and upper quarters, but the royal city stood fuller now than it ever had before.

In anticipation of two of the most significant events of their lifetime, commoners and nobility from all kingdoms of the Halos had flooded the city. Every guest house, high house, steam house and whore house was packed to the roof and ablaze with lanterns and sound, storytelling and music. The recent murder of King Sirion Barthos of Anacharasis, last of the old kings, and the whole royal family, had brought about the first King's Hearing in over fifty years – the coming together of all the rulers of the Halos to witness the choosing of the new king of Anacharasis. It was an historic moment, rivaled only by the magnitude of the second event. The time of contemplation was over, and at any moment the Lord Liege of Corinthia would be naming his princess. Ramses felt a hollowness in the pit of his stomach, a sure sign of unwelcome sobering. All the light and sound and song around him only served to remind him of what he missed the most.

Ramses again felt the cold breeze brush against his skin like fingertips. He turned and saw a staircase leading down to the lower balconies. He went to it and from the top of the stairs he spotted August standing there, below him, half in the shadows, looking out over the city. The humblest man with the greatest mind, a warrior rider able to defeat with words before ever raising sword. Ramses' skin prickled.

"*Tato*," he said, descending to join his father.

August turned to look at him and smiled. His eyes sparkled with delight even as they were shadowed by the deepest despair. They stood together in silence for some time before August said, "I've always been partial to the darkness, even when I was your age."

"I remember," Ramses said.

August gave a short laugh. "Do you?"

"Of course." Ramses could smell the wine heavy on his father's breath.

"Some days, when you were very small, I thought you'd never go to sleep. And then when you finally did, I just wanted you to wake up again." August's eyes crinkled heavily at the corners when he smiled. "But tell me, son, do you often stand atop a balcony so open to touch yourself?"

At first Ramses didn't understand what he was saying, then he glanced down at his naked body and back up again quickly.

"No. I'm not here for that. I'm just ..." He searched for the right words.

"You know they have a perfectly equipped harem house in this building?" August said, a tease behind the words.

"I know, I was just there. That's why the state of undress. I left quickly. I felt a cool breeze and sought it out."

Except now the night was still as the dead.

August's eyes rested on him a moment longer, dancing the way they always did, before he looked back out over the city.

"So how long has he been going out unattended?" he asked quietly.

Ramses' shoulders sank. "Who?"

August smiled. "You tell me."

"I have nothing to tell."

"Nothing is not much."

"Nothing is nothing."

"Well. Should the Lord Liege be the person I am thinking of and the person you know nothing about," he lowered his voice to a whisper, "I would highly recommend advising caution."

"How can I advise him of anything if he'll neither talk nor listen?" Ramses' frustration burst out of him before he could censor it. He cleared his throat. "He's different ... things have changed."

He met his father's eyes, then looked away.

"Time changes all," August said softly. He rested a hand on Ramses' shoulder briefly before moving past him toward the staircase.

"Resist touching yourself in public, son," he said from halfway up.

"I'll do my best, *Tato*," Ramses returned meekly.

"Do as I say, not as I do," August added in a whisper, glancing over his shoulder, the mischief back in the eyes of a man known as much for his parties as for his genius. August stepped into the shadows, becoming the darkness as soon as he touched it.

Ramses stood alone again, a heaviness in his chest as he thought of Titan, Lord Liege of Corinthia. Almost two years had passed since they had feasted in the Halls of Ma'at in Ironeye to celebrate Titan's coming of age at thirty. At the ceremony the Lord King Osiris had deemed Titan worthy to marry, and commanded him the task of finding a wife for himself and a princess for the realm. It was law that he was forbidden to cut his hair or beard or partake in any pleasures that may cloud his judgment until the night of his wedding. Titan had been given the traditional two years to contemplate his decision, and Ramses could understand why he had taken the full time. Not only did he need to find the one woman among millions whom he could love above all others, he also needed to consider how his choice would affect the Kingdoms. Titan's choice of wife would change the whole face of the Halos. It could cause offense and resentment, it could see alliances, already shaky in the current political climate, dissolve and war erupt. So it had been two years since Titan had touched a woman. Two years since he'd tasted wine, smoked a cigar, since he'd danced or even shaved. Two years of being hairy, sober and constantly hard. It was enough to send any man into mental recession. But Titan wasn't just any man. So instead of going out of his mind, he had been going out of his window – unattended by his Companions or any of his periphery guards.

Ramses had discovered these doings only by a twist of chance. Titan was masterful at vanishing and covering his tracks; where he was going or what he was doing, Ramses had still not been able to discover. He'd just been counting time until Titan made his choice, hoping the company of his new wife would change things. August's warning suggested more urgent attention was required. But how could he approach Titan on matters so serious when these days they spoke only about trivialities? Time had gotten between them in a way Ramses would never have believed.

Looking back, he could see where the end had begun. Just as the fire forges iron into shield, the Amkalai, the training camp, had molded Titan's body into layers of steel muscles and scar tissue. He'd trained in the general camp with all the rest of them at first, and then by himself, his tests more grueling, his punishment more severe. Ramses remembered well, each time Titan had returned from the trials he was bloodied, bruised and starving. Sometimes his broken bones were protruding through his skin. Sometimes they'd been that way for so long that they'd set into wrong angles. Ramses had stood beside him while Marcos, physician to the Lord Liege, had re-broken and reset them. The first few times Titan had raised his voice to the gods, seeking mercy, but with time his yell became a grunt, then a murmur and then nothing.

With time, he changed. Somewhere out in the Barbarian Plains the joyful, quick-minded, golden-hearted brother Ramses loved so well vanished. It was the price of enduring and inflicting terrible suffering, and when Titan's time of First Trial was done, he emerged at fifteen years, silent, serious and hardened, man not boy, a Liege on the way to being worthy to stand as successor to the throne of his father. The rift between them had begun then, and with passing time only grown wider and more impossible to cross.

Ramses fidgeted with the rings on his fingers, twisting them around as his eyes searched the royal city.

"Where are you?" he murmured.

Chapter 5
Titan

HYDRIA

CORINTHIA (CORINTH CITY)

He smiled easily and laughed out loud. It distracted from his eyes. He put himself at the center of all attention, promising much, telling everything. He had a hundred thousand amusing stories, a million secrets *just for you*. His charm was disarming, but Titan saw him for exactly what he was. His words were red. Their mist hung in the air around his face as he told another lie. The merchant slipped an arm around the girl and she giggled but stepped away modestly to avoid his embrace. She didn't see the way his lips twitched, snarled a fraction into contempt, because by the time she looked back he was smiling again.

The pair strolled down the Street of Initian. Hundreds of candlelights twinkled in the sunset glow. Bakeries, wineries and fineries lined the smoothed stone streets, filling the air fragrant and sweet. Gold clinked, and people lounged, laughing in unhurried conversations. Wine flowed.

A gust of warm air stirred the vines climbing all over the stone surfaces. The merchant casually plucked a flower from one tendril, a moonlight blossom, white with pink inside. Titan heard all conversations at once, and all apart. He could recall each of them, word for word, at any point from now until forever. His mind was a lock, but this man was a trap. Titan heard him say to the girl, *"This flower reminds me of you – so beautiful! You glow like the stars. You must be a princess. Are you telling me your real name? Surely you are a princess."*

She laughed and Titan heard screams. In his mind he saw every possible avenue of action from here, this time only two paths. Sometimes there were many more, but for this girl, only two. She could leave now and go home. She'd walk through the door and greet her mother, who had been sitting up to watch for her, sewing now so her daughter wouldn't realize she'd been waiting and worrying. She'd go to her room where an aging, shaggy hound, toothless and poor of sight, was stretched out beside the bed. Its tail would flip-flop at her return. She'd pat the dog's head, then go to sit in front of her mirror and smile at her reflection. She'd met a man and he was perfect. The only harm that would come to her then would be her disappointment when he never came calling again.

The other avenue. Blood. Pain. Death.

She chose without realizing, following the merchant's lead, bedazzled by the shine of his words, leaving the lights of Initian and heading toward an ordinary door in an average street that led down into darkness. Titan followed. He wore a black suit of armor with helm and full-metal zivas locked down over his face, and over that a hooded cloak, gray-black, a common type that workmen wore. It blended with the crowd. On his back he carried heavy metalsmith's tools to account for his hunching over. People noticed a man who stood head and shoulders above everyone else. People also noticed a man with five armored guards, so his *ata-ajua* were spread out, following him over rooftops and down side roads, except Argos. He remained Titan's shadow, from beginning to forever. They trailed the pair all the way to the door. Titan had been seeing it in his dreams for a full two sevens now and had just caught a sense of the merchant tonight. Those red words made him, they betrayed him. Above them, a man appeared on his balcony and whistled a long note and then another two shorter ones, summoning his children back for supper from their play in the streets. Similar calls were going up all over the city, each one slightly different. Dread wormed its way through Titan's stomach. Some children would not return. Some parents would be waiting forever. There stood a predator among them.

The merchant pushed open the door. The girl went to step inside, then hesitated, and her paths suddenly leapt from two to three – she was running away through the streets, the man chasing, but before she had a chance to break away the merchant shoved her back against the wall, pressing a cloth soaked in crushed maiden lily against her nose. Her legs gave way and she slumped down, unconscious. The merchant checked around him, then hoisted her up over one shoulder. Still smiling, he vanished into darkness and closed the door behind him.

Titan heard the bolt shunt locked and he let several moments pass, then he was moving again, swiftly now, to the door. He lifted his hand and held it just in front of the handle. It shuddered and flew into his grasp, breaking the lock. He cast it aside onto a pile of refuse in the alley and levered open the door. The first step inside brought a gust of odors, burning flesh, spilled blood, bad breath and fear – sending images crashing through his mind, but he cleared them with a silent repetition: *Service to the Lord King, Honor in Battle, Sacrifice in Brotherhood, Sanctity in the Afterlife* ... The Warrior Way. He and his *ata-ajua* descended.

The stairs were sparsely lit and long, but soon the sounds were echoing from below. Shouts, thuds, screams, clashes, shield and sword, fist and flesh. Proper arena sparring had a particular rhythmic sound to it; these noises were sporadic, desperate. The howl of an injured animal rang loud, piercing, and a deafening high-pitched squeal sounded in Titan's mind, splitting enough to make him grimace, the sound of suffering. It drove him mad. His steps quickened. The end of the staircase was blocked by two foreigners, Anacharasi at a glance. They held themselves with import, chests puffed, arms bulked out, faces full of challenge and reproach.

"Password?" one demanded.

Red words.

Titan cut them down so quickly, so silently, that no one in the underground fighting pit noticed at all. He dropped their bodies to one side behind a table and entered. One glance around from under his hood captured everything. Seven fighting pits, five person, two animal, each staging their own brutal battle to the death surrounded by crowds of screaming betters. The majority were not Corinthian, and Titan was tempted in that moment to think his people better than this, but he knew well that all manner of men, good and corrupt, existed in every race, and indeed he spotted several Corinthians there. They would not be spared judgment.

He moved among them, glimpsing one of the animal fights through the gaps in bodies. A brilliantly colored peacock was dominating against an all-white opponent. The white was beautiful, terrified. Its screams made Titan's head pound and his teeth ache. He forced his eyes away, pushing forward until he caught sight of the merchant. He was on the other side of the room, disappearing through another doorway. Titan glanced over his shoulder. Argos was right there, and the other four were around him, Afton and Ruan on the left, Herra and Sention on the right.

He made for the door and passed through into a hallway, narrow and bare. The farther down he walked, the heavier fear gathered around him. Titan spotted handprints in blood in the shadows of the walls. A sense of great foreboding constricted his chest. He paused, seeing light up ahead, spilling through a second doorway. He lowered himself to a crouch, his *ata-ajua* echoing his movements behind him. They silently inched toward the door. Titan peered around the corner to see the merchant standing in front of a table, the girl still slung over his shoulder. At the table sat a much younger man, wearing spectacles and an expensive cloak. A book lay in front of him in a circle of light cast by a lantern. He was staring up at the merchant.

The merchant clapped him on the cheek and said, "Don't look so frightened, my young Damius." He dumped the girl down beside the table, unfurling a length of chain from the shadows and locking it around her wrists.

"She looks upper," the younger man said, his accent provisional Armenite.

"She is upper, and the price will be upper too," the merchant responded.

"And the attention will be greater."

"What attention?" He gestured around them with exaggeration. "You see anyone watching us?"

Damius pulled a face, unconvinced. "I'm just saying, we don't want to end up like Savege. Harlow Darro has come to this city, everyone is talking. Not to mention the eyes of the Lord King and Liege."

"Harlow godsdamned Darro!" the merchant spat. "I've told you before, he doesn't exist. He's fictitious, boy, just a tale told by the Anacharasi to give them fear advantage over the Drauls – and fools all over have been swallowing it up. A man cast in iron, who rides with a giant at his side? The Unbreakable? The Sword of the Sky? Really, you'll buy this? Come on, Damius! And the Lord King, great bronzed *abram*, sits atop his grand throne, looking down on us, taking from us and giving nothing back but the right to gaze upon his ugly face!" He pounded his chest. "We should be so honored! It's their fault, the Lord King and his blessed son. This is their doing! They give us nothing so we have to make our own. It is our right! We are the new kings, claiming our right! Who will miss one or three whores?"

"They're ladies," Damius corrected him. "And their parents just might."

The merchant snorted, "What are they going to do? What can they do to us?"

Behind the table a door opened and both men tensed. A bearded man poked his head around the corner.

"Yes? What?" the merchant demanded.

"They're here," the third man said.

The merchant and his young assistant exchanged a glance, then leapt into action. The merchant dragged the heavy table aside, kicking away the mat from beneath it to reveal a trapdoor. He raised it and headed down. Titan heard shuffling, then a woman cry out in pain. He felt a beast inside of him arising and he clenched his fists to restrain it.

Damius called down the trapdoor, "If they're marked they'll be worth less."

From behind his spectacles, his eyes went to the girl, the merchant's latest catch, where she lay on the floor, and Titan saw a moment of doubt there, a moment where he considered saving instead of condemning her, but then the moment had passed and the gold was back in his sights. The merchant emerged, dragging a line of chained women, eight of them, and one little boy with his mother. The boy was sobbing, terrified, and the merchant struck him hard in the back of the head, where the bruises wouldn't show. Titan flinched at the blow. He clenched his fists so tightly they were shaking. His grandfather, Apollo the Almighty, had taught him that a man who fears he is not man enough becomes a sadist who hates the weakness he fears within himself. He attacks the innocent and the defenseless first.

The door on the other side of the room opened up again and the bearded man entered with a group of others. Buyers. Almost without a second glance at the merchant or Damius, they crowded around the captives and started examining them hungrily.

"They're all in fine condition," the merchant announced.

One of the buyers, a man with shoulder-length hair and sharp yellowed fingernails, took an interest in the new girl, who had now awoken, groggy and gasping with shock. He took her face with one hand and said, "You have beautiful eyes."

Red words. And Titan saw a flash of vision, a wall of jars with eyes floating inside them, and screaming in the background. Sweat broke on his brow behind the zivas as the beast inside him strained against its chain.

The boy whimpered as another buyer seized his mother roughly by her shoulder.

"What would you do to save your child?" he growled.

"Anything, anything, just let him go, please. Please! I beg you, Warrior."

That made them all laugh. They knew what they were and it wasn't warriors. Titan had seen enough. Enough to know no one there had anything but the most sadistic intentions. All paths ran to blood.

Enough.

Titan rose out of the shadows and stepped inside the room. All eyes were immediately on him.

"Who are you?" the merchant demanded. "Get out!"

Titan spoke to the women, keeping his words low and common to conceal his voice. "Move back and look away."

As soon as they started stepping, he struck, Argos with him. Titan destroyed the buyers first, his sword cutting through them without resistance. The merchant tried to run away during the confusion, but Argos caught him hard and kicked him into one corner, the blow, though restrained, shattered bones. The merchant started crying, sobbing, dragging himself along the floor.

"This is not my fault. It was him." He pointed at Damius. "He blackmailed me. I demand a proper trial before the court. Do you know who I am? I demand —"

Titan cut him down. There was no justice in it. It was just an end. Damius stood in the corner, saying nothing, his face set, keeping his composure unlike his business partner before him.

Titan approached him, seeing his own reflection in the young man's blood-splattered spectacles. He raised the tip of his sword to Damius' neck.

"Where are they?" he growled.

Damius eyed him, "Who?" he asked, his voice breaking.

"The rest of the missing women and children."

The young man shook his head. "These are the only ones we have."

"What have you done with the others?" Titan pushed the tip against his skin and red blood spilled out. Many more than eight women and one boy had vanished.

"There aren't any others. This is our first time. We knew only one other man in the skin trade, but he was killed by Harlow Darro."

Titan could hear he was telling the truth. Lies had a different sound to his ears.

"Are you ... Darro?" Damius asked, tremulous.

Titan flicked the sword and took his head off fast. The captive women were huddled together, hiding their faces, their chains clanking. Titan went to them and broke their locks. One of the women whispered, "Gods bless you Warrior Darro. Gods bless you." She kissed his armored hand.

He freed the little boy, who was staring up at the darkness beneath his hood, searching for his eyes, but they were well concealed behind the zivas. No one would mistake eyes like his.

"The Unbreakable," the boy whispered, and his mother pressed her hand over his mouth, clutching him closer, her every breath half a cry.

"Pause here a time," Titan spoke to the women in a lowered voice, "until you hear silence from beyond this room, and then come out."

Titan and Argos left the room, the other four *ata-ajua* falling into step with them as they reentered the main pit area. Here Titan paused and looked around the chaos. What manner of man reveled in the suffering and degradation of others? Everywhere Titan looked, he saw red pouring from open mouths.

"Spare no one but the captives," he commanded his *ata-ajua*.

He closed his eyes and started moving. When he opened them again, the whole area was cleared, silent, with bodies everywhere and blood flooding the floor. There was a captive kneeling in front of him with his hands raised, eyes wide with terror, Titan's sword inches from his neck. Titan withdrew his sword and the man scrambled back to where a gathering of other prisoners huddled in one corner. He turned at a movement behind him and saw the women standing in the doorway, hands over their mouths and faces, horrified.

"Go up the stairs and out. Go to your homes or to a shelter, don't delay," he told them all. "Go!"

The prisoners fled, helping each other. No one looked back, except the boy.

Titan sheathed his sword, not his own, which was distinct, but another made for the purpose of secrecy. He stood in the middle of the carnage, turning in slow circles, his breath loud in his ears. The law stated that any accused must have a trial. There must be evidence. They must be tried and judged with accordance to the law. He knew it to be true. He knew why it was important, but his heart denied both logic and reason. What his heart told him was that once certain lines in life are crossed, there is no going back, and there should not be any going forward either. Men such as these must be stopped. As the Lord Liege he must uphold the law at all times, but as himself, he was the law, the trial, and the executioner.

A high-pitched scream pierced his thoughts and he turned fast, looking for the sound. He spotted feathers beneath a pile of rubble. Titan crossed the room and dug out the white peacock.

As his hands clasped onto it, the screaming subsided. His touch, he knew, blocked pain. He smoothed a hand along the bird's back to a bleeding wing.

A snarl came from the shadows beside him as a huge mountain dog emerged, bloodied and salivating, starving, its eyes on the bird. It alternated between growling and whimpering, wounded from fighting, as terrified as it was angry.

Titan clutched the peacock in one arm and extended his other. The dog immediately lunged forward and tried to bite him. He caught it by the scruff and felt the animal's body relax and the trembling subside. The dog leaned forward and rested his head on Titan's leg. The poor beast was so weary.

"Now we leave this place," he murmured. With the bird and the dog and his *ata-ajua* behind him, Titan ascended out of the pit into the night.

* * * * *

Secrecy was not permitted. Words were bitten back, emotions withheld, certainly and always. But secrecy, the type of secrecy involving hidden tunnels beneath the city, and unknown chambers beneath old dungeons, that was not done. And if it was, it was either by Kís, spies, whose very existence relegated them to the shadows, or by the crooked and evil inclined. But a prince who hid, who wore a mask, who disguised himself, embraced the shadows, welcomed solitude and craved silence? Such a thing did not exist. What Titan was, he knew, could not exist.

These thoughts ran through Titan's mind as he stepped with his *ata-ajua* up from the tunnel into his hidden chamber. The wall closed behind them with a boom, the locking mechanisms snapping back into place. The heavy scent of candle wax and aged parchment lingered in the air. Titan closed his eyes, taking a moment to compose the ill-ease and guilt inside himself, while his *ata-ajua* removed the tools from his back, as well as the cloak and black armor.

He lifted off his own helm and took it over to where Argos was hanging up the rest of the suit. He placed the helm at the top and stood blinking, taking a moment for his eyes to adjust to seeing a full picture and not just through the slits of the zivas. He stared at those two empty spaces and they stared back. This was what people saw when they looked at him, just as they did when they looked at his *ata-ajua*, except his guards never removed their helms. In all the years they'd walked together he'd never seen their faces. They wore identical armor, they were the same height, they walked the same, fought the same, but strangely, to his eyes each of them looked completely different.

Titan rubbed a hand along the rough angles of his chin. His own face felt more like a mask than his mask did. Other suits of armor hung all around the walls. It had taken numerous prototypes to get the design right, concealing Titan's physique effectively while still allowing enough free movement to fight. His thoughts turned to the animals they'd brought up from the pits. He'd given them into the care of a healer known to him. Sention started to clean the blood off his armor, while Herra brought Titan a bucket of water. He stripped bare, casting aside undergarments soaked with sweat, and washed briefly. Afton and Ruan started preparing his clothes, while Argos brought over a cup and held it up to Titan's lips. He smelt the lemon and salt and turned his head away. He didn't have a feeling to drink or eat anything. His appetite was not as it had been, neither was his sleep, and had not been for a long time. He waved the offering away, but Argos grabbed the back of his neck and pushed his face to the cup, holding it there until he relented and drank. He grimaced as the sour, salty mix burned his throat. Argos made him take some more before putting the cup aside. He then took an orange and started to peel it.

"I'm not hungry," Titan told him.

Argos continued on, and fed him pieces while the others helped him re-dress – subs and cintus, breastplate, arm irons, shin irons, boots. He strapped his own calteus over both shoulders, feeling his weapons now lying cold and firm against his back. Over the top he fastened his royal cloak. Argos went to the wall, slid out a brick and pulled the concealed lever behind it. The wall of armor sank down and out of sight, locking into place before the waters started flooding the room.

As the platform where they stood rose up, Titan stared down into the dark waters. They'd set it up to deter even the most curious of intruders, but the water didn't repel Titan as he knew it should. He'd even at times, as a child, tried entering the waters deeper than his knees. Argos had always held him back and kept anyone from seeing it. He'd hadn't realized at that age how odd it was to like water.

Titan lifted his hands and examined them, his mind returning to an earlier worry. What existed inside him did not exist. Even as he knew it did, it could not. The red mist he saw, the paths he knew, the way he remembered, the spark in his touch, his influence over metal and the way his moods shifted the weather and could bring lightning from the sky. All this could not be spoken of, it could not be brought into the light. By the old law, man was man and gods were gods, and no powers but those of sword and muscle were bestowed on man, elsewise it was a trick from Methusael. It was evil and existed only for the destruction of mankind. Titan closed his hands, feeling a weariness across his shoulders and a heaviness in his heart. At times he was certain that he walked the righteous path, and at others he was filled with doubt and confusion. Maybe he was evil and it was only a matter of time before it overtook him.

The platform came to a grinding stop and a drawbridge lowered. It seemed to come from solid wall, but as they walked across it, the wall opened into another chamber. The design of the chamber was not Titan's – he'd copied it from papers recovered from Harlow Darro's quarters during the investigation into King Sirion's murder. Darro was Sirion's former Kí, his chief spy, as well as the prime suspect for his slaughter.

The *ata-ajua* entered first, four of them lighting lanterns, while Argos went to another switch. Blank walls slid out and rotated around, revealing plans, designs and research, and a table lifted from the floor with a map spread out across it. Some were Darro's work, including the map, but the rest were Titan's own findings on the illusive Kí. On inspection of Darro's chamber at the palace in Asta, royal city of Anacharasis, one thing had been apparent to Titan: it wasn't Darro's real chamber. It had been skilfully set up with enough work and belongings to make a convincing cover, but Titan had realized quickly that what he'd come to know of the man did not fit with what he was seeing.

Titan stood at the table and looked down at the map. He understood the manner of masterful work, his father and grandfather were legendary, but he'd never encountered a mind like Darro's. The former spy's approach to strategy was singular. According to the accounts of Sirion's surviving officials, it was Darro who had orchestrated the entire travesty against the King. Yet they could produce no evidence, nor even many facts at all about Darro, other than what was known of the nature of all Kís – they were more often than not individuals with significant skill who could not be part of official office because something was wrong with them, whether it be that they were bastard born, deformed, drunkards, or hiding secrets of other varieties. Titan had tried to uncover Darro's secrets only to be met with endless rumors.

Some said monster, some said hero – the Unbreakable, the Sword of the Sky, The Scourge of Morcvara – who had freed tens of thousands of slaves from the alleged illegal mines in the regions of Nisitseri and Morcvara on the borders of Draul and Cytisus. Some said there was none more skilled in combat and on horseback, others said he was a shambling deviant who put others to task while he profited from the glory. Some even more outlandish rumors claimed he was cast in metal as a child and had survived to now living fully coated in impenetrable steel, and that he rode with a grotesque Cytisian giant as his guard, who wore the skulls of men around his neck on a chain.

Rumors. And behind the rumors he'd found something even more peculiar, a solid wall of silence formed by those who had actually seen or met Darro. It was a silence that hadn't been moved by promise of payment or stern word, a loyalty that, in Titan's experience, could never grow from fear. It was respect, in the true sense of the word. It was clear Darro had risked himself to save lives. Not just once, not even a thousand times, but more.

Titan had himself only once glimpsed the person he believed was Darro, and from a great distance. Titan had been riding through the Kingdom of Armen, neighbor to Anacharasis, and had seen from the top of a hill a herd of wild horses spooked and charging toward the edge of a cliff. His heart had sunk into the acid of his stomach. He was a rider to his very soul, and he was helpless to stop them. He couldn't get to them in time, and even if he could, any movement behind them would only spur them on faster.

Then he had spotted it, a figure running across the plain, faster than should be possible, bending light and speed around him in ways Titan had never seen before. He had caught up to the herd, entered it and vanished, and then appeared again as he'd sprung onto the back of the prime stallion, leading the stampede. At the very edge of the cliff, Darro had managed to turn the stallion's head and run the herd back toward the plains to safety.

A rider can't ride an unbroken stallion, no one can enter a wild herd without getting crushed, nothing can turn a crazed stampede, no one can run that fast, and yet Titan had seen it with his own eyes. Who else could it have been except this brilliant shadow? Another person who couldn't exist, but did. Titan didn't deny it to himself, he did feel an affinity with the spy.

Titan studied the map. Over the top of Darro's lines he'd drawn his own design. It was his first plan for the war that he felt was inevitable, lines of truth that mapped out the plot he knew was tightening around him and his kingdom. War was coming, but behind that he'd also marked in the places from where the women and children had been vanishing, all throughout the city and the extended kingdom. He, not Darro, had been the one to bring justice to the first skin trader and now the merchant, but both had been dead ends. There was something else out there haunting the darkness of the night. He closed his eyes tightly, willing the truth to come to him. Who was it? Who? He could almost see an image, but it kept to the shadows, refusing to form fully.

The beast he felt within him roared, suffocated by frustration and infuriated. Titan slammed his hands down on the sides of the table and pushed back. Immediately, shame caught him. Loss of control was not acceptable, but he was barely able to hold himself in. He felt Argos' hand on his shoulder directing him to the staircase out of the chamber. He pulled away. He needed to stay. He had to keep working. Argos grabbed him again, this time tightly, and by both shoulders. Titan knew all too well that his First did not care what he wanted or did not want, only what he needed, and he was completely uncompromising.

"I'll go," Titan said, holding up his hands, and Argos immediately released him. He moved for the stairs while the *ata-ajua* concealed the truths of the chamber and then joined him. The staircase took them all the way up through the center of his residence tower, all the way to his garden on the flat rooftop. Making sure no eyes were on him, he climbed out of the hollowed tree trunk where the secret entrance opened.

He took a deep breath from the hot night air, immediately feeling his composure returning to him. A soft whinny sounded behind them. Titan turned as Simeon Ishboseth Farahman XI, gleaming like diamond satin in the moonlight, trotted up to him. Titan embraced his stallion, pressing his face against his neck, and Farahman rested his head down on Titan's shoulder.

The splendor of Ironeye and the lights of the royal city shone all around them. Titan swept his eyes across the upper quarter, pausing on the common ladies still waiting outside the gate, the line so long it stretched beyond where he could see, all the way down the hill into the old quarter and farther out into the plains. They waited there day and night in the hope that he might see them. It was a thought that made him truly uncomfortable. Tomorrow would be filled with hopeful proposals from the noble women and then he would have to choose his wife. He massaged a pain in his head. How could he choose when the person he wanted was a figment in his mind, just a thought, a feeling without a face – just a forgotten memory? He believed he had met her in his life, had known her and loved her, but perhaps in childhood, before he'd understood what it meant, and now he didn't know who she was, or where to find her again. And time was running out.

Keeping a hand on Farahman, Titan walked through the garden, contemplating, until he reached a place where a statue stood alone in the center of the garden. In the darkness it looked like the real man, so much so it made Titan's steps falter and he stopped. Originally the statue had been carved into the temple wall among the likenesses of other former kings and warriors. Titan had never admitted it aloud, but he'd developed a loathing for seeing the statue there. At first he had avoided looking at it, but the more he'd avoided, the more he'd felt compelled to look. And the more he looked, the more he hated it.

That figure pressed into the wall, that wasn't the Almighty. Apollo of Ironeye didn't stay inside, he was a restless warrior, always outside, under the sun, under the stars, always moving among his warrior riders, always watching over his people. But now he was trapped in a rock prison. It felt like a tomb, though everyone knew that his real tomb stood empty. And so one night, Titan had gone in and taken the statue and brought him here, under the sky, where they had sat together many times when Titan was young.

He crossed over and stood in front of the statue with his head bowed. Even now, he half expected to hear the Almighty's voice. Even after all these years. If anything, the grief was worse now than when he was a boy, the longing more desperate, the confusion deeper. Titan raised his eyes to the likeness. Up close, it truly looked nothing like the Almighty. No statue or portrait of him, and there were thousands throughout the city and kingdom, ever looked like him. His face without the spirit was someone else's face entirely. But it was all that was left of him. When a king dies he leaves behind his armor, his sword, his horse, their presence a comfort to his people, something left to hold when there is nothing left of him. But when a king disappears, he takes everything with him. A sharp pain in his chest drove Titan to his knees. He rested his head on the feet of the statue and closed his eyes, allowing himself to believe, for half a moment, that it was really him. That he was still there. That he had never left.

In the distance, thunder rumbled.

Chapter 6
Harlow

HYDRIA

CORINTHIA (CORINTH CITY)

Her chin was doing all the ridiculous things chins did when people were losing a battle against their tears. All that jiggling and wobbling. She made an embarrassing choking sound, shaking from the effort of holding back a cry of emotion so violent it felt volcanic. Harlow stared up at the sky, blinking and holding her treacherous chin. In this night shadow it might just pass as a contemplative pose, an intellectual pondering, or at least she truly hoped so. If either Aron or Vitali caught her crying, they would never *ever* let her forget it. She knew exactly what Aron would say, with that look in his eyes, mischief overlaying anger: *Harlow Darro doesn't cry, does he?*

Anakis shuffled behind her and placed one heavy hand on her armored shoulder. She tensed on instinct, but then relaxed into the touch and laid her hand over his. They stayed like that until she caught herself. Harlow cast her eyes back down to the Lord Liege, Tarrus of Ironeye, where he knelt before a statue of the Almighty. The tears sprung back immediately and she had to look away. As far as watching over the Titan to make sure no one was assassinating him, it wasn't going very well. How could she protect him if she couldn't even look at him without breaking down?

Harlow blew out deeply, then clenched her jaw. It was hard to feel anything without feeling everything, which was a problem when all she wanted to feel was nothing. But the sight of him resurrected the past, even parts of it she didn't realize she'd forgotten. The furious night sky growled above them and she looked upward into the darkness with mistrust. They hid at the very highest point of Ironeye, the temple tower, inaccessible by all accounts, but if lightning was going to strike, they stood vulnerable. She looked back to Titan, his *ata-ajua* around him, still as statues themselves. Harlow leaned back against the legs of the stone stallion behind her, carved into the roof of the temple. The Corinthians believed that after life, warriors rode from the Halos into the Blessed Plains, where their trials were over, where death would be no more – no more mourning, no more crying, no more pain.

When she had first arrived in Corinth with the brothers and Anakis, they had taken cover atop the Lord King's tower to watch the ceremony marking the calling in of the Halos' kings. Corinthians were fond of ceremony. She'd been unsure of what to expect of herself. Just riding to the King's City had disturbed all sorts of feelings inside her and she couldn't predict, upon seeing the Titan, what other emotions would suddenly decide they needed a showing after lying dormant for so long. She hadn't cried a single tear in over twenty years, and now …

So she'd been tense, aware of the unmapped territory she was treading. The warrior riders had filed into the square, and then the periphery guards, companions and *ata-ajua* with the Lord King Osiris and the Lord Liege at their center. What she'd felt, maybe there wasn't a word for it, like a person standing outside of a room and looking in, wanting to be inside, but knowing they never could be. Then all the royal and noble women had entered to start the dancing. Titan had stood on the palace steps watching the festivities.

The last time Harlow had seen him, he was a boy riding across The Rise, where she lived then with Aron, Vitali and their grandmother. Vitali had forbidden her to go into the town to watch him ride through. There was no tolerance for oddities in those parts of the Halos, not then and not now. And she was as odd as odd got. But she'd felt there was no option, she had to go, she didn't have the words to explain at the time but she felt such a wild desperation to see him, as though seeing would bring back the Almighty. She would have walked through fire, leapt from a cliff, thrown her own life down, even at that age, for Apollo of Ironeye. She loved him. Looking back there was, of course, no rationality in thinking Titan could bring his grandfather back, but at the time it had seemed a possibility.

She remembered tearing through the forest, running as fast as the metal would allow, terrified she'd miss him, and then coming up on the side of the road well out of town so that no one would see her. She'd looked one way and then the other, fearing the worst, but then she'd seen the cloud of dust in the distance coming toward her. It was him. She'd started waving her arms around and couldn't stop as the Lord Liege and his party rode closer. When they were near enough, he spotted her with those eyes in the image of his grandfather's, eyes that could harden to iron and look into a person's mind. She couldn't say what he saw when he looked at her, possibly just a little boy dressed up in full armor jigging about, certainly he wouldn't have seen a little girl cast in iron crying behind her permanent mask. She'd endured a lot of pain by then, and a lot of scorn. But whatever Titan saw, as they rode past, he took one of his pinion knives from his calteus and threw it down to her. A gift – and they rode on.

It was just a small knife, usually used in games more than anything, but she'd held it in her hand and it had changed everything. There was suddenly hope where she'd seen only darkness. There was suddenly pride when she'd felt only shame. A future grew from one act of kindness toward a strange and lonely child by the side of a dirty road. It was for this reason that she hadn't know what to expect on seeing him again after all this time.

He'd stood on the steps as the women danced before him and as they swirled around him she'd felt – call it what it was – jealous. Some of the girls were truly beautiful, their dresses, their hair, their jewelry – they looked like princesses. Harlow had wondered who Titan was looking at and what he was feeling. In general, beauty didn't trouble her. There was no place or need for beauty on the path they walked. Mostly she wanted to be terrifying, not beautiful, but in that moment she'd felt like a disgusting animal, and it had been shameful how quickly she was reduced to self-loathing and doubt – after everything.

She sighed again and cast her eyes back to the Titan. He had cut such a strong and majestic figure at the first ceremony, but now he truthfully appeared exhausted. He rested his head on the feet of the statue Almighty. It was nothing like the Lord King, nowhere near big enough, and that disturbed her. It was just a statue, but it wasn't, as well. It was all they had. She realized from watching Titan that she wasn't alone in her extended mourning. So many years had passed and still everyone was struggling to accept he was gone. Not just struggling, but permanently broken by it.

Apollo the Almighty had been a once-off, larger than the world he walked through or the life he lived. He was light, time and space itself, drawing people into his presence. He was rest and safety for the tormented, the tired and forgotten, and every nightmare come true for those who meant to harm the innocent. The King. Her memories were dismembered, destroyed by torture, but if she even dared to close her eyes she was right back at the beginning all over again, clinging to the rocks with Naro beside her, the saltwater burning their eyes, filling their mouths, choking them to death.

She couldn't remember getting there, but she certainly remembered arriving. The boat had shattered on the rocks and left her clinging, bleeding fingers torn to the bone, holding Naro to stop the foal from being swept away. Shapes had moved atop the cliff, help, rescue, she'd thought, and she'd screamed to them, her small voice drowned by the roar of the waves. Then the arrows had come skimming through the air. She was target practice.

One had nicked her hand and she'd let go. They'd been swept away, tumbled brutally beneath the surface without relent. When she crashed into something solid, she'd believed it to be rock, but then a hand had wrenched them up out of the water. They'd gasped, sucking air into their lungs hard enough to break ribs. It was a man, and he carried them back to shore. Gigantic waves crashed over them, some with the forms of sharks and other water-dwelling monsters hidden inside them, but the man didn't falter. He never lost his grip, never stumbled, and nor did the five armored soldiers around him.

Harlow remembered trying to hold on to him, but her hands were too torn up. Her blood streamed down his neck, but when she touched him, her pain vanished and she just felt cold enough to freeze, and probably would have if not for the furnace that seemed to burn at the core of this man's body. At the top of the cliffs, the archers had gathered. She remembered seeing the light washing over their startled faces as the clouds rolled across the moon. The man put Harlow and her foal onto his horse. She'd rested her face against the great stallion's spiky mane and heard a swipe and zing, then another, and then silence. The man returned and the stallion started moving. She had lifted her head and seen the archers lying on the ground behind them. She'd thought at the time that their helms had come off, but it was their heads as well. That was the beginning.

In the middle was two years of learning everything she knew now that was of any worth – how to ride, how to fight, how to win and to accept defeat, how to speak and write and read in High Corinthian and many other languages, how to think logically and illogically, how to strategize, how to plan for war, how to feast, how to starve, how to be brave, how to trust again when trust had been so broken. How to love, how to lose. Wrong and right. Dark and light. He'd taught her everything.

And then came the end. All stories had an end.

Harlow stared down at the Titan as he lifted his head and stood before the statue.

"Are you crying?" a voice whispered from beside her. She jolted inside, but showed no outward response.

She turned to Aron, standing in the shadows, with the face of a boy and the eyes of a killer. She snorted. "What are you talking about?"

Morrison, Aron's blue alarm bird, ruffled his feathers from his perch on Aron's shoulder.

"It just looked like you were, you know, wiping a tear." He gave her a grin and made a tear-wiping motion across his face.

She definitely was.

"I definitely was not."

"Just some dust in your eye perhaps?" Aron stepped closer. "Sweat from your brow? A solitary raindrop?"

"Keep laughing, Aron of the Rise," Harlow said lightly. Too much protest was always obvious.

"Harlow Darro doesn't cry," Aron said. "Does he?"

"No. Never," Harlow said, smiling.

"Why are you now smiling?" Aron asked, still smiling himself.

"Why are you suddenly so interested in my emotions?" Harlow returned.

"I asked you first."

"And I you second."

He looked down to Titan and his face turned serious. "Apollo of Ironeye."

Harlow nodded. "The Almighty."

Aron shot a glance her way and then nodded.

Aron understood loss. He had become closely acquainted with it, and picked up a bag of tricks for dealing with his own darkness. Aron Storon. If one asked him how he was faring, he'd always say okay, because he hadn't been okay for so long that not okay was now his okay. He laughed a lot and hid in the sound. And when they'd found him trying to hang himself, Harlow had warned him if he ever tried it

71

again, she'd put her sword through his throat for his troubles. She hadn't meant it of course, but he had truly meant to die that day.

Harlow smelled beer, a pub meal and cheap perfume moments before the shadows stirred again and Vitali appeared, looking far more full and self-satisfied than he should have. A headwing moth suddenly fluttered down near his face and he did a jig, waving his hands around and making Aron snort with laughter.

Vitali stopped and glared at them both. Harlow shook her head.

"What?" he demanded.

"Garlic chicken on your breath, the brothel on your clothes, cheap wine exuding from every pore of your skin."

Vitali started to shake his head.

"Don't waste my time with your denials, Vital," Harlow said. "I told you both, we need to be invisible. If I can smell you so will the guards, so will the *ata-ajua*, so will the Titan's enemies."

"I went to the steam house. If I still smell then it's the way I smell. You smell too, you realize that?"

"She was crying as well," Aron put in.

"Crying!" Vitali demanded, so loudly that Harlow almost drew her sword. They all ducked low. Harlow peered over the ledge toward the Titan. He wasn't looking. The temple tower was at a perfect height for sound reduction, to see but not be seen.

She looked back at the brothers and Anakis. "I know it's been a while since we did such close work, and I know we're all rattled, for our own reasons." She looked over them. No one but Anakis met her eyes. "But we need to tighten up. No excuses. War is stirring, the assassins are sharpening their steel, the Kís are all over the place. If we're not on our game, he'll end up dead. Understood?"

"Understood," the brothers repeated.

Harlow turned back to where Titan stood.

The end.

The memory of it was corrupted as well, moments missing, out of order. Mostly black and white, the pain had overwhelmed her. When the Almighty left the camp and never returned, the Drauls invaded. King Vitor-Petacula's armies were looking to claim the Almighty's body, his armor, his metals and jewelry, whatever they could get their filthy hands on. Word of his disappearance had spread with stealth. Harlow was left with the women, but she didn't stay. She'd gone to find the Lord King, and been found by the Drauls instead. They took everyone they captured to the death camps for questioning. Their words were burned into her mind. *Where has he gone? Who killed him? Where is his horse? Where is his armor?* The same questions, over and over again. Everyone was put to the question. Everyone was put to the sword – women, children, infants even. No one was shown mercy.

When they tied her up by her legs above the molten iron, she'd held her silence, even as they'd lowered her closer and closer and the steam started to burn and the pot spat fierce sparks of metal up onto her skin. She'd barely felt it, so sure had she been that Apollo of Ironeye would appear and save her again. Before they could finish the task, the Anacharasi army attacked the death camp. The inquisition fled with her still tied up, but by ill-chance the rope around her legs took on too much heat and snapped. She crashed against the side of the pot headfirst and it fell, tipping the boiling iron all over her.

One does not survive being cast in iron. One does not rise from that.

Vitali found her. He was a young Anacharasi soldier with a brutal father he hated but obeyed and a frail mother he loved but couldn't save. She was Corinthian by birth. And so the confusion of his life began. An Anacharasi soldier with a Corinthian heart beating inside his chest.

Harlow could imagine Vitali's face when he had found her there under all that metal. If there was ever a man who lived in hard reality and hated variations, this was him. She'd made eye holes in the metal mask. How? She didn't recall. But according to Vitali, he heard a sound and knew she was alive.

He'd stood there staring at her for quite some time. He claimed it was only a moment, but she knew Vitali well, it would have been much longer than that. Strangeness confounded him. He was the most reluctant, angry hero of them all. Vitali Storon would have loved to be a villainous rogue, brutal without question. He hated his conscience and his heart, if he could cut them out and continue living he would.

She looked back to the brothers. Vitali was threatening Aron under his breath and Aron was sniggering. Harlow's frustrations erupted.

"Anak, if you will," she said to Anakis, who stood behind the brothers. The giant man bent over and clunked the brothers' heads together solidly, leaving them both reeling.

"Aron, go to the Armenite camp, watch Ravana Nazar. Vitali to the Anacharasi camp, watch Gorse. *Just. Watch.*" She emphasized the words.

Vitali's eyes burned in the darkness. "Traitorous scum of the earth. Methusael take him. He's —"

"I know." Harlow cut him short. "Watch him. They'll make their move."

"I still don't believe the princess Ravana is involved. She's far too lovely. She wouldn't hurt a fly," Aron said.

"Pull your head in," Vitali snapped at his brother. "You think all scheming women are ugly, do you?"

"Watch her," Harlow said to Aron. "We know she's up to something. And go carefully, remember where you are."

Aron nodded. "All the women at the inner gate makes for easy entrance and exit. I've never seen a line that long in all my life."

He looked over the ledge toward the Lord Liege. "He's not *that* handsome," Aron added. "He's tall. He's a warrior, no doubting that, but look at his nose, will you!"

"He's the Lord Liege of Corinthia," Vitali said. "He could look like a squashed turd and all the women would still want him."

"Not *all* the women!" Aron objected.

"Yes, *all* the women," Vitali insisted.

"Harlow's a woman. She doesn't want him."

"Harlow's not a woman."

Vitali glanced at Harlow. "Well, you're not. Not really, not a proper woman. Why are looking at me like that? You know what you are."

"Get going. Both of you," Harlow growled at them.

The brothers vanished off in different directions. Harlow stayed where she was, listening to them go as she resumed her vigil over the Titan. Vitali was yet to make the acquaintance of tact, but his words were true enough. She was a woman who had lived as a man for all her life.

The deception had not been intentional. When Vitali had found her, he'd just assumed she was a boy, for no other reason than the common assumption that boys were stronger than girls, so anyone who could survive such horror must be male. She'd even forgotten herself that she was a girl until after she'd been in the Anacharasi camps, training as a soldier, for several years. At that time, as she was leaving childhood and entering another phase, she'd looked around and thought, *I don't belong here. I don't want to be here. I don't want to fight. I don't want to be with the boys. I want to be with the girls.*

She'd told her commanding officer that she thought she was actually a girl. At first he had not responded, and then when she had repeated herself he'd said to her, *As a man you can fight, you can serve, you can ride – you can rule. As a woman you're of no use to anyone deformed as you are. All you can do is put yourself in a dark corner so that everyone can forget you exist. So stop lying or you will be punished.*

Anakis moved behind her and Harlow looked up at him. He patted a hand on her helm and she knew he was worried about her.

"It's okay, my friend," she murmured.

There wasn't a gentler soul than Anakis, trapped in a more terrifying body. The opposite of Vitali, he yearned for love and acceptance and only received fear and hate. No man had any right growing to his size and height. Giant. Outcast. Monster. Just like her. Just like all of them. They were oddities that only made sense together.

Below the tower, Titan finally started moving back through his garden with his *ata-ajua* and stallion. Harlow rose to her feet to see him reaching the stairs that would lead to his inner residence. He'd stand well guarded in there. When he vanished from sight, Harlow turned to Anakis and said, "Time to test these out."

Behind her, she shook out long wings. Harlow stepped up onto the tower ledge and jumped.

Chapter 7
Eli

AQUAIS

SCORPIA (THE MANTICORE FACILITY)

Eli shut his eyes and turned to face the interior of the hangar. He moved with a deliberate slowness, monitoring his emotions and composing himself as he went. Over the past year-cycle he'd come here countless times, so many times that nothing about it should have been astonishing or shocking to him, yet every single time he set foot in the place he was like a giddy kid. He was determined this time to be nothing short of cool and composed – *cool and composed*.

He completed the turn, then opened his eyes. He clung to cool and composed for approximately half a buzz of a firefly's wing and then it all came crashing down around him and he was standing there, mouth gaping, eyebrows shooting for the sky like it was his first time again, and he had to conclude that it was impossible not to be stunned by the sheer, incomprehensible magnitude of the *Scorpian Manticore*. It was enormous, an immensity of machinery, a metal mountain, a flying city – it was like Scorpia sprouted wings and took off. Obviously that was a slight exaggeration, considering the *Manticore* was only taking up part of one of the 997 living levels of Scorpia, but for a person standing in front of this megacraft, feeling like a speck of dust in comparison, it didn't seem like such an overstatement.

The whole front of the craft had been hinged aside, revealing the multi-layered interior where Drays performed their respective jobs and duties, which at present mainly revolved around the repairs of the *Manticore*. The ship had sustained major damage in its desperate escape from the tunnels of Kullra Fornax pursued by the Arequium Mors and the humans and creatures the Mors were inciting to chase them.

Eli tried to focus on one level of the craft at a time, but it just went up and up and up until the workers looked like ants and Eli's neck started to hurt because he was straining his head back so far. He looked down, then glanced around to check if anyone had noticed him acting like such an amateur. But maybe that was the thing, he wasn't an amateur, he knew exactly what it took to make a craft fly, so he understood the mind-blowing genius of the *Manticore*'s design and the skill that it would have taken to get it in the air and keep it there. And that genius could mainly be attributed to the *Manticore*'s captain, Shah-Jahan RaAhura.

Eli gulped a little. He had sincerely tried not to feel intimidated by the Dray leader, he'd gone into each and every conversation with Shah-Jahan silently shouting motivational phrases to himself. "*You can do this! You're a professional! You're a soldier! You can do at least seven consecutive push-ups*

– *maybe six. Definitely no less than four!"* But unfortunately every time he'd come face to face with the man himself – well, things had gone downhill from there. Not to the Diamond/ Copernicus level of downhill, but like a really embarrassing first date, or a job interview where all the wrong things are said coupled with a plenitude of raucous, inappropriate laughter. Shah-Jahan just had that effect on him, and as a combined people the Drays made his skin crawl. He didn't mean that to sound horrible and racist, more accurately, they made him feel as though his face was being analyzed by a high-powered microscope while he worried about having something hanging out of his nose, or stuck in his teeth, and struggled not to do anything embarrassing.

Drays were highly developed communicators, which meant that during conversations, they weren't just hearing the words being spoken, they were also reading in minute detail every expression, pupil flicker and body twitch. They were smelling pheromones and micro-odors that most others had no idea even existed, and hearing nuances to the words that no one else could detect.

On top of all this, they were also a communal mind, a very rare organization of family all linked up to each other through a central person via psychicsonic energy. And their central person was also their captain, Shah-Jahan, head of the family and pilot of their craft. He was the most powerful mind of them all, and the connection he held with each member of his clan was so strong it was palpable. Walking through the *Manticore* felt like walking through a forest of invisible spider webs, the web being their psychic *rete* or connection, and the fact that Eli could physically feel their minds talking to each other gave him the creeps. He wasn't sure why, it just felt *sticky*, for want of a better word.

Even so, Eli could have spent a lifetime studying the Drays. They were fascinating, in a really terrifying sort of way, for many reasons, not least of all the fact that they seemed to be the only race who were immune to the influences of the Arequium Mors. Even more than that, it had been foretold, according to the Nÿr-Corum survivors, that Shah-Jahan could defeat the Indemeus X. Unfortunately the ancient and haggard foreseer who had told him of this future had been agonizingly cryptic and had died moments after the telling, having only the breath to murmur the words *Apollo Corinthia*, which at the time had meant exactly nothing to a young Shah-Jahan.

He had pretty much pushed the incident aside until the Arequium Mors had started hunting him, and then the whole horrible story had unfolded. Eli knew if he could just get one of the Drays to let him run some tests on them, nothing invasive, just basic harmless things, he might be able to come up with a vaccine or block against the Arequiums. He might even be able to figure out the connection between Shah-Jahan and the Indemeus, but the Drays were nothing if not secretive and guarded and they couldn't have been more mistrusting if they tried.

Eli could understand why, but it was so extremely frustrating. Literally the whole universe hung in the balance and they could be the key to its salvation. The commander had told Eli to have patience, so he'd attempted to stop himself salivating over every Dray he saw, but he really couldn't help but drop questions and fish for answers at every opportunity. Which was perhaps why Shah-Jahan was so guarded around him. As far as information went, the Dray captain hadn't come to the party at all. The team only knew about the prediction and about Apollo Corinthia because one of the survivors, Saint Croy, had told them.

Eli's ensuing frenzy of research had led to nothing, even Beatlebee's crow book came up blank, until he had repeated the name Apollo Corinthia to Silho and a light had come on in her eyes. Silho told him that Lecivion had mentioned the name Apollo to her in Omar Montanya. He'd said – and Eli had written down and re-read the words so many times they were branded into his mind – *"The North of Hydria still stands after the four barbarian kings, Apollo of Corinthia, Kleomedes IV of Thesolon, Sphairos of Armen and Sirion of Anacharasis, made an unwitting pact with the ratha demon king, Mordan-Grieg, which resulted in the sparing of the North."*

After finding no leads from there, Eli had gone to Ev'r and Ismail and asked if they could use their scullion skills to see anything in the past about this King Apollo of Corinthia. They'd delved deep into the combined memories of their bloodline and Ismail had seen Apollo with a map, splitting it in five. He'd described the map and Ev'r had recognized it. Year-cycles before, she'd glimpsed one piece of the map in the Vestibule Shrine in the desert mountains of Al-Serrah, and so a quest ensued in which monsters were met and matched and moved aside and the map piece was recovered – and then three more pieces after that, from other equally inaccessible locations.

The team had taken the pieces to Shah-Jahan. He had touched them and, through the *rete*, which connected into the past as well, he'd seen a lot of disjointed things, demons, a man imprisoned, desolate lands and destroyed cities, nothing that made sense yet, but Eli was sure if Shah-Jahan pushed himself a little further he could see more detail. But he didn't seem to be making a serious effort, and Eli wasn't sure why.

He clutched the wooden case to his chest. This partial map was their only link to Apollo of Corinthia, who was their only link to how Shah-Jahan could defeat the Indemeus, which was really their only hope. It was convoluted and confusing but Eli was determined not to be discouraged. What he really felt like doing was barging onto the *Manticore* and demanding that Shah-Jahan take another look at the map pieces, a good, hard look, but what he was going to do was crawl in there and beg, on hands and knees if necessary, for him to do it, because he sincerely didn't want to see anyone else die.

He had intended to wait for the rest of the team to arrive before entering the *Manticore*, but with the storm, the Wing Ripper, the Indemeus X, he was so jittery he could barely stop shuffling. He couldn't just stand there or he would explode or collapse, or both, either simultaneously or consecutively. Plus, with the weather and the traffic, the others could be delayed for who knew how long. As the thought entered his mind, his com buzzed and he looked at the message. It was from Diega – *We're delayed*. Well, that was that, he couldn't wait any longer. Eli burst forward into movement, heading deeper into the hangar past Drays carrying metals and materials, conferring with each other, working on smaller crafts and other projects surrounding the *Manticore*. Eli gazed at them all with interest. Their clothing was made from some kind of black reptilian hide and it gleamed in the light and blended with the shadows. None of them paid him the slightest attention, keeping their dark and glowing eyes averted while he tried to stop himself from wiping their psychic webs off his face.

It was with substantial relief that he spotted a familiar face in the crowd. Darius DeCavisi, another of the original human survivors. Original, because they were the ancestors of a group of humans who had left Scorpia during the Devil's Age, just before humanity began breeding out into the animal bloodlines to survive, so they were really the only "pure" humans left, with no bloodline marks. Eli headed straight for Darius and found him crouched beside his machine, a very primitive hover bike which they called a dragger. According to the survivors it had been one of the main sources of transport in their city.

Both Croy and Darius had been law enforcers in Nÿr-Corum, Controllers, partners, though now they weren't on speaking terms, or at least Darius wasn't speaking to Croy. Eli didn't know the complete story of what had happened, but it was pretty obvious that there were intense feelings on both sides, as well as a possible love triangle involved. Such triangles seemed to be a pervading theme of Eli's life at that moment.

Croy was an absolutely stunning girl with pure white hair that had a silver shimmer to it. She wore it short, like Ev'r, and she was the type of powerful and fearless woman that got Eli's heart beating a little too fast. Croy and Darius had obviously been close, but now when they were together she would step forward, he would step back, she would look away, he would look at her, she would look at him, he would look away. He was extremely angry and she was hurt and sorry. Eli could see they were both suffering and wanted to be close again, but Darius couldn't get past his own anger. Relationships. Seriously, who needed them?

"Darius," Eli called out to him. Darius looked up with sweat dripping down his face and his forehead smeared with grease. As soon as their eyes met, Darius looked away. That was something about him that Eli found interesting, he always avoided eye contact. Which was a shame, because he had fascinating eyes, a green-blue aqua with a faint glow to them in lowlight and from certain angles. Darius was half Dray, though if Eli said that aloud he would likely get a punch in the face for his trouble. Darius flat-out refused to accept he was any parts Dray, even though it was obvious he was, and he exerted most of his anger rigorously ignoring all the Drays around him, even though they were everywhere. He made it quite clear that he wouldn't still be there at all if he had anywhere else to go. The city was completely foreign to them and the sun fried their sensitive skin. Plus, Croy was there, though Darius would never admit that was a reason not to leave. He claimed he hung around because he didn't trust any of the Drays not to touch his stuff.

Eli glanced at Darius' workbench and saw he had the AAF weapons manual Eli had given him weighed open to a middle page. Darius had been a weapons expert in his own city, but the weaponry in Scorpia was a million times more advanced. Eli had given him the manual to help upgrade his knowledge and he had responded with "not interested", though clearly he was. Darius saw him looking and moved over to the bench, surreptitiously shifting the book away. The man had skill and heart, but he was also proud and probably the most stubborn person Eli had ever met – and between the commander, Silho, Diega, Jude, Christy Shawe and Ev'r Keets, there was some seriously tough competition. In truth, Eli felt sorry for him, standing there with all that was left of everything he knew and understood scattered around him in a small circle. He was like a man clinging to a crumbling raft with a tidal wave of change rising up before him.

"Hi," Eli said, realizing he was staring. The survivors spoke a dialect of ancient Urigin that was quite different from the evolved language, but close enough to understand with some effort. Eli had taken the liberty of writing it down and learning it to try to make the survivors feel less alienated.

"What's happening, Junior?" Darius grunted, examining a machine part on his bench.

He called Eli *junior* because of his height, even though they'd figured out he was older than Darius by several year-cycles at least, but Eli didn't actually mind at all. Junior was a far better option than some of the names he'd been called throughout his life. Mosquito boy, runt boy, shortstop, squirt, smidget, widget, niblet, stumpy, stubby, plug, plip, blip, plop, wee-wee-pee-pee, slipper sleeper sleeps in slippers so small, and, most recently, snacksize, were among the least explicit. And it really didn't help that his last name was Anklebiter.

Besides, an almost friendly nickname from someone who seemed to utterly loathe everyone else was difficult not to appreciate. It felt like Darius was reaching out in whatever way he could manage, so Eli returned his greeting with, "Controller DeCavisi." He saw the side of Darius' mouth twitch slightly. No one else called him by the title he had held before he'd come here and become known as "one of the survivors".

"What are you doing here?" Darius asked him, eyeing the blue stripes and purple dots of Eli's bloodline marks.

Eli sighed and said, "I need to see him."

Darius' expression immediately soured and he turned his back on Eli, muttering, "Off you go then."

"We're not getting anywhere with the map," Eli said. "And Meteor just vanished from the sky – that's the sixth planet to go."

Darius' back tensed, and after a moment he glanced over his shoulder. "Six now?"

Eli nodded. "And that's not counting the ones we can't see. Things are desperate, which is why I *desperately* need to see him. Even though getting any information out of him is like milking an antagonized male dragon."

Eli's words brought a shadow of a smile to Darius' face despite his best efforts to remain furious.

"He's in the subsidiary control room," Darius finally said. Despite denying he was one, as a Dray, Darius could sense where Shah-Jahan was at all times.

"The one near the blue room?" Eli asked.

Darius shook his head. "Another one near the center of the craft."

"Is that near the mess hall?"

"Nowhere close," Darius said, and Eli's frustration peaked.

"I know you like – I mean – *don't like* – going on the *Manticore* and I don't blame you at all, but please, *please*, can you show me where he is? If I go on there alone I'll get lost, and the Drays are as helpful as electrodes to the nipples."

Darius snorted, and started to say no, but then seemed to reconsider. He lowered the tool he was holding and said gruffly, "Let's go then."

"Thank you!" Eli exhaled with relief.

Darius headed off and Eli followed him, weaving through the Dray workstations all the way to the ramp leading up to the first level of the *Manticore*.

"You know, I've been wondering this for a while," Eli said, trotting at Darius' side to keep up. "The 'Scorpian' bit of 'Scorpian Manticore', do you think that came from here, Scorpia? Did the Drays know about the above lands?"

"Yes, they knew," Darius said.

"So it was just the humans kept in the dark, so to speak," Eli said, realizing too late that it was a very poor choice of words.

Darius glanced at him with his "enough talk, Junior" expression, then looked away. So Eli held his tongue, and followed him through the congested halls of the ship, pushing through the invisible webs of communication everywhere.

Darius finally slowed as they turned into a corridor and saw guards blocking a doorway, their dogs beside them.

Usually Eli had an affinity with dogs but these canines weren't the usual. They had glowing eyes and two mouths, one in the normal place and another in the middle of their neck, and they could bark and bite with both, and they really didn't take kindly to sweet talk. They were savage and wary animals, and like no breed of dog Eli had ever seen. Apparently there were many foreign animals aboard, but Eli hadn't been permitted to view them, even though he was itching to. As they approached, the dogs' ears pricked forward, and they started growling. Eli put his hand in his pocket to steady Nelly, but she was sleeping soundly.

Darius stopped a distance from the guards with Eli beside him. "He needs to see your captain," he said curtly.

The guards eyed them with suspicion and one said, "Then he'll wait."

"Go get him," Darius said, then raised his voice. "Now!" As he commanded it, the webs of the *rete* shivered around Eli and the Dray guards each took a step back. The dogs growled, but before the conflict could escalate, a figure appeared in the door behind them. Croy. Darius looked at her, then immediately away. She stared at him, so many emotions crossing her face.

"Darry what's wrong?" she asked him.

"You're on your own, Junior," he muttered to Eli, then turned his back and left, with Croy watching him go. When he had vanished, Croy turned her gaze on Eli, burying her feelings and saying, "Hello Eli." She crossed her arms.

"Hey there." He waved, then lowered his hand self-consciously. "I need to talk to him."

Croy gave the slightest wince and glanced back over her shoulder. "Give me a grain ... a second." Eli knew Croy had been making a real effort to learn Urigin and adapt, more than any of the other surviving humans. She turned back into the room, giving him a glimpse of the impressive scar on the side of her head. Croy had confided in Eli that before they'd been able to escape their city, Nÿr-Corum, there had been a confrontation between Darius and Shah-Jahan that had ended with Darius giving her an ultimatum: either he shoot Shah-Jahan or himself. In desperation, Croy had put a gun to her own head and pulled the trigger. Shah-Jahan had managed to grab her as she'd fired, and the shot had just grazed the side of her head. Croy had told Eli that in hindsight she couldn't believe what she'd done, but that it had been a spur of the moment, irrational decision.

Eli waited a second, then another five minutes, which felt like five centuries.

All the machinery inside the *Manticore* made it hot and stuffy, and sweat started pouring down his face. His stomach growled loudly enough for the dogs to hear, and they tensed on their chains, eyeballing him, and snarled back. Eli glanced behind him, looking for an exit strategy in case things went south, and then suddenly he desperately needed to use the bathroom. He had to cross one leg in front of the other while the Dray guards continued to ignore him. Finally Croy stepped back through the doorway and signaled for him to come. He hurried forward. The guards and dogs didn't try to stop him as he passed, just sniffed and growled some more.

As Eli entered the room, his attention was immediately drawn to Shah-Jahan working in one corner. He and a few of his men had dragged a large chunk of engine out of the wall and he was elbow-deep in components. The *Manticore* was designed without a conventional engine, the entire craft was an engine within itself. It was extremely complicated.

The Dray captain was shirtless. He had the hard muscles and the scars of a soldier and he was slicked with sweat. Eli felt well and truly intimidated, but desperately tried to hold onto his composure. He hadn't actually seen Shah-Jahan physically working on the craft before, and it made him worry that maybe they were planning to leave Scorpia. If the Dray left, they would lose the only hope they had. Eli clutched the wooden case harder and swallowed back his anxiety.

Eventually Shah-Jahan glanced at him. Croy had once described his eyes to Eli as fire reflecting over dark waters and that was as accurate a description as any he could think of. They left Eli gulping.

"Captain RaAhura," he greeted him, trying for less butt-kissing and more carefully respectful, and perhaps not succeeding.

"What do you want?" Shah-Jahan responded. His tone wasn't promising, but Eli pushed forward, determined.

"I'm not sorry – I mean, *I am* sorry – to disturb you, I really am." He took a second to try to slow his breathing as Shah-Jahan's eyes scrutinized every minute detail of all he was consciously and subconsciously doing. "Is there any way you could possibly have another look at the map pieces?"

"No," came the firm and immediate response, and then he turned back to his work and the conversation was officially over.

Eli shot Croy a desperate glance and he could see by her eyes that she was frustrated by Shah-Jahan as well. She shook her head, thinking, then walked over and placed a hand on his shoulder. Eli saw the other Drays in the room bristle at the touch. Apparently Drays and humans had been enemies since the beginning of time, possibly before, and the fact that the captain was keeping company with a human woman was causing some major feather ruffling. But Shah-Jahan stopped and turned to look at her, and something unspoken passed between them in the *rete*. Croy wasn't part Dray like Darius, but a Dray bone had been implanted in her leg and it gave her some communication skills, as well as immunity to the Arequiums. As they continued to look at each other, Eli started to feel as though he was intruding on an intimate moment, again. Eli was an expert across several fields and according to some was seen as the city's foremost scientific mind, but what he felt he was truly gifted in, his true super skill, was busting in on people during their intimate moments. In that, he was the undisputed master. Unfortunately.

Under Croy's silent influence, Shah-Jahan seemed to relent and turned to face Eli again. He approached the central bench, vanishing for a moment in the shadows before stepping out into the light and stopping on the other side, larger than life.

"Bring it here," he ordered, and Eli hurried forward. He placed the case on the bench and unclipped it, carefully opening up the lid. Inside sat the four pieces of Apollo's map beneath a layer of protective glass. Eli glanced over the torn and worn parchment. The writing was tiny and in a language he had never seen before. Over the year-cycle he'd decoded the language, deciphered the alphabet, and taught himself to speak it. But unfortunately, some of the translated words and sentences were also in a code of their own, which he hadn't realized until Diamond had pointed it out.

"I was working on this bit last night," Eli immediately rushed in, pointing to the top, near a tear. "And I think maybe, *maybe*, it's talking about a sword. I mean the word is only partially there, and it was coded, so it's hard to say for certain, but the word 'Finsgini', at least, I think that's what it is, means, I think, length of steel, which in some cultures would otherwise be known as 'sword'. And referencing several ancient map-making techniques, I believe the lines of the map are all converging on this word, which means it is the X point of the map, the central importance of the whole document. So I thought if you could look inside the *rete* around the map for anything to do with a sword, that would … that would be great."

He took in a deep breath and looked up at Shah-Jahan, but he wasn't looking at the map. His eyes were closed and he wore an expression of pain. Croy noticed as well and stepped closer to him, worry tightening her face. Her eyes suddenly shifted to the door and she whispered, "There's something out there. Beyond the gate."

In the dark of Croy's eyes Eli saw the reflection of a shadow descending on a small, hunched form. His mind immediately jumped to their serial killer. He gasped, got caught up in himself and spun several times in useless panic, then lunged for the door. He crashed through and ran, only realizing Croy was with him when she overtook him, leading him to the ramp out. They thundered down the ramp and raced through the hangar. Eli caught movement from the side as Darius came leaping over a bench to join them. The three of them crashed out the front door, startling the Watchers there.

"There's something outside the gate!" Eli yelled at them, his voice drowned out by the water gushing like a storm from above. He didn't wait to see if they'd heard him, just took off across the square toward the watchtower, ripping out his electrifier as he ran. When he reached the gate his hair and clothes were drenched, and as his hand touched the metal he heard a terrified, agonized scream that gripped his neck with horror. He grabbed hold of two jutting bolts and leapt up to reach one of the spyholes in the gate. He jammed his eye against the hole as the screaming continued, a long, high desperate note piercing the air. He looked one way and saw nothing, then the other, and within his small circle of sight, through the dark and rain, beneath a streetlight's glow, he saw a gigantic, clawed hand clutching something in mid-air. Eli spotted blond curls and sparkle and his heart seized.

"Diamond!" he screamed.

He leapt down and stood for a moment, hyperventilating, then his rational mind kicked in and he shouted up to the watchtower.

"Mo-Mo! Mo-Mo! Mo-Mo!"

The Watcher's face poked out the interior window.

"Open the gate! Open the gate!"

"I can't!" Mo-Mo screamed back. "There's a threat – I can't."

"Open the trutting gate – open it!" Eli shouted at him, but Mo-Mo just continued to shake his head helplessly, as Diamond's screams went on and on. Croy, Darius and the Watchers stood around Eli, unable to help.

In desperation, Eli threw himself at the gate, then raised his electrifier to blast it even though he knew it would just glance off the shield. *The shields!* he thought. He'd designed them, he could override them. He threw his electrifier down and whipped his computer system off his belt. With shaking hands and water dripping into his eyes, Eli rapidly hacked the facility system and shut down the entire security grid. The gate sparked and the huge locking system suddenly snapped off. Eli threw himself again at the gate and strained to slide it aside, but it was so huge he couldn't shift it, even though he was screaming and straining with everything he had.

Darius pushed in beside him, his shoulder to the steel, with Croy and the others behind them. Together they struggled until they shifted the massive structure. Eli rushed to the opening and squeezed out.

The place where Diamond had been was now empty. He stared at it in horror before hearing a whimper from above. He looked up and saw Diamond high in the air, still in the monster's clutches. Blood was pouring down with the rain. He grabbed for his electrifier, but realized he'd dropped it on the other side of the gate, so went for his blade instead and started hacking at the bind around his wings. They burst free and he leapt up into the air and sped toward the demon creature that held Diamond in his grasp.

"Let her go!" he yelled, darting in with his blade. He stabbed toward the Ripper but the blade went straight through it as though it were made of water, and it gave no response at all. Eli immediately changed tack and grabbed hold of Diamond, who lay limp in the creature's arms. He wrestled with the Ripper, struggled with all his strength and fury, but its grip held fast. From below, Croy and Darius opened fire on the monster, but its shadows just consumed the shots without effect. The Ripper released a call, a long echoing *ech ech* sound. Clutching Diamond in his arms, Eli stabbed wildly. His efforts seemed to cause no actual damage, but the creature suddenly released Diamond. Eli gripped onto her, trying to fly backward, but then he felt the agony of the Ripper's claws puncturing his shoulder. Diamond slipped from his grasp and fell. All Eli could do was scream.

A blinding light fell over the scene as the *Ory-6* broke out of the mist above and sped right for them, with the commander hanging out one window shooting, and Silho out the other with her hand raised, using lightform. Eli felt the creature shudder, but then Silho slumped back inside the craft and Eli felt an excruciating pain as the creature grabbed one of his wings and twisted. He couldn't even scream. His senses blurred as he realized this was it. This was the end.

Chapter 8
Ev'r

AQUAIS

MATADORI DESERT (THREEGULLS)

Ev'r and Ismail made it to the entrance of Threegulls and passed beneath the bone arches unchecked. They moved swiftly through the streets until they reached the center of the town. There they found the Broken Mother, a statue from the Postmesatonic Era. It was made of pure monalith steel, the heaviest substance in the world, and had somehow ended up out here in the middle of the Matadori, lying on its side, half buried in the sand. The gigantic figure's face was covered in lines and fissures, almost like a real woman aged by the desert's unpredictable moods and foul temper. Ev'r stared for a moment into the Mother's cold, empty eyes, then dropped her attention to the shrine of fresh and wilted desert flowers and other gifts encircling the statue. Certain scullion tribes, like the Shineriver Coyote Tribe of Threegulls, believed the statue had god-like powers, especially regarding fertility, and they worshiped it as their deity and protected it with their lives, which was why they were going to be really upset when she and Ismail smashed it to pieces. The Broken Mother was just about to get a whole lot more broken.

Ev'r smiled to herself as she reached into her pocket and took out the burrowing device implanted with a biochemical detonator that Snacksize had given them.

"Think this will work?" Ismail said, staring doubtfully at the gigantic woman.

"It's Snacksize," Ev'r said. "It'll work."

She stepped forward, trampling the offerings, until she reached the statue's face. She pressed the burrower onto one of the eyes and clicked it to start. Immediately, the machine's pincers dug down into the steel and went to work hollowing out a space. The tiniest part of Ev'r felt discomfort as she watched the little machine do its job. This was one of the oldest pieces of art in Aquais, and they were destroying it. Then again, if the whole planet was to be devoured by demonic forces anyway, what was art? As the burrowing bug vanished from sight, Ev'r stepped back to Ismail and the two of them stood, holding their breath, waiting.

"Should we be taking cover?" Ismail suddenly said, after they'd been standing there for some time.

The statue shuddered and they both threw themselves sideways. Ev'r skidded behind a rusted speedway platform that someone was using as shelter around their dug-out toilet. She almost skidded face-first into the black pit, stopping herself just at the edge. The smell made her grimace. She braced, expecting a highblast explosion, but after several moments of nothing, she lifted her head above the platform, just as

Ismail did from behind a pile of bricks close by. They looked at each other, then back at the statue. It shuddered again and then disintegrated to dust. Ev'r stared. She'd witnessed disintegration before, but never of monolith, and never done so wholly and beautifully that the object simply turned to dust. She heard Ismail curse and knew he was thinking the same.

Ev'r stood and brushed off her pants, then stepped out to where the Broken Mother once lay. She spotted the deactivated bug among the debris and picked it up.

"You, I'm keeping," she told it, and slipped it back into her pocket.

Ismail lifted his head, hearing something her ears couldn't. "Movement."

The suns were rising fast now, the gray veil evaporating from all around them. Soon the worshipers would return to the scene, and the eyes of the lookouts would turn back their way. Ev'r grabbed the compact shovels from her pack and threw one to Ismail. He caught it and shook it out to full size and they started digging. In his vision the final piece was here, somewhere beneath the Broken Mother. As far as Ev'r was concerned this was it, the last handover to Snacksize before they could walk away for good.

The two of them dug fast and it wasn't long before Ev'r's shovel hit something solid. Ismail threw down his shovel and dug with his hands around the object, and they soon pulled up a small wooden chest. Ev'r brushed off the black wood and studied the images etched in the sides. She'd never seen this type of wood before in Aquais, or the images. In his vision, Ismail hadn't seen who had planted the chest or exactly how they had managed this seemingly impossible task, but he said he'd gotten a sense of something – armor, and a sword. Ev'r placed the chest onto the sand and put a finger to the latch, pausing for a moment to check for traps or tricks before flipping it up. Ismail tensed beside her. She took the sides and raised the lid and a smile spread over her lips. Inside, on red velvet, sat the final piece of the map. The scent of old timber filled her nose.

"This is it," she said to Ismail. When he didn't reply, she glanced over at him and felt a surge run through her. He was kneeling in the sand, his body tense and shaking, his head tilted up to the sky and eyes completely whited out, deep in a vision.

"Not now," Ev'r murmured, darting a quick glance around them. She wanted to grab him and shake him, but couldn't. If she touched him now she risked splicing into his vision, which could cause them both serious and permanent brain damage.

The raised voices of the worshipers returning echoed around her, closing in on all sides. Ev'r cursed.

"Ismail!" she called into his face as loudly as she dared. "Ismail, snap out of it! Come back! Wake up!"

He made a murmuring noise as though he was trying to wake, then jolted out of the trance. He gasped once and slumped motionless down onto the sand.

Ev'r cursed again. She couldn't carry him without using dark magics, which she hadn't used since coming back. As much as it left her feeling defenseless, and as much as the magics called to her, if she was the same as the witch who had destroyed them in the first place, there was no future for them. Not because either wanted to leave or would leave, but because love couldn't exist with fear. And as much as he tried to hide it, Ismail was still terrified.

"Okay, get up!" Ev'r slapped his face lightly, then again more firmly. "Ismail! ... Trutt!"

The voices were right on them, almost to the square. She had to get them to cover.

Ev'r grabbed a cloth from her pocket and used it to extract and wrap the piece of map and store it in her bag, then she grabbed Ismail's arm and slung it around her shoulders. Heaving with the full force of her natural muscles, she managed to maneuver him into a draggable position and shuffle back inch by inch through the sand. She dropped Ismail momentarily to force open the door of a burned-out, abandoned shack beside the square, then seized him again and dragged him through.

A fierce sweat had broken on her skin and she was panting heavily, the beat in her chest rivaling the robotic thuds of Ismail's heart. She closed the door and straightened up, breathing relief – they'd made it just in time. But then she froze. If they were inside, why was the desert wind blowing as though they were outside? And why did she feel eyes on her back? Ev'r turned. The shack was just the front wall of the place and nothing else. She stood in front of a crowd of at least a hundred Shineriver Coyote Scullions, all staring at her with hostility and suspicion.

"Definitely losing my edge," Ev'r muttered.

A voice shouted out from the square just beyond the wall.

"The Mother is gone! The Mother is gone!"

Screams and wails of grief followed, and Ev'r gritted her teeth. All the eyes locked onto her were now murderous. No one moved a muscle. These scullions were not the sharpest tools, but they could put one and one together. Stranger sneaks into town, Mother is destroyed, stranger is prime suspect. Nothing like desecrating someone's fanatically held religious beliefs to bring out the worst in them.

Ismail groaned and started to stir. While Ev'r stood eyeballing the crowd, he struggled to his feet, glanced around them groggily, blinked, then glanced around again. Clarity rushed to his eyes.

Without hesitation he drew his electrifier and shouted out in the common scullion tongue, "Back off." He aimed the weapon at the crowd. "I said back off."

In a clatter of metal, a hundred electrifiers were simultaneously drawn and pointed back at them.

"Nice going," Ev'r said to Ismail.

A massive tremor ran through the ground, rattling all the shanties around them, bringing unstable board, steel and brick crashing down.

"You broke the sacred bond. You are both cursed forever!" one of the old women in the crowd screeched out, and the others all joined in, screaming and yelling – *cursed, cursed, cursed.*

The words didn't rattle Ev'r at all. There was a scullion saying – *If I cried about every dog who barked at me in the streets I would have drowned in my tears year-cycles ago*, but Ismail's chest had started to heave. Time to fly.

Ev'r raised her com to her mouth and spoke into it. "Gypsy to us."

She waited for the response beep and when she heard nothing, looked down and saw the *Gypsy Rose* was not on the radar, something was malfunctioning. Ev'r swore.

Another tremor, stronger this time, shook the entire town. Ev'r's teeth rattled together. Ismail looked over at her and said, "Something's rising."

Ev'r looked down at the shaking ground. Something was definitely rising. Her bet was a massive, angry Skither, woken rough from its beauty sleep by their charge blast.

"Run?" Ismail asked.

"Run," she confirmed.

They lunged out into the crowd. Ev'r fought with her blade, striking fast and hard, cutting a path through the scullions.

Ismail used his fists. He was a powerful telepath, but the vision had wiped him out. They were severely outnumbered, the only advantage being that there wasn't room for everyone to attack at once. A few of the scullions stupidly opened fire, but Ev'r ducked low and the shots struck down others in the crowd instead.

She stayed down and pushed through. The third tremor was so violent it knocked people off their feet and fractured the ground across the square. People suddenly became aware of the rising threat. They forgot about her and Ismail and started to flee.

Ev'r made it through the crowd and around the back of another building. Ismail collided with her and their eyes met. She saw the look in his dark stare. They needed to be gone – *now*! Ismail gritted his teeth and she heard bone snapping and fracturing as his wings cut out from his shoulder blades and through his skin. He grabbed onto her, squeezing the breath out of her.

They shot up into the air and electrifier zaps rang out around them. One struck Ev'r in the leg and she bit her lip, tasting blood. As they flew higher, she heard another tremor shake Threegulls, but this one didn't stop. She looked down to see a gigantic hole opening up all around the entire town. It grew bigger and bigger until a huge mouth with hundreds of rows of teeth broke out of the sand, swallowing everything and everyone who had not managed to get clear. The Skither shot up toward Ev'r and Ismail. Ismail looked down and saw it too. He yelled out and beat his wings furiously to get them clear of the monstrous beast, but it was rising too fast. Ev'r grabbed the nuclear grenade from her jacket and pulled the pin, dropping it down into the gaping tooth pit below. The explosion made the creature shudder, and it slowed slightly, but didn't stop.

"I have an idea!" Ismail shouted.

"Is it a good idea?" Ev'r yelled back.

"Not particularly!" he replied. He suddenly stopped flying and they dropped down toward the monster's mouth. Ev'r's stomach leapt up into her throat. They freefell all the way to the rim of the mouth, then Ismail shot sideways. It only took the Skither a moment to realize they were clear of its jaws and redirect sideways too, but its effort bought them time. Ev'r heard a bleep.

"The *Gypsy*'s coming," she shouted.

The transflyer zipped across the sky, faster than sight, zigzagging around the Skither's head and roaring to a hover just below them. The roof slid open and Ev'r and Ismail dropped down. As soon as they were inside, Ev'r yelled, "Kick it up!"

The *Gypsy* responded, shifting to hyperspeed and burning a path across the sky, way too fast for the Skither to catch. Ev'r looked back into the gray distance and saw the gigantic form slumping back down into the crater that used to be Threegulls. So much for a low body count. Ev'r collapsed back in the pilot's seat, a sensation coming over her that her face and jaws were gigantic. It was a hangover from her time as a Ravien, at times she still felt the size and weight of her head as it had been. And then there were the memories and dreams as well. Enough to make any person afraid to close their eyes. The feeling passed and she straightened in the seat.

"Where were you?" she asked the *Gypsy*, taking over from autopilot. "Do that again and I'll sell you for scrap!"

Her leg was throbbing where she'd been shot and her pants were soaked red. Ismail lay beside her, his eyes closed, face pale.

"Hey!" she called to him, knowing not to touch him until he regained himself. His eyelids flickered open and horror stared from behind his gaze. A chill crept across Ev'r's skin. She held her breath, waiting for him to speak.

"Eli," he whispered.

The word lingered in the silence between them.

'What about him?" Ev'r forced herself to ask.

"He's dying."

A spike ran through Ev'r's chest. "Where?"

"The underside – the *Manticore*. Now."

"We're way out," Ev'r said, checking the craft's readings.

Ismail's eyes darkened, and he said, "Go. Help him. Try."

"Follow me there," Ev'r said, and he gave a nod, straightening in his seat, ready to take the controls.

Ev'r pulled her scarf up over her nose and her dark vision glasses down over her face. She shut her eyes and let out a long breath, whispering the enchant that would sink her into the Murk, the gray drift of magics behind reality. She felt herself falling backward into the slipstream. Her mind told her to fight it but she let herself fall, and everything around her became gray and distorted. Hazed forms like giant creatures thrashed through the mist. It had been a while, and it took her a moment to acclimatize, but then she was running across the Matadori Desert, faster even than teleportation.

She spotted forks of electricity ripping up the gray-green ahead of her and she knew she'd reached the storm over the city. She broke downward, searching for a sense of Snacksize. It hit her all of a sudden as she literally collided with something that leapt out of nowhere, a monstrous and pulsating formation which, as she hit it, twisted and convulsed into a duplicate of herself. Ev'r knew immediately what she was dealing with, a haunt, a reflector, a stubborn tumorous infliction of a creature. It dug down like a tick wherever it went and was all but impossible to kill because it existed in the Murk. No outward weaponry could touch it and no magics could confound it because its best defense was to mirror its attacker and reflect the damage back onto them. But what most people didn't know was that the haunt could still be injured, it just took a lot more effort. Ev'r stared at the haunt, seeing her own extremely smug smile spread across its face. She returned the grin and the haunt's smile faltered. Its defense only worked on people who were afraid of pain.

Ev'r threw a crippling curse at her reflection and felt her legs going out from under her. The haunt fell as well, and as it did, Ev'r threw another curse, and another and another, in an unending stream of attacks. She felt each one in her own skin, tearing, twisting and burning, but she didn't stop and didn't pause, until the haunt gave a desperate scream, a harsh echoing sound, and vanished, dissolving into the murk. Ev'r crashed out as well, into reality, right beside Snacksize. He was lying facedown in a streaming gutter, his back a mangled mess of blood and flesh. She grabbed him up and hauled him over. His face was gray, his eyes staring into nothing. She shook him hard.

"Wake up!"

Eli twitched as running steps exploded out from all directions and the trackers crashed in beside Ev'r – Kane, Silho, with her head gushing blood, and the fairy breed they called Diega. They all took one look and knew what Ev'r had known. They recognized death when they saw it.

"His lights are almost gone," Silho said.

"Take us through the Murk to Headquarters! All of us!" Kane commanded Ev'r. He hated dark magics as much as Ismail, and Ev'r hated Kane as much as he hated dark magics

– but this was Eli Anklebiter. Ev'r stood, lifting his limp body in her arms.

"Hang in there, Snacksize," she whispered, and sunk them all into the gray drift.

Chapter 9
Ramses

HYDRIA

CORINTHIA (CORINTH CITY)

August's warning had compelled Ramses to leave the harem house immediately and gallop straight back up to Ironeye. Despite his body's great objection, he'd run to Titan's quarters with full urgency. There the Lord Liege's Captain of Periphery Guard had informed him that he would be shown in as soon as Titan gave response to their knock. Then Ramses had spent the remainder of the night perching on the hard-as-rock chair outside the chamber, his head nodding down to his chest every few moments and jolting back up with thwarted sleep.

By dawn his posterior was completely numb and his mood almost as foul as the taste in his mouth. Titan wasn't there. Where he should have been. Where his guards thought he was. But they weren't saying anything, and neither could he. Ramses rubbed his stinging eyes and sighed deeply. The shuffling and rustling of a messenger running up the corridor drew near, and Ramses leaned back against the wall, crossing his arms, assuming the messenger was heading to Titan's chamber and wishing him silent, cynical good fortune. But the footsteps stopped in front of Ramses. He raised his eyes. The young messenger was red in the face, breathing hard, and staring at him as though he couldn't believe his good fortune.

"I've found you!" he said, then realized the disrespect of his words and dropped to one knee. "Forgive me, Warrior. I'm truly sorry. It's just I've been running all the over the city. I didn't think I'd find you in time."

Ramses considered him for a moment, then said, "In time for what, boy?"

"In time for the hearing, Warrior." The messenger swallowed hard. "There's a delicate situation."

"Involving who?"

"A friend of yours." The boy shifted uncomfortably and lowered his voice, "He's asked to remain nameless."

Ramses' thoughts immediately jumped to Titan, but he knew the Lord Liege would never send some green kid to call him.

"Please, the situation is quite dire," the messenger begged.

Ramses grunted. He didn't want to leave now. He had to see Titan, but no one would dare summon him in this way unless it really was dire. He glanced at the royal guards standing in front of Titan's chamber doors.

"I'm going for a few moments and I will return," he told the captain as he stood. The captain gave a sharp nod and said, "Understood, Warrior."

Ramses stretched his legs out, groaning as blood rushed back through his body. He indicated for the messenger to take the lead. The boy set off at an eager pace, leading Ramses through the palace, all the way to the quarters of the Lord King's Warrior Riders, where Ramses himself resided. They bypassed both the doors to the Absolutes, the warriors from the generation of the Lord King, and the Centurions, those of the Almighty's generation, and entered the quarters of the Furious, Ramses' peers. The boy stopped at the head of a hallway lined with doors.

"If you would please, Warrior. It's the room at the end," he said, glancing at Ramses and then quickly away.

Ramses continued down the hall by himself, coming to a closed door. He knew the rooms in this wing of the quarters should be unoccupied, spares in case of need. His suspicions prickled, unsure of what he could expect to find on the other side. He twisted the handle and the door swung inward. Ramses stepped forward and saw Leor, his friend and fellow warrior, standing naked with his manhood stuck in a pottery jar, white arse cheeks gleaming in the morning sun.

"What am I looking at?" Ramses asked.

Leor startled as though he'd been asleep on his feet and turned to face Ramses, his expression equal parts extreme relief and sheepishness. He gave a strained laugh.

"Rams ... there's a slight problem."

"So I see," he said. He walked over and, yes, it was definitely stuck. He looked at his friend, unimpressed. This was the second time in the last four-sevens that he'd had to rescue a warrior from a similar predicament. Some men were known for their physical might, others for their intellectual prowess, but evidently Ramses had become known as the man to summon when a warrior, in all his ridiculous drunkenness, sticks his cock into something he shouldn't and gets it stuck.

"Why?" Ramses demanded of his friend. "Are there not enough women in this city that upon the offer of silver, bronze, or even a nice word, will have their legs open faster than light itself? Why this?"

Leor searched for his words, his face well red. "I became confused on wine," he finally came up with.

"Confused on wine!" Ramses said. "Confused on wine is public singing, it's challenging walls to fight, forgetting where you live, it's telling random commoners that you love them, it's even bedding a woman so unattractive that upon seeing her at dawn you startle back with such force that you do yourself a physical injury. Confused on wine is not fucking livestock, food or objects. That's something else entirely!"

Leor sighed and lowered his head, saying meekly, "I couldn't be bothered to go out – you understand."

Ramses grunted. To say he didn't understand at all would be a lie.

He inspected the jar more closely and his mind calculated the exact angle and force he'd need to strike it with in order to spring the seams in two and prevent sharp shards from injuring Leor. Ramses saw everything around him as the composite of many shapes, each shape in constant motion. It wasn't until he was well into childhood that he'd realized not everyone saw the world as he did. And that it was a gift.

"Well there's nothing for it," he said to Leor. "We'll have to smash it."

Leor's eyes widened. "Smash it! To Acheron with that! I called to you because I knew you'd come up with something better. I could have thought of smashing it myself."

"Judging by the fact that you have your cock stuck inside a jar, I question your ability to think at all!"

Leor sighed. He wanted to say more, but wisely held his tongue.

"It's turning purple," Ramses told him. "You've created a vacuum inside the jar and there's no room to grease the opening. It's either crack the jar open or have your cock fall off in your hands."

Leor paled so much that Ramses thought he would pass out. In that distracted moment, Ramses took the opportunity to seize the jar and strike it firmly on the table in front of them. It split clean in two.

Leor stared down in disbelief. Then he laughed, and tried to hug Ramses.

"Don't do this ever again!" Ramses shoved him back. "And if by chance you do, I am not the man to call. Repeat – cock stuck – do not call me. I am not the man."

"You *are* the man," Leor proclaimed him.

"No!" He gave Leor a final stern look. "Imagine if you'd had to go before the Lord King like that!"

Leor's face fell and Ramses felt some pity for him. "Just be smart from now on – understood?"

"I will, I promise," Leor said.

Ramses left the room and heard his friend's giddy laughter of relief behind him. He had to grin. Seriousness didn't suit his face at all.

Suddenly, the horn and trumpets rang out throughout the palace, a particular note, summoning the Companions of both the Lord King and the Liege to the upper rooms for preparation for a Hearing – in this case, The King's Hearing. Ramses cursed. His teeth felt furry, his face scratchy, his armpits were offensively fragrant, and there was a wine stain on his tunic.

He had planned to go before the hearing after having a steam and dressing in his finest, or at least something clean, but there was no time now. The Lord King awaited no man.

* * * * *

Ramses thundered down the narrow side steps. This staircase was more commonly used by palace attendants than warriors, who preferred the palatial front stairs for leaving and entering the main buildings of Ironeye. Currently, however, Ramses was less interested in how elegant his exit appeared and more in how fast he could move his body without causing himself heart failure. He knew he needed to train harder than he currently was, drink less, eat less, smoke less, but the knowing and the actual doing were not connecting.

He crashed out through a door and into the courtyard beyond. It was overgrown with shade trees and heavily laden grapevines. Hordes of blue-tail wasps buzzed through the air. Ramses looked up toward the sun to check the time. It was not long past dawn, but already the heat was thick and heavy. He wiped his forehead and flicked the sweat off his hand, running across the courtyard and through the outer door to the west quadrant.

Across the open square stood the main training arenas, full of warrior riders engaged in practice and strengthening. Ramses sent out a long low whistle and kept running toward the Tower of the Upper Rooms known as Cirles. The thunder of hooves sounded immediately behind him, becoming louder and louder, until Arah galloped up level with him, whickering a greeting. Ramses grinned at his stallion, then lunged sideways and leapt up into the saddle. The moment he was seated, his focus sharpened and everything around him took on a brighter color. It was the way of the Rider.

"My friend, my boy!" he said, giving the bay stallion an affectionate slap on the neck. He gave him full rein and Arah took off, only to swerve suddenly to avoid horses and riders cutting out from a doorway beside them. The other riders pulled up hard as well, with much stomping and blowing from their stallions as they circled each other.

"Brothers!" Ramses said, seeing his interceptors were actually the other three Companions of the Lord Liege.

"Here you are you *abram*!" Hammer swore at him as his stallion tried to nip Arah, who sidestepped nimbly.

"Good morning to you too, brother," Ramses returned.

Mohammad, Hammer to the Companions, and anyone else with a death wish, glared at him with burning eyes, his mouth a hard straight line. Ramses truly loved his eldest cousin, but honest to the gods Hammer had been so serious for so long that it seemed smiling just once might crack his whole face into a thousand pieces. And the fact that he hadn't had a woman in over two years really hadn't helped. Hammer had taken it upon himself to abstain in solidarity with Titan. But abstinence did not become him. Neither did the beard. Beside Hammer, the other two Companions, Mohammad II and Morchetti, gave him much a kinder greeting. Mohan's expression was friendly and apologetic, Chey's amused and wicked. They looked how they lived.

"*Cursil ios*," Mohan said.

"*Cursils ios*," Ramses echoed his greeting. High Corinthian did not translate easily to any other language of the Halos, but was most closely related to Common Corinthian, and his greeting was similar to *my cousins*, though the emotion of the original was completely lost in translation.

112

Without command needed, the four of them started off at a trot toward Cirles.

"Where have you been? We've been seeking you everywhere!" Hammer demanded, riding beside Ramses.

"Seeking me everywhere is the new fashion, haven't you heard?" Ramses said. "And where exactly is everywhere, because I was most certainly somewhere."

Chey snorted from behind them. "Can't find Ramses of Ohai, look to the closest whorehouse they say."

"Can't find Morchetti of Praden, look to where he's polishing his own sword," he sent back, making a gesture.

Chey laughed. "That doesn't rhyme at all, you're a terrible scholar."

"*Se*," he agreed in High Corinthian, "but a solid warrior."

"*Se*," Chey gave him that. "But nowhere near as solid as me, *cursil ios*."

"Oh really?" Ramses dropped Arah's pace suddenly and came even with Chey's stallion, darting a hand out to flick his cousin's ear. Chey warded him off with a block.

"Don't touch the hair!" he warned, smoothing along the shaved sides of his head.

"If you women are finished!" Hammer growled. "We've already wasted enough time looking for him."

"Why would you look for me?" Ramses asked. "I have ears, do I not? I would hear the summons as I have for every day of my entire life before this."

"This day is of great import. I need to lead you in," Hammer said.

"Lead me in?" Ramses laughed incredulously. "Perhaps while you're at it you can wipe my ass and breathe for me as well!"

That made the other two laugh, Chey out loud and Mohan discreetly. Both received a dark look from Hammer.

Though Hammer and Mohan were blood brothers, both named Mohammad after their warrior grandfather, they couldn't have been more different. While Hammer was black of eyes and hair, Mohan was fairer, with blue eyes, a rarity among Corinthians. Hammer often mocked him for it, saying the gods had turned them blue because he'd spent too much time crying. Mohan was by far the most full-hearted of them, and he had suffered the most in the yards of the Amkalai, the training camps that all Corinthian warrior riders resided in from seven years to thirty. When it came to the matter of emotions, Hammer felt nothing, Chey admitted nothing, Ramses could rationalize everything, but Mohan always searched for the deeper truth in life, and the journey had left him desperate.

"Just so you know, I was awaiting the Lord Liege outside his chambers. He didn't call me in all night," Ramses told the Companions.

"There was another mass slaughter overnight in a fighting pit," Chey said. "Darro again, they're saying. The Lord Liege was no doubt in consultation or thought over this."

"He was where he was," Hammer growled. His stallion, Illios, flattened his ears and threw his head furiously in reaction to Hammer's foul mood. *Two bodies – one heart – horse and Rider.* Ramses studied his cousin. He had heavy lines across his forehead that aged him beyond his thirty-five years.

"You should take a woman," Ramses told him as they trotted on.

"The most important of days and you're thinking with your cock – why am I not surprised?" Hammer responded without looking at him.

Ramses snorted. "Honest to the gods if your mood gets any darker, the sun will turn black. Heed me, take a woman. Abstinence is not our burden to carry."

A second trumpet note blasted out throughout the palace grounds, a second and final summons.

"Ride!" Hammer bellowed. He flicked his reins and Illios lunged into a gallop, sending stone and sparks flying from his steel clad hooves as they disappeared around a sharp bend.

"He acts as our command, not our equal," Chey said, maneuvering his stallion closer to Ramses as they rode. "I've had enough."

"We serve the Titan, not the Hammer," Ramses reminded him.

"So he can say all he wishes and we hold our tongues like attendants?" Chey shot back.

"Don't pay him any mind, his balls are blue," Ramses said.

"Black, by the sounds of things."

"Quite possibly."

Ramses clicked his tongue to Arah and the stallion took off, Chey and Mohan right behind him. Their path took them across the front of the palace, close to the great gates where guards were allowing palace attendants to enter. There were massive crowds of common girls waiting there day and night in the hope that the Lord Liege might spot them. Chey perused the girls as the Companions rode past, smiling at the ones who took his interest, and they gazed back as though they looked upon gods. They screamed out, but both Ramses and Mohan kept their eyes to the front, not wanting to falsely inflame any fragile hopes, or start a stampede.

They galloped past a line of bakers lugging bread and rolls on their backs, heading up the hill to deliver for the grand feast that night. Chey snatched off a loaf as they flew by. He ripped it in half, taking part for himself and throwing the rest across to Ramses with a grin. He stood in his stirrups and caught it, ripping it in two again and then throwing the other half to Mohan. Ramses stuffed the bread in his mouth and urged Arah on faster as Cirles rose up before them. Titan would be there at the top. Ramses felt discomfort worming its way inside him. He had many things to say, but how?

* * * * *

As luck would have it, or not, Ramses didn't need to rush to compose his speech. He had plenty of time while he and the boys sat outside the upper rooms, awaiting Titan – plenty of time to think and plenty of time to realize he still truly had no idea what to say. Waiting was, by its very nature, annoying, but it gnawed at Ramses for a whole other reason. The Lord Liege rarely kept the Companions waiting – he had always been careful not to use time as a weapon. So this was strange. The others didn't seem to even notice, but Ramses felt so on edge that he was literally sitting on the edge of his seat. The others didn't notice that either.

Ramses' eyes wandered restlessly around the room, over the statues, plaques and the maps on the walls. When he was little he'd called this the round room because it was circular, built in the shape of the tower. It was full of reminders of the past, mostly from the reign of the Almighty, Apollo of Ironeye. So many feats the great King had accomplished. He had changed the whole face of the Halos. The history scrolls told that upon his coronation at the age of thirteen years, the first act of the Lord King Apollo was to bring an end to slavery, he decreed, "No man is permitted to enslave another, or a woman, or a child". His deniers cried out – *"it can't be done – society will fall to ruin"* – who would make their food, run their messages, wash their clothes, tend their animals and fields, clean their houses, empty their toilets? Who could they beat when they were angry, drag to their beds when their wives were indisposed, blame for their mistakes and their deliberate evils?

To their questions the Great King had replied, "I do not care. By my law it is done and all who stand against me will die."

And so they did.

After this, he abolished the old calendar and wrote the new one, which was easily read and understood by all – not just the scholars and priests, but the common people as well. He had initiated great advances in medicine and scientific belief, in food growth and water storage. He had designed the aqueducts below Corinth City and now throughout the realm, freeing the Corinthians from the need to buy water from the mountain king and elevating modern Corinthia far above all the other empires of the Halos.

"It's begun!" Mohan shouted from where he was standing beside the windows, staring through his looking glass.

Ramses and the others leapt up, rushing over to watch the royal families enter the interior gate and proceed into the Halls of Ma'at.

"Anacharasis first?" Chey said with some surprise.

"Of course!" Hammer replied. "It is their king to be called, and so they proceed first. Did you ever listen during lessons?"

"Occasionally. And if the teacher's terrazzo had not afforded such a clear view to the ladies' steam house I would have listened much more. I'd be a scholar by now!"

Ramses laughed at that and felt the tension breaking, sharp in his chest.

"Small group," Mohan murmured, his eye glued to the looking glass, as the representatives of Anacharasis entered. King Sirion Barthos and all of his immediate family line were gone and in their absence stood what was left of the king's former officials, now rallying behind the sole surviving member of the royal line of Barthos, a distant cousin's distant nephew, Yorem Gorse. Gorse had a solid reputation as a warrior and it was fully expected that he would take the throne.

Behind the Anacharasi came King Maneam Nazar of Armen and his representatives.

"Is Ravana there?" Chey snatched the glass from Mohan.

"Well is she?" Ramses asked after a moment. Much had been spoken of the Princess Ravana over the last years. Until now she had been too young to put forth a proposal to Titan, but she had just recently come of age at sixteen. Rumor said she was the most beautiful girl in the Halos, with the body of a goddess and the face of an angel. Ramses felt a flicker of hope. Perhaps she would be the one to bring Titan's walls crashing.

"No, just the men," Chey told them. "But if it's true that she is the most beautiful girl in the Halos, one thing is clear, she didn't inherit her beauty from her father."

Chey held the looking glass up to Ramses' eye and he choked at the sight of King Maneam. He was only the age of the Lord King Osiris, but he seemed double if not triple that. It looked as though all his muscles had slumped down to his gut, which made him stoop over and hunch. They said he drank too much, and even as Ramses had the thought, he saw the king put a flask to his lips. Ramses stood up straighter and pulled in his own stomach.

"He hasn't entered the arena in years, you can see how dull his armor is from here." Hammer clicked his tongue in disapproval.

Ramses noted the king's breastplate and arm irons did look dull, particularly compared to the gleaming figure of King Tiberios of Theselon riding in behind him. Theselon was the closest realm to Corinthia and Tiberios stood a blood cousin to the Lord King Osiris, through their mothers. Like the Companions, he held all the characteristics of a plains Warrior Rider, tall of height with a sharply defined muscular physique, dark skin, dark eyes, and that big nose that no one could seem to successfully breed out of their family line, no matter how many other races they mixed in. Ramses was admiring Tiberios' spectacular stallion when he heard Chey curse loudly.

"Look at his face, will you? It looks like he's just unearthed a maggot in his supper."

Ramses turned his attention back to the gates to see the royalty of Kirith-Jerom were entering, led by King Gideon, ruler of all the mountain ranges that separated the plains from Cytisus, the drowned swamp beyond the Halos. The features of the mountain people were far different from the plains. The trees hid their skin from the sun, so they were paler, with mostly fair or red hair, some with a tinge of green or blue to it, all blue of eyes, tall and slim, angry and proud, wearing animal pelts for clothing. To Corinthians, wearing death on their bodies was bad fortune.

Ramses eyed the head of the mountain lion that King Gideon wore on his shoulder. It was a big head – a lot of bad luck. The king himself had fine gray hair and his beard, groomed and shiny, came halfway down his chest. Ramses knew his eyes were the palest of blue and right now they were narrowed with disdain. Ramses took a look through the glass when Chey offered it, providing an even closer vision of Gideon's displeasure.

"Well, none may say that the man does not know how to maintain an impressive sneer," Ramses said.

"And an impressive grudge at that," Mohan muttered.

"Well, it's only been twenty-five years, these things take time," Ramses said dryly.

Before the Almighty opened the aqueducts, the only water the plains empires had access to was that which they traded for with Kirith-Jerom. The Kirithi had collected the rain in big barrels and sold them to the plains for a big price. It had been their main source of income. But the aqueducts had crippled the trade and economy of the mountains, leaving a very bitter taste in the mouth of their king. Gideon would never have had the courage to stand up to the Almighty, but it was many years since Apollo of Ironeye had sat atop the throne – and many years of brewing hostility.

This hostility was shared and fueled by the final king to enter through the palace gates, and in this case, Ramses used the term *king* very loosely. King Vitor-Petacula of Draul, the soggy boglands that bordered Anacharasis on one side and Cytisus on the other, rode through on his mule, bouncing around so much it looked as though he was about to fly off. The Companions burst into laughter.

"Honest to the gods, he looks like a monkey riding a porcupine," Ramses said.

That made Chey and Mohan laugh louder and even Hammer's lips twitched toward a smile.

"Go on Hammer – smile – you know you want to!" Ramses tried to force a smile onto his cousin's face.

"Get off, *abram*!" Hammer growled.

Ramses gave him a playful shove and turned back to watch the rest of the Draul royalty enter. He found himself shaking his head. If Ramses were to generalize, and he did so liberally, he would propose that Drauls were primitive and brutal interbreeds, with abhorrent practices, which the Almighty had abolished when he'd allowed Draul to join the King's Circle, but once again, that was many years past. The Lord King's spies were currently investigating rumors that of late many of the old practices had crept back in. Including the slave mines.

Ramses took the looking glass from Chey and peered through, watching Petacula sliding off his mule. The king was sunken and sallow, with a drawn-in, used-up face. Suspicious eyes stared out from beneath saggy lids. His skin, tainted yellow from the yarok the Drauls ate as a staple, was hidden beneath a thick layer of greasy make-up. It made the Draul king look dead and half rotted, ghastly white with blood-red lips and drawn-on eyebrows, oily hair combed over his balding head. Ramses couldn't help but think if this man was the best Draul had to offer, no wonder they had never dragged themselves out of the bog.

"Wait!" Mohan called out and made a lunge for the glass. "She's here – Ravana Nazar."

At that they all started grabbing for the glass, even Hammer moved closer. Ramses managed to get it to his eyes and caught a momentary glance of the Armenite princess. That brief glimpse was enough to see the rumors were true. She was a genuine beauty – long, shiny dark hair, large eyes, full lips and fuller breasts in perfect balance with the curves of her hips. Her mother, the Queen Raflessia, stood slightly out from her circle of supporters, looking like a woman clinging to her youth with a savage sort of denial that only made Ravana's beauty even more vivid.

The princess wore a tiara of gold and diamond, glittering gems and pearls adorning her hair and dress, arms and neck, so many that she glowed and sparkled with every move she made. Chey snatched back the glass and he and Mohan had a tussle over it, reduced to giggling boys by the sight of the princess. Ramses saw Ravana wave to the common girls at the gate and they were calling out to her in praise and adoration, as though Titan had already chosen her as princess, and truly she had something so magnetic about her, even from this distance, that in that moment, Ramses felt sure she would be the one.

Behind them, the doors to the interior chamber opened and the Lord Liege's periphery guard started to file out into the round room. The Companions immediately composed themselves and formed a line. The guards took their positions, there was a pause, then he appeared. The Lord Liege. Tarrus of Ironeye. The Titan. The Companions went to their knees, feeling the presence of their royal cousin wash over them. All men lived and died, some men achieved greatness, but very few were born great, with strength enough to fill every space of every place they went. This man, grandson of the Almighty, was one, he radiated like the sun. His presence alone chased away pain and fear.

"Rise, brothers," Titan said, before they'd even gotten all the way to the ground. Titan had never held any fondness at all for prolonged ceremony or glorification. A stab of pain made Ramses falter as he stood. When he wasn't with Titan, his anger at his cousin could build up like a rising poison inside him, but then he'd see him like this, and be reminded of the truth of Titan, and all the anger would just dissolve, leaving only sadness. Sadness that he'd ever held any anger against his cousin and sadness that things had become so broken.

Titan and his *ata-ajua* walked over to stand in front of the Companions, and Ramses made full effort to look him in the face and keep his turmoil hidden. While Titan's father, the Lord King Osiris, had taken to his mother's side, with the narrower eyes and lighter skin of the Theselonians, Titan had thrown back to the Almighty's appearance, even inheriting his grandfather's eyes – two irises and two pupils in each, very overlapped but still visible, with fine lines of gold running through both dark centers.

It was widely told that at his birth, the birthing priests had announced that Apollo of Ironeye was not fit for survival because of his eye aberration, and that his father, the Lord King Ahasuerus, had ordered him taken away. It was said that Ramses' own grandfather, Aramasas, little more than a boy at the time but already a high advisor, had raised word in the newborn's favor, convincing the Lord King that the baby's eyes were not a defect but a blessing from the gods. It was said that Lord King Ahasuerus was utterly unmovable, but that Aramasas had been unrivaled in intellect, then and since. He had saved the Almighty's life.

"Brothers," Titan said, his voice filling the round room. "Are you are well?"

"Well, Lord Liege," Hammer responded first.

"Well, apart from my eyes being offended by the sight of the Draul king trying to ride," Chey said. He still spoke to Titan as he had when they were boys, and at times Ramses felt so jealous of the ease between them.

"*Ivar*," Titan responded in High Corinthian with a word that could mean many things, even opposite things. It could mean yes or no, agreement or disagreement. It could be used to express humor, or to draw someone's attention, all depending on how it was said. Titan used it now to indicate that Chey had been heard.

Ramses studied his cousin, looking for any suggestion as to where he had been that night, and he felt the gaze of Titan's First of the *ata-ajua*, Argos, watching him through the eye slits of his full-metal zivas.

"Today's meeting will not be without discord," Titan told them. "At times you will need to exercise restraint. We cannot be seen to be provoked, no matter what is said."

The Companions all straightened up at Titan's words.

"Is it decided? Are we going to war?" Chey asked boldly.

"There will be a meeting following the hearing, in the Lord King's chambers, to discuss all matters. The Lord King has recalled all his Kís to attend."

Ramses felt a tingle in his spine. If the Lord King had recalled all his spies then it seemed that war was imminent. He could feel from the tension of the other boys that they were thinking the same. He glanced at them and noticed that Hammer was staring at the stain on Ramses' tunic with a look of heavy disapproval creasing his brow.

"And you wonder why we had to come and find you!" Hammer growled.

Ramses' shame sparked his anger from nothing to blazing inside him. He felt like smashing his fist into Hammer's face.

"As we rode in, Rams was already on his way, we did not need to find him," Mohan leapt in to defend him. The only time Mohan ever stood up to Hammer was in defense of Chey or Ramses. Hammer glowered at him and said, "Silence yourself, you wouldn't have even been able to find your dress armor if I had not assisted you. You're a disgrace to our father's name the way you act!"

"Who do you think you are?" Chey shot back at Hammer.

Titan watched them argue for a moment before commanding, "Kneel!"

The Companions hit the floor so hard the sound rang in the air for some time before Titan asked, "Are you all kneeling equally?"

"Yes, Lord Liege," Ramses responded in unison with the others.

"So stand as equals," he commanded. "And know that you are and always will be seen as such before my eyes." He spoke to them each in turn. "Hammer, your devotion keeps me; Mohan, your search motivates me; Chey, your strength steels me; and Ramses, your humanity ... frees me."

Titan locked eyes with Ramses, and Ramses saw a momentary, unexpected pain in his royal cousin's stare that made his heart skip. Titan never showed pain. Ramses had all but forgotten he could suffer at all. Ramses blinked, as close to actually crying as he'd been for longer than he could remember, and he wasn't even sure why. He lowered his eyes, and when he looked up Titan was removing his tunic. He motioned for Ramses to do the same. Ramses obeyed and Titan gave him his clean tunic, taking the soiled one and pulling it on. Titan's larger breastplate covered the stain, but Ramses felt terrible inside. His clothing was stinking and Titan's was fresh.

"Lord Liege," he said. "It's my fault I have not changed, to have you bear that is shame on me."

"I'm not ashamed of you," Titan said clearly. "And if I am not, you should not be either. Besides, I know you were helping one of your fellow warriors out of a situation and did not have time to change."

Sometimes it surprised Ramses how quickly Titan knew of everything that was happening in the palace and the city.

"Hammer," Titan said, "embrace your brother – he is the one and only you have, and when all the gold and fury are gone from this world, he will be your only remaining truth."

Hammer stepped forward and he and Mohan hugged.

"Heed me," Titan warned, and the Companions gave unified affirmation. Then Chey smiled and said, "We just saw your wife to be. The rumors are true, she shines like the sun. I tell you, she's the one. Your bed won't be cold for much longer."

Titan gave a measured nod and said, "We shall see."

Ramses heard from the words that Titan didn't wish to speak further on it, but Chey continued. "She'll give proposal today."

"Her and many others," Mohan added. "We'll be listening to love poetry and strumming harps until sundown."

Ramses stifled a groan, barely. Titan gave a neutral, "*Ivar*." But Ramses knew his cousin found the elaborate displays of love as excruciating as he did, even more so, because all the songs and poetry were about him.

The trumpets sounded again, summoning them to the Halls of Ma'at.

"It begins," Titan said. He nodded to his Captain of Periphery Guard and they all started toward the stairs. As they descended, Ramses pushed closer to Titan, past Argos.

"Lord Liege," he spoke with lowered voice. "I sought to speak with you last night. I attended your quarters."

Titan glanced at him and said, "Yes. I've had much to think on. We will speak properly after the hearing."

Ramses started to step back, but then a sudden urge made him persist. "When you're inside a room I know it, even if I'm outside. You weren't there." He felt his heart speeding up. He was broaching a topic that was never spoken of. If one was to touch Titan with bare skin, which was not done as touching him at all was forbidden, they would feel the sharp shocks of something emanating from him, and it was a similar feeling that Ramses spoke of, for the first time ever. Ramses felt like he was boiling beneath his clothing.

Titan paused his step for a moment as the guards opened up the doorway leading onto the walkways to Ma'at.

"We will speak properly after the ceremony," Titan repeated without looking at him. Ramses felt himself hit a solid invisible wall and crash down. He dropped back beside the other Companions as Titan stepped out onto the open walkway. The common girls beyond the gate caught sight of him and erupted into screaming, loud enough to deafen sound itself.

"Here we go," Chey said to Ramses, clapping him on the shoulder. Ramses gave a quick smile, but inside he felt emptier than ever.

Chapter 10
Titan

HYDRIA

CORINTHIA (CORINTH CITY)

Titan stared at his reflection in the golden doors of the Halls of Ma'at, surrounded by his *ata-ajua*, his Companions and the periphery guards. The image shivered and changed, and there in the gold stood all the stolen women, staring at him. There were tears in frightened eyes, creased brows, bitten lips, fingers worrying across bruises and wounds. The picture shivered again, back to him, and he saw Ramses watching him closely. Their eyes met for a moment in the reflection and Titan felt a tight pressure across his chest. Ramses had spoken his mind all of a sudden, and at a time when they were surrounded by others. He'd broached such dangerous territory, speaking of things they'd never spoken of, and for good reason.

Titan knew what his cousin was feeling without him saying it, and it tore him inside to know that Ramses felt there was a rift between them. Ramses thought that it was because of the training, and his position as Lord Liege, but it had nothing at all to do with that. The truth was, Ramses managed to keep up a completely convincing front while being profoundly unwell. No one knew the whole story, aside from the Lord King. No one knew that Ramses trod the thinnest line of sanity, that he had never allowed his mind to register, let alone accept, what had happened. That was the distance between them – the unspoken. And Titan was acutely aware that in ways he had failed his cousin. He had been so scared to send him over the edge that he had withdrawn. Not knowing the right things to say, he had said nothing, but that had been a mistake. He'd treated him carefully, which was opposite to before, when they had sparred constantly in the arena and with their words. They'd been inseparable as boys and now life had separated them. Death had separated them.

Titan heard the cry of a golden eagle from far above and looked up into the sky. He saw a figure in full shining armor standing on the rooftop of the cathedral above them and felt a jolt. A glare of light momentarily blinded him and when he blinked to clear his eyes, the figure was gone. Had it truly been Harlow Darro or just a product of his sleepless mind? There came an announcement, short and sharp, at the door behind them.

"The Lord King!"

Titan dropped immediately to his knees, all his guards and Companions with him, except for Argos and the *ata-ajua*, who always stood. He kept his head bowed low as heavy footsteps crossed the marble floor and stopped at his side.

129

He saw the faces of children staring up at him from beneath his feet, pressing their hands against the marble, screaming. His chest tightened so much he could barely take breath.

"Rise," the Lord King commanded.

Titan stood and came face to face with his father.

"My king," he said in High Corinthian, the only one who could use these words when it came to the king.

"My son," the Lord King responded. And under his stare, Titan felt both a fortifying of his strength and an immensity of self-doubt. His father was a fortress, impassable, unshakable, but there was no openness between them. For all the riches of Corinthia, honesty was a luxury neither of them could afford, and though he fully understood why, it didn't stop him wishing things could be different.

Quintus unlocked the doors to the hall and walked in. The murmuring coming from the chamber dulled down to silence and Quintus' voice rang out.

"All kneel in the presence of your *capostati*, the King of Kings, the Lord King Osiris Thiair Isten Fa-Ma'at al-Attinas al-Rahotep nas-Cyus-nas-Apollo Al'Maktoub and his rightful son, the Lord Liege – Tarrus Saheen Esesi Fa-Ma'at al-Attinas al-Rahotep nas-Apollo-nas-Osiris Al'Maktoub."

At the sounds of mass movement the Lord King stepped forward into the chamber and Titan followed him in. The immensity of the gathering took him momentarily by surprise. He was accustomed to commanding Corinthia's vast armies, but never to presiding over a royal audience this large. It was tradition that during his time of contemplation, he must lead all hearings, even the King's Hearing today, as a way of proving himself before the Lord King. He knew many present would not take well to him speaking instead of his father, but it was not a matter of choice.

Titan went to his throne and, after the Lord King was seated, sat down looking over the high and low courts of Corinthia, separated into the three generations of Centurions, Absolutes and Furious. Titan felt an onslaught of thoughts and images hit him, a hundred thousand pathways of possibility opening up all at once. He turned his eyes toward his father and it all stopped, and he was able to focus.

"All rise." He gave the command and all the royalty and nobility in the hall took their seats. Even with the Kiom bearers lining the hall with their feather fans it was stifling hot, more like a steam room than a great hall.

Titan began. "Kings of the Halos. The Lord King Osiris of Ironeye, your King of Kings, has called this Hearing to bring forth discussion on the murder of King Sirion of Anacharasis and on the succession of his throne. Here also lies opportunity for you to bring any matters of import before Corinthia."

Before Titan could proceed further, Quintus returned to the center seal and bowed low, awaiting a response. Titan signaled for him to speak and Quintus rose and announced, "If it please the Lord King and the Lord Liege, there are several ladies seeking proposal – Lady Tara of Theselon, Lady Viki of Theselon, Lady Becca of Anacharasis and Lady Alana of Anacharasis ..."

Quintus paused, then announced, "and Princess Ravana Nazar, daughter of King Maneam of Armen."

Titan felt the ripple around him. People were sitting up straighter and looking at each other with knowing smiles. They were convinced, as Chey had been, that she was the one. Titan steeled himself for what was to come. He knew no one realized just how excruciatingly embarrassed he felt during each and every proposal. There had been so many. He nodded and the first ceremony began.

The first four proposals proceeded as usual, in a haze of silk and song. The ladies presented gifts, fabrics and jewels and artworks of great worth, before Titan and the Lord King, as a symbol of their sentiment. They demonstrated their talents in songs and dance, then spoke at length of themselves and their good qualities. Then they bowed and waited for Titan's sign and then it was over.

As Lady Alana of Anacharasis left the chamber, the music for the entrance of Ravana Nazar began. It was traditional Armenite music and began a royal procession so elaborate and lengthy that it was almost like a wedding entrance itself. Titan waited with all others gathered as the princess's ladies and cousins and friends and seemingly friends of friends, and possibly every woman in Armen, walked down the aisle. Finally, in a flurry of the finest silk veils and the scent of vanilla, the princess appeared in the center of the chamber with the abrupt cessation of all music and sound.

She bowed low before the Courts and Titan could sense so many eyes on him, watching his slightest move, waiting for any reaction at all. He gave them nothing. The gifts began, and continued, huge towers reaching for the vast ceiling. After the last of the coffers of gold were brought forward and placed down, the music restarted and Ravana and her ladies danced and sang in an extravagant show that made the presentations of all the other proposing ladies seem like common jigs. It also ran far longer than all the others combined, coming to a conclusion with an Armenite song of love, which Ravana sang beautifully by herself.

After its final note, the princess took the center again to speak of her own worth. It seemed there wasn't a talent, hobby or skill she hadn't accomplished. She spoke of the depth of her heart and mind, of her other favorable qualities, and of the strength and honor of her bloodline. At the conclusion of the proposal she remained standing, looking toward Titan as though she fully expected to be shown some kind of special interest. Maybe she thought he would offer his hand for her to kiss, or even that he would pronounce her his on the spot. In that moment he felt pity for her. She was beautiful and elegant and talented in what she did, but she was definitely not the one. She was too young, half his age, and although this was lawful, it left him uncomfortable. To his eyes she looked so delicate and fragile that the foremost thought in his mind was that he'd snap her with one touch.

Titan waved her away, causing a murmur of general confusion to run through the hall. He heard every word around him and fought to block it out. Ravana's face fell and she cast a confused glance at her mother, Queen Raflessia, who hurried forward and ushered her from the chamber on a much flatter note than she had entered.

Once the women had cleared, Titan returned swiftly to the business of the Hearing.

"Yorem of Asta, come forward and give word on the death of your king."

Yorem Gorse immediately stepped out from the line of Anacharasi officials and spoke in well-practiced and precise Corinthian, his voice ringing loud and clear around the chamber.

"King of Kings – Lord King of Corinthia and Lord Liege of Corinthia," he began. Titan could see approval in the eyes of many people watching Gorse, they thought he would make a fine ruler. And he did cut a strong figure, if not for the red mist pouring out of his mouth with every word.

"Many sevens have passed since the heinous murder of our eminent king. His cruel demise has thrown our realm into a chaos from which it struggles to recover. Today I come to prostrate myself before you with full respect, to beg that I may be elevated to my rightful place on the throne, so that I may bring about new order to Anacharasis, to bring comfort to its children and re-establish the peace it has lost, and in my crowning I vow that my first act as king will be to bring you, *capostati*, the head of the vile traitor Harlow Darro, murderer of our king!"

The mention of Darro stirred a massive disturbance among the gathered royalty and the fury of the room ignited. Only the Corinthian courts remained silent and composed.

Out of the rabble of united outrage, a voice spoke up, abrasive and slurred, speaking Corinthian so poorly that one would be forgiven for thinking it must be a Draul commoner, but Titan knew from past meetings who the speaker was. King Vitor-Petacula stepped forward.

Titan saw many of his warrior riders around him, including his Companions, clenching their jaws. A king should speak not only their own language but all languages and war codes, and educate themselves above and beyond all others. The fact that the king of Draul hadn't even bothered to learn the language of the *capostati*, the official language of all the lands, and came here now with such extremely poor skill, showed a complete lack of respect. Titan was neither surprised nor angered. The Almighty had said that the man who enrages you owns you.

"Don't worry," Titan overheard Chey whisper to Hammer, who sat so incensed his face was red. "The chances that Petacula can even read and write in his own language are extremely thin."

Beside Chey, Ramses snorted, concealing his smile.

Petacula continued, not waiting for the signal to speak. "Darro is pestilence, a plague, slime and filth on the soles of our boots. Each of us have brought before you – Osiris, King – evidence that this is so. He has murdered a king of the Halos! And yet Corinthia has done nothing to bring this traitor into check. Right now, as I speak, Darro plunders my land." He thumped his chest. "Terrorizing my people – taking what is mine to fuel his mongrel army. I pay homage tax to Corinthia for hearing and protection, yet here we stand in a time of need, and I see nothing being done in our aid!"

Petacula's words had been so direct and so insulting that all the gathered royalty and their courts had frozen at the sound of them, fearing Corinthian retribution. But Titan could see the Lord King from the side of his eye and his father was utterly unmoved by the insult. *A king acts, he never reacts.*

Titan responded, though Petacula refused to address him or even look at him, staring beyond him to the Lord King.

"Shall I take from the force of your words, King Vitor-Petacula, that you are in possession of new evidence against Harlow Darro? Because to expect the Lord King to send forth his riders on previously dismissed rumor and secondhand witness would be more than the most lack-witted of men would expect with consideration to the law under which we all live."

Though Titan delivered it with complete composure, it was still a slap to Petacula's face and he surely felt it, blinking with indignity and outrage, but before he could respond, King Gideon of Kirith-Jerom spoke up with his cold and over-pronounced words.

"The king of Draul is not alone in his sentiments against Darro."

Petacula's face took on a superior expression and he crossed his arms. Titan saw Yorem Gorse nodding.

"Darro and his collection of traitors and abominations move about my mountains with no respect for my sovereignty.

They go wherever they please as though they own whatever land their feet touch. They respect nothing and no one. Is it not true, Lord Liege of Corinthia, that if a man spat at your feet your men would in an instant take his head? Well, Darro is spitting daily right in my very face – he killed Sirion, and yet Corinthia makes no move."

At that point Maneam of Armen spoke up also, starting, then pausing to cough violently before continuing hoarsely, "I've see the traitor Darro and his giant riding through my lands also—" he coughed again. "They ride where they please with no heed to authority or respect."

"That's four accounts," Petacula called out, holding up three fingers. "Of four kings no less – one from his grave! What more do you require, Osiris King? Or do you doubt the words of myself and the kings who stand here now before you." He almost pointed at the Lord King, but stopped himself just in time. Warrior riders all around Titan were reaching for their swords.

Titan held up a hand to bring the Hall to order. A memory came to his mind – he saw with full clarity the Almighty stopping on his way through the city upon hearing the sounds of an animal trapped in a drain hole. He'd knelt down beside the drain and put his hand in to retrieve the trapped cat, tiny and starving. Titan had seen the officials from Armen, visiting at the time, exchanging mocking glances, incensed that a great king would lower himself to such an act. When Titan told the Almighty of what he'd seen, his grandfather had said, "So much of life is spent stumbling in the darkness of uncertainty, but when I am hated by men such as these, I know I am walking the righteous path."

Darro was hated by men such as these, with a heavy red fog all around their mouths that no one else could see.

"I have heard your words, kings of the Halos," Titan said. "And I answer with a question – did any of you present here, or any of your people who are willing to stand before the courts of Corinthia, see with your own eyes former Kí to King Sirion, Harlow Darro, strike down the king or command anyone to do so?"

Titan could see many there wanted to speak, but no one did, fully aware that lying to the King of Kings would see their heads removed instead of Darro's.

"Kings of the Halos," Titan continued. "Royal inquest found no evidence that Harlow Darro was responsible for the slaughter. Each of you has the right by law to cut down Darro should he directly insult your name or trespass on your lands, but if you desire the Lord King to send his warrior riders forth then you must produce evidence. Equally so, if Harlow Darro presents before me with evidence of his own against one or many of you, then you will be the ones to stand trial for King Sirion's death."

He heard it then – fear – a high, thin note and a flashing of uncertainty in the eyes of many gathered there. Not even Vitor-Petacula was lack-witted enough to say anything at that point.

At the back of the huge chamber, through the arches of the entryway, Titan saw the orange glow of the setting sun. Great relief streamed through him.

"Night is upon us," he announced. "The hearing will adjourn for those of you who have prayers to offer your gods, and at darkfall the feast will commence. Tomorrow," he paused, "I will open the gates of Ironeye to accept proposals from the common ladies."

This time, not just murmurs of surprise but a commotion of shock flared up. No king or liege before him had ever opened the gates for the common women to be heard. Titan spoke over the noise. "Once all the waiting ladies have had their turn, the hearing will recommence. You will be informed of the exact day as it comes. For today the hearing is officially closed."

Titan saw Yorem Gorse and the Anacharasi crowd casting around looks of veiled uncertainty and frustration. They'd expected Gorse to be crowned that day. *You'll never sit as king,* Titan thought silently as Quintus announced their departure and he followed the king out of Ma'at.

They paused there in the outer hallways as the Companions and the guards took formation around them. Titan could see his Companions were looking somewhat stunned, and also furious about what had been said in the hearing. The Lord King's face gave nothing away, but Titan could read his silences well enough to know he wasn't displeased.

There was the shuffling of a commotion behind them and Titan heard a voice call out to him, "Lord Liege!"

He turned and saw Ravana, crying, fighting to get through his periphery guards, with her mother trying to hold her back. "A word. Please."

The distress but also the determination in her eyes made him distinctly uneasy. Mercifully, the Lord King started moving and Titan turned his back on the princess and followed. Her calls chased him down the hallways.

Chapter 11
Eli

AQUAIS

SCORPIA (LIBERTYTOWN)

When Eli was a kid Grampy had often said "time was a relative". What he'd meant was that *time was relative*, but he'd thrown in the "a" because he was overly fond of putting "a"s in front of as many words as he could in a sentence. It was one of his things. So Eli had grown up thinking that somehow he must be related to time itself, in some kind of strange imp-breed way that everyone understood, but no one could ever explain. It wasn't until later on that he figured it out – time was relative. Two minutes at school felt like two eras, two minutes eating ice-cream were over in a blink. Two days could pass as he sat at his desk inventing and he would think it had only been two hours. Two minutes lying on a stretcher, awake but keeping his eyes shut because he was afraid to open them? To quote gran'pa, "time was a dragging".

His eyelids fluttered up and a hazy light stung his eyes.

"He's awake." Diega's melodic voice echoed above him and her hair brushed his cheek as she leaned in close.

Eli stared up into her eyes and saw fluttering purple eyelashes and rainbow skin, the colors blurring together.

"A human-breed of horse blood walks into a bar and the bar keeper says, 'Why the long face?'" Diega said.

Eli smiled, he couldn't help it – that one always got him – but then he grimaced.

"My everything hurts," he groaned, his voice croaky.

"Stop moving then," Diega replied.

"What happened? Where's Diamond?" He looked around him and saw he was back at the Trackers' Headquarters in one of their medical rooms.

Diega nodded toward the door. "Intensive, in the civilian ward."

"I have to see her." Eli tried to sit up, but Diega pushed him back down.

"That's a negative. Don't even think about it," she said with force.

"I told her not to go outside the gate," Eli whispered, feeling sickness building up inside him.

"Trutting imp-breeds. They never listen." Diega smiled, but there was an edge to it.

Eli stared at her, fragments of the attack returning to him.

"It's bad, isn't it?" he said.

Diega dropped her gaze for a moment, then looked back up at him and said, "You've lost a wing."

Eli had known something was coming, but the news still knocked the breath out of him. He felt Diega holding his hand.

Behind her the doors slid open and the commander and Silho rushed in. Eli was vaguely aware of the commander checking all the medical equipment around his bed. Then the sound of his voice roused Eli from his shock.

"We didn't expect you awake for some time."

"You can add anesthetic resistance to your list of strengths," Diega informed him.

"And take flying off it, I guess," Eli murmured. Silho tensed up, but the commander said, "For now, yes."

For now and forever. Wings weren't like normal limbs, they were like brains, once taken, they couldn't be replaced.

"I need to see," Eli told him.

"It's too soon to walk," Diega said, but Copernicus ignored her and helped Eli to sit and then to maneuver out of bed. He stood swaying on his feet and the commander held his arm as he wobbled toward the mirror on the wall. Diega and Silho moved just behind him, as though they expected him to drop.

He approached his own reflection wearing a short surgical gown, white legs sticking out underneath, mouth open, gawking at himself. He closed it and licked his lips. His front seemed unscathed enough, a few scratches and bruises here and there. He turned his head one way and then the other. There was a long red mark on the side of his face, where a gash had undergone quick-regen. His hair was shaved and so was his beard. He felt a regretful twinge. It would only take him another lifetime to grow it back.

Eli breathed in deeply and forced himself to turn his back to the mirror and look over his shoulder. The open back of the surgical gown gave him a clear view. Where his left wing had been, there were several long lines of stitches and a whole bunch of anti-pain patches. His wing was completely gone. Eli felt his heart pounding in his throat and his body going hot and cold. His legs gave out from under him and the commander grabbed him, holding him up. Silho hugged onto him as well and Diega put a hand on his back. He wasn't sure how long they stayed like that, but when his senses returned to him, his face was squished up against the commander's chest and he'd vomited all down the boss's shirt.

"I'm so sorry," he said, realizing.

Copernicus shook his head. "Don't be sorry, Eli. Not at all."

"He can douse himself with boiling water and disinfectant later," Diega put in, getting a look from the boss.

The doors to the room slid open and Ev'r and Ismail stepped in. They immediately saw Eli's damage. Ismail clenched his jaw but Ev'r didn't react at all.

"Nice dress," she said.

"I do my best," Eli replied faintly.

"I probably would have gone with underwear though."

Diega snorted, "Now, everyone knows *that's* a lie, Zingara."

"Rich, coming from you, fairy girl," Ev'r threw back.

The tension between the two groups was never far beneath the surface, but a long, loud trumpeting sound from Eli's stomach brought the building argument to a close. The commander helped him back to the stretcher bed and he sat down on the edge, shivering. Diega took his heavy military coat off a nearby hook and wrapped it around him. It was torn and covered in blood and he could see she immediately regretted putting it on him.

"I need to see Diamond," Eli appealed to Copernicus.

"After," the boss said, as firmly as Diega had, and he guessed from their reaction that she wasn't in a good way.

"How are her lights? Do you see the darkness around her?" Eli asked Silho.

Silho shook her head and it looked authentic, but Silho was an accomplished deceptionist. Eli had always said you can't lie to a liar, but Silho could lie convincingly to pretty much anyone.

"I told her not to go outside," Eli choked up again. "We couldn't get the gate open." Diega made him lie down, but he shot back up almost immediately.

"Nelly! Where is she?"

Everyone looked at each other and no one answered.

"We didn't see her," Diega told him. "But then again, we didn't really look – a bit busy saving your life to worry about the rat."

Eli felt his panic hit the roof and he tried to get back out of the bed. "I have to go! It's storming. She's afraid of thunder and she won't find her way back from there!"

Both the commander and Diega restrained him, though one of them would have been more than enough.

"I'll go and find her," Silho told him.

"No," the commander said firmly. "You'll remain here."

Silho gave him a look but complied. The tension between them hung silent and uneasy.

"Your mother wouldn't have taken that," Ev'r said unhelpfully from where she and Ismail were standing near the door.

"My mother's dead," Silho responded, her voice flat.

The doors opened again and Jude entered with several Androt soldiers.

"Eli!" he said, running to the bedside, with SevenM, his arachnid robot, perched on his shoulder, feeding images back to Jude's mind. SevenM stared down at Eli with his many mirrored eyes. He made a sad sound.

"Are you alright, Eli?" Jude said, searching over him for injury.

"He's lost a wing," Diega spoke up, and Jude's blue eyes stretched wide. He put his hands to either side of his neck in shock. The others had all blunted their reactions, but the truth was, imp-breeds who lost wings never usually survived very long after.

"This is your fault! You kept pushing him!" Jude shouted at Copernicus, the shoved him.

The commander kept his feet, and returned the accusation with a cold silence. Jude tried to come at him again, but Diega leapt in between them.

"His fault? If you hadn't been distracting Eli with all your guilt trips and demands —"

"You are not pinning this on me!" Jude yelled, trying to push past her.

"No!" Silho intervened as well and caught an elbow to the face.

Copernicus started to react but Ismail got in first, his glowing red eyes locked onto Jude. "Watch yourself," he growled.

The Androt guards armed their electrifiers and took aim at him. Eli could feel the powerful psychic energy surging from Ismail.

"They're machine-breeds, remember," Jude said to him. "Your mind tricks and dark magics don't work on us."

"No, but this will," Ev'r said, drawing her machete, the Morsus Ictus.

"Stand down!" the commander ordered everyone.

"You can't control them," Jude told him. Then he shouted at Silho, "Can't you see yet what a monster he is?"

Eli's head ached and his heart was pounding from the horrible tension between them all.

"A monster?" Diega yelled. "This monster has saved your skin more times than you can count!"

"Only because it suited him to do so, because I always did as he said. As soon as people start questioning him, he throws them away – like Eli!"

"*Fsx*," she swore at him in Fenlen. "You're trutting crazy! He didn't throw Eli away! And he didn't throw you away either. You turned on him, and on us."

"Of course you're going to defend him," Jude snorted. "You never cared at all about me, did you? It's always been him."

"Wake up to yourself," Diega said. "Silho doesn't want you, and Copernicus never wanted me. That's trutting life, Jude. And I did love you, but unfortunately you couldn't accept that. We didn't break up because of him. We broke up because you tried to kill yourself and you didn't give a second thought to how I'd feel about that!"

"I was trying to save the world," Jude said, his voice losing some of it's fury.

"So?" Diega said. "That doesn't make any difference."

Jude started shouting again and Eli clutched his stomach, feeling increasingly sick as the yelling continued.

"Stop," he whispered, unheard. Then he raised his voice, crying out, "Stop!"

That made everyone pause.

"If you don't stop fighting I swear I'm just going to lie down here and die! I don't care about my wing," he lied. "But you're all tearing me apart!"

Jude's eyes immediately softened. After a moment he nodded to his guards to lower their weapons. Once they had, Ev'r sheathed her black blade.

Shawe appeared in the doorway behind them eating a sandwich, chewing with his mouth open, a cigarette tucked behind one ear.

"You still alive then?" he said to Eli, only mildly interested, in the response.

"No … I mean yes," Eli said.

The former gangster king grunted. He stomped into the room and said mockingly to Jude, "Your highness." And then, more teasingly than mocking to Diega, "Sunshine." He glanced at Silho and thought better of saying anything.

"The gangland's buzzing," he told the commander. "K-Ruz is organizing a hunt for the creature."

"Yeah, good luck to him," Diega snorted.

"I told him he's dreaming, but you know kitty. He knows everything."

A violent gust of energy suddenly swept through the room and Luther materialized with his big shaggy white wolf, Moses. The cross-bred Midnight Man descended on Eli with a hug so tight it made him gasp and fart at the same time. Luther immediately released his grip and stared down at Eli with his striking yellow-green python-blood eyes, his face shifting, as it did, between the frightening appearance of a Midnight Man and his human-breed side.

Moses licked Eli's fingers and whined softly. Luther saw Eli's injury and winced, then he held up a hand for Eli to wait and pulled a squirming bundle of fur out of his swirling shadow cloak.

"Nelly!" Eli cried out, and she leapt into his arms. He cuddled her tightly. Her fur was damp and she was shaking.

"Thank you! Thank you!" he said to Luther.

Luther patted Eli heavily on the head.

After a moment the commander asked the Midnight Man, "Anything?"

Luther shook his head.

"What about from your outposts?" the commander spoke to Jude, his voice tight. "Have they seen anything?"

Jude started to respond aggressively, but then caught sight of Eli and changed his tone. "No, Commander Kane, they have not."

"The gangland?" Copernicus asked Christy.

"Trutt all," Christy said. "Like I said, K-Ruz is organizing a hunt."

Ev'r snorted near the door, looking up from under her fringe of white blond hair. "Well aren't we all just one big happy family now."

Eli tensed. He loved Ev'r dearly, but she dearly loved conflict.

"You ain't my trutting family, stinking scullion scum." Shawe took the bait.

Ismail growled, bristling.

"Or mine," Diega backed Shawe. Ev'r looked between them, amusement playing in her green eyes.

"I say this with no care or consideration for you at all," she said to Diega. "You can do better than Christy Shawe."

"Big words, considering your history. You've been bedded by every man in this room," Christy said. "Except for him," he nodded to Jude. "Nobody wants him, even if he is the king."

Jude clenched his jaw.

"And not me either," Eli put in. He was trying to protect Ev'r's honor, but it didn't quite sound right.

"Aren't you a girl?" Shawe said to him.

"Yes – I mean *no* – no I'm not," Eli replied, insult adding to critical injury.

"You sure?"

"Yes, I'm pretty sure," Eli said.

Shawe started to question him again, but both Silho and Luther flared up, Luther becoming a dangerous looming shadow and Silho's eyes starting to burn. Nelly dove headlong into Eli's pocket and curled up in there.

"Okay, relax." Shawe backed down, shuffling to the other side of the room.

Eli sighed and rubbed his stinging eyes, noticing then that his weapon belt was hanging up on a nearby hook. A red light was flashing from one of his monitors in a particular rhythm. Eli froze, staring at it, not believing it.

The commander noticed. "What is it?"

Eli reached out for his monitor and Silho quickly handed it to him. With numb fingers, he fumbled with the switches and started checking the readings. It was quite clear. Devastation and fear ran cold through his chest.

"Eli?" Copernicus asked. Everyone was staring at him.

"The detector. The darkness – it's ... it's started." This was it. It was actually happening.

"How long?" Ev'r asked.

Eli shook his head, wordlessly.

"We don't know," the commander responded for him. He addressed the team. "We'll return to the *Manticore*. Shah-Jahan will talk," he said, with no give to his words.

Diega lifted her com off her belt and dialed in.

"Commander Santana," she said when it picked up. "We're coming back down to question the Dray captain. Make sure we have backup there in case."

The Ohini Fen soldier, Santana, paused before saying, "There's an issue here."

The commander took Diega's com and said, "Kane here. Speak."

"The *Scorpian Manticore* just vanished."

"Define 'vanished'."

"One moment there and the next gone. The whole facility is completely empty. There's no one left. At all."

"When?" Copernicus demanded.

"A few moments ago. I was just about to call you," Santana said.

"Understood." Copernicus said, massaging his forehead. "End."

Eli's throat tightened. "King Apollo's map! I left it on the *Manticore*."

"Trutt!" Shawe cursed, slamming his fist into the wall and shattering the plaster.

"You don't need the map, Eli." The commander said and tapped his temple. "It's all here. Calm yourself. Copy it down."

Eli nodded. The commander was right. He always was. Eli had a photographic memory and he'd studied those pieces so many times. Silho handed him a pen and paper and with a shaky hand, he redrew what they had of the map.

"Well, it's here," he said once he had finished, "but we still need the last piece. I can't finish the translation without it. It still doesn't make any sense."

Ev'r stepped forward and slipped a piece of paper into Eli's hand. He unfolded it and saw it was the final piece. He stared at her in amazement, and she gave half a smile.

"Now we're even, Snacksize."

Everyone pressed in close as Eli lay the final piece onto the paper, completing the king's map. He quickly translated the words of the map, finding in the final corner a full sentence. "On these hallowed grounds I stand," he uttered.

Silho gasped and started to shine with white light.

"Stop!" the commander gripped her shoulder and said, "Repeat the words!"

Silho closed her eyes and managed to control the change with the illusionist enchant she used to anchor herself, but it left her gasping and swaying on her feet.

"No one say it aloud! It's an access enchant to open a portal," Copernicus said. He looked around the group. "Arm up. Everyone. We're going through to find Apollo of Corinthia. It's our only lead. Eli, you're staying here, coms and intel, same as always, as much as you can handle. Luther, keep with Eli." The Midnight Man nodded and Eli felt tears prickling his eyes.

The commander turned to Ev'r and Ismail, and Ev'r said, "Don't look at us, Kane. We've done what we promised and now we're out." Her eyes met Eli's and she said, "We can't stay."

Eli had known this moment was coming, but it hit him so hard, all he could do was open and close his mouth silently.

"Come with us!" Ismail said to Silho, but she shook her head.

"Alejan. I can't leave him," Diega spoke up, realization dawning across her face. Eli had never heard her sound so panicked before. It hardly sounded like her at all. "I can't just go!"

"If we don't go, Aquais will be taken, and so will he," the commander said. "You remember Omar Montanya?"

"He's with the old lady, right? He'll be fine," Shawe put in.

"He's my son! I can't just leave him with the nanny!"

"He'll be fine," Shawe repeated.

"I'll take care of him!" Eli jumped in. "Luther can go get him and bring him here. He loves Moses and he won't be afraid with me, I'll make sure of it."

Diega's colors were flashing brightly and Eli thought he saw a tear in her eye.

Luther signed, "I'll get him now." The Midnight Man vanished.

"Everything will be okay," Eli tried to comfort her, but the words sounded hollow. They were about to be attacked by the Arequium Mors and have their whole planet dragged down into a hell realm. Everything would most definitely not be okay.

Eli looked up and saw Ev'r and Ismail going out the door.

The words burst out of him, "Don't go!" Ev'r hesitated, looking back.

An *ech ech* sound echoed around them and one whole wall blew out as the Ripper plowed into the building. Eli was slammed off the bed and onto the ground, debris raining down on his head. He felt the monster descending on them, and knew it was impervious to the electrifier shots ringing out around him. It would kill them all. Eli clutched the map parchment and in panic shouted out the words, "On these hallowed grounds I stand!"

A blinding white light engulfed the shattered room and Eli felt himself falling, tumbling, crashing downward at a terrible speed, until a force propelled him out of the blazing lights of the portal. He tried to keep his balance, running forward for a dozen out-of-control steps before tripping and face-planting into thick, poo-brown mud, or possibly, from the foul stench of it, just thick brown poo. Eli wiped the gunk out of his eyes and looked around him. Alarm filtered through his shock, gradually at first and then in one solid punch that made him scramble up, gasping.

A foreign land stretched out in front of him, a barren mud plain with a few straggly trees, hemmed in by a primitive, ramshackle fence, broken in more places than it was solid. And the light ... Eli peered up into the sky and saw one very distant white sun, which cast a cold and almost eerie glow across entire the land, as though a monster storm or some kind of apocalyptic happening was brewing. It wasn't anything like the Aquaian light, which meant this wasn't Aquais. Eli's heart was hammering so fast it hurt. He'd just jumped worlds. He spun around, searching for the others, but there was no one. Just him. Alone, in the middle of a wasteland with a chill breeze on his bare backside. Eli felt something smooth and hard beneath his feet and gazed down. Skulls and other bones lay half buried in the mud all around him.

"Not good," Eli whispered.

Chapter 12
Ramses

HYDRIA

CORINTHIA (CORINTH CITY)

The walkway between the Halls of Ma'at and the Lord King's chambers at the center of Ironeye was so heavily guarded that Ramses and the other Companions were forced to walk single file, and even then had to press through the lines of soldiers. The Lord King's private quarters were always guarded, no one was permitted to even approach the doors unless specially summoned, but it had never been this intense. Ramses had known every warrior there for all his life, but as they walked through, there was none of the friendly banter that usually went on. The Companions were watched with the same scrutiny as a stranger would be. More guards crowded every rooftop, hallway, entrance and exit of Ironeye, making sure no one was going anywhere without the Lord King's permission.

The Companions climbed the steps to the doors of the inner chamber and stopped there to wait. No one had spoken much on the way over, each of them silently burning over what had happened in the hearing. Words were too soon and not enough.

Ramses turned to look out over the palace grounds. The music for the feast had already started up, the drums pounding heavily in the distant halls; over that came the recital of evening prayer from the temple and the rumble of thunder from above. Gray clouds were rolling over the orange and red of the sunset, and Ramses could smell the coming rain, as well as the succulent scents from the feast foods cooking in the palace kitchens. He watched the smoke from the steam houses rising into the air and his stomach growled with a savage reminder that just wine for breakfast, lunch and supper was not acceptable. As he was contemplating this, he smelled another odor that became increasingly heavy, until Ramses was forced to cover his nose. This gas was enough to turn even the hardest stomach. Chey was trying unsuccessfully not to look guilty.

"Really?" Ramses said.

Chey raised his eyes and said, "What?"

"Is it possible that we should be subjected to the smell of shit? What have you been eating?" Ramses demanded.

Mohan laughed quietly beside Chey and Ramses continued, "Must have been down at the Draul camps eating their yarok."

Chey scrunched up his face with repulsion at the thought of the Draul's vile yellow root vegetable. Ramses had tried it once himself and spat it all the way across the room. His tongue had never tasted right since.

"Vitor-Petacula keeps crying on about the strength of his soldiers, and truly I tell you Drauls must be the most fearless warriors of all the Halos to partake in such a repulsive diet," Chey replied.

Both Ramses and Mohan laughed, but with restraint under the eyes of all the guards. Hammer would have usually thrown them one of his glares of thunder, but he had remained quiet and restrained since the round room.

"And even yet I'd rather eat their yarok for every meal than take one of their women to my bed," Chey added, smoothing his hands along the shaved sides of his head. "Did you *see* what Petacula was trying to pass off as a princess? If he'd put a dress on a bog swine it would have been a more appealing sight."

Ramses grunted in agreement. The word *Draula* in High Corinthian meant *unpleasing woman* – coincidence? Ramses thought not.

"Come now," Mohan said. "The women aren't *that* bad."

Chey gave him a crazed look. "Did you smell them?"

"It's the marsh waters," Mohan said. "It taints their skin. But I assume it washes off with time."

"Don't bet on it," Chey grunted.

Draul's lands ran into the diseased Cytisian Swamps, also known to Corinthians as *Censangue*, which meant bloodless, and also *La – there –* as opposed to *here*.

"Besides that," Ramses added, "do you really think you should be passing judgment on bad smells?"

Chey snorted and said, "My shit smells like a bed of roses compared to the Drauls ... the nerve of Petacula and that mountain goat, Gideon. To Acheron with them both. Methusael take them."

"*Se*," Ramses and Mohan agreed, exchanging a glance. War was coming – they could all feel it.

The great doors opened and Quintus appeared.

"Companions. You may enter," he said, and they stepped in, following him down the red carpet of the entrance hall, built of ancient and grand architecture, with sandstone pillar and soaring roof dimly lit by lantern fire. The walls were lined by the sacred armor of all the kings to have reigned in Corinthia before the Lord King Osiris, all except one. Where the Almighty's armor should have stood, with his sword on the wall behind it, there was an empty space. They all avoided looking at it.

Quintus opened up the inner doors and gestured for them to wait as he entered to announce them. They stood in silence, listening to his voice ring out, announcing their full names, before he returned and gave the signal that they were allowed in. Ramses stepped through the door and around the corner into the Lord King's private meeting chamber. It was much smaller than Ma'at, but it was built in a way that fascinated Ramses, so many shapes and edges and interlocking pieces to the walls.

The Companions went to their knees and heard Titan calling them back up. Ramses stood again, his eyes drawn to the Lord King Osiris sitting on his throne, which was carved from Corinthian marble. The sides were in the likeness of galloping stallions and the Lord King sat there, his heavy arms resting on the stallions' backs. When Ramses looked at the Lord King, it felt like he was being drawn toward him, ineluctably, toward his eyes, which were so fierce it felt like they were melting back Ramses' metal and skin, his pretense and bravado, to the truth of his heart.

The king was a force of nature, so powerful that peripheries and surrounds seem to blur around him, and all others lost focus. Like his mighty father before him, he made people stand in awe no matter how many times they stood before him. Ramses resisted the urge to wipe his face, sweating more now than he had been in the full blast of the sun. The chamber stood packed full, with the Lord King's *ata-ajua*, his Companions, one of them Mohan and Hammer's father, all his advisors and as many Kís as Ramses had ever seen in one place at one time. He hadn't realized that the king even had so many spies. Titan and his *ata-ajua* were standing in the center of the room in front of the Lord King's great marble table.

The Companions moved down to stand beside Titan, and Ramses saw he was studying a strategic map embedded with battle code. He didn't recognize the code, and couldn't decipher it just with his eye, but he knew the hand of the map to be Harlow Darro's. It was very distinct, very skillfully constructed, seeming simple on the surface, but with so many layers of strategy that every glance brought something new and unconsidered to sight. Darro was said to be a master strategist and here lay proof. It was the most complete map by Darro's hand that they'd yet seen.

Ramses glanced over at the Kís. If Ramses was to be kind, he would say, at the very kindest, they were an extremely odd collection of individuals. He wondered which of them had uncovered this treasure. Ramses could tell by the way Titan leaned in so closely to the table, studying and memorizing each and every line, that he was greatly impressed, and Ramses felt an unwanted twinge of jealousy. Impressive was not a word he'd use to describe himself. Wine-stained, yes. Impressive? No.

The room sat in absolute silence while Titan analyzed the map, and Ramses felt the Lord King watching his son. It made him think of the day they had been released from the Amkalai after the first trial. Attending the brutal training was tradition and honor, but when Titan had first been brought before the Lord King after many long years away, Ramses had wondered if perhaps, just perhaps, he had glimpsed, for a moment, sadness in the Lord King's eyes.

Maybe some part of him had mourned the loss of his boy, or maybe the look was something else – sorrow that his second son would never have a chance to stand with such greatness. Titan's brother had been born wrong. As the law demanded, he was outcast to Cytisus, taken and left beyond the halo of sanctified lands, and he was not spoken of since, as though he'd never existed. But once, August had whispered a secret truth to Ramses, that before the Lord King Osiris had ordered the baby be taken away, he'd broken custom and held his little son and named him Arisef. In High Corinthian it meant "return to me".

Titan straightened up and turned his attention toward the Kís.

"Good." His word was high praise and they all bowed.

Titan then approached the king's throne and lowered his head, awaiting his father's word.

"Speak," Osiris commanded.

"Lord King, the code of the map supports our evidence. The mines have been reopened in the Kingdom of Draul."

The chamber stirred in anger, but the king just gave a silent nod.

Titan continued. "It also supports our evidence of the alliance between kings Maneam of Armen, Vitor-Petacula of Draul and Gideon of Kirith-Jerom and throne contender Yorem Gorse."

Ramses breathed out heavily through his nose, his anger building again. Beside him Hammer clenched his jaw, and Chey his fists.

"The Kís also bring confirmation that Darro and his companions have been attacking mine sites, liberating slaves. Darro's companions have been sighted as Aron and Vitali

Storon, brothers, and former soldiers in the Anacharasi army, Darro's left and right from when he was Kí to King Sirion. The third companion has been sighted as a man of large proportions, origins unknown."

Titan paused, removing a scroll from his tunic. He moved up the stairs to his father and bowed low, offering him the parchment. The Lord King took it.

"This is my position," Titan said. "Darro had no hand in the slaying of Sirion and the royal family. I believe it was by the hand of Yorem Gorse, in conspiracy with Vitor-Petacula, Maneam and Gideon in a bid to form a union of their kingdoms against Corinthia. They wish to destroy us. Only Theselon still stands our ally."

It was a huge call, and the heaviest of silences hung over the chamber as everyone watched the Lord King and Titan.

"This is my true belief," Titan continued. "It is clear in my mind. And I put forth that Corinthia should declare war."

The words rang out loud and true and Ramses felt a shiver run through him. It would be the first war of the Barbarian kingdoms for over a hundred years – Theselon and Corinthia against Draul, Armen, Anacharasis and the mountains. It left them the superior warriors, but greatly outnumbered.

The Lord King sat back in his throne studying Titan's parchment, which would be the initial strategy of the war. He spoke after some time.

"What is your first step?"

Titan paused, his eyes moving around the room as he thought. "The Hearing awaits word on the succession of the throne, but Gorse must not be given the power. If he is not the legitimate king it provides immediate weakness in their armor. That is the reason I made announcement that the common ladies would be permitted to propose. To extend time."

"Time," the Lord King repeated.

"Time for me to find Harlow Darro. I believe Darro will provide strong advantage in knowledge of both the enemy and their lands. He knows the secrets of these places unlike any other."

Ramses swallowed. It was another strong call, considering he was talking to the Lord King.

"*Ivar.*" A voice rang out from the gathered advisors. It belonged to a Centurion, Billios, known for speaking his mind, in or out of turn. He was known to be completely inappropriate but had been the Almighty's closest friend.

"If Darro was going to present evidence or even to make himself known to us, we'd already have him. Kí by name, Kí by nature, he's not coming in easily."

"Agreed," Titan said. "Which is why I propose, Lord King, humbled before your wisdom, that I be sent myself to locate Darro and bring him in."

Ramses felt himself caught off guard by Titan's words, his surprise reflected over the faces of the king's companions and advisors, well used to showing nothing.

"You forget, son," Billios spoke, taking huge liberties again. "You'll be expected to sit through the proposals of a hundred thousand common girls then announce the name of your wife. Don't you think they might notice if you're not there?"

"I forget nothing, Warrior," Titan corrected him lightly. "Darro must be found, as we stand on the brink of war. I put forward that my companion, Mohammad—" he indicated Hammer, "take my place during the proposals. With enough distance of throne and dimmed light, we would pass easily for one another."

Ramses saw Hammer's muscles lock up with the honor of Titan's proposition.

The Lord King ran a hand down his chin, considering Titan's words.

"My permission is granted," he said, after what felt like a very long time. "Go, Tarrus. Bring Harlow Darro to me. Mohammad, you will stand in as the Lord Liege's double throughout the proposals."

"Yes, Lord King," Hammer said, bowing.

A feeling of panic sprouted inside Ramses and grew by the moment. August's word rang loudly in his mind: *caution.*

"Lord King," Ramses spoke up. All eyes in the room turned his way. He lowered his head and waited until the King granted him to speak.

"Please, Lord King. I beg, humbled before your wisdom, that you allow me to accompany the Lord Liege on his search for Darro. I stand his Companion, now and always."

The Lord King's eyes burned into Ramses' face as he considered his words, then he gave an almost imperceptible nod and it was decided. If there was a word for feeling simultaneously terrified and greatly relieved, Ramses was uncertain what it was, but his legs felt weak and his hands shaky.

"Clear the chamber." Titan gave the command and Ramses moved out of the room with the rest of the gathering, leaving Titan alone with his father.

* * * * *

Ramses waited in front of the chamber doors long after the other Companions had gone to attend the feast as they were expected to do. It was well into dark when Titan finally emerged with his *ata-ajua* and periphery guards. He headed down the steps, pausing a moment as he saw Ramses on the last step, beneath a flickering torch.

"Brother," Titan greeted him. "You were not expected to await me." His words were not harsh in any way, but they touched raw wounds inside Ramses' mind, making them feel like a reprimand.

"I had hoped to speak with you, Lord Liege," he said, hearing the uncertainty in his own voice. "About personal matters."

Titan took him in for a moment and Ramses braced himself for refusal, but then Titan said, "Best we talk alone then."

He nodded toward the walkway to his quarters and Ramses fell into step at his side. They walked together in silence, through the crowd of guards, the new shift just turned for the night watch. All the warriors bowed before Titan and he acknowledged them. When they reached Titan's tower, he ordered his periphery guards to spread out across the steps, and he and Ramses climbed all the way up to the rooftop courtyard. Ramses knew it was Titan's favored place in all the palace. It always had been. By the time they reached the top Ramses' legs were aching and he was trying to hide how out of breath he felt. Titan's stallion, Farahman, whickered a greeting as soon as he spotted them and trotted over, putting his face down to Titan's.

"Look at you old boy," Ramses said, patting Farahman's velvet nose. "Living the good life."

The stallion nudged him playfully, following after them as they walked deeper into the garden. The red moon of Mascald blazed high in the sky above them, and below, the sounds of feasting echoed all over the palace and city.

"It's been a while since we've ridden together," Ramses said, finding his words uneasily.

"Too long," Titan murmured in response, his face obscured by shadows.

"It's hot." Ramses wiped his forehead.

"*Se*," Titan agreed. "The rains are returning." As he spoke, Ramses felt a drop of water on his neck and another on his cheek. He resisted the urge to wipe them off. Most believed that Acheron was a place of burning fire, but to him hell was water. It was *Mĕthmalay*. Bringer of death.

"Good news," Ramses said, trying to sound positive. "It will be good to know the aqueducts run full again."

They stopped beside a lantern under Titan's gigantic quercus tree, which in light stood fully covered in vivid red and pink flowers. The blooms crunched under their feet, giving off the scent of honey.

"The rain comes from *Mĕthmalay*," Titan told him and Ramses felt a shadow cross his heart. Rains from the mountains meant good fortune, but rain from over the sea meant a change was in the near future. It could be good or bad, but it would be inevitable.

Silence held between them until Ramses said, "Ravana Nazar ... She's quite lovely."

Titan didn't respond and Ramses thought he must wish to avoid the topic, but then he spoke quietly.

"Tell me. Has there ever been a woman you considered taking as your wife?"

The question surprised him. Titan hadn't asked him any personal questions for years. The rain pattered down on the leaves above them and the ground steamed beneath their feet.

"No, never," he admitted. "How are we supposed to choose just one and do so with a true heart? How can I vow to love when I don't feel it? When I don't feel anything?"

"Here-in lies the question," Titan said.

Ramses stared across the garden to where the black stone statue of the Almighty stood in silence, surrounded by the night.

Titan followed the direction of his gaze.

"Do you remember him?" Titan asked, taking Ramses again by surprise.

The truth was, he couldn't remember Apollo the Almighty at all. In truth, a lot of his childhood was lost to him. He blinked and saw an image in his mind of his own grandfather, Aramasas, all wildly overgrown gray eyebrows and sparkling eyes, holding up a royal coin and saying, "Fetch us another drink my boy. Go on, one for me and one for you."

Over the years he had fetched his grandfather enough wine to drown a mountain, enough that the troubles of life and the darkness of the old warrior's memories had blurred and become irrelevant. And even when Aramasas had been falling down drunk, he'd still been wiser than the wisest man in any realm. He had stood as first advisor to the Lord King Apollo, and the stories he would tell of the Almighty were unequaled in color and detail, so real that the Lord King seemed to walk among them again through his words. Ramses had found his grandfather lying dead on the floor of a harem house, his heart stopped mid-fuck. It was not the death of a warrior rider, not the death he'd deserved, but the one he had created for himself. Ramses had dragged him out to the street and put his sword through Aramasas' heart. He'd told everyone his grandfather had fallen, heavily outnumbered, defending a woman and her child from skin traders. August had realized the truth immediately, but he had held his silence. He'd let Ramses tell his story as many times as he needed to, until the ringing clash of sword as his grandfather fought to the death for a righteous cause became real.

"Aramasas said, 'Never a man existed like he, a man who could show the greatest of mercy and not be weakened by his love – a man who could enforce the most brutal of punishments with his own hands and not be corrupted by the blood. A man with one foot in the Blessed Plains and the other in the fires of Acheron, standing in perfect balance.'"

Titan nodded. "I remember him saying that."

"You stand in the Almighty's exact likeness," Ramses said to Titan in sudden impulse. It was high praise and he meant every word.

Titan turned his eyes to Ramses, but it was too dark to see exactly how he had taken it.

"Go, brother, join the feast," he said after some time. "There is much on my mind."

Again the words held no dismissal or reprimand, perhaps only the suggestion of fatigue, but Ramses' mind told him he was being dismissed, rebuffed, and it hurt badly.

"There was a time," Ramses spoke with effort, "that we would speak our thoughts to each other always."

Titan nodded.

"When did we stop trusting each other?" He'd uttered the words before he could filter them. He expected some kind of strong retort from Titan, but instead he said quietly, "How much do you remember?"

Ramses felt a stirring of the most uncomfortable feeling inside him. He opened and closed his mouth, unable to make any sound. While he stalled in attempt, there came a fluttering of wings beside them and a stunning white peacock landed on a branch of the quercus tree, in a circle of lantern light. It looked right down at them and released a mournful cry. Movement behind them made Titan and his *ata-ajua* turn swiftly. Ramses looked as well, and saw Princess Ravana Nazar standing there in the moonlight. A white lace veil covered half her head and her long white dress sparkled, even in the darkness. She moved gracefully toward them and

Ramses could see in the flickering flames of the lantern that her face was tearstained and eyes misted. He hadn't heard her approaching them and wondered how she'd slipped past Titan's guard. She stopped before them and lowered her veil.

"Forgive me Lord Liege," she spoke in a whisper, far different from the confident voice she'd presented with at the hearing. "But I must speak with you."

"Princess Ravana," Titan answered, his voice harder than Ramses had expected. "I did not summon you here."

"Please, Lord Liege," Ravana said, her voice tremulous. "I wanted to tell you, that ceremony, it was not of my design. My mother keeps pushing me into things I don't want to do. I wanted something simpler, where I could tell you of my true heart. I've loved you since I was a girl, when you first visited our royal court." She touched her heart. "You were so kind to me."

Ramses was moved by her expression, but when Titan responded his voice remained stone. "Princess Ravana. I did not summon you here. Return to your quarters immediately."

Ravana stared at him, tears rolling down her face.

"Lord Liege," she sobbed, losing her composure.

"Return to your quarters, now," Titan commanded her.

She lowered her head, weeping into her hands. Ramses made move to go and comfort her, but Titan held him back. After a moment of uncontrolled crying, Ravana stopped suddenly, raising her face to them. Before Ramses' eyes, her expression shifted from heartbroken to disdainful. She stared at Titan with contempt.

"What?" she finally spoke, her voice different once again. "Am I not pleasing to you? My face, my hair, my body?" She ran her hands over her breasts and down her sides. "Is my smile not white enough? Am I not young enough for you?"

Titan gave no response and she continued, walking closer to them. "You," she growled, "stand most imperfect and so glorified, and we are forced to crawl before you across the floor to grovel at your feet. But you don't even see us."

Titan held his silence still, and Ramses shifted, feeling extremely unsettled. His imagined emotional outburst to Titan was being spectacularly outdone.

Ravana was shaking now with anger, and she raised her voice to a shout. "You drive us to doubt ourselves. You drive us to hate ourselves, to seek desperate measures!" She grabbed her hair and ripped it clean off, exposing a much less luxurious clump of patchy, limp hair beneath. She threw the wig down on the ground and Ramses stared at it. If he wasn't mistaken, there was a real scalp still attached to the hair. His stomach clenched.

"Where are the children?" Titan growled from beside him, and Ramses stared at him, confused.

At that, Ravana gave a hard laugh. "Your eyes are the most unflattering mirror I've ever looked into, Tarrus of Ironeye. But that will change."

She closed her eyes and gave a guttural snarl beneath her breath. The lanterns flared all through the garden and suddenly many women appeared from nowhere to stand behind Ravana. Ramses startled back, recognizing some of their faces as the women reported to the courts as missing. Titan and the *ata-ajua* drew their swords.

"What's happening?" Ramses uttered, drawing as well.

"Don't expect help," Ravana spat at Titan. "Your guards are all dead."

In a flash of light, a person dropped from the sky onto the railing of the courtyard. A warrior with armor shining like white fire in the darkness, his face hidden by a full metal zivas like the *ata-ajua*. He held up a glowing silver sword. Darro.

Ravana spoke, her voice strangely distorted, sounding like more than one voice. Her eyes were rolling back in her head, showing the whites.

"Put it down and your death will be quick."

Darro's voice rasped from behind his zivas. "I appreciate the consideration." He stepped down from the ledge. "Really I do. But I'm afraid you can't break my armor. My sword, on the other hand —" he held his brutal looking weapon up to the light – not a solid sword, but many smaller blades coming off a central blade, "will show you your life and then your death, and the meaninglessness of both, all in the wake of its strike. And I would return your offer of such kind mercy, if only I believed that filthy excrement-guzzling pustules such as yourself deserved any."

Ramses sensed movement beside him and turned quickly to see two more warriors creeping up on Ravana from the other side while Darro distracted her. One held a finger up to his mouth, gesturing for silence.

Ravana snarled and Darro said, "I see I've gone and used too many words. Allow me to clarify."

The hidden warriors leapt out and Darro swung his sword, cutting through a row of the gathered ladies. Ravana released an ear-piercing screech and the ground beneath them trembled. Her form seemed to expand, and then it appeared to explode into a deluge of water that crashed down on top of them. Ramses was knocked off his feet and landed hard, gasping, saltwater filling his mouth and nose. He panicked, screaming out and losing hold of his sword. It clattered from his hand and washed away.

"Help me!" he cried out to Titan, who tried to shield him, but Argos and the *ata-ajua* had Titan, and were dragging him away. Ramses grabbed onto his leg, trying to hold on. They heard a voice coming at them through the confusion, a distorted, groaning chant, many voices in one. Titan tensed and stumbled backward as a black hand with hugely elongated claw-fingers shot out of the darkness and seized him.

Titan's stallion began screaming and rushed in, trying to protect him, but was rebuffed by a sudden explosion of water. Powerful geysers exploded out of the ground, propelling Titan's *ata-ajua* into the air and dragging them back down into the building with gigantic water hands. Argos managed to fight his way back to Titan, but then the water around him froze completely, locking him in. The building was shaking, bits falling off and falling in all around them. The ground beside Ramses collapsed. His hand slipped off Titan's boot and he fell. As he did, he saw Darro diving through the water and ripping Titan out of the clawed grasp, swooping him upward into the sky. He saw Titan going up and up, while reaching back toward him, shouting out his name. Ramses crashed down with shattering force and his senses blacked out.

PART 2

Chapter 13
Eli

HYDRIA

FARNORTHERN HALOS (NÒ)

"Okay," Eli whispered to himself. "Do something. Just move."

He rubbed his face vigorously, trying to shift the haze from behind his eyes. The commander's voice spoke from his memories – *arm up and assess for immediate threat.*

Eli grabbed for his electrifier, but ended up with a handful of hospital gown instead. Then he remembered. His electrifier was back at the *Manticore* facility, his weapon belt was back at Headquarters, and all he had was his bloodied jacket.

"If there had been immediate threat you'd be dead by now," he told himself sternly. "Get it together. Next step ... find cover and evaluate available resources."

Ducking low, and feeling ridiculous as he did so, given that he'd been standing out in the open, completely exposed, for a good few minutes already, Eli ran through the mud, hobbling as sharp pieces of bone dug into his bare feet. He ran across the field to the closest ragged tree and dived behind the trunk, realizing on closer inspection that it was made up of a series of twisted vines with a gaping hole between them, so anyone on the other side could clearly see him hiding there. He sank down lower, sickness pounding through his body, and started counting back from forty-six to stop himself from passing out. He woke some time later, facedown in the mud.

He spluttered and wiped his face, trying to shake his head clear, then pushed a hand into his pocket, touching Nelly's soft fur. She was coping with the near-death experience and headfirst tumble into another world in the same way she coped with everything else – by having a snooze. At least she wasn't panicking. Eli started checking through all his other pockets, searching for weapons. He laid everything he found out in front of him, pausing to do a quick inventory – minty breath spray, a spanner, several parts of a transflyer engine, a crumpled tissue, his badge, a plastic spoon, a scrunched piece of parchment, a novelty toy from a kid's meal he'd purchased at Gappys, two half-finished inventions of little practical use and a whoopee cushion – so, all in all, a pretty useless collection of randomness. He unfolded the parchment and found a note in Diamond's handwriting that she must have slipped into his pocket in the *Stardust*. It said – *You*. Eli stared at it for a moment, then closed it quickly, refusing to be overcome by emotion. He blinked hard, looking around him. The place had an air of destruction about it, as though it had been hit multiple times by war and reduced to only the ruins of ruins. The atmosphere itself felt sickly, neither hot nor cold but something in between, with a lukewarm mist, sticky rather than wet, drizzling constantly from the sky.

"Focus," Eli whispered, forcing himself to check the last of his interior pockets. His hands closed over something round and firm and his heart fluttered. Eli dragged out his telescopic sights. The lens had cracked, so he'd put it into the secret pocket to fix later and forgotten all about it. He saw immediately that all its higher functions were fried from the portal shift, he could smell the burnt components, but the basic function would still work. He stood cautiously and pressed the sights to his eyes, scanning his surroundings, desperately hoping to find the rest of the team, though he didn't even know if they'd come through or not. The cracked lens moved across empty spaces on all sides until they happened on a blurred form. Eli darted back to it and manually adjusted the sights until the shape came into focus. It was a person, possibly a man, and it looked like he was raking the ground. Eli judged he was about six klicks away.

A sound echoed out across the desolate plains – an *ech ech*. Eli looked up with horror. A sharp twinge ran through his back where his wing had been. The sound came again and Eli spun around, scanning his surroundings for the Ripper. It must have come through with him. On the upside, that meant it wouldn't be terrorizing Scorpia anymore. On the downside, it was there with him looking to finish the job it had started – and Eli was armed with a plastic spoon and a whoopee cushion.

"We have to get out of here!" Eli whispered to Nelly. He rapidly gathered up all his belongings and stuffed them back into his pockets, then took off running in the direction of the stranger. His body kept urging him to break into flight and he kept remembering that he couldn't, and checking over his shoulder, expecting the Ripper to appear right behind him any moment. He didn't know if the faded sky and sticky drizzle constituted enough of a storm for the Ripper to be able to attack, or if that mattered at all in this new world, or exactly how it had mattered in Aquais either. His chest and sides were burning with stitches, but he pushed himself on. Finally, he came within shouting distance of the stranger and called out in Urigin, breathless, "Hey there!"

The man continued his work, now lifting a hoe over his shoulder and plunging it down into the ground, raking the tool back and then doing it again, drudgingly, mechanically. It immediately seemed strange to Eli, especially considering there was not a plant in sight, but he dismissed his ill-ease and ran closer before saying, "Hello – excuse me?"

Again the man didn't turn or register he'd heard, even though Eli was close enough to see his arms. They were weather scorched and covered in thick blond hairs. He had no bloodline marks.

"Excuse me?" Eli said, when he was almost right behind him. "Sir, can you hear me?"

The man turned suddenly then, and Eli caught a very brief glimpse of a face that reminded him of a highly wrinkled pig before the man brutally smashed the end of his hoe right into Eli's nose, knocking him out cold in the mud.

Chapter 14
Ramses

HYDRIA

CORINTHIA (CY CYRENE)

Ramses woke rough. Weak of limb and shivering, the metal of blood in his mouth. The effort just to lift his head racked him with tremors and sent pain stabbing through his neck and face. His vision blurred and cleared and blurred again as he stared through vague slits. Everything was gray. He blinked, and very gradually his senses returned to him, until he realized he was lying down and looking up. A storm threatened in the sky above, darkness rapidly devouring the blue. He heard a horse's snort and the clop of hooves, and felt himself swinging, but wrapped on all sides by fabric. He had no idea of where he was or how he'd gotten there, and as he tried to remember, a sudden falling sensation made him bolt upright. He burst up out of the sling and saw a flash of two faces turning sharply toward him, two men riding horses with him slung between them. Strangers.

He lunged for the edge of the sling and crashed out at the horses' hooves, making them shy sideways and rip the sling across. He covered his head with one arm and went for his sword with the other, but his hand didn't connect with the hilt. He rolled over, trying to get to his feet, but something was stopping him. The riders' boots thudded down beside him. Out of the corner of his eye, Ramses saw that one had a long dagger hanging from his belt in the Anacharasi fashion. He made a grab for it and managed to pull it free. The strangers leapt on him, restraining his arms and chest. Hoods partially concealed their faces. He fought hard, but found himself weakened, and they wrestled the knife from his grip.

"Easy! Easy!" One of the men tried to calm him as he fought on with every bit of strength left to him.

"Get off me!" Ramses shouted at them.

"Lower your voice!" the other man growled.

"We mean no harm," the first man said. "We're trying to help you."

"Who are you?" Ramses demanded.

"Stop fighting and we'll tell you!" the first man spoke again.

"Tell me and I'll stop fighting!"

Still keeping their hold on him, both men dropped their hoods back, revealing faces Ramses did not immediately recognize, but seemed familiar. The elder man had a receding hairline shaved short, and a soldier's hard face. The other was leaner and fairer, boyish at first glance, but his eyes told a different story. There was a subtle similarity to the two men, even though they were very different. The younger had a shiny blue bird riding his shoulder.

"Aron Storon," the younger of the two men said. The elder just returned Ramses' stare with as much if not more suspicion.

"The Storon brothers," Ramses said. He blinked at a wave of faintness, fighting to stay focused. "You're Darro's men?"

A memory came to him, a white bird and the gleaming warrior standing on the ledge. For some reason Ramses started laughing – he had no idea why.

"He's taking a turn. He's caught something." The elder brother, Vitali Storon, leapt back, covering his mouth.

"He's not turning, he's laughing," Aron said, keeping where he was.

"Then he's mad," Vitali said.

"Perhaps ... but aren't we all?" Aron said quietly. "Easy," he said to Ramses again as he started coughing until tears welled in his eyes and began rolling down his cheeks.

"He's definitely got something. Get back from him you *abram*!" Vitali said.

Aron stayed beside Ramses and took a bottle out of his cloak. He tried to put it to Ramses' lips, but he turned his head away, still coughing. He recognized the smell of vanilla poppy, a common cough suppressant, but still refused. When he managed to catch his breath, his chest ached. What had happened? He closed his eyes and saw Titan writhing in pain. Panic shivered through him. He looked from one brother to the other and to the blue bird, staring at him with eyes sharper than most people he knew. It tilted its head to one side.

"Where is he?" he demanded. "Where is the Titan?"

"With Darro," Aron told him.

"Why? What's happened? Why am I here?" He tried to sit up but Aron held him down.

Ramses' anger surged and he stared at the brother with outrage. Aron's eyes didn't mirror his anger though, they showed only pity. Vitali cleared his throat and went to tend the horses, who had stopped nearby. He kept his back to them, fixing the sling.

The wind rustled through the long grasses around them and Ramses smelled saltwater. He turned his head and saw they were atop a plateau, a cliff overlooking the ocean. The closest Cy to Corinth City was more than a sevens ride away – how long had he been out? Panic and sickness swelled inside him.

"Do you remember that Ravana Nazar attacked your Lord Liege? Do you remember falling a great distance?" Aron asked, keeping hold of Ramses' shoulder.

"Yes," he lied.

"You've been injured," the brother told him.

Ramses noticed a bandage on his arm. "It's just a scratch."

"Not your arm," Aron insisted.

Ramses glared at him, not sure what he was getting at but with a bad feeling spreading all through him; heart, chest, gut.

Aron helped Ramses sit up. The world spun around him. He looked down, at first seeing nothing wrong, and then it struck him – one of his legs was stretched out, the other … it was missing from the knee down. Just a stump remained, bloodied at the end. He stared at it, seeing it, but not believing what his eyes were showing him.

Aron's voice came from somewhere beyond and far away.

"We did our best to save your leg, but the break was terrible. It went septic."

Ramses gave Aron a savage shove away from him, making him topple backward. His bird fluttered to keep his perch. With the whole world rocking and spinning around him, Ramses tried to stand, again and again, but couldn't.

Aron grabbed his shoulder and said, "Stop. You'll injure yourself further."

But he couldn't stop. He thrashed on the ground, gasping, unable to get a breath. Vitali rushed back in to help restrain him.

The cold wind gusted again, stirring the grasses, and Aron's blue bird made a squawk. Both brothers looked around them, bodies tense. Hooves clattered in the distance. Ramses slumped back, closing his eyes tightly. He felt the brothers lifting him up. All this was just a nightmare. He would wake at dawn to find everything back to right. He would wake. Everything would be alright.

Chapter 15
Titan

HYDRIA

KIRITH-JEROM (AGHAMORE VALE)

Titan saw the ground rushing up toward him, lit by three circles of fire. He broke free of Darro's grip, drawing his sword as he fell, and landed heavily, going to one knee before finding his feet. He swiftly closed the gap between himself and Darro as the former Kí swooped in on his winged contraption. It was unlike anything Titan had seen before. It had borne them across the Barbarian Plains as though they were golden eagles. Never had he imagined or even dreamed that he would soar through the sky like that, but now he meant to take the advantage before Darro had a chance to stabilize. Many times, as they'd crossed the plains, he'd requested and then demanded that Darro turn around, return to Ironeye, to Ramses, to the Lord King, but Darro had held to his own direction. As much as Titan admired the elusive warrior, it was clear he had his own agenda. And Titan had to assume that if Darro wasn't with him, he had to be against him.

Darro touched down and as soon as he was within range, Titan struck out with a blunt blow to the side of Darro's helm, meaning to knock him off balance without causing serious harm. Darro's wings shot off behind him with force, and in a blink he had sword to hand and was sidestepping Titan's strike. Titan spun as Darro raised to counter. He anticipated a strike force from Darro equivalent to his height and mass, but the spy hit with far greater power. It had been almost his whole lifetime since anyone had posed serious competition to Titan, in the arena or out, aside from the Lord King, but Darro's blow made him catch his breath. It jarred his arm backward, forcing him four steps in retreat to keep his balance.

He retaliated immediately, a strike downward that should have driven Darro to his knees. Titan had a clear height advantage, but Darro blocked with an upward blow, and their swords collided with a grind of steel and a spray of sparks. The force of the impact sent them both three steps back. Titan paused there, a sudden awareness distracting him. It was the absence of movement, stark and unnatural. Since he could first walk, his every step had five echoes – Argos, Afton, Ruan, Herra and Sention. His *ata-ajua*. But now he stood alone, in the middle of a forest humming with insects, beneath the dark open sky and blood red moon. His attention snapped back to Darro, but the Kí had lowered his sword and was standing beside one of the fires, waiting for him to get his bearings. Unafraid of him – just waiting.

Titan stared at Darro's full-metal zivas and heard Ravana's words – *your eyes are the most unflattering mirror*. He could see himself mirrored in Darro's armor. His breastplate was damaged and hanging askew and his tunic torn and bloodied. There was a wound on his chest. He looked down and saw that a mark, roughly in the shape of a farmer's pitchfork, had been scratched or burned into his flesh. He could feel a dull ache in the wound and saw that it was not bleeding but weeping. Titan touched his fingertips to the liquid and held it up to his nose. Saltwater. *Mĕthmalay*. It sent a chill through him.

"I must return to Ironeye," he said to Darro.

"You cannot," the Kí responded, his voice a rasp from behind the zivas.

"I must. Do not stand to stop me," he warned.

When Darro didn't respond, Titan started moving in a slow circle around him. The Kí stepped with him, keeping the distance between them. It was clear from the readiness of Darro's pose that as soon as Titan tried to turn his back, Darro would be on him.

"Heed me!" Titan commanded.

As the words left his mouth, he broke away fast, running through the forest. He could outrun any warrior, but glancing over his shoulder he saw Darro was right beside him, keeping up without effort, and he recalled seeing the Kí moving with unnatural speed across the plains to stop the wild horses. Titan pushed himself faster and ran for some time, with Darro alternating from one side of him to the other, before he realized he was being herded. He knew this truth for sure as he broke out into a clearing with three more campfires. He drew his sword and spun around to engage Darro again, but as he did, huge arms closed over his and lifted him right off the ground. Titan fought with fury, no one had ever lifted him off his feet before, but as he struggled, the grip only constricted tighter. He looked up and saw a fearsome face looking down at him, the eyes pits of shadow in the firelight. Titan had read of the Gigantus, but he'd never seen one.

Darro moved toward them, light reflecting off his armor.

"Lord Liege Tarrus of Ironeye, meet Anakis of Abigar. Anakis, if you will my friend," Darro said.

The giant, Anakis, bent forward, lowering Titan to the ground with care. He placed him down on his stomach and held him firm with one hand as Darro shackled Titan's arms behind his back. Titan tried to struggle, but Anakis' grip was immense and he could only squirm as Darro locked him down.

"Do you realize what you're doing?" Titan asked, breathless from the pressure on his back.

"I'm fully aware, Lord Liege," Darro responded.

"You're committing treason. I have given you an order."

"And I have heard you. I understand you believe you must return to the palace, and that you will not stop until you do, which is why I must detain you," Darro said.

He took Titan's sword from where it lay beside him, and started unstrapping the calteus from his back.

"Do not do that," Titan warned him.

Darro continued, removing his weapons and also fishing around beneath his breastplate for his secondary short sword and around his thighs for the knife strapped there.

"Anak," Darro said, and the huge man lifted Titan back up to his feet, staying him with one heavy hand on his shoulder. Titan tested the chains around his wrists and found them fastened solidly. As Darro slung Titan's calteus over his shoulder, Titan noticed he had one of his own. It was the Corinthian way of fastening weapons, not Anacharasi.

"You're Corinthian," Titan said, seeking a way to reason with the Kí.

"No," Darro replied, and Titan heard no lie, nor saw any red mist coming through Darro's eye slits or from his giant guard's mouth. But then, he had not seen any from Ravana either.

"You were raised in Corinthia," he said.

"No," Darro responded again.

The big man, Anakis, gave a grunt and Darro said, "We can't risk it, my friend, we need the light. What now moves in this darkness is more worrying than Gideon's men. We'll go under and ride at first light, as swiftly as possible. If his *ata-ajua* live, it won't take them long to find him."

Titan's heart gave a solid thud. *If they live.*

Darro lit a lantern, then put out the fires. He led the way through the trees and shadows, moving more deeply into the forest. Titan noticed that Darro and Anakis moved as though they'd been walking as a pair for a very long time, and his thoughts turned again to Argos. Frozen.

Darro and the big man stopped and Darro began stomping on particular places on the ground in a sequence of moves until a tunnel opened up in the seemingly solid earth in front of Titan's feet. Darro nodded, and before Titan could protest, Anakis lifted him and dropped him into the pit. He slid on smoothed surface down and down, landing on a pile of sacks in the darkness. He smelled the sweet fragrance of hay. There was a mighty thump as Anakis landed just behind him, then Darro after that, holding the lantern. Anakis put a hand again on Titan's shoulder and directed him to sit in one corner, while Darro triggered the tunnel collapse above them. With their entrance now closed, the small underground chamber appeared to have no way out. Anakis stood beside Titan, having to hunch to stop his head from hitting the ceiling, watching Darro as he moved around the cramped space, opening up hidden compartments in the walls. He lit a small fire and put a pot with pieces of metal inside it into the flames.

Titan grimaced. The dull ache of his wound was intensifying into pulses of sharp pain radiating out through his chest. An agonizing heat seared through his stomach and traveled along the side of his groin, all the way down his legs to where it pooled, stinging pins and needles, in his feet. Titan understood that he had been poisoned. He was well acquainted with how that felt, and had been trained to develop a resistance to many poisons by taking them in minute doses over a long period of time – not enough to kill him, just enough to make him wish he were dead. He was also well versed in pain, but he'd never felt anything like this. His stomach was in such violent turmoil that it felt as though the skin was truly tearing apart. A groan escaped him and Darro's attention turned his way. Anakis also responded, crouching down to check on him. He put a hand on Titan's head and patted him, as though trying to comfort him.

Titan caught sight of the giant man's eyes. There was a profound sadness in them that reached to the core of Titan's heart. He saw a flash of image, a young boy, already bigger than a fully grown man, at the bottom of a dark pit, tied by the wrists to a turning mill. He was covered in injuries, scars upon scars upon fresh wounds, gruesome afflictions from torture. The boy was looking up toward a distant light, far above him, and he could hear men climbing down into the pit, hear their laughter, and though he was bigger than all of them, he was terrified beyond words of what they were going to do to him. He started crying, but then a figure appeared from out of the shadows beside him, a short boy wearing metal like a second skin. The boy raised a sword in his hands and Anakis cringed back as he brought the sword down on the binds, cutting Anakis free. He said, "Come with me."

Titan broke out of the memory in more pain than he'd ever felt in his whole life and saw Darro standing over him, watching him. After a moment of silence, he knelt down in front of Titan and put a vial of warm liquid to his lips. It smelled truly disgusting.

"What is this?" Titan gasped.

"Venom from the spidersbane cobra, fermented leech blood and a special type of Draulia mold."

"What?" Titan said, horrified.

"Are you in pain? This will take it away, almost instantly."

"Nothing takes pain away instantly."

"Except your touch," Darro said, making Titan look up sharply, shocked despite the pain. Darro took the opportunity to quickly pour the concoction into his mouth. His pulled back, spluttering, his mouth tingling all over as though covered in tiny crawling spiders. The sensation traveled all the way down his throat to his stomach and then out into the rest of his body. It was an awful feeling, but Titan noticed himself sitting up and unclenching his fists, still chained behind his back, as his pain vanished almost instantly. He felt like an enormous weight was being lifted off his shoulders. Darro unstrapped his damaged breastplate and cut away the tunic, inspecting the wound. Titan concentrated on the Kí's zivas, looking for pathways, for intention, for the truth of him.

"Whatever you're doing," Darro said, "stop. You'll bring them to us. Trust me."

The Kí's words were alarming. No one had ever seemed to *feel* what he could do. Except Ramses. He remembered seeing his cousin falling all that way and felt a horrible, twisting fear inside him. He heard Farahman's scream.

"My companion, Ramses of Ohai," he said.

"He's with my men. Two of the finest warriors in the halos."

"*Ivar,*" Titan said. "I heard they were drunken and undisciplined."

"One would have thought, Lord Liege, that you were above pre-judgment," Darro said.

"Are you saying it's false?"

"Oh no, it's truth enough," Darro laughed. "But that doesn't change anything."

"Remove these," he ordered, rattling the chains behind him.

Darro continued inspecting the mark and Titan felt his frustration, his fear and grief erupt.

"Darro – heed me!" His voice bellowed in the enclosed space and Anakis grunted. So far the man had been a gentle giant, but the look that came into his eyes said that when it came to protecting Darro, there was a whole other side to him.

"I'll remove them if you swear on your father's name, Osiris of Ironeye, that you won't try to leave here or return to Corinth."

Titan held his silence and Darro said, "Then for your own protection, they remain!"

Titan lowered his head to contain the feelings thrashing inside him. Darro left him and returned to the metal he was melting over the fire. Titan stared at the warrior he'd spent so long studying, copying and admiring, who was now keeping him prisoner.

"The Unbreakable, The Sword of the Sky, The Eternal, The Scourge of Morcvara?" he said, and noticed Darro pause at the last name. "Is it true?"

"Which part?" Darro asked.

"You were cast in iron."

"Yes." He spoke the truth.

"Impossible."

Titan heard him laugh from behind his zivas. "Why did you ask me then?"

"How did it happen?" Titan asked.

Darro looked up from the fire. "I was dropped in smoldered iron as a child. I survived, and here we stand."

"Your armor is not affixed now."

"No," Darro agreed.

"How?"

"It reached a certain time that I outgrew the armor and it started to crush me." He paused, stirring the metal. "So we found a man – a madman by all accounts. He designed an experiment to free me – fire and water. Now the only metal left is in my neck, set there, somewhat inconveniently, for people who wish to behead me."

"And there are no small number of those."

That made Darro laugh aloud again. "I judge the virtue of our path by the number of corrupt trying to kill us. Currently it's extremely virtuous."

"And now Ravana Nazar as well," Titan said. "What do you know of the manner of her trickery, of her crimes?"

"I know nothing for certain," Darro told him.

"You may not know with all certainty but you certainly know all. I've studied enough of your works to know that."

Darro paused at that and took his time in responding. "The truth is heavy, and especially so when it's dressed as impossibility."

The turn of phrase struck Titan as strange. Darro spoke Corinthian as though it was his mother tongue, yet the words he used and the way he used them felt like he was reinventing the language to his own pleasing, and it grated on Titan immensely. Darro spoke like he was on show, with a mocking turn of phrase in almost every sentence.

"You take too much liberty with my language. I will hear the truth – plainly. I will hear it now!"

His voice growled in the walls around them and Anakis stirred again. Darro gave him a slight shake of his head.

"At your command," he replied. "Lady Ravana Nazar is a *Samyaza*."

Titan narrowed his eyes. It felt like an old word and although he didn't know the language, he understood what it meant, as he understood all languages without the need to learn them, a legacy from the Almighty. The word meant *witch*.

"*Nea*." He rejected the notion, using a word in High Corinthian that meant he was rejecting everything about it.

"You saw with your own eyes," Darro said.

"What did I see?" Titan asked him. "A trick of perception – science, poisons, hallucination – all this, yes. Magic, *nea tetishina*."

"I'll assure you, Lord Liege, that it does exist," Darro said. "Do you really believe it's just the gods and man and nothing in between?"

"All the history scrolls throughout time have spoken of the falsehood of this *magic*. It is not real. It is myth, stories, lies. There is no unnatural in our world."

"What about you?" Darro asked directly. "What about the Lord King Apollo of Ironeye before you?"

Titan stared at Darro. "What are you saying?" he asked, his voice dangerously quiet.

"Look at your chest," Darro said. He walked over to Titan and used a stick to draw the mark there in the dirt in front of him.

"It is the Thirteen Prime, Belphanganor's Prime."

Titan looked up at Darro. He had never heard of it before.

"The mark is a sign that you've been encroached by a demon's familiar."

"Encroached by a demon's familiar?" Titan repeated, hating the sound of the words. "What does that mean?"

Darro turned back to the fire and Titan lost his control again and shouted at him. "Speak now!"

Anakis stood up with a deep grunt.

"I will speak!" Darro said. "But only if you listen! And not as the Lord Liege of Corinthia, Tarrus of Ironeye, but as a person of intelligence and wisdom who should know enough about the world to understand that there is much you don't understand. And much you do that you deny!"

The Kí's response silenced him, and after a few moments he said quietly, "I'm listening."

"Ravana is not a person anymore, she's a *Samyaza*, she's a demon's conduit."

"What does that make me?" Titan could feel the mark throbbing like a heartbeat.

"Hunted."

"Why?"

"Because a witch has marked you as her own. You belong to her now, and she will collect."

"What has she done with those women? Where are all the children she's taken?"

"*Samyaza* eat human flesh, and gather dependents to do their bidding. Glooms. Shadows of the people they were."

Titan lowered his head. *Eat human flesh.* He couldn't believe what he was hearing.

"So they're all dead?"

"They're all dead," Darro confirmed. "You did everything you could to save them. You didn't know. Neither did I."

The words hung in the air between them as Darro continued to stir the metal.

"What do you mean to do with me?" Titan asked Darro after a long silence.

"I mean to keep you alive," The Kí replied, with an edge of weariness. "Is this not obvious?"

"In all this, my life is not of any import. The Lord King must be informed so that he can protect our people."

"As long as you have that," Darro said, "she'll be able to find you. You can move fast and out of sight, but it's still only a matter of time. We have to remove it or you'll just take your destruction back to the palace. Think and remember what happened back there. She collapsed your entire tower with her rage."

Titan thought on Darro's words. He spoke the truth. A terrifying truth.

"Remove it how?" he asked.

"I don't know exactly. I remember reading something about this a long time ago, but all the scrolls are in my base in Oas Havre. It's an old mine in Anacharasis."

"Could you not have brought the relevant scriptures with you?"

"Surely! Lugging around several thousand scrolls would not have drawn attention to us in the least," Darro said. "I didn't expect this. I thought they were hunting you in regards to the rebellion against Corinthia. I didn't expect a *Samyaza*. I would never have inflamed her if I had. I made a mistake."

Titan paused at Darro's confession. It was very unusual for a warrior to admit mistake. They were taught against it.

"May I see the wound?" he asked.

Darro walked over, crouching down so that Titan could see his would reflected in Darro's armor. Titan reacted instantly. He broke out of the chains around his wrists and grabbed Darro's helm, squeezing it in, not with the strength of his arms, but using his way with metals, which did as he bid. He'd never used it so openly, Darro made a sound as his helm constricted painfully around his head. Anakis shot up, his huge axe in hand.

"Keep back," Titan warned him.

The giant's chest heaved and his brow furrowed deeply, his hands working the handle of his weapon.

"Easy my friend, calm yourself," Darro managed to say, though his voice was strained. "He won't kill me or he'll be trapped here."

"Make path to the surface and I'll release you," Titan told the spy.

"Let me treat your wound. If we block it, it will slow Ravana down."

"Make path – now! I wish you no harm in this world, believe me, Darro, but I will allow nothing to stand in the way of my returning to Ironeye."

"I mean only to stand in the way of your death, Lord Liege," Darro said.

"Heed me," Titan commanded. "Take me to the surface." He increased the pressure of his hands a fraction and Darro staggered from the pain.

"Anakis – if you will," he uttered.

The big man set his eyes, black with fury, on Titan and he saw a flash from the past – the boy cowering in a corner while the child Darro brought him food. He saw the boy frightened of a storm and Darro hugging him. He saw him running up a hill, through a field, smiling and carrying Darro on his back. Anakis took his axe and swung it hard against the wall, shattering rock and opening up their way out.

"Move," Titan commanded Darro and the Kí obeyed, stepping out of the chamber and into a tunnel leading upward. Anakis kept close as they ascended, holding up the lantern. The closer they came to the end of the tunnel, the heavier Darro's steps grew, until they reached the boulder blocking the entrance and he pulled back, refusing to go any farther.

"We don't know what's out there," he said.

"Open it," Titan commanded Anakis. The giant man held his place, so Titan squeezed his hands once again, reinforcing the urgency of his request. Darro grunted and Anakis moved quickly to obey.

"Don't say I didn't warn you," Darro said as Anakis heaved and shoved the boulder aside.

Early morning light, birdsong and fresh mountain air flooded the tunnel. It was a beautiful day outside, perfect for a fast run home. Titan stepped out into the light. From above, the forms of women dropped down to block the entrance of the tunnel. For a moment they appeared ordinary, aside from the way they were all hunching in, but then they screamed in unison, their faces contorting horribly, water hurtling out of their mouths in powerful jets. Their curse sent Titan crashing into the side of the tunnel. He struck the rocks hard and landed on his back. He tried to move but found himself frozen, poisoned, his mark pulsating with agony and gushing saltwater. It ran down over his neck and he felt it tightening like hands. He couldn't even raise his head. The sounds of the creatures were closing in on him.

Chapter 16
Eli

HYDRIA

FARNORTHERN HALOS (NÒ)

Eli gasped and struggled to sit up. Pain shot through his face and down his neck and he felt a hot stream gush from his nose. It was throbbing, and whistled when he breathed. Broken. He slumped back down, groaning, and when he tried to lift a hand to his face, he discovered his arms were tied at his sides. He struggled against the rope, but it was knotted so tightly his wrists were pulsating. Eli silently cursed himself. He'd been stupid – *perhaps overly optimistic*, Jude may have said in the past – but straight-up stupid was the truth of it. He'd projected through a portal into an unfamiliar world and instead of keeping himself hidden until he figured out where, what and when, he'd dashed headlong toward the first guy he'd spotted to ask for help. And that person, a crazed, snaggle-toothed yokel raking a mud paddock, had knocked him out and tied him up. Stupid. Stupid. Stupid.

Eli quickly glanced around him, searching for something he could cut the ropes on, but all he could see from where he lay was dirty straw. He moved carefully, aware of the growing ache in his shoulder. The patches were still containing the worst of it, but when they lost effect, he'd be in a world of pain. Eli closed his eyes for a moment, trying to steady himself. As he did, he noticed the floor beneath him rocking from side to side, and heard a sound like trudging feet, and a heavy trundling of wheels. He looked up to a close wooden roof and bars on all sides. As his mind put all the pieces together, he realized he must be in the back of some kind of prison cart. The stink of rancid body odor and urine was so pungent and raw, it made Eli's eyes water.

The cart hit a bump and Eli tumbled across the boards and hit against something warm and spongy. He rolled onto his side and came face to face with a huge hog with a muddy, hairy snout and sharp tusks. It gave a few concerned grunts and snuffled his face, spreading mud all over it, then it nipped Eli's shoulder. He gasped with pain and tried to shuffle and roll away, bumping into something else behind him. He quickly tilted his head back, for a second confused by the face he saw – then he wasn't confused, he was just horrified, because he was staring directly up at another pig's backside, and its tail was twitching in an ominous kind of way. He rolled again, as fast as he could, but another bump send him tumbling back against the pig's behind. It grunted and rounded on him, and then there were two gigantic hogs snuffle-grunting at him curiously.

"Nice piggies," he whispered to them, trying to get to the side of the cart so that he could work his way up to sitting.

His nose kept whistling as he struggled to control his breathing, then a terrible thought came to him.

"Nelly!" he hissed. He maneuvered his hand, trying to pat at his pocket, but he found his jacket was gone, along with everything in it – including Nelly. A dizziness threatened to knock him out, but he counted back from forty-six, forcing himself to focus this time.

"Nelly?" he whispered. "Nelly, where are you?"

Both pigs grunted in response.

"Nelly?" he repeated, as loudly as he dared, and the pigs grunted even louder.

He tried to shush them and a harsh voice barked out from somewhere beyond the bars. At the sound the hogs backed away into the shadows and Eli flattened himself to the ground, the side of his face pressed into the muddy straw. He noticed the hay near to him shifting, and a little face peeped out.

"Nelly!" he whispered urgently. She cast a fearful glance around them, then scurried across to where he lay, hiding at his side.

"The ropes," Eli said. Nelly crawled along to his wrists, where she started gnawing on the binds. She cut through them quickly and Eli ripped his arms free, rubbing the deep ridges in his skin. He scooped Nelly up and put her down the back of his hospital gown where she could hide under his wing. He felt sharp little claws tickling him and heard muted whimpers coming from somewhere behind the hogs. He dared to lift himself up and peer over a bale of sticks. A small group of weather-beaten women cowered at the far end of the prison cart. He didn't recognize their race and they had no bloodline marks. Their faces were all creased up like the man's had been and their eyes were wild with fear, looking beyond him, through him, to the outside.

He followed their line of sight, through the bars and out to where a group of men in chains stumbled beside the cart, being herded by the wrinkled swine-like person who had knocked him out. And on a second glance he really did look like a human-breed of pig blood who had thrown way *way* back to his animal ancestors. He had the snout and the tusks growing out of his mouth, long floppy ears and the thick fair hairs all over his body. His face was so creased up his eyes were almost lost in folds. Eli thought he had an almost sad and wistful look to his face, as though he was a misunderstood man trying to find his way in the world, if not for the bloodied cleaver strapped to his heaving stomach, and that hoe that he kept belting into the prisoners every time they stumbled. Eli's own blood stained the end of its handle, and he felt the heat of anger rising as he watched the man tormenting his captives. His nose whistle increased in speed and intensity until he felt the cart slowing. The slower it went, the more urgent the cries from the women sharing the cart became, and Eli got the distinct feeling things were about to get a lot worse.

He peered through the bars as the ground shivered and quaked and then broke open beside the cart. A group of creatures scrambled out with an array of weird and wonderful appearances – an amphibious-looking man, an eagle-faced girl, a very short monkey-like person, but the group that followed them were less wonderful and more terrible. Spiky, clawed, ghoulish predators – lesser demons – began circling the prisoners and the cart, snarling, snipping with pincers, drool dripping from long fangs. The ground trembled again as a final monster emerged, one that made all the others look cute and cuddly. Eli heard the women crying out *ratha* and he recognized the word. Lecivion had told Silho that ratha demons had invaded Oren Harvey's world and destroyed it.

The ratha roared, shaking the ground, and Eli ducked lower behind the side of the cart, staring at the demon. He was clearly a killing machine. Every part of him was formed like a weapon. His skin was made up of small armored scales with razorblade edges. He had two mouths – one smaller, full of jagged needle teeth, and a larger one around that with fangs. Spikes grew out of the ratha's chin, on his wrists, knees and shoulders and all down his back to a long whip-like tail. There were horns on his head and the sides of his face and he had only two legs, but four arms, a smaller pair and a longer pair, almost touching the ground, each with huge clawed hands. He used his limbs interchangeably with alarming dexterity for such a hulking beast. Three sets of eyes moved independently of each other, with a fourth on the back of his head. Even its ears grew to a fine thorn-like point on the end.

As the ratha bellowed, the captured men suddenly rebelled, breaking wildly free from their binds and trying to attack the demon. The first to get free ran at the ratha. The monstrous creature breathed into the man's face, a cloud of toxins, which made him crash immediately to the ground, convulsing. The next man, the ratha spiked through the shoulder. He fell as well. The ratha kicked the third man down with large flat feet made for blunt-force trauma. The fourth escapee ripped a hidden knife from his garments. He actually managed to slice off one of the ratha's hands while the demon was occupied with another man. Eli gasped as the hand regenerated immediately. The ratha spun around, lashing out his tongue like a long snake. It wrapped around the man's neck and dragged him to the ratha's mouth. The demon creature lifted him up in the air and bit him clean in half with his massive jaws.

Eli looked away for a moment to compose himself before forcing himself to look back. The last man had abandoned the attack and was making a run for it. The ratha spat out an almost invisible chemical net, which landed over the man and brought him crashing to the ground. The demon rose up on large black wings and retrieved the man, dumping him down with the other prisoners. Aside from the one the ratha had bitten in half, they all lay on their backs, breathing but unmoving. Eli could hear the women's muffled sounds behind him and he watched on, as helpless as they were to stop the horror.

He thought for a moment that at least the worst was over, but he'd thought too soon. The ratha proceeded to remove what appeared to be insectoid creatures out of his mouth, one after another, and force them into the prisoners' mouths. The parasites looked to be attaching themselves to the captives' tongues. Eli had completed extensive research on parasites and isopods and their human-breed equivalents during military studies into mind weaponry and defense, but never participated in any live tests or experimentation due to the potential damage of hosts. It was extremely invasive and extremely cruel. He didn't want to look away in case he missed something crucial he could use to escape, but his stomach churned horribly and his eyes watered and he had to count backwards again to stop himself from passing out.

He clutched the bars, trying to mentally distance himself from what he was seeing. He stared at the parasites themselves. They had white, blobby bodies and almost comical little faces, with arachnid-like limbs curled up underneath them. Cute almost, if they weren't biting off people's tongues and fastening themselves to the muscles there instead. Once all the men had been converted, the ratha made a sound and the prisoners staggered to their feet in unison. Some of them had come around, and Eli could see their eyes swiveling around in panic as their bodies moved out of their control. Others were still out, and their heads lagged to their chests even as they stood upright. As the final action, the ratha stuck his sharp-ended tail into each of the captives' necks and injected in some kind of live maggot-like larvae that Eli could see squirming and pulsating behind their stretched skin. He gagged. It was too much, but he didn't have long to cringe. The ratha gave a command and the swine man came to the back of the prison cart and flung open the doors. He and several others of the ratha's entourage leapt into the cart and started flinging everyone out, including the two big hogs.

Eli was launched into the air and tumbled into the mud right at the feet of the hulking ratha. He kept his head right down, feeling the monster's hot breath on his back as a toxic smell overcame his senses. Nelly was so still, but he could feel her heart racing a million beats a second against his back. The ratha moved away from them, toward the pigs. Eli scrunched his eyes shut and blocked his ears, not wanting to hear their suffering, but when he heard nothing he looked over his shoulder and saw that they were completely gone, and the ratha was smacking his lips.

The captive women had been thrown down all around Eli, their bodies emaciated and filth-encrusted, just like the men. Eli had no idea what was going to happen, and his eyes searched the ground, desperately hunting for anything he could use as a weapon. He spotted a long femur bone half buried in the mud and inched his hand toward it, but before he could reach it, the ratha grunted another command, then the ground opened and he vanished.

Eli breathed out heavily, not believing the demon had actually left without maiming them or injecting them with his terrible squirming spawn. He almost didn't register when someone dragged him to his feet and forced him into line with the women. He came back to his senses as they started walking, with the men, now slaves inside their own bodies, trudging beside them and the ratha's underlings all around. Behind them, the swine man had turned his cart and was trundling back the way they'd come. It took a good long moment of walking in line for Eli to realize what had happened, and as he did, he had to slap a hand over his mouth to hold in the hysterical laughter. He was in the women's line. He'd been spared before the demon, and the creatures thought he was a girl. For a man who was trying to be as manly as possible, to still be mistaken for a woman was a rather cruel blow to the ego, but after what he'd just witnessed, Eli was more than happy to keep his head down and attempt his most feminine walk ever.

The creatures pushed them on and Eli took careful note of the land around them, memorizing every landmark in case he needed to retrace his steps. This place, the land of King Apollo, was exactly as Shah-Jahan had described it – ravaged, destroyed, with glimpses here and there of a formerly powerful and beautiful world. There were solitary arches, waterfalls running brown, and the most striking remanent – gigantic warrior-like statues, some sunken into the mud, some on their sides, most missing heads or limbs. They walked directly past one of these towering relics, and Eli found his head was up to the height of one carved big toe.

As his pain levels soared, his feet started to slow and his legs locked up. His mouth hung open because for some reason it hurt more if he closed it. One thought kept Eli moving: *Apollo of Corinthia*. Shah-Jahan had seen a prisoner, a man, it might be him, he might be here. They knew he and the other kings had made an unwitting pact with Mordan-Grieg, king of the ratha demons. It could have ended with Apollo as his slave, and if it had, Eli was, however accidentally and horrendously, on the path to finding the one person who may know how to stop the Indemeus X. He made his sole focus putting one foot in front of the other and he whispered a constant prayer to the Khaiti god – *please give me strength* ...

The group struggled up the side of a mud hill and when they came to the top, Eli stared in awe at the sight below them. A flat plain ran into the hazy distance, where he could just see the outline of a wall, and halfway there sat the most gigantic skull and bones Eli could ever imagine. An entire city had been built beneath the skull, and Eli could just make out the tiny forms of people moving around there. In the gray skies above, thousands of birds swarmed over the skull city.

The demon's underlings kept the group moving down onto the plain, where they soon joined with other scavenging parties heading back toward the skull, each with their own prisoners and produce. Lecivion had told Silho that Oren Harvey's people had all been killed, and Eli wondered where these prisoners had come from. Perhaps other portals, or other lands of this world, he couldn't be sure.

Suddenly something swooped down and seized the woman walking behind Eli. He had thought the forms in the sky were birds, but he looked up into a snarling face as the monster snatched the woman and dragged her screaming into the sky. The other women cried out, and blood rained down on their heads.

Eli kept his eyes to the ground, trying to block out the brutal violence around him. He didn't look up again until they started climbing and he saw they were directly in front of the giant skull, which was even more immense and astounding up close. He imagined whatever creature the skull had belonged to must have been the biggest in the universe. The thought was mind boggling.

His group of captives were herded with the other groups into a packed open marketplace right at the front of the skull city, where the towering buildings appeared to be carved from one solid piece of rock rather than built up from separate pieces. They were beautiful really, pieces of artwork in their own right, but the smell was overwhelming, such an undiluted, pungent odor that his eyes were watering constantly. It was a foreign smell, almost what he imagined earwax might smell like if it could somehow go off and start to rot.

He huddled down as the groups began to be separated – men in one direction and women in the other. The women cried out, and their screaming wrenched Eli's heart in all directions. He tried to keep blocking it out, focusing on moving forward as he and his group of women were crammed into train-like carriages tethered to creatures that looked like a cross between a horse, a dog and an ape. Eli made sure he stood right beside the wall, where the boards were slightly parted and he could feel the air, however offensive, wafting in.

Their door slid shut, casting them into darkness except for the slivers of light coming in through the rough-built walls, and the carriage took off, swaying from one side to the other as they headed downhill. Eli put his eye to the slit in the wall and looked out. He could see large poles like tree trunks with fire at the top lighting a narrow path along a cliff face. Far ahead of them, he saw a line of other carriages rattling along. As he watched, part of the path ahead broke away, plunging two carriages into the black abyss below. They fell silently, tumbling through the void, until they vanished. Eli felt his stomach clench in so tightly it almost rivaled the pain in his shoulder. He leaned his head against the boards and closed his eyes, trying to control his breathing, trying to stay calm or at least not dissolve into hysterics. He drifted without wanting to and jolted awake to find himself in the same position, the carriage still lumbering on. He heard the commander's voice in his thoughts. *Establish enemies and allies.* Eli gazed around him in the dim light. A hard-faced muscular looking woman stood directly beside him.

"Hello," he ventured in Urigin, which was supposed to be the universal language. She immediately turned her back on him. He looked to the other side where a shriveled lady, almost shorter than he was, peered at him from the folds of her wrinkled face. Her pig snout was less pronounced than the man who had captured Eli, but her ears were long and floppy.

"Hello." Eli nodded to her.

To Eli's relief, she gave a nod back, and even smiled, showing almost no teeth except one brown straggler.

"Where are they taking us?" Eli whispered.

She leaned in closer and grunted as though she hadn't heard, so Eli repeated the question into her ear.

She grunted again and gave a response so muttered Eli could barely decipher it.

"Service?" he tried.

The lady nodded and smiled again.

"Service, like – serving food?" Eli asked, acting out "food serving".

The woman looked at him in puzzlement.

"Food. Food, like breaking bread, ladling soup, chopping vegetables?" he tried again, going through a full range of culinary motions, each one producing more confusion and possibly horror on his neighbor's face.

Finally, the dawning of comprehension came into her eyes and she waved her arms around.

"No, no, no." She tried to say something but then held up a hand to mean stop, and consulted the woman beside her.

"Service," the other woman said, much more clearly, and thrust her hips in a way that really left no doubt as to what they were serving – or, more like it – servicing.

Eli's heartbeat kicked up a notch.

"Not good," he said to himself. "Not good." He jammed his face back against the board, looking around frantically. He had to get out, now, before one of these demons decided they required servicing from the pretty, slim girl in the white dress.

The carriage came to a slamming halt, throwing Eli and all the women forward. Eli smashed his head against the wall and landed badly on his shoulder with a pile of bodies on top of him. He was sure he'd felt stitches popping, but didn't have time to check before the door was reefed open and the women herded out, some flung if they weren't moving fast enough.

Eli jumped down quickly, keeping in the center of the pack to avoid attention. He looked around – they were in an underground area with burrowed out tunnels, lit by fiery torches. The air was very thin and had an acerbic aftertaste. A laugh drew his attention and he peeked through the crowd to where a bearded man stood among a group of others. He was a lesser demon, Eli was sure of that in one glance – he had pale green glowing eyes, no hair on his head, just patterned skin, and big horns. He had rings through both pointed ears and a flat nose with nostrils that extended over the top of the bump as well as under. He was sneering with pointed teeth and held a vicious looking whip in one hand. It actually looked like it was moving on its own, and his jacket appeared to be made from someone else's skin.

The shriveled lady who had spoken with Eli in the carriage pushed his head back down and hissed into his ear with sour breath, "Gibbit." She nodded with meaning, her expression warning Eli: this was one to avoid at all costs. Eli nodded his thanks, trying to keep his eyes to the ground, but then the person beside Gibbit captured his attention so abruptly it literally took his breath away.

She looked like an angel. A scarred, tattooed, scowling angel. The girl caught him starring and came toward them. Eli felt everyone melting away from around him the closer she came, but he couldn't take his eyes off this stranger. When she stood right in front of him he breathed, "You're beautiful."

She raised her fist and punched him in the face, and Eli hit the ground, out cold, for the second time that day.

Chapter 17
Ev'r

HYDRIA

FARNORTHERN HALOS (LAUREION)

Sinking through the Murk was painful and disorientating for the uninitiated, but a portal jump was cerebral chaos and sensory anarchy for anyone. The way a portal shrunk and shifted space and distance was completely incompatible with the cardiac rhythms of most beings, and the circuitry of most machines. Upon breaching the secondary portal into whatever land Snacksize had catapulted them to, Ev'r landed in a sweating, cursing, furious mess with Kane's knee in her back and Christy Shawe's stinking arse right in her face. She shoved out of the scrummage to find all her weaponry and coms fried and smoking, and no doubt seven year-cycles taken off her life as well.

Ismail dragged her up to her feet and into his arms, growling, "We can't be here!" His eyes were wild in the way they became when panic had set in.

"We're leaving," Ev'r assured him. She turned to the group and made directly for Brabel, getting up into her face and demanding, "Send us back, now!"

Silho stared her down with the same formidable green eyes as her commander mother, Oren Harvey. Ev'r knew Brabel was harboring some kind of silent resentment against her and Ismail for not wanting to spend time with her, or whatever she'd imagined should be happening. But they couldn't stand to be near her – Ev'r because she generally disliked her and Ismail for his own reasons. He felt extreme guilt that when they'd met Brabel as a kid out in the Matadori, they hadn't told her that her so-called carer was selling her out to the Omarian prince who eventually ended up snatching her, torturing her and trying to kill her. They hadn't helped her. But as Ev'r had told Ismail, they owed Silho Brabel nothing, less than nothing. Who was she to them? What had she ever done for them? Brabel was too young and dumb and consumed with her own self to give a trutt about anyone else, but expected everyone to be crawling all over themselves to get to her. That wasn't going to happen. Neither Oren Harvey's legacy nor her blade, Solace, hanging from Brabel's weapon belt, intimidated Ev'r in the least.

"Brabel, I said send us back," she growled, putting a hand to the hilt of her own blade.

"Can't," Silho said. "My skills are down."

"What do you mean *down*?"

"Mine too," fairy girl said beside Brabel. "There's stars here," she looked up. "But I'm getting nothing from them."

"I have nothing as well," Kane confirmed, throwing his burnt out electrifier down and drawing his blade. He glanced at Shawe, who grunted, "Can't hear a thing." He picked up a huge boulder beside them, lifting it high above his head before slamming back down. "Arms still work though."

Ev'r whispered a basic enchant, trying to access her magics. There was no response at all and her hopes sunk. She turned to Ismail and he shook his head.

"We're being blocked. I'm feeling something." He narrowed his dark eyes. "But it's very filtered."

"There must be an augmentor here," Kane said.

"I thought augmentors could amplify skills, not block them," Silho asked.

"They can do both," Kane told her. "I can feel my senses coming and going – it's an augmentor who isn't in control."

Ev'r sighed and shook her head. "We're stuck. She can't open a portal."

"I don't open portals, Keets. I am the portal." Brabel gave her a look.

"Great, Brabel, or at least it would be if you worked. Right now you're trutting useless!"

Silho's eyes darkened dangerously as she shifted momentarily to light-form vision, and Ev'r felt a drag of strength leave her before Brabel's skills were cut short.

"Do that again," Ev'r threatened her. "Try it."

"Where's Eli?" Ismail suddenly said. Everyone turned to look for the short soldier.

"Eli!" Silho called out.

"Shut it!" fairy girl hissed at her. "We don't know who's here."

The place looked like a disaster zone, shattered buildings, ground trudged to sludge.

"Spread out," Kane commanded. "Find him."

Ev'r turned with Ismail and they headed across the flat plain behind them to where the ground dropped into a slope.

As they walked, Ismail held Ev'r tightly to his side, his breathing ragged.

"I can't lose you again," he whispered to her. He dragged her to a stop and hugged her against him, crushingly tight. With her head against his chest, Ev'r could hear the thuds of his robotic heart. A sudden terrible thought came to her. She pulled away and put a hand over his heart. He understood what she was thinking.

"It didn't stop," he uttered. "Why?"

Ev'r shook her head. Everything else mechanical had been wiped out. The thought made her icy all over. And angry. It could all end again so quickly. Death was death and right now, together, this was the only paradise they'd ever see. They shouldn't have stayed to help. They shouldn't have been involved in this. She would never have made this mistake before. Whoever this new Ev'r was – she hated her. She was going to get them killed.

Ismail's eyes shifted over Ev'r's head. "There's someone down there."

She turned. "Who is it?"

"It's coming and going," Ismail said. "I can't—" he tapped his head.

"So let's see," she growled, drawing the Morsus Ictus and moving toward the drop. At the rim they saw a flash of reflection. It wasn't Snacksize, it was the Ar Antarian King of Aquais, Jude, holding his shut-down robot like a baby and standing over the two Androt guards lying on the ground. Ev'r could see even from that distance that they were both dead, but Jude, a cross-blood machine-breed, looked mint. To their left, the trackers and Shawe were also heading down the hill.

Jude looked up at their approach, his blazing noble blood eyes doing a fast inventory of the group.

"Where's Eli?" he called out.

"That's what we're wondering," fairy girl responded.

The group gathered around the fallen soldiers. Kane checked them for a pulse and pronounced, "Dead."

"Why is he not smoked too?" Ev'r asked, nodding to Jude, but thinking of Ismail.

"Organic metals react differently," Jude said, casting a look down at his robot and struggling to keep his composure.

"You'll rebuild him," Silho said softly, getting a sideways glance from her boyfriend and boss, his eyes like a storm.

"He's not here," Ismail said. "I keep getting flashes and I don't sense him anywhere."

Kane nodded in agreement.

"Where is he then?" the Fen asked.

"Forget him, where the trutt are we?" Shawe looked around them with suspicion.

"Forget him, just like you forgot Alejan?" Diega said. "Do you even care that we left him back there? We just left him!"

Shawe gave her a crazed look. "He's with the old lady. Her entire house is a playground."

"He's not with her. Luther went to get him, which means he's there – with a Midnight Man and no Eli!" She raised her voice.

"He's not a full Midnight Man, besides, he has that dog. He takes care of that."

Fairy girl rounded on him, "What are you saying? He takes care of the dog, so he can take care of a baby?"

"Lower your voices," Kane ordered, but they both ignored him.

"He's not a baby. He's a year old. He's virtually a grown man!"

"You don't care about anyone, do you?" The fen's rainbow skin flared up bright and Shawe laughed at her, making her eyes turn red. She started to scream something else when the ground broke open at their feet and a creature burst out. Ev'r reacted instantly, slamming the Morsus Ictus right into its throat, under two foul gaping mouths. The creature tried to breathe some kind of toxin in Ev'r's face, but she ducked, ripping the blade sideways and half taking off its head. It should have been enough to end it, but as soon as the blade ripped out the other side, the creature healed.

"It's a demon!" Ev'r shouted to Ismail. "Everliving!"

It meant it was immortal, except for one weakness only, and they had no idea what that was. The demon lunged forward, trying to gore Ev'r with one of its many poisonous horns, its eyes flashing in a way that was meant to blind her. Ismail snarled and sent a blast of psychic energy toward it. Even filtered through an augmentor, it was enough to send the demon stumbling back. Brabel hit it too, with a flash of lightform, not strong enough to do any serious damage, but it pushed it back one more step. Shawe grabbed it around the neck, his skin too thick to be pierced by the horns, and Kane struck it hard in the back, tearing up his hand on the demon's scales. Jude got a hit in too with the strength of his metal prosthetics. Neither made much of a dent. The demon rounded on Kane and whipped its tail toward him, but Shawe intervened, landing a massive blow to its chest that put a hole straight through it and sent it crashing facedown into the mud. Ev'r took the chance and cut its head off with one strike. Jude booted the head far into the sky, while Shawe dumped the contents of his flask onto it and a spark from Silho's mouth set it alight.

"Run! There's cover above!" Kane commanded. No one needed a second invitation. They only had moments before it would shake the fire and regenerate. They sprinted back up the hill toward the place they'd first entered this world.

"There!" Ismail pointed ahead of them to a ruined building lying on its side in the mud. They reached the gaping entrance door and piled in just as a roar went up behind them. Shawe grabbed a fallen pillar from inside the house and jammed it up against the doorway to block it. Kane gestured for everyone to get down and keep their mouths shut. As though they needed to be told.

Ev'r grasped the Morsus Ictus is her hand and ducked down low, peering through one of the many cracks in the building. The demon appeared at the top of the hill and started searching for them, first one way and then the other, up and down. It broke into the air, beating powerful wings, trying to get an aerial view.

As formidable as it was, this demon breed evidently didn't have very good senses, fortunately for them. They'd had a lucky break taking it by surprise, but Ev'r got the feeling they wouldn't be so lucky the next time. She'd never seen this type of demon before.

"It might be a ratha demon," Silho whispered. "If we've jumped into the right world."

"Your mother's world," Jude said, his eyes meeting Silho's. Ev'r could see Kane clenching his jaw.

The demon slammed down again. It took a sword that was strapped to its back, a heavy jagged red weapon. It held the sword up into the air and bellowed with both mouths, the sound vibrating through the air and the sword lighting up like a beacon. From the hill behind it, other twisted creatures started scrambling up to join it, demon familiars from the look of them. They were a bunch of underlings so freakishly butt-ugly that it looked as though they were having a competition to redefine the term. If there was anything worse than demonic hordes it was their trutting servants – not smart enough to rule, not dumb enough to die. Ev'r would be glad to help them out there. She tightened her grip on the Morsus Ictus.

The demon sent his servants out in all directions. It would only be a matter of time before one of them stumbled across their clear and obvious hiding place.

"We need to take stock of weaponry, make a plan, and find another way out," Kane said, watching the familiars disperse. "Farther down." He pointed into the darkness behind them.

"Not us," Ev'r told him. "We're going our own way."

He gave her a look that said she and Ismail hadn't actually been part of the "we" he was talking about in the first place. The trackers and Shawe started to make a move, but Kane put a hand up to stop Jude following them.

"Not you. You're not one of us. You go your own way with them."

Fairy girl looked away and Shawe crossed his arms over his chest, but Silho said, "No. Where can he go?"

"That's not my concern," Kane responded, his eyes cold. "And it shouldn't be yours either."

"He's getting off easy. Do you know what happens if a gangster turns against his boss?" Shawe put in.

"What are you talking about?" Brabel questioned Kane more directly than most people would ever dare. "He won't survive on his own against those demons. None of us could with our skills down."

"He's already dead to me," Kane said. Ev'r had to admire the commander's ability to hold a proper grudge, most people folded all too easily.

Jude dropped his head. "Don't worry, Silho," he said softly, clutching his dead robot against his chest. "Go with them."

Brabel stood there between his majesty and her commander, completely stuck. Jude looked like a kid whose ice-cream had fallen on the ground just as he took his first bite. Kane's gaze was slicing strips off Brabel's face.

"Why don't you both trutt off together and Silho can come with us?" Ismail spoke up, his voice a growl.

"She's not welcome with us," Ev'r said, feeling a flash of something sharp and green that couldn't be anything but jealousy.

"We're going. Jude's staying – and you're staying with him. Permanently." Kane said to Brabel, his voice low and icy.

Kane, Diega and Shawe turned and headed farther down into the ruins of the building.

"Go with them, Silho!" Jude urged her. "Tell him you're sorry. He can protect you. You have a better chance with him."

Brabel's eyes were burning, flames glistening in the green of her irises as she watched Kane walk away. She rounded on Jude and said, "Do I look like I need protecting?"

"Now you're talking," Ev'r said.

"Trutt off Zingara!" Silho growled at her. "Do what you do best – leave when a person needs you the most!"

"Straight to the heart," Ev'r mocked her, and Ismail put a hand on her shoulder to quieten her.

Brabel turned her furious stare back to Jude and said, "We can't stay here. We have to go farther in."

Jude nodded. He hoisted his robot higher and said, "I'm sorry, Silho."

"Don't be sorry. Be a tracker. We have to find Apollo of Corinthia or Aquais is going to sink. You didn't see it in Omar Montanya, but it's —" Brabel lost her words for a moment. "It's hell."

"We'll find him," Jude promised, his eyes glowing bright blue in the dim light.

Brabel nodded, but her expression was already defeated. She cast the slightest of glances toward Ismail and then the pair headed off.

"Come on." Ev'r put a hand on Ismail's powerful arm. "Let's go, once and for all."

"What about Eli?" he asked in their native scullion tongue.

"We can't help him. You said it – he's not here. Which means he's back in Scorpia or some other trutting planet. How can we get to him?"

Pain flashed through Ismail's stare and Ev'r felt it in her own chest. "He saved us. And Silho helped him."

Ev'r started talking but he cut her off. "She was the only one who told Eli he could bring you back, who believed in him. Even I didn't." His words became heavy and his eyes misted. She hadn't seen him cry since they'd reunited – she hadn't seen him cry ever – and it almost broke her right there. They hugged each other, squeezing so tightly.

"We stay with Silho this time," Ismail whispered to her. "We right our wrongs."

"We can't stand Silho."

"It's not like that," he told her. "She's *consan*."

Ev'r shook her head. *Consan.* She hated the scullion term. It didn't make sense to her at all – a stranger who is family? A kindred spirit linked through rebirth? She didn't believe in any of that stuff, though Ismail always had.

"We're going to end up dead." She told him the truth as she felt it.

He pulled back and they looked into each other's eyes.

"We need to stay," Ismail said. "I feel it."

"Then promise me we go together this time," Ev'r said, her voice catching. "You're not leaving me again." Her fingers dug into his arms, clutching tight.

"Never again," he promised, resting his forehead down onto hers. After a few moments of silence Ev'r said, "I guess it makes sense to stay near Brabel. She's our only exit off this rock."

She looked down into the darkness of the ruins, where Brabel and Jude had vanished.

"One big happy family," she whispered.

Chapter 18
Ramses

HYDRIA

CORINTHIA (DOM FARRY WEST)

At Ironeye, Ramses' sleep had more often than not been broken by the stirring of whatever beauties he'd taken to his bed the night before – either that or the haunting melody of the Dawn Bird, exquisite turquoise and orange pheasant-like creatures who came to roost on the rooftops of the palace at sunrise. This morn he woke to a rooster's insistent raucous crowing and to Vitali Storon pissing into a pot in a circle motion.

He found himself still lying in the sling, which had been laid out on the ground behind a barn structure. Ramses could smell the thick scents of molasses and pig's muck. Somewhere in the distance a sheep herder was calling instructions to his dog, and kids were laughing. The aroma of fresh baked bread floated over the top of everything else. Ramses' stomach cramped up with hunger. He knew there were several small farming villages on the plateau hills of Cy Cyrene – Cormac, Irial, Bram and Dom Farry, each with only several hundred inhabitants or less.

Aron squatted nearby, studying a map spread across the bare ground. The brothers' horses grazed in an open field just beyond. Aron's blue bird turned on his shoulder to look at Ramses, tilting his head one way and then the other. It made him remember. Everything. Guilt crashed down on him so heavily, he felt crushed to the ground. He remembered Titan under attack and him just lying there, crying, unable to move, not helping him at all. Because of all the water. And then the fall.

Ramses tried to shift his legs but couldn't. Dread flooded hot through his body and he lay there, hardly able to breathe around the horror. Vitali put the piss pail down beside Aron and said, "There. Now as I was saying – Morcvara, Czernobog, Crnoborg, Mukesh, Shemal, Bogwart, Ainmire, what do these all have in common?"

Aron sighed and continued examining the map until Vitali clicked his fingers right under Aron's nose and the younger brother responded, without enthusiasm.

"They're all mines we've closed."

"Yes," Vitali said. "But more importantly, no! Look! They form an arrow pointing at Kasav. That's where Darro has taken him." He stood back and crossed his arms, satisfied, but Aron just stared up at him.

"I have no idea what you're talking about."

"That's because you're an imbecile!" Vitali snapped back. He wiped his forehead, sweating profusely even though the wind was cold up here and he was at rest.

"There's no arrow," Aron said. "And we know where Darro will go – Oas Havre."

"It's too obvious."

Ramses listened in, studying the men they called the right and left hand of Harlow Darro. Vitali had a steel glare and a warrior's body, cut strong from combat. Aron was unusual of face, boyish from some angles and quite menacing from others, clearly bred across races. A scar ran down over one of Aron's eyes, preventing it from opening fully, and Ramses thought by the way he was looking at the map, favoring the other side, the eye may be blinded. His expression seemed to change moment to moment compared to Vitali, who appeared to have only one fierce look for all emotions. And their accents were slightly different as well. They both spoke Corinthian fluently, but one had a heavier Anacharasi accent than the other. It was a subtle difference that not everyone would pick up. The two brothers continued to argue, with Vitali becoming increasingly agitated and Aron becoming increasingly amused.

"Keep going, whelp – keep pushing and I'll teach you a lesson," Vitali threatened his brother.

"What lesson?" Aron laughed.

"Something about how fast I am," Vitali said.

"So fast you've left your hair behind," Aron teased him.

Vitali's anger boiled over and he swung a punch, which Aron dodged. He fell back lightly on his hand and noticed then that Ramses was watching them. Ramses dragged himself up to a sitting position. He grabbed for a nearby stick, brandishing it, then he saw his half leg and his stomach turned.

"Why did you bring me here? Why didn't you take me to my father at Ironeye?" he demanded. "He would have healed me!" August was the most revered physician in all the Halos, like Aramasas before him. He would have set the break no matter how bad it was, and controlled the infection.

"We were under attack and had to flee or forfeit your life," Aron told him.

"This should not be! You should have taken me to him!" Ramses insisted.

The brothers exchanged a glance, and the younger spoke in common Anacharasi.

"Maybe the strike to his head?"

"Or he's caught crazy," Vitali muttered.

"It's not contagious," Aron replied. "Or I would have caught it from you long ago." He picked up the piss pail and brought it over to Ramses. "I need to cleanse the wound again."

"Get away from me." Ramses threatened him with the stick. "I won't be subjected to your barbarous antiquated practices."

"Well unfortunately this is all we have, so it's this or more infection."

"Return me to Ironeye." Ramses struggled to keep his head up, groggy with pain and fatigue. "My father will fix this."

"Your father is dead, Ramses of Ohai," Vitali said.

Aron tried to quieten him, but the elder Storon continued. "He's confused. Coddling him will just confuse him further." He spoke again to Ramses. "Warrior Augustus of Ohai is dead – many years now."

"We're sorry," Aron added softly.

A cold feeling ran through Ramses' body. *Dead?* He drifted somewhere dark in his mind, then came back to Aron unwrapping his leg, preparing to douse it in piss. Ramses shoved the bucket away, right into Aron's face.

"I'm leaving! Try to stop me and you'll see," he threatened. Using the stick, he managed to struggle up to one foot.

He swayed there for a moment, then fell forward and landed flat on his face, smashing his nose painfully. He grappled with the dirt, trying to get back up, but he just couldn't. The pain was beyond compare. He hadn't fully appreciated it before, but now it hit him so hard he gagged and if there was anything in his stomach he would have lost it. Aron and Vitali grabbed him under his arms and hauled him up and back onto the sling. He collapsed there, panting, gagging, clutching his stump. Aron tried to feed him some medicines.

"Get away!" he snarled, tears misting his eyes. He was a hard warrior, a Companion of the Lord Liege, and now he couldn't even stand on his own two feet. Then he realized he didn't have two feet anymore, and fresh white-hot pain ripped through him. He was completely defenseless against it.

Aron managed to get some liquid down his throat, which gradually took the edge off the agony until he could breathe again without gasping. The blue bird on Aron's shoulder squawked.

"Already, Morrison?" the younger brother asked his bird. It tilted its head in a way that looked like a nod.

"To Oas?" Aron asked Vitali.

"No! Too obvious I said," Vitali shot back.

"Only to us!" Aron said. "It's the only place Darro will go. It's the only place that might hold them back."

Vitali turned away. "It's so far. They won't make it," he muttered.

Aron gave his brother's back a knowing look and said, "Then we'll meet them on the road."

Vitali sighed, his shoulders dropping.

Aron spoke to Ramses. "Darro will keep your Lord Liege with him."

"He won't abide by that," Ramses said, his voice weakened. "He'll return to the Lord King as he should."

"It would be far too dangerous for that. Darro will take him to our stronghold, Oas Havre."

Ramses knew that Titan wouldn't allow himself to be *taken* anywhere, but he felt too sick to speak the thought aloud. Without further discussion, the brothers grabbed one end each of the sling and started to lift Ramses up.

"No," he said feebly. "I'll ride."

"Not a chance," Vitali told him.

"Actually, it may help him," Aron disagreed.

"We need speed. We can't be stopping every few moments to drag his carcass off the ground!"

"He's a warrior rider! Even if he can't walk he will ride!" Aron said it so strongly that Ramses felt a stirring inside him.

"He can't ride behind one of us. It's too obvious," Vitali said.

"So we'll buy a horse here."

"All they'll have here is done-with nags and unbroken mountain ponies."

"Vital, we're not trying to win the Parrish Plains Medal," Aron said, with exasperation. "It's just for him to ride. If we have to run, I'll have him behind me."

"Make it quick then," Vitali grunted, letting go of the sling.

"First," Aron said to Ramses, "a disguise." He hurried over to his horse and dragged off a pack, which he brought back to them. "A smith is always easy."

He dragged a common cloak out of the pack and wrapped it around Ramses' shoulders, pulling the hood down low over his head. Aron grabbed a larger stick from the wood pile and dragged Ramses up, letting him test his weight on the log, while keeping hold of him.

"Lean on me. Keep your head down and for the love of the gods, don't speak," Aron instructed him. "You're straight out of the royal palace and as obvious as flatulence during silent prayer. We're wanted and being hunted by all and sundry near and far, and if they capture us, they won't take you back to Corinth. They'll use you for bargaining. You know how close to war we all stand – not to mention whatever near finished us on that rooftop."

"Yes, don't mention it," Vitali muttered darkly, making an old-fashioned Anacharasi warding gesture. He took a flask out of his bag and had a long draft.

"Cough medicine," he said, seeing Ramses watching.

"Where's my calteus?" Ramses asked, realizing it wasn't on his back.

"We had to cut it off and leave it there," Aron told him.

"I see a farrier." Vitali nodded to a place beyond the barn. "With a horse yard behind it. Can you move?"

Ramses nodded, even though everything inside him said no. He limped, leaning heavily on the crutch and Aron's shoulder, as they descended the slope toward the farrier. Ramses blinked as plateau winds straight off *Mĕthmalay* stung his eyes and sent a chill of dread through his body. The town itself was little more than a collection of cottages and huts. Ramses could hear the blows of a metalsmith's hammer on steel, the moos and bleating of livestock and the shouts of children running through the village, playing. He heard them saying, *"I'm Darro." "No, I'm Darro." "No, I am this time!"*, all of them fighting to be the infamous Kí in their pretend battle. Someone's grandmother had to come bustling out of one of the cottages and break up the squabble with her broomstick.

It was always the most legendary warriors, usually the kings, that the youngsters of the time wanted to be, and Ramses felt an inner murmur of surprise that it was now Darro. Their play reminded Ramses of his childhood with

Titan and the other Companions, and the memory brought a lump to his throat. Where was Titan? Was he with Darro, as the brothers said? Had he even survived? He knew something unnatural had attacked them, something that shouldn't be, but was. Memories returned to him of black clawed hands and chanting voices and he pushed them forcibly from his mind. It couldn't have been real.

Ramses and the brothers entered the very small market area of the town, which had a limited range of foods on display, fruits and vegetables, some dried meats, bread, eggs and cheese and pots of boiling stew and pottage.

At the very end of the market street they found the farrier's yard, where one horse stood for sale – a white-faced gray draft horse, gelded and clearly well into his twilight years, but still sturdy. Corinthian warhorses lived to over a hundred years, many outliving their riders or dying at their sides, but working horses like this were lucky to see even thirty. Horses weren't meant to be passed around like tools. They attached their soul to their rider, and being sold over and over again shattered them. This gray's eyes looked tired and detached, weary and sad as he blinked at them with long white lashes. Ramses ran a hand down the gelding's neck, reassuring him. The geld responded immediately, lifting his head and snuffling Ramses' hand. Horses knew the sound of a true rider's heart beating. Vitali made a show of inspecting the horse, clicking his tongue and shaking his head.

"How much?" the elder brother finally asked the large red-faced farmer who stood watching them, trying to pretend he wasn't.

"How much you paying?" the farmer asked.

"Four bronze." Vitali started low.

"Four bronze! Lost your mind I see. I paid four times as much for this one."

"What, twenty years ago? He's on his last legs," Vitali argued.

"I'll get more selling it for meat."

The farmer's words offended every fiber of Ramses' mind and body. He felt like spitting into the man's face, but a look from Aron made him keep his head down instead. The blue bird, Morrison, sitting atop Aron's shoulder, croaked a warning. Vitali clenched his jaw tightly and said, "Four. Final offer."

"Nine or nothing, you'll not get far with injury like that." The farmer nodded to Ramses' leg. "And you'll be grateful when you can slaughter it for roasting."

Ramses had to swallow hard again. He couldn't believe they were standing on Corinthian land and hearing this blasphemy.

"Four or we walk," Vitali said.

"So walk," dismissed the farmer, with a Theselonian hand-sign that was equivalent to *kiss my arse*.

Vitali turned immediately and marched off. Ramses didn't move, he had no intention of leaving the gray at the mercy of this turd.

"Wait, wait," the farmer called Vitali back. "Let's call it even and say eight."

"Four," Vitali said.

The farmer looked at Aron, opening his arms, appealing for a better price, but Aron just shrugged.

"Fine, six – it's daylight robbery," he said.

"I'm paying four," Vitali said. "If you could have gotten more you would have already."

The farmer spat in disgust, but then untied the geld's reins and threw them at Vitali. Vitali retaliated by throwing the coppers at him, making him scramble in the mud to retrieve them.

Vitali led the gray over to Ramses and Aron and positioned it so that Ramses could grab hold of a fence and hoist himself up. He struggled to do it, but neither brother tried to help, knowing how shameful it would be for him if they did. The gray stood patiently as Ramses made several attempts, grunting in agony as he bumped his leg. Finally he managed it, and as soon as he sat upright on the gray's back he felt some measure of improvement. It was extremely strange riding with one leg, but he found he was still able to keep his seat. Rain started drizzling from the gray sky, dampening Ramses' cloak as the winds blew in from the mountains.

He leaned forward and patted the geld's neck as it climbed the hill back up to the brothers' horses.

"My Grayweather boy," he murmured to it. "That's your name from now on. Grayweather. You'll never be sold again."

The geld's ears twitched and he gave a soft whicker. Ramses thought of Arah and of Farahman's screams on the rooftop, and his hands starting shaking on the reins.

As Aron and Vitali mounted their stallions, the alarm bird Morrison made a louder, more urgent squark and they heard the sound of fast approaching hooves in the distance.

"Still chasing," Aron said.

"Chase on, *abrams*," Vitali snarled.

He clicked his tongue and his stallion took off up the larger hill behind the town leading to the flats of Cy Sandel in Theselon. Aron and Ramses followed him. As they rode over the rise, Ramses looked back and saw soldiers riding into the Dom Farry. It was a mixed group, from Anacharasis and Armen.

"We're hunting the murderers of King Sirion," their leader announced to the townspeople in a voice full of self-import.

Ramses immediately recognized Yorem Gorse, the contender for the throne himself.

"Wanted far and wide," Ramses said to Aron as they vanished from sight.

"Absolutely. Just not in any of the good ways." Aron gave him a quick grin.

"What part did he have in the happenings on the rooftop?" Ramses asked him, and Aron's smile soured.

"Enough to know that you and your Lord Liege may be with us. Gorse hasn't involved himself personally until now."

"Is he—" Ramses searched for another word but settled for "unnatural?"

Aron's eyes shifted, as uncomfortable hearing it as Ramses was saying it. "I really don't know," he admitted.

"He'll have his day," Vitali said, turning suddenly onto a more hidden path winding around the hilltop. "Whatever he is."

"I can't remain with you," Ramses told the brothers truthfully. "I must return to Ironeye. I know that the Titan will do the same. He won't agree to leave the kingdom, no matter the consequence."

Aron gave a measured nod and said, "Darro won't allow him to put himself at risk. He'll be going to Oas whether he agrees to it or not. Trust us – we know Darro."

Ramses didn't like the sound of his words, but didn't let on. Thoughts flowed fast through his mind. Even if he was at full physical capacity, Grayweather wouldn't be able to outrun the soldiers' horses. They wouldn't make it back, and then Ramses would be taken and he'd be neither at Ironeye nor finding Titan. He concluded that the best decision he could see was to stay with the brothers, for now.

"How long until we reach your stronghold?" Ramses asked.

"We'll have to take the hard roads to keep out of sight," Aron told him. "It may be a while."

Ramses' thoughts turned again to Titan. He looked out over the hills of Cy Cyrene and whispered, "Where are you?"

Chapter 19
Eli

HYDRIA

FARNORTHERN HALOS (BLED)

Light filtered through Eli's unfocused gaze. He blinked once, then again, as forms took shape from the nebulous drift around him. For a moment he thought he was in his laboratory, sitting at his desk, but everything was off-kilter, un-angled, nothing was where it was supposed to be. It didn't make sense. Confusion seeped through the fog of his mind, pursued closely by fear, then memory – the portal, the ratha, the city beneath the skull. Eli's awareness suddenly spiked, and his surroundings crashed in on him with clashes of sight and light, sounds and scents melded together and horribly discordant all at the same time.

Panic compelled Eli to struggle toward standing, but hands held him back. Two women were sitting beside him, trying to calm him, one of them the old woman from the carriage. He let them sit him back down and hunched there, shivering in the cold heat, blinking burning eyes, the pain in his back growing until it was a physical weight pushing him down. He gritted his teeth and leaned low, trying to find relief, but there really wasn't any to be found. Nelly moved beneath his remaining wing, her little paws tapping on his back as though trying to comfort him. It helped to know he wasn't alone, but at the same time, it was horrifying to know he'd dragged her with him into this nightmare.

When he felt strong enough, he raised his eyes and looked around. He and a large group of women were crouching in a cell. It had been dug out of the dirt and the ceiling was very close above. No one could stand up straight, nor could they sit very comfortably, because the dirt was wet and sludgy. Rusted bars enclosed the front of the cell.

Eli wondered how long he'd been out. He was quite used to fainting, but not with the assistance of someone's fist. His nose gave a long whistle, drawing some looks. He covered it and felt the dried blood caked around it. Gritting his teeth, he crunched it back into place. Immediately a strong sense of smell returned. The air was thick with the scent of musty earth that reminded him of spectral-breeds and also of his hideout beneath his grandparents' place when he was a kid. He'd spent hours there imagining and inventing – and yes, hiding from gran'ma too. She hadn't been able to fit underneath to drag him out, although she'd tried once and ended up getting stuck, with her dress riding up to her neck, flashing her long old-fashioned bloomers to the entire neighborhood. Grampy fell over in the street laughing and spent the night in his shed with his hat collection. He was thrown out on a fairly regular basis.

The bar doors of the cell suddenly burst open and Eli flinched back. The women on either side steadied him. In walked the beautiful girl who had punched Eli in the face, keeping toward the front of the cell, where she could stand, and even then the tips of her large red feathered wings brushed against the roof. Eli's heart did a dance inside his chest and he couldn't tear his eyes away from her. She didn't look like anyone else he'd ever seen, with dark mahogany hair and very pale silver eyes that glowed in the darkness. She had bumps on her forehead like horns that had never broken through, and hundreds of rings and pieces of metal piercing her face and body. All the skin he could see was tattooed with violent bleeding pictures that on their own were alarming, but together formed a beautiful tapestry across her body. The old woman beside him pushed his head down again as the girl's eyes flashed their way.

"Sanfrass," she whispered. "Bad."

Sanfrass, Eli repeated in his mind. It was a lovely name. He couldn't help but sneak another peek at her, and as he did, he caught sight of a pale figure beside her. It was a spectral-breed, a type he hadn't seen before, with faint glittery bloodline marks and a binding band wrapped tightly around her neck, stopping her from using her skills. Behind them the demon, Gibbit, walked in with his writhing whip in his hand and the rest of his entourage around him.

"Listen up," Gibbit shouted in a dialect of Urigin, close enough to Eli's dialect for him to understand most of what he was saying. "Today is an exhibition. The king himself will be attending. That means you will *all* be on the floor. That means you will *all* bathe and scrub your filthy bodies clean – as clean as they get, anyway." His entourage sniggered. "And do I really need to tell you what will happen if you disappoint me?"

Eli sensed the women drawing back, away from the master slaver.

"Well, do I?" he shouted, and lashed out with his snake whip, striking one of the women across the face and opening red gashes in her skin. She gasped, then started convulsing, thick blue veins rising all around the wounds.

The other women pressed back, away from her. One of the women stumbled and fell, revealing a small child she had been hiding under her dress.

"What do we have here?" Gibbit said, seizing the little girl, who started crying out for her mother. "Take her." He threw the kid back to his group. The mother shrieked and leapt up, trying to get to her daughter, but Gibbit flung her back down. She kept trying to stand, over and over, screaming out her child's name, and he kept kicking her down, laughing.

The kicks were getting increasingly savage and Eli's heart was pounding. He couldn't just watch a woman be beaten to death. He darted in and as she crashed onto the ground once again, he grabbed her around the chest and whispered in her ear, "Stay down or he'll kill you and you'll never find her."

The mother started to push his arms away, but then collapsed against him, sobbing. Eli hunched low over the woman, keeping his head down. He could feel Gibbit's eyes burning into his neck and he braced for pain. Gibbit booted him hard in the side, sending him sprawling at Sanfrass' feet. He pretended to be knocked out in the hope they would leave him be. Imp-breeds could play dead better than any other race, they could even stop their own hearts for a certain amount of time, and then restart them.

"Sanfrass, Octavia," Gibbit said. "Get these maggots presentable."

The master slaver left with the rest of his enforcers and Sanfrass yelled out in Urigin, with a heavy accent that Eli couldn't place, "Get up!"

She gave Eli a kick, but it really felt more like a token nudge than anything too savage, he thought. He shook his head as though he was coming to and rolled over. His side was throbbing. His friend from the carriage helped him stand and they shuffled out of the cell. He kept his eyes down as he moved past Sanfrass and her spectral-breed friend, Octavia. He really wanted to look at her, to talk to her, but realized it would be an extremely bad idea.

Eli kept to the middle of the group as they were herded down a narrow dirt tunnel to an area with a slate stone floor and pipes in the walls, dribbling out water. All the women started stripping off, but Eli was acutely aware that he could not be seen naked. So he used his speed, reduced though it was, to dart in and out of the crowd and keep cover behind the women, hiding from the eyes of Sanfrass and Octavia, who were standing on a ledge above the bathing area, watching. Eli's feet splashed through the puddles, and droplets of rusty-tasting water rained over him. He was very tempted to have a drink, his throat so dry and sore, but he was wary of what might be in the water.

The women were leaving their soiled clothes and re-dressing in slightly less soiled clothes that had been piled by the door. Eli did the quickest change in history, with Nelly still huddled beneath his wing. He swapped the hospital gown for a brown sack dress, which he hoped would be far less appealing. While the women finished up, he kept to the shadows beneath the scaffolding where Sanfrass and Octavia stood. He couldn't help but steal glances upward at Sanfrass' boots. They were knee high and seemed to be coated in or made from metal. There was a screaming skull etched into their soles. Octavia had bare feet, as most spectrals preferred.

More boots thunked on the scaffolding and Eli heard the hiss of Gibbit's snake whip. The women hunched lower and moved like frightened animals in his presence. Eli himself pressed closer to the wall, watching as Gibbit and Sanfrass' boots separated from the others and moved away. He slid along the wall, following them. They stopped and he heard Gibbit whispering something, but he couldn't quite hear what it was. Eli moved around carefully so that he had a clearer view. He saw Gibbit kissing Sanfrass' neck and his stomach growled unhappily. She was holding him as well, and smiled when he looked up at her, flashing sharp incisors. He smiled back, then took hold of the metal ring through her nose and pulled it so hard, it brought her to her knees.

The violence was so sudden and horrendous that Eli froze, watching as Gibbit grabbed Sanfrass' neck, squeezing hard and making her choke. He yanked her face up to him and pressed his lips down on hers. Eli could see her shaking in pain. Something snapped inside him, and he grabbed furiously at a piece of loose rock at his feet. He lifted it to throw it at Gibbit, but the demon had already lost interest and moved on. Sanfrass was struggling to her feet, with Octavia helping her. The spectral looked down through the gaps in the grating and her pale eyes saw Eli standing there and captured his rage. He gulped and dropped the rock, darting back into the shadows. He felt her eyes following him and expected her to shout out or to tell Gibbit, but she said nothing, just stared without blinking until Sanfrass gave the order for the women to move along.

From the bathing room, the group was pressed upward through more winding, dark tunnels. The farther up they went, the more the ground seemed to tremor beneath their feet. As a light appeared up ahead, they could hear the muffled roar and chanting of a crowd. Water started dripping on them. A drop fell on Eli's arm and he wiped it off, leaving a red smear. It was blood, not water, seeping through the ground above.

Eli's stomach churned and twisted. He didn't know what lay ahead of them – torture, death, being molested by a monstrous demon. He gulped, his throat constricting. The group broke out into the light at the same time as another bunch of slave women appeared from a tunnel beside them, and more women from others all around, filtering into a single line, climbing upward. The noise above them was almost deafening.

Eli stepped off the top step into the chaos of a fight arena. Spectators – ratha demons, other demons, and an assortment of predatory and dangerous-looking creatures – crowded the benches above the dugout pit below, where two gigantic lizard-like men were grappling in the sand.

Eli's eyes darted around. Some of the women had obviously been here longer, and he took note of what they were doing. Some were finding demons to offer their bodies to, but there was another group serving food and drinks. That was definitely the group Eli wanted to be in. He moved quickly and nimbly attached himself to one server, helping her carry some empty plates all the way up to where the kitchen was. He took it from there, rushing drinks and food around the arena, not stopping long enough for anyone to even get a good look at him.

As he worked, he gave his kleptomania a longer leash than usual. With hands faster than sight, he pickpocketed, swiping a number of blades and other implements from the spectators and hiding them under his wing, aware that Gibbit, Sanfrass and Octavia and the other slavers were gathered above, watching.

Eli continued in a whir of movement, blocking out the smells and shouts and grisly sounds from the fights below. Then something caught his eye. It was a section of the stadium across the pit from where he stood, front and center, and divided off from everywhere else by a line of huge boulders and a gathering of ratha guards. Inside the area, a group of demons sat around a table, working on something spread out across the tabletop.

A man sat at the head of the table, and Eli was struck by how ordinary he looked. He really stood out in the sea of bizarre. He looked like a human-breed with a common blood type, like dog or cat, wearing ordinary human-breed clothes, trousers and a shirt, unlike the ratha demons, who had thick leather skirts or loin cloths, or the other spectators, who frankly looked like they were all on their way to a sadomasochistic orgy. Eli wasn't in the habit of casting judgment, but the man just looked way out of place. Even the way he was sitting, with one leg casually crossed over the other and his hands clasped in his lap, seemed odd. Eli continued watching him out of the corner of his eye as he worked. He saw one of the demons at the table lean over and say something to the man, and he smiled in response. It started as an ordinary, even attractive, smile, but kept widening until it reminded Eli of a carnival clown with a huge demented grin. His old phobia of clowns was immediately reignited, and he found himself staring at the man's mouth. A roar from the crowd shook him from his trance. Below in the arena, a pack of oversized wolves were fighting a bear and had almost brought him down. Eli flinched and looked away, escaping into his mind until a silence fell over the arena. Eli lifted a platter then paused, seeing that the out-of-place man had stood up.

"Who is that?" he whispered to one of the other slaves.

"King," she said, her eyes flashing fear.

Mordan-Grieg, Eli thought. King of the ratha demons. Mordan started to speak flawless Urigin, and his voice was rich and pleasing to the ears.

"Ratha, fellow demons, lesser demons, scroungers, slavers, enforcers, ravagers, parasites and slaves – yes, even you – you are all in for a treat today. May I have the honor of presenting Apollo of Corinthia." He paused, then raised his voice. "The Almighty."

Eli felt his body lock down as the words rang out around the stadium. *Apollo of Corinthia!*

A door below in the arena shrieked upward and two ratha stepped out onto the sand, dragging between them a towering man wrapped in chains, with a mask fastened around his head. The silence was absolute as the demons led the man into the center of the circle, where they stopped and removed the chains. They put a sword into one of his hands, then ripped off his mask, backing away and fast as they could. King Apollo of Corinthia struck out at them instantly, effortlessly wielding the huge sword and beheading one of the ratha before he was out of range. The demon hit the ground then regenerated, and scrambled to get away.

Eli sensed nervousness, even fear, radiating from all the demons and creatures in the stadium – they seemed to be pressing as far back in their seats as they could, while Eli stepped closer to the edge of the seating area, his eyes fixed on the king below. He was a huge, muscle-bound man with a long gray beard and matted gray hair, and scars all over his body. But it wasn't the way he looked that was drawing Eli in, it was the feeling he got upon seeing him. It seemed crazy, but it was a feeling of having been alone – hurt, exhausted and terrified – and seeing someone who loved him ahead. It was like seeing home. Tears misted his eyes and he almost lost it.

Barred doors all around the fight arena rattled upward and a horde of lesser demons and creatures rushed out to battle the king, but the fight was really over before it even began. King Apollo cut them down powerfully and completely with no fancy steps, no savoring the moment, just hard, fast blows of his sword until he was the last one standing. The silence in the arena took on an awkward edge, as though the gathered demons didn't know whether to applaud or just run in terror. Eli saw Mordan, grinning in anticipatory pleasure, register that it was already over. His smile dropped and his shoulders sagged. He got back to his feet and said, without any of his earlier showiness, "Take him back! And clean up that mess!"

Ratha demons descended on the king and he fought back, decimating whoever came before him. If they hadn't been ever-living they wouldn't have stood a chance, even with all their armor and inbuilt weaponry, but they healed fast and by sheer numbers overwhelmed him. One trapped him in a chemical net while others pinned him down. They bound his arms in chains, forced the mask over his head and dragged him back through the doors. Even then, Eli had the distinct feeling that they'd only captured him because he'd allowed it.

He was so engrossed, and overwhelmed that he'd actually found Apollo of Corinthia that he didn't feel his dress being lifted from behind. He did, however, register the indignant yell from the demon doing the lifting, who had been expecting to see a female body and was met by something else entirely.

Eli stumbled back, realizing his error, as the demon menaced over him. Behind them, Gibbit and his group of enforcers, including Sanfrass, heard the commotion and started toward them. Gibbit's eyes flashed murderously. Eli felt like every demon face in the stadium had turned their way. He made a quick decision and grabbed the railing of the seated area, leaping over and down to the fight arena below. He didn't dare try to fly in case Nelly and the weapons he'd gathered fell out, so instead he plummeted, crashing sideways into the sand.

He leapt to his feet and sprinted across the open space, leaping over bodies and avoiding the arms of the underlings there cleaning up the carnage. He jumped onto the opposite wall and clamored up to the railing, then cast a glance over his shoulder to see the slave master and his enforcers leaping over seats, running to get to him. Sanfrass beat her feathered wings and lifted into the air, her silver eyes fixed on Eli. Without properly turning back around, he jumped over the railing, stumbled and collided solidly with something ahead of him. He found himself kneeling at the feet of Mordan-Grieg, the ratha King.

Eli's heart sank. Of all the places that he could have climbed back up, it had to be right into the king's section. Mordan was looking down at him with something that looked like angry amusement in his eyes.

"I'll deal with her, your majesty," Gibbit panted as he reached them.

Eli's eyes darted around and he caught sight of the papers on Mordan's table. It was the blueprint of a locking mechanism, a vault maybe, and he could see they were trying to figure out its breaking point, and failing.

"It's based on a Saint Lander's cross," Eli rushed in, speaking to Mordan. "Two strikes up, two across, and then a half circle down. You'd have to cast an incision onto the half circle and trace it down from there – anywhere else and it's a dead-end and the structure will fail, either immediately or soon after."

Mordan's eyes shifted to the papers and then back to Eli and the amusement became calculating. His eyes flashed a bright light and Eli looked away, momentarily blinded. Mordan went to the papers and traced Eli's instructions over the blueprint with his finger. From what Eli could see from the papers on the table, it was far simpler a solution than the one they'd been working on. Eli crouched low, feeling the weapons under his wing, ready to grab one if things went as badly as he was anticipating.

"Interesting," Mordan said, then let out an unexpected peal of laughter. He rubbed a hand over his face. Gibbit tried to breach the circle of demons around Eli to grab him but Mordan turned suddenly and his tongue lashed out like a whip, striking Gibbit's neck. The enforcer squealed in pain and scuttled back. Eli bent even lower as Mordan stepped back to him, surrounding him with a heavy chemical stench, which saturated the air. He sat down on his chair right in front of Eli and said, "*Him*, not *her*, right?"

Eli gave one very careful nod, using everything he had to keep his hands in front of him and his hysterical giggling behind his clenched teeth.

"Of course you are," the ratha demon king said, leaning in to study Eli's bloodline marks.

"Aquais?" he asked

Eli nodded again.

Mordan gave a knowing look. "Yes, I've been expecting a few of you to jump through in the next little while – considering ..."

His words sent a chill through Eli's chest – considering their world was being consumed by the Indemeus X.

"Fairy-breed?" the demon king asked.

"Imp-breed," Eli said through numb lips.

Mordan sniffed. "Same thing really."

Imp-breeds and fairy-breeds were completely different, but Eli nodded, letting the lie happen naturally.

"Well," Mordan said, bouncing his arms on the sides of his chair. "Wherever you came from, whatever you are, your mind—" he looked into Eli's eyes as though they were windows, "is clearly brilliant."

Eli saw something moving across Mordan's forehead beneath his skin disguise, and an insectoid's hairy leg poked out one nostril for a moment before disappearing again.

"And I need more brilliant around here – considering." He looked around the table and then back to Eli, shaking his head as though they were sharing a joke about the others. "Trouble is, there aren't any chairs left." He took a sharp red dagger from his belt and handed it to Eli. It was hot to the touch and much heavier than it looked. "So you'll need to get yourself a chair."

The demons around the table glared at Eli and Mordan's eyes demanded blood, but Eli's mind found another way. Grampy was a carpenter and mason when he'd still been able to work and Eli had spent many an hour helping him in the workshop while he was supposed to be at ballet. With that skill behind him, the thought of the carved-out houses they'd just seen, and hands so fast they were difficult to watch, he went to the nearest boulder and rapidly cut himself a chair. When he was finished, he pushed it to the table and sat down.

Mordan's eyes widened and he looked somewhat dazzled. He laughed out loud and put a hand over his mouth, leaning his elbow on the table. Eli cautiously slid the blade back over to the demon king. Mordan took it and then, still smiling, slashed the throats of his two closest advisors. Eli gulped hard and tried to block out the sounds and the blood. Mordan booted them out of their chairs and indicated for everyone to close the gap. It was a lesson, Eli understood. Mordan had demanded Eli to kill, Eli had gone his own way, and so now two were dead. Mordan slid a piece of paper over to Eli with a complex gravitational equation on it.

"A solution to this by the day's end," Mordan said. "This is where you nod and say 'yes, your majesty, I won't disappoint you' – nod your head, there's a good boy." He spoke to the ratha guards beside him. "Give my little friend his own room … and a pair of pants."

The guards assisted Eli roughly to his feet and dragged him away toward doors at the back of the arena. They passed Gibbit and Sanfrass. Gibbit was killing him with his eyes and Sanfrass was looking at the ground. She had blood running from her ear, down the side of her neck. One of her rings had been pulled right out, tearing the skin. Eli had the awful thought that she would be punished in his place and he was helpless to stop it. The pain in his heart rivaled the pain of his back. Octavia stood behind Sanfrass, her eyes still fixed on him.

"I'm so sorry," he whispered as he was pushed past her.

Chapter 20
Titan

HYDRIA

KIRITH-JEROM (AGHAMORE VALE)

A sudden crack of sound and an intense flash of light drove Ravana's glooms back. Titan saw shadows growing larger before him in the chaos and heard Darro's rasp.

"No time for dignity, Lord Liege."

Anakis swooped Titan off his feet and cradled him like a child in impossibly strong arms. Titan tried to fight it, the dishonor of being carried horrifying him even through the haze of the poisons, but his strength failed him. An ear-piercing screech blasted out from behind them, sending a chill all the way through Titan's body.

Darro and Anakis broke into a run, the big man clutching Titan tight against his chest. Scuttling, scrambling sounds pursued them down the tunnel.

"Here!" Darro called out and the pair slowed. There was a grinding of rock against rock. Anakis shuffled forward and Titan felt him pressing into a small space. Titan's hand brushed against stone.

"Brace, Lord Liege," Darro's voice came to him.

The ground dropped out from beneath them and they plummeted down at a dizzying speed until they landed on a spongy surface that cushioned the blow. Titan immediately smelled horses and heard soft whickers and hooves stamping in the darkness.

"Put him up with me, Anak," Darro said, and Titan felt himself being hoisted up on a horse's back. As soon as he was seated he felt a portion of his wits returning to him. Even though he couldn't see his hand before his face, he knew many things of the horse just by the touch and scent of it. She was a mare, young – only 30 years at most – well fed and well cared for. She wore no bit or saddle, just a halter and full combat armor. She was shifting her weight anxiously but otherwise awaiting her rider silently, unlike the stallion beside them. He was pressing in close, whining and nickering constantly. Titan could smell the heavy fear beneath his armor. The stallion stood tall, but young, unbroken and frightened, throwing his head all over the place. Titan expected him to start bolting or thrashing about in the enclosed space, but the stallion held. Four more horses could be heard in the darkness behind them. Darro leapt up behind Titan, clutching him around the middle and locking his legs over Titan's to hold him on.

"Naro, go!" Darro commanded and his mare leapt forward, the stallion right beside them. Titan heard a cart rumble behind them, moving fast, not on trundling wheels but sliding. He hunched low over the mare's neck, pressing his face against her withers. Horrendous pain ripped through his body, radiating from the mark. It felt like he was being skinned alive by a knife within his chest. He clutched at the prime and groaned. Darro put a hand on Titan's shoulder as he urged the mare, Naro, to run faster, lunging into full gallop in the pitch dark. Titan sagged low, slowly slipping into unconsciousness. He could feel the mare compensating, keeping him on. She was a warrior's horse and Darro a powerful rider, in control of his horse's every move, even without saddle or bit, even in this darkness.

Titan heard Darro's voice from afar. "*Service to the Lord King, Honor in Battle, Sacrifice in Brotherhood, Sanctity in the Afterlife ...*" He repeated it and Titan joined in, his lips fumbling over the words as his voice failed him. The Warrior Way brought him back from the edge, an anchor to the Lord King through all things.

The ground beneath them changed. Darro brought his horse to a sharp halt, paused a moment as Anakis' cart slid up close behind them, and then slashed out with his sword. A gasp escaped Titan's lips as they suddenly swung forward in a headlong rush. High shrieks like bird calls echoed behind them and then a wave of water struck them from the side like a wall of shields. The stallion started screaming, the cart horses were blowing hard, but Naro pushed forward silently. Titan could feel hands in the water, grabbing him, trying to drag him under. He clung to the mare, fighting a rising terror inside him. Only the sound of Darro's voice speaking to his horses, urging them to fight, kept him from panic. Naro's hooves clattered on rocks as she found solid ground.

"Anakis!" Darro called out. "Go right! Don't stop!"

Titan heard the cart take off as Darro broke sharp left.

"Naro, Winta. Run! Go! Run!" he urged his horses.

Both the mare and stallion responded immediately, pushing even harder than before, thundering through the darkness of the tunnel with the sound of rushing water just behind them. Titan could hear voices screaming and chanting. Suddenly the tunnel vanished from around them as they blasted out into the light and into mid-air. They started falling and Titan felt his heart crash upward into his throat, but then Darro pulled a lever on Naro's armor and wings extended out on either side of them. Darro pulled a rope triggering the lever on the stallion's armor and his wings shot out as well. The air caught beneath them and stopped their fall, now rushing them upward. Titan blinked, the light and air blinding. The water behind them broke out from the tunnel and Titan turned to see a blurred image of the women leaping toward them, walking on the water as far as it would take them, then falling into the deep canyon pit far below. Darro changed the direction of their wings and they soared away over the treetops.

* * * * *

Warrior riders understood, all that is to be known of a man's heart can be read in his companion beast's eyes. Darro's horses had run against their fear, against every natural instinct, for their rider. They'd even ridden the sky. They trusted Darro implicitly. And that type of trust could never be forged by a cruel man. Titan held that fact with full certainty, even as Darro tied the last knot on the ropes binding his arms behind his back. They'd landed on a rocky outcroft above the Aghamore Vale and ridden to another of Darro's hidden places, behind a waterfall.

Titan grunted again, doubling in on himself as the pain of the mark hit him in immense and all-consuming surges.

Darro dropped down beside him and poured another dose of his horrendous concoction into Titan's mouth. Relief swept through him, leaving him flattened on his side. Darro spoke from above him.

"When I told you that tapping the source of your power would bring them to us, I was not lying."

"*Nea tetishina,*" Titan uttered stubbornly, even though he knew full well his power did exist. He could not accept speaking of it in such open and ordinary ways.

"Believe as you will, Lord Liege," Darro said. "But I'm telling you, refrain. Our escape was more luck than anything else."

Titan sensed the Kí move away from him. When he was able, he maneuvered up to sitting, and tested the ropes behind him. Darro had tied them skillfully, not tight enough to hurt, but leaving no give. Titan watched the spy tend to his horses, talking to them and praising them for their bravery. Naro stood still, with her ears forward, attentive to Darro's words. The young stallion, Winta, was another story. He was jittery and bumping his head against his rider as though in need of more reassurance. Titan thought of Farahman. He could remember choosing him when they were both small and new to the world, and now. His chest felt so tight his could barely breathe.

"My stallion," he said, and Darro looked over his shoulder.

"I think he made it down alive."

"The tower was flooded."

"Yes," Darro confirmed. "But horses can swim well, even Corinthian horses."

"The sounds he was making."

"He was scared for you, but he'll sense that you're alive. One heart —"

"Horse and rider," Titan finished the Corinthian saying.

"Your *ata-ajua* will use your stallion to find you – or your Lord father will."

Darro started removing his horses' armor, revealing two of the most magnificent beasts Titan had ever seen. He knew all the breeds of the Halos, but he'd never witnessed anything like them. The shape of their bodies, the length of their legs, and their coloring were all unique. The mare was black silver and the stallion white gold, and their manes and tails were long and flowing, unlike Corinthian war horses. There were tufts of hair all around their hooves and their eyes were ink black. He could feel the stallion now watching him as Darro strapped feed bags over their noses. The Kí left them to eat while he started a fire, the waterfall over the entrance to the cave consuming the smoke before it could escape into sight. After a short while, Darro lifted a heavy boiling pot over to Titan and sat it down beside him.

"Lie back as well as you can," Darro said, pressing him backward on his bound arms. "Do you need something to bite down on?"

Titan shook his head, looking up at the dark slits in Darro's full-metal zivas. The thought came to him that if Darro had truly been cast in iron and then freed again through fire and water, he must be horribly deformed beneath his mask.

"Brace," Darro ordered.

Titan gritted his teeth and tensed his muscles, and Darro poured the liquid metal over his mark. It seared his skin and sizzled the water oozing from the wound. The pain was intense but brief, controlled by Darro's medicines. The Kí assisted him to sit back up and he examined the wound. The shape remained but the ridges were now filled with set metal.

"Will it hold?" he asked.

"For a time," Darro said. "Hopefully long enough for us to get to Oas and find a way to be rid of it for good."

Voices, muffled by the thunder of the falls, sounded in the vale beyond. Darro went to the entrance of the cave and then returned.

"Gideon's soldiers?" Titan asked.

The spy nodded. "All the regents are leading their men down to the plains to assemble for war."

The words sent a prickle across Titan's skin.

"Was it Yorem Gorse who betrayed King Sirion of Anacharasis?" he asked directly.

"Gorse, Maneam of Armen, Gideon of Kirith and Vitor-Petacula," Darro confirmed. 'And now they're uniting against Corinthia."

"I'm aware," Titan said.

"Are you aware of the army they have hidden beneath the ground? Cytisians that Vitor-Petacula has been bending to his own will for many years."

Titan felt the shock sweep through him, but kept his expression unchanged.

"Vitor-Petacula looks like a jester but he's far from it," Darro continued. "How do you think his line has managed to keep a kingdom alive on nothing but swamp mud and shite?"

"How many heads?" Titan asked, his mind formulating war strategy as they spoke.

Darro made a sound behind his zivas. "Four hundred thousand – at last count."

Titan's breath caught in his throat.

That number, plus the armies of Draul, Anacharasis, Kirith-Jerom and Armen, put Corinthia and Theselon at great statistical disadvantage. It changed the face of the war and the entire strategy required to win it, but the strategy could not be changed if the Lord King did not know.

"You must untie me. The Lord King must be informed. You can see that, Darro, can you not?"

"It appears, Lord Liege, that either your ears or your mind are still not functioning," Darro said. His response made Titan clench his jaw – he was unprepared for the disrespect, especially at a moment as grave as this.

"I'll repeat myself again, and pray you're listening," Darro continued. "You cannot return to Ironeye. A witch has formed a union with you against your will and she's looking to collect, do you understand? We cannot even send out a bird for fear it will bring her to us."

Titan held his silence, letting the fury of his eyes respond for him, and Darro went and gathered items from places hidden in the walls of the cave. He came back and set a jar of balm and a sharp shaving knife down at Titan's side. Titan wondered why the Kí would want to shave when his face was so concealed, but held his breath in anticipation of seeing Darro's true form. It wasn't until Darro put the knife to Titan's own beard and started slicing that he realized his intention.

"No!" Titan bellowed, louder than he intended. "I cannot shave until my marriage vows!"

"You can't marry anyone if you're dead, Lord Liege," Darro replied, continuing his work. "The fastest way to Oas Havre from here is through Dolma. You need to look like someone else."

Dolma was the royal center of Armen, and Ravana Nazar's home city. To go there now seemed madness.

"I can wear a helm and zivas," Titan said, as more and more of his beard fell into his lap.

"All helms are removed at the city gates," Darro told him. "I'm sorry, Lord Liege, this must be done."

Darro's words were final and his knife fast. When the beard was short enough, he spread the balm over Titan's face and shaved him clean, then did his hair as well. The air on his skin felt incredibly good, but inside he felt so wrong.

"Had you made a choice on the matter of your bride?" Darro broke the silence as he started lightening Titan's skin. "Not Ravana Nazar, I'll hazard a guess from her reaction. You might have tempered your rejection so she felt less inclined to kill you where you stood."

Titan's ire rose. "This *affect* that you practice in your speech," he said, "is entirely unnecessary with me. I'm neither your enemy nor your judge. Why were you in Ironeye?"

"With war imminent, we expected an attack on you."

"And why would you take it upon yourself to stand in guard over me?" Titan asked. 'Are you not Anacharasi?"

"I seek the righteous path," Darro replied in the Corinthian way that meant much more than the words. "And no – I am not."

Darro proceeded to disguise Titan, setting clay over his nose to change the shape and using dark liquids to hollow out his face. He spread another balm around Titan's eyes that made the skin tingle and swell.

"What is this substance?" Titan demanded, his eyes starting to water.

"The slime from a giant bristle worm and the sting from a tiger-tail wasp. It won't leave permanent damage."

Titan could see his reflection in Darro's armor and didn't recognize his own face. The spy tied a bloodied rag around Titan's head. "When we get closer to the gates or get stopped, we'll use this—" he held up a small vial, "and your eyes will temporarily swell shut." He went and removed garments from his horses' packs, the wears of an Armenite leather peddler. Darro cut off the rest of Titan's tunic and wrapped the new clothes around his shoulders.

Once Titan was dressed, Darro started twisting screws and adjusting levers hidden under panels in his own armor.

"What are you doing?" Titan asked.

"I'm going to vanish into thin air," Darro said.

The front of the armor hinged open unexpectedly and Darro stepped out of it, twisting his helm in a particular fashion to unlock it and then lifting it off his head. Titan stared for a moment, not believing what his eyes were showing him. Darro was neither a deformed man nor an Anacharasi man, nor a Corinthian man – he was not a man at all. He was a woman. Pale, even more so than the mountain dwellers, with dark red hair tied in a knot on her head and eyes a shade of green he had never seen in real life, only in ancient mosaic artwork of Farnorthern women.

"You're a woman," he said.

"As I said – vanish into thin air," Darro replied, his voice much softer without the echo of the helm. *Her voice.*

Exactly what feelings twisted and churned, broke over each other and bled together inside him, Titan was unsure, but anger was there, confusion, shame … He felt like a fool.

"I see you're angry." Darro adjusted the metal yoke she wore around her neck. She untied her hair and let it fall long, into unusual waves, curls and tangles, around her shoulders.

"When you present as a man, you are deceiving the people who believe in you," Titan said with steel in his voice.

Darro wrapped an Armenite commoner's tunic around her body and fastened it with a piece of rope. "That tone of voice was the same one you used to tell Ravana to leave. One would think a man of your intellect would learn something from past mistakes."

Her voice mocked him and her eyes measured him and found him wanting, a seasoned warrior's stare from a woman's face. And her hair was long, but shaved at the sides like a man's. Her unorthodox and contradictory appearance made him truly uneasy.

"You live a lie," Titan said.

Darro snorted and her stallion, Winta, put his ears back. "When a man is a Kí, he is a spy, an asset to the kingdom. If a woman is a Kí, she's a liar? Really?"

"There are no woman Kís," Titan said.

"I beg to differ." Darro cast him a look under her eyelids. "Besides," she said, turning now to disguise her horses. "Are you sure you're the right person to teach me on deceit? It's a nice collection of armor you have beneath the palace."

A rush of heat burned through Titan's skin. She was so very direct, so very derisive.

"I do as I do to try to help people I would not otherwise be able to reach – not to deceive anyone," he said.

"And why do you think I'm doing this?" Darro asked. "For fun? For pleasure?" She cast a glance back his way. "If my conscience allowed me, I'd get in a boat and sail from this land and never return."

"I don't believe you," Titan said. He didn't hear a lie in her words but at this point, he didn't trust either Darro or himself to know the difference. "You enjoy this game. You enjoy fooling people. Your words tell me that, even as you swear otherwise."

Darro's horses were fast taking on the appearance of work horses. The stallion's ears were still pressed back and he'd started pawing the ground, angry, as though he understood Titan's words.

"Well, you know what they say?" Darro took her time to respond. "Every Kí with the perfect disguise will search forever for that one person who can see through it." It was an old Corinthian saying and it was talking less about actual spies and more about love. Darro looked back at him, and he couldn't read her expression.

"If you're trying to seduce me," he said, "I'd advise you to stop. I would never accept a woman who can lie as easily as breathe."

Darro paused while strapping up the stallion's hooves.

"Ever thought," her voice was soft, "that there must be something truly broken inside you, to only feel like yourself when you're pretending to be someone else?"

The sharp barb struck its target.

"You know nothing of me," he said.

"Nor you of I."

"So hold your tongue."

"Hold yours!" Darro said, rounding on him. "You'd be using it to pleasure a witch right at this moment if we hadn't intervened."

Titan blinked, unsure of how to even respond to that. Before he could try, his attention was distracted by a shadow appearing behind the waterfall. It grew rapidly larger and closer, until Anakis stepped through. The giant went to Darro and embraced her, thumping her back like two soldiers would. Then he looked down at Titan and his stare darkened and fists clenched. He went to move toward him, but Darro held the giant back. Anakis grunted.

"I know," Darro muttered darkly. "Trust me. I know." She took a vessel of a dark dust-like substance from her pack and poured it all over her hair, following it with a jar of water from the falls. Her hair changed color to black. She tied it at the base of her neck and cleaned the dark stains off her face. Titan watched as she skillfully used her pastes, clay and make-ups to completely transform her face into that of an Armenite commoner at least three times her age. When she was done, she quickly repacked the saddlebags and spoke to Anakis.

"Through Messel, Anak – meet before the Sentinels." The big man gave a nod. He reached out and put a hand on Darro's shoulder.

"It'll be alright," she reassured him. He grunted. "Oh, I will," she said. "If he makes a wrong move." She glanced at Titan.

Anakis took hold of Winta and Naro's reins and started to lead them deeper into the cave, casting hard eyes down on Titan as he passed him.

"Anakis," Darro called, and he paused to look back. "Be careful."

They looked at each for a moment longer, words passing between them unsaid, then he kept moving.

Darro came over and crouched beside Titan, avoiding the burn of his stare.

"Travelers on the road don't smell this fresh. They stink."

She yanked the cork out of the bottle in her hand and Titan jerked his head away from the smell that leapt out.

"Let me guess, the spray from a skunk cat on heat and the sweat from a mountain gorilla's balls," Titan muttered.

His words caught Darro by surprise and she laughed out loud, then stopped.

"Worse."

She sprinkled the liquid onto Titan's tunic and her own, then cut the ropes around his wrists. He went to touch his face but she slapped his hand away before he could smudge the disguise. Nobody had slapped him on the wrist since he was three years old. Darro held a dart up in front of Titan's face.

"This poison will knock you flat as soon as it touches your skin. I'm accurate. Try to run and you'll see."

"What happens if it gets on your skin?" he asked, a threat behind his words.

"Nothing. I'm immune," she returned.

"What do you want from me?" Titan asked her, and Darro gave him a look that said they'd already had this conversation.

"No, I understand you're trying to keep me alive, but why? What do you get out of this?"

"I told you," Darro said. "I walk the righteous path and all who walk the righteous path —"

"Are brother," Titan finished. "I know. But you are not a man, so we cannot be brothers."

Darro's eyes focused on his.

"You're trying to keep me alive, but does it matter what I want?"

"If I was convinced that you had full understanding and comprehension of the nature of the threat against you, then yes, but I'm not," Darro told him.

"Why do you need to be convinced? It's my life."

"I really don't think you've seen much death, Lord Liege," Darro said, in that way that sent his anger through the roof. He controlled it.

"I've seen enough," he said.

"Then come." She stood up. "To Dolma."

"Into the lion's mouth?" Titan asked.

"No, the witch's," Darro said, flashing a grim smile.

Chapter 21
Eli

HYDRIA

FARNORTHERN HALOS (BLED)

As the guards dragged Eli through the tunnels, the fear of had what happened, what could have happened, and what needed to happen materialized into very real pressure bearing down on his damaged body.

"Calm down," he whispered, and clenched his hands to stop their shaking. He cast his eyes around, searching for focus, for direction in the pitch dark where everything looked identically black. He almost started giggling hysterically, but slapped a hand over his mouth.

Diamond's face came into his mind, her voice whispering, *"Don't forget to fly ..."*, just the way she'd said it as he and Ismail had been entering LaNoria with the strong possibility that neither would be coming out. The meaning of the imp-breed saying was complex, but could be very loosely translated to "keep breathing because I love you".

Part of him had known the truth since he'd woken at Headquarters.

A part that he'd ignored.

Diamond was gone.

Eli doubled over, feeling like a giant fist had slammed into his gut. The demons dragged him on by his arms while he sobbed, trying to muffle the sound but unable to stop, the grief completely overwhelming him. He wasn't sure how long he cried, but when he finally stopped, his eyes were swollen and burning and his chest ached so badly every breath felt like shards of glass stabbing his heart.

He rubbed a shaking hand over his face. The guards had taken him deeper into Bled, where the flame torches were even sparser and the darkness stretched on until Eli felt suffocated by it. Lights flashed across his vision and it was several moments before he realized they weren't in his eyes, they were on the walls. A shaky smile touched his lips. Fireflies and glow worms twinkled in the darkness. As he passed them, Eli brushed a hand across the shining forms, picking up some of the glow bugs and putting them on the inside collar of his dress, so quickly the demons didn't notice.

They reached a corridor of cells, and as the ratha pushed him toward an open door, he caught a glimpse of someone through the bars of the last cell, wearing chains and a mask. *The King.* Eli silently counted the number of cell doors between his own and King Apollo's. Then, with a push from one of the demons, he found himself in a cave-like cell with black rock walls, a chair and table, a candle, and a drain in one corner. It was a dark, claustrophobic space, but all things considered, it could have been a whole lot worse.

Another lesser demon came in and put water, a slab of bread and bloody meat, parchment and ink, and a pair of trousers big enough to cover his legs three times down on the table. Then the guards left and locked the door behind them.

Finding himself alone, with his mind racing, Eli stood up and sat back down about twenty times before he forced himself to stop. Nelly poked out the top of his dress and wound around his neck.

"I'm sorry I got you into this, girl," he whispered. He patted her soft fur and felt his heart rate slowing and his logic returning to him. His drug patches had lost much of their potency and his pain had increased, but so had his clarity. He'd actually known the answer to Mordan's problem as soon as he'd seen it, but he'd learned from the commander that letting an enemy see your full hand is a mistake. So he took the quill and dipped it in the ink and filled the parchment with equations and workings out, as though it had taken him some time and effort to reach the answer. Once he was finished, he stood cautiously and moved toward the door of the cell, standing on his tiptoes to peek through the bars.

There were no guards directly in front of his door but he could smell the ratha odor in the air. He inspected the lock and saw that he could definitely pick it, especially with the bunch of blades and other implements he'd collected at the arena, but he couldn't be sure that there wasn't a guard somewhere close out there who would bust him. He needed another way out. He looked around the cell, his eyes settling on the drain. He went over and examined it, finding it less primitive than he'd thought it would be. It was a large, round metal pipe with a grid over the top. Eli used one of the blades, made of sapphire, to pry up the grid. He moved it aside and peered down into the darkness. The smell was foul, but not unbearable, and just on eyeball estimation Eli thought his head could fit through it. He had leaned farther down to cautiously test his theory, when the blade he was holding suddenly clattered against the side of the pipe, dragging his hand with it. Eli gasped and whipped back his hand but the blade stayed there, the metal parts of it magnetized. Eli's eyes widened and he reached for the blade, having to use pressure to take it off. He felt the pipe with his hand and found it vibrating.

"It's an electromagnate," Eli whispered to Nelly with excitement. Someone who could harness magnetism was close by, and he was charging up Eli's cell. A plan formed in his mind and Eli acted quickly, boosted by a flash of hope. He removed his dress and cut strips off the long trousers, using them to tie the various metal implements onto his arms and his knees. Then he lowered himself feet-first into the pipe. The metal weapons clung to the walls of the pipe, allowing him to shuffle slowly downward instead of hurtling headlong without control.

But before he could begin his descent, he heard a rattling at his door. Eli leapt up. He didn't have time to undo all the weapons, so he threw the dress back on over it all, kicked the grid back into place and dashed to the chair, leaping into it so quickly it rocked onto two legs and almost toppled over. He righted it just as the cell door swung inward and several guards entered. They snatched up the parchment along with Eli and marched him out. Fears tore through his mind as the guards led him even deeper into the heart of the buried city. Had Mordan changed his mind? Would he be killed before he had a chance to reach King Apollo? As they walked, Eli picked up on a distant sound echoing in the tunnels behind them – *ech ech*, *ech ech*. His blood ran cold. The Ripper had found him.

It was with some relief, but mostly terror, when they reached a gigantic black door that opened up into someone's workshop, cluttered with books and scrolls and contraptions that reminded Eli of his own laboratory. The guards left Eli standing in the middle of the room, holding his parchment, then backed away quickly, vanishing. Eli could hear a muffled voice somewhere beyond a wall of books separating one section of the chamber from another. He inched toward the sound and peeped around the books, and saw Mordan-Grieg talking to a dark form made of smoke or mist.

For a moment an eyeless face solidified in the mist and Eli's stomach lurched. He'd seen that face once before, when they'd brought the commander, Silho, Diega, Christy and Caesar back from Omar Montanya. The form of a man, who they'd believed was the Indemeus X, had chased them through the portal and tried to drag them back down. And now the Indemeus was here speaking with the demon king. Eli couldn't believe his eyes. He started shivering and couldn't stop. He couldn't make out what the pair were saying, but Mordan's body language suggested that he was upset, maybe even pleading.

The misted form of the Indemeus flared, and Eli jolted, backing away from the books until he struck the side of a table. Stretched across it was what appeared to be a map of the universe. Heavy black lines running across it had separated it into distinct bands. The bands were numbered first wave, second wave and so on. Eli studied the map, seeing that each band had a number of planet names inside it. The second wave included Praterius and Omar Montanya, and in the third wave he read Bandos, Eumaios, Eradanis, Meteor and Aquais. In the seventh he spotted Hydria, the world where he now stood. He realized with a start that this was the Indemeus' plan – this was his blueprint for destruction. Eli felt eyes on him and instantly took a step back. Mordan-Grieg was standing behind him, a smile plastered on his face and his eyes flashing a warning. Eli felt the sweat breaking out on his skin. What if Mordan found all the objects strapped to him? Nelly crouched under his wing, trembling.

"I realize I gave you until day's end," Mordan said, his voice genial, "but I changed my mind. Have you solved it?"

"I haven't finished it," Eli rushed. "I mean, I *have* finished. It's not perfect, but I think I've solved it, at least I hope so." He offered the parchment to Mordan and he took it, watching Eli a moment longer before lowering his eyes to the paper.

"So you have," he said. "Well done. What's your name?"

"Eli," he said.

"Don't like it. Your name from now on is Tick."

"As in the ectoparasite, or the sound a clock makes?" Eli asked before he could stop himself.

Mordan gave his too-wide clown grin and said, "Neither. What do you think of the outfit, by the way?" He pulled at the skin of his cheek like a mask and it stretched wider than it should, his eye socket moving off his eye.

"It's very – convincing," Eli managed.

Mordan let the skin snap back into place and said, "Good. That was the look I was going for."

The demon king's gaze shifted to the table and the Indemeus' blueprint.

"Do you know what you were looking at?" he asked Eli, who recognized more dangerous territory.

"Yes – I mean *no*." Eli's face broke out into guilty red blotches.

"Yes or no, Tick?" Mordan's eyes flashed.

"No – no – I have a speech impediment. I'm sorry."

"Oh, that's unfortunate," Mordan said, almost kindly. "Do you know what my usual cure for a speech impediment is?"

Eli shook his head.

"Cut the head off – no more impediment." He grinned, and Eli gulped.

"You're looking at the work of the Indemeus X – do you know who that is?"

"No," Eli said very convincingly.

Mordan nodded and murmured, "Of course he doesn't. Let's just say it's a plan but there's a problem – here-ish." He pointed to the darkness between the second and third band. "And this," he waved the paper Eli had given him, "is part of the solution, a very small part. The Almighty was working on it, before he decided to become less ... *cooperative*." He spat the word out. "He's the reason we're all still here," Mordan continued. "His mind – there's no one quite like him, no mind quite like his – until now." His eyes fixed onto Eli's face.

"You'll continue his work. You'll finish it. Say yes, not no, Tick. Or just nod if you're too scared."

Eli nodded.

"Good boy." Mordan patted him on the head. "Yes, good," he added in a much more bestial tone, as though he was talking to himself, his hand still resting on the top of Eli's head. Eli tensed, expecting something terrible, but Mordan seemed to snap out of it.

He aimed his grin at Eli. "Now, what can I do for you? I'm firm but fair – no, I truly am, I am a fair man."

You're not a man, you're a demon wearing a man, Eli thought.

"Tell me something you want."

"I'm happy just to serve you," Eli said, trying not to sound too much like a suck-up.

Mordan laughed. The sound was out of sync with the movements of his mouth, and Eli's skin crawled.

"Come on now, Tick, everyone wants something. Tell me what you want – anything, you can have it."

Eli's mind ran through many things – home, the Ripper, the trackers, Sanfrass. He knew Mordan would almost certainly twist whatever he said. But the demon king was waiting and he had to say something.

"When I first came in, when they put me with the women. There was one woman who had a child with her and they took the girl away. What I want is for them to be reunited safely and given mercy – living mercy. That's what I wish for," Eli said.

He saw something move in Mordan's gray stare. Not the showing of some creepy tentacle or parasite, but emotion, just a momentary sliver.

"Done. Get to work – Eli," Mordan said in a monotone without shifting his gaze from Eli's face.

The guards swarmed back into Mordan's quarters and gathered up Eli and all the paper Mordan pointed to.

After they left Eli in his cell with more water, more bread and more ink so he could find them a way to bring about the destruction of the universe, Eli's mind whirled back around to the drain. He needed to get to King Apollo and he needed to get them out, right now. He had a feeling he wouldn't survive his next encounter with the demon king.

Chapter 22
Ramses

HYDRIA

NORTHERN HALOS

THESELON (TRADERS ROAD)

A thousand steps were lost behind them. Ahead lay ten thousand more. The road they traveled appeared awash with molten gold as the sun sank ever lower into the night. Soon the whole world would be lost to the shadows, and to the despair that darkness brings. They had been riding for a good two sevens straight now, eating, sleeping and pissing from the saddle. As Aron had said, they were taking all the hard roads, constantly changing their disguises, and still every time they even thought about stopping, the alarm bird Morrison started squawking. They were being hunted without relent. Ramses gritted his teeth as a sharp pain surged through the leg he no longer had. It made him light-headed and he leaned heavily on Grayweather, who whickered, distressed by his pain. He patted the geld's neck to reassure him as the feeling passed and he could breathe again.

The brothers rode ahead of him, Vitali in the lead and Aron just behind. Over this time, Ramses' clarity had come and gone. The more he remembered, the more confused he felt, but there were two things of which he was now absolutely certain. One, if someone, somewhere, felt inclined to inscribe a list entitled "The Things that Annoy Vitali Storon", it would be without a doubt the longest list in the history of existence, and, two, Aron Storon knew each and every item on said list and he took a certain quiet pleasure in randomly enacting them and watching his brother boil.

It had begun shortly after dawn that day. First it was the tapping – Aron drumming a tune on his saddle until Vitali shot back a glare, at which point Aron proceeded to sniffing, giving a brief, sharp sniff every few moments, on and on and on. Vitali finally glared at him again with severe annoyance, which led to Aron grinding and clacking his teeth, which upon another stare became flicking, and then chewing, and then scratching. When Vitali snarled at him, the scratching changed to coughing, then throat clearing and then humming, which soon became singing – but it wasn't until now, after a full day of teasing, as Aron began singing a song and alternating between the female and male parts of the tune, that Vitali truly snapped.

He spun his horse around and with a maniacal yell charged at Aron. When he was close enough, he leapt off his stallion and tackled Aron from his saddle. They went rolling down a ditch into a field below, exchanging punches as they went. Ramses kept riding. The brothers threw down frequently enough for him to know there was no need for concern. Their horses continued plodding forward as well, and Morrison flew up and perched on Aron's empty saddle. The blue bird looked back at Ramses and raised its eyebrows. How a bird could have eyebrows he did not know, but this one did. Aron had told him they'd found Morrison on the border of Cytisus. Ramses thought about the white peacock that had flown to the rooftop before Ravana had appeared. It had seemed to be warning them. He shivered and drew his raw-spun cloak closer around his body.

The thin, rough fabric did little to shield him from the wet wind sweeping from the icy peaks of Kirith-Jerom. The great mountain ranges loomed over them, casting far shadows across much of the outer plains of Theselon. Even in the full heat of Mascald, these shadows were cold and the nights freezing, made colder still by the constant drizzle from the tumultuous sky. The brothers ran back up from the ditch, Aron with a split lip and in high spirits, Vitali a black eye and blacker mood.

"Judging from the map we'll make Finnanbar before middle night," Aron said, as he jumped back onto his horse.

Finnanbar and its closest neighboring town, Birr, stood due east of Leon, Theselon's capital city, directly on the old trade road between the capital and the mountains.

"What do you think Morrison?" Aron asked the bird, who for once remained silent.

"We might be in luck, Ramses of Ohai." Aron grinned at him.

Neither were large towns, but they were the largest they had passed through in many a day and that meant there was likely an inn, maybe even one that served food. The thought of a hot supper, even a turnip soup or a stew, made Ramses' mouth water. They'd been existing on a poverty diet of stale bread, pickled onions and pottage, a gray gruel the commoners made of moldy oats, for so long he didn't think he could stand to take one more bite, but then hunger would hit hard and he'd go back to it with gratitude.

From thoughts of food, his mind leapt to the possibility of a bed, even a simple straw bundle or a mat on a dry floor seemed like the greatest of luxuries compared to sleeping on the run, battling the cold, the bloodsucking bugs and the threat of capture. Ramses licked his dry lips and grimaced. His breath was so awful one puff would be enough to kill a man. On the positive side, the stink nicely complemented the rank odor of the rest of his body, unbathed, unshaven, with clothes so filthy they clung to his skin. They were pretending to be skid-poor farmers looking for work; the role really didn't require much acting. A bitter laugh escaped him. In such a short time everything had changed. Vitali shot a look at him. He wasn't a man who tolerated random laughter. Or anything.

"Do you think Finnanbar may have an inn?" Ramses asked, his voice embarrassingly tremulous. He hoped the brothers hadn't noticed, but they could scarcely miss it. He cleared his throat.

Vitali gave a grunt and Aron said, "That means yes in bog swine."

Ramses smiled despite everything, cracking his lips and making them bleed. The taste of iron filled his mouth. He looked up as the sky rumbled above them and the winds gusted from the mountains, bringing with them the scent of more rain. They rode past an old beggar shambling along the road and Ramses took some bread from his saddlebag and threw it down to him as they passed. He caught it with a grateful noise.

Ramses dragged his cloak tighter again and wiped a hand across his nose. The urge to seek a toilet struck suddenly.

He knew he had a limited time to act before soiling himself disastrously in front of the brothers. He pulled on Grayweather's reins, sliding off the geld's back and grabbing his walking stick. He hobbled and slid down the side of the ditch and into the sugar cane field below, seeking some measure of privacy. He leaned heavily on his stick and squatted down. When the terrible pressure began to subside he cast his hand around in the dimming light, searching for a leaf. Soon after they'd started out he'd had the extreme misfortune of using the wrong leaf for wiping, and the experience was still strong in his mind. He felt across the backs of the leaves he touched, avoiding the hairy ones. His hand closed over a large smooth leaf. *Perfect*, he thought. He didn't hear the rustle of sugar cane behind him or the creature drawn in by his scent. It wasn't until a low rumbling growl sounded right behind him that he realized he wasn't alone.

Ramses froze, holding his breath as the growl continued, building force. He gripped his walking stick hard as the sound broke off into a snarl and the cane parted in a rush. Ramses used the stick to propel himself sideways and he landed on his back with the beast already on top of him, saber-sharp teeth snapping toward his neck. He shoved his stick sideways into the mountain lion's mouth and it bit the stick clean in half. Ramses tried to wrestle the gigantic creature's face away from him but it strained forward, hot breath on his face. Suddenly the creature was shunted to one side and Ramses saw the beggar standing over him, holding up a flaming stick, which he waved in the cat's face. It blinked into the heat, snarled, then took off.

"My gratitude," Ramses said to the beggar, who looked down at him. Ramses saw in the glow of the flames that it was August.

"*Tato*," Ramses said, reaching up for him.

Before August could speak, Aron and Vitali came crashing through the cane, swords in hand.

"What was that?" Aron said, his voice raised. "It sounded huge!"

"A mountain lion," Ramses said.

"Are you hurt?" The younger brother inspected Ramses while Vitali kept lookout in case the cat returned. There were some claw and tooth marks on his arms, but nothing serious.

"You're one lucky man, Ramses of Ohai," Aron told him. "How did you fight it off?"

"With luck," Ramses murmured. He looked around for August, but he was gone.

Morrison swooped down onto Aron's shoulder and released his high-pitched warning.

"Come on!" groaned Aron in frustration. The brothers grabbed Ramses up, one on either side of him, dragging him up the ditch.

"Gideon's men, no doubt," Vitali grunted.

As they mounted with haste, Vitali said, "Forget Finnanbar, we'll ride west for Taor. It's more off the track and Kirithi are less likely to check their own towns. West." He pointed.

"Indeed, west," Aron confirmed.

"As I just said."

"Except you're pointing north. That's west," Aron indicated.

Vitali's eyes narrowed. "Don't think to tell me the manner of direction, whelp. I was navigating these forests before you were even a thought." A leaf, dislodged by a gust of wind, fluttered down near Vitali's face and he cut it down with his dagger as though he was cutting down the foulest of foes.

"Just ride!" he snarled.

They lunged into a gallop and Ramses cast a glance back, searching for the soldiers. Instead he saw August, standing by the side of the road.

Chapter 23
Ev'r

HYDRIA

FARNORTHERN HALOS (LAUREION)

It hadn't been the most joyous of reunions with Brabel and Jude. The two groups had exchanged half a glance and a few words and then separated, sitting on opposite sides of the cavern room they'd found to hole up in. Not long after, Christy Shawe had appeared from farther down, where the other three had stopped, and said, "Which one of you freeloaders is coming with me on first watch?"

Ev'r gave him the crudest gesture she knew, while Ismail just growled. Jude had already opened up his robot and was trying to bring it back to life using components from his own arm. So Silho was the only option.

She headed back toward the entrance with Shawe.

Ev'r stretched her legs out in front of her. They'd re-gened her wounds from Threegulls and from the haunt, but they were still aching.

"You should rest," Ismail said, going through the packs, discarding everything electronic to lighten their load and taking inventory of what they had left. He handed her a packet of swivels but she waved it away.

"I'm not hungry or tired," she said.

"I know," Ismail replied. "But you should eat and sleep while we can."

"Only if you do," she said. He gave her a smile and put his arms around her, dragging her down onto the dirt and holding her close. She traced a finger along the three bloodline marks of his genetic heritage, the scullion Blackwater Wolf, the bloodline they shared, along with human-breed shark and bat blood. Her touch came to rest on his chest, scarred deeply with the symbols of dark magics. Behind them his robotic heart thudded solidly.

"Are you angry at me for using the magics?" she asked him straight.

"No," he said. "Why would I be?"

"You hate it."

"I do hate it and I always will, but you were using it to try to save Eli, and then us ... Is it even dark magics when it's used for that?"

Ev'r thought over the question. Ismail had never really asked about magics before and she wanted to give an answer that wouldn't disturb him. "I don't think of magics as dark or light. I just see those words as a way for others to understand it. Dark curses can be used to save someone by inflicting injury on someone else, and light enchants can manipulate otherwise positive things, like love, for selfish purposes – it's just that the witches that use the dark are usually malevolent." She could feel Ismail's body tightening. "For me it's the intention behind the curse or enchant that matters. It's the fundamental stand, and it's a choice the witch makes, not once, but every time they use magics."

"Do you—" Ismail struggled with the words. "Do you ever feel like hurting someone just for the sake of it?"

"No," Ev'r responded. "Except Shawe."

Ismail snorted.

He pulled her even closer and said in a smaller voice, "Sometimes I feel like hurting people just for the sake of it, but I don't think that's really me, I think it's just the militia in my head ... and the witch. I can control it. I guess that's what matters?"

He sounded so uncertain and Ev'r said, "Neither of us started off wanting to hurt anyone." Remembering them as children hurt, but she forced herself to let the memories in. "Did we?"

"No," Ismail agreed. He held her hand, and their fingers locked together.

"I blame you," she whispered.

"What's new?" he murmured, kissing her.

They lay in each other's arms until Ismail fell into a restless slumber, then Ev'r sat up. Her head felt heavy again and her thoughts were flipping fast, like the pages in a book. She slid her journal out of her pack. Transferring the images and words from the book in her mind to the book in her hand had been one of the only things that had helped over the year cycles. She opened the journal and flicked through to a blank page, then started drawing. When she finished, she saw a sketch of a Ravien staring back at her. She wrote beneath it: *Ravien; Class: Demon, Subclass: Draconis, Order: Were.*

Ev'r closed the book on the picture and stood. She lay her coat down over Ismail and rubbed the chill in her arms, smoothing across the gold bands she wore over her bloodline marks as she headed down toward the sound of tinkering.

The Ar Antarian sat by himself on a boulder, still working on his arachnid robot. One of his arms was all opened up, his handsome face set in concentration. He looked up at her.

"Keets."

"You think it's a good move disabling yourself now, right when you may need every strength you have, just to save a robot?"

"SevenM's not just a robot."

"That's exactly what it is. No matter how many names you give it."

"I don't expect you to understand, Ev'r," he said quietly.

"Why, because I'd never be stupid enough to think an inanimate object loves me?"

His back tensed and his hands faltered, but then he let it go and said, "Machine-breeds are people too. It's a fact; it doesn't require your agreement."

From farther down the cavern they heard the murmur of Kane and the Fen talking.

"Remember," Ev'r said. "You wouldn't have turned on him even if it meant your life, and look at you all now."

Jude nodded. "Things change. People. Like you. The old you would never have gone after those map pieces unless it meant gold for you, and you would never have come for Eli."

To hear her thoughts spoken aloud unnerved her more than she wanted to admit, even to herself. The old her was the Ev'r who had survived everything.

"You care for Eli," Jude told her, looking up from his work. "Love changes you, sometimes for the better, sometimes for the worse – but it always changes you."

"Poetic. You should write a book that no one will buy. Your brother was a poet too, and a philosopher, and look where it got him," she said, speaking of Jude's half-brother Kry, who had led the machine-breed rebellion against the Ar Antarians before Caesar K-Ruz had ended him.

Jude nodded and said, "He was also a megalomaniac and a psychopath. I've made my peace with my past, my family, my history – maybe you should too."

The words struck a place in Ev'r's chest that she hadn't expected. She gave a faint smile to hide it and said, "Noted, your majesty."

She left Jude to his tinkering and truth bombs and headed farther down the tunnel. Picking fights with pacifist intellectuals was completely unsatisfying. She stepped quietly as she neared the next room. Kane's skills were out, which meant he wouldn't sense her footsteps or her body heat as he usually would. She peered around the corner and saw the two of them sitting, facing each other, the Fen stitching up the wounds in Kane's hand and talking about her adopted Omarian son. If the Fen was looking for comfort she was looking in the wrong place. The neon glow from their plant-derived light source made the scars on Kane's face stand out thick and white. No one could survive scars like that and stay warm and fuzzy.

Kane put a hand on his own shoulder and squeezed.

"Something out?" fairy girl asked.

He gave a nod and she stood up and moved behind him, massaging his shoulder.

The touch started out perfunctory, trying to push back in whatever had pushed out, but then, as Ev'r watched, it became something else. She saw them almost falling into it, that motion, that closeness, that contact. It was hypnotic in a way, and the touching flowed to kissing and the kissing became passionate and then she pulled his pants down around his ankles and Ev'r looked away. She really didn't need to see it all. It didn't make her hot or even amused, it just made her feel bad inside, for many reasons.

She left them to it and headed back to Ismail, then stood at his feet, looking down at him sleeping, tormenting herself with thoughts of how it would feel if she saw him with another girl, until a clatter of rocks woke him with a start. He swung a punch before he realized there was nothing to hit.

"Ismail," she said to steady him and he blinked, catching himself, as Christy Shawe barged into the room. He was holding a glowing gem the shape of a star and looking very pleased with himself.

"Shift's over," he grunted. "You two are up."

"Is that for me?" Ev'r asked him, pointing to the rock.

He snorted.

"Fairy girl?" She gave him a sickly-sweet smile.

Shawe's cheeks reddened and he said, "She's worried about her kid."

"I wouldn't worry about that. Kane is in there comforting her in the full-body kind of way."

The gangster's face fell before he could hide it and he started blinking as though he'd been hit in the face with pepper spray.

"Fair enough." He struggled to maintain his tough exterior while he was backing away. As he turned and left, he threw the gem against the wall and it shattered into a million glittering pieces.

"When people without hearts discover love," Ev'r smiled at Ismail.

"Maybe someone is saying that about us," he told her, always the more reasonable one.

"People can say whatever they like," she replied and leaned in to kiss him.

They heard more footsteps. Ev'r thought it was Shawe returning to pick up the pieces of his pride off the ground, but then Brabel came around the corner.

"The sun's dropping. We can move out in the cover of dark. Can you still use your echo-location?" she asked Ismail.

"Yes, but it's coming and going. My nocturnal sight is still working though," he added.

"Good. Jude has some nocturnal capacity too, if he hasn't disabled it. We just have to know we can keep going if the Canderlight fuse extinguishes. Mine broke in the jump, Diega has the spares. I'll have to get one from her," Silho said, sounding as though she'd rather do anything but that.

She started to move past them, but Ev'r stepped into her path and Ismail stood up as well.

"You don't want to go down there," Ev'r said.

Silho eyed her with suspicion, and Ev'r could see the thoughts running through her mind. "Why not?"

"Your commander and the Fen are busy," Ev'r told her, and it was much less fun than it should have been. To Brabel's credit she didn't even flinch, but her skin heated up so quickly that Ev'r had to step back. Silho went to go around her, but Ev'r stopped her again.

"You don't want to go down there," she repeated.

Silho stared her down, her eyes fiery. Ismail shuffled forward, clearly unsure of what he should be doing. Brabel pushed forward again and Ev'r grabbed her burning hot arm. Silho moved fast, pulling free of Ev'r's grip and then shoving her back against the wall. Ev'r had thought that without her skills Brabel was basically useless, but she'd been quickly proven wrong. Brabel was still strong and fast – the real deal, as people said. She'd already been tested more times than a soldier triple her age. It was just lucky, Ev'r supposed, that the girl was currently incapacitated. Maybe it was lucky they both were, clearly neither of them was the "talk first" type. Jude walked in, watching the exchange with wary eyes, his robot in a sling behind him.

"Let me explain something to you," Ev'r said. "You go in there and tear up the place, you're just going to end up embarrassing yourself. Do you understand? It's all about control with Kane. If he can't control you, it'll punish him far more than going in there and kicking his face in. Pain, violence, they're his old friends – that's his world."

Brabel let go of Ev'r and stepped back.

"And let's face it," Ev'r continued. "If you wanted an easy ride you would have chosen his highness over there, not Copernicus Kane. You knew what you were getting yourself into."

Silho stared at Ev'r with those blazing eyes, then turned and left the way she'd come in.

As she went, the Fen and Copernicus Kane appeared on the other side. Jude moved away from them, avoiding eye contact.

"Who's fighting? We heard sounds," fairy girl said.

"No one," Ev'r said. "Those sounds were just the echo of you two pounding each other."

A thud came from the entrance to the ruins above.

"Trutt," Ev'r cursed, snatching up her bag. Shawe had unlocked the door. Silho wasn't going to kill Kane, she was just going to get herself killed instead. The group ran up through the ruined building until they found the entrance.

Silho and Shawe were standing on the hilltop some distance away, silhouetted against the dim glow of the Hydrian sun, sinking small and green in the far distance. Shawe was smoking, one hand in his pocket, and Silho was crouched down touching the ground and reading patterns in the dirt.

"I'm getting stronger bursts of skill back," Ismail said as they walked over to them.

"Me too," Ev'r agreed. "The augmentor must be doing something different. You got something?" she asked Brabel.

"A flash of Eli," Silho said, her voice sounding flat. "Look," she said, pointing down to the plain below. "He ran through here."

Ev'r couldn't see a damn thing except bones, but Silho was an elite desert navigator. If she said there were tracks, there were tracks.

"Is he alright? Is he alive?" Ismail asked.

"Somebody grabbed him," Silho said. "Smashed him in the face."

A heavy uncomfortable silence hung over the group. They needed Eli there to break the tension with some bodily malfunction, but he'd been snatched. Eli was harmless. He wouldn't stand a chance.

"Are we at least in the right world?" the Fen said.

Silho stood up, but didn't turn. "This is it. I saw him too, King Apollo, chained up like Shah-Jahan described."

"Did you get a direction of either of them?" Kane asked Silho, business as usual.

"Due north, both of them."

"Maybe the same place?" Diega suggested.

Silho nodded. "It's crawling with ratha."

"We arm up and fall out," Kane gave the order. "All of us."

"Does this make us official trackers?" Ev'r said dryly. "I feel honored."

"Shut your mouth, Keets," the Fen warned her.

"Shut your legs, fairy girl," Ev'r shot back. "And just so I'm aware, is it tracker policy to stab your teammates in the back at the first possible chance, or is that just you being a podsucking gadfly?"

"Fall out," Kane repeated firmly before Diega could shoot back.

He stepped around them, close to Silho and she moved away to the other side of Shawe, the two of them moving off together, not waiting for Kane to take the lead. Ev'r looked around at the rest of them as they walked down the hill – blinded by rage, paralyzed by fear, overcome with desire, crippled by doubt, fooled by love ... Was there any emotion above dead inside that didn't render a person completely incapacitated and utterly useless? All the tension put her on a razor edge. The new her was one big raw nerve. It was trutting unacceptable.

Chapter 24
Harlow Darro

HYDRIA

ARMEN (DOLMA)

If the right time to completely expose oneself to judgment, humiliation and disdain does in fact exist, then it had been that moment. Just before that moment, she'd struck against a solid wall within herself – she didn't want to be faceless anymore, so she'd shed the armor and the mask and showed him her real face. The Titan's reaction had hurt, and not in the sense of passing insult or hatred from enemies, both of which had entirely no effect on her, but the kind of hurt that had made her question everything about herself and everything about life; the kind of hurt that ate into a person's soul and spread doubt like a disease into every part of them, making them feel unworthy of life.

And then somewhere between Aghamore and Dolma, Titan attempted an apology. Attempted, because kings and lieges didn't apologize – ever. They never recanted or admitted error, and the words Titan had said were so foreign to him that he'd almost had to say them in a different accent from his own just to get them out. Luckily they were dressed as Armenites so he had that excuse for sounding so strange. It was awkward enough as it was. Harlow lowered her head to hide her smile in the scarf around her neck. Titan sat beside her on Anakis' cart, holding Alban's reins while the big workhorse pulled them forward along Votan Road, the final stretch to Dolma.

Titan had said something along the lines of, *My reaction was rash and born from pain and frayed wit – if I had been under normal circumstances it would have been very different.* And since that admission, he'd been trying to converse with her civilly, clearly attempting to understand her, and it helped. Just the words alone had ended the pain and doubt inside her, but it was also frightening. How could one person have so much sway that she would change how she saw herself based on his words? If it was the Lord King Apollo himself, then she would have felt safe in his wisdom, but the Titan? He wasn't the same man. The world was still surprising for him and he didn't even seem to know himself, so how could he know her? And why should she let him have the power to hurt her so badly? So she hadn't spoken much of any import to him as they'd traveled their road, just answered in the way a Kí does, many words, no substance. He'd realized, but still kept trying.

"Look, the walls of Dolma," Harlow said, and Titan glanced up from the shadows of his hood. Until now they hadn't encountered much on the hard roads they'd chosen, mostly just people flooding out from the capitals and pointedly minding their own business. There'd been only a few shady characters, with whom they'd dispensed quickly, and a handful of soldiers, who had ridden past with full haste, most of the blockades and military action concentrated on the more common stretches of road.

And there had been no sign of Ravana Nazar or her glooms, other than the occasional chill across their backs. This wasn't necessarily a good thing. The iron on Titan's mark had held well, but now it was weeping again and needed to be refilled. They just had to make it through the gates.

Harlow started to prepare, unfolding her tonic pouch on the floor in front of them. She selected a few vials – more sting for Titan's eyes, more stink for their clothes and the powder that would make their breath powerfully foul and their teeth turn brown. They already smelt fetid, and it was about to get worse, but it mustn't be overdone. It had to be repellent, but not utterly unforgettable.

While Titan handled the reins, Harlow applied the tonics to him – more pain syrup, more color around his swollen eyes. Her fingertips brushed against his skin and she felt a buzzing that muted all her aches, pains and worries and left her feeling light. The relief was addictive so she had been touching him as little as possible.

"Now this," she said in an Armenite accent, holding the breath powder up to his nose.

He jerked his head away and she said, "It wears off."

He gave her a savage look, so she tipped it into her own mouth, then breathed on him. He grimaced and she laughed.

'What's wrong?" she said, huffing the words out on purpose. "Is there something wrong?"

He pulled away. "That's truly repulsive."

"Oh yes," she said. "And we're going to need it."

She offered him his portion and he reluctantly took it, turning his white teeth brown and black and making him splutter.

Harlow smiled again. She lowered the bloodied cloth over his eyes and said, "Let me take over." Harlow put her hand on the reins, but he resisted. It was not in his nature to be a passenger, but it just wasn't realistic for a blinded man to be driving a cart. And they had to realistic, or they would be dead. She took the reins.

In the distance, the walls of Dolma had appeared stunted, but they grew ever-larger until they consumed the entire land and sky before them. Unlike some walled cities, where the walls were blank defense only, Dolma's outer walls were made up of buildings with open windows and many levels of housing. And the walls were not straight but staggered and uneven, as though one building had been built on top of another, and another after that, onward, without any regard for color, order or style. It was not majestic or beautiful like Corinth, or vast and ordered like Asta in Anacharasis, but it was formidable nonetheless, a gigantic metropolis sprawling across the Barbarian Plains with no sign that it planned to stop growing any time soon. Eagles circled high above the walls and red flags flapped in the winds, two long flags on either side of the entry gateway and many smaller ones from the windows and building tops.

The closer they rode the greener the ground they trod, nurtured by the run-off from the city. The first smells to hit Harlow's nose were iron and grilling pig meat. She saw Titan twitch. Corinthians didn't eat pigs or fish, considering both meats unclean. Harlow had found her own appetite for all meats had dropped off after she, Anak and the brothers had been in exile many years back. They'd been starving out in the Cytisian swamp and had happened across a drifter who had offered them a soup. They'd taken it with full gratitude and reveled in it, only to be told afterward that the meat had been man-meat.

"We're closing in," Harlow whispered to Titan as they joined the line of people looking to enter the gates. It was not as long as she'd anticipated, the traffic out seeming far busier.

"Relax your arms," Harlow said as the cart shuffled forward and Alban started snorting dust off his nose. Titan tried, but it wasn't in a warrior's training to relax anything.

"Clench your fists, now release them," Harlow tried. "Feel the difference?"

He gave a nod, managing to drop his tension a little. They rode forward in silence until it was their turn with the guards, who looked fatigued and bothered. It was close to shift turn and they'd had enough.

"Papers!" one guard barked at them. "Why do you seek entrance to the city?"

Harlow took their forged citizenship out of her tunic and handed it down.

"It's warm because it's been beside my breast," she said in the commoner's tongue. The guard caught a whiff of her body odor and breath and winced. "I see." He opened the papers delicately, trying to touch them as little as possible, glanced over them, then threw them back to her.

"The levy on all traders has gone up – you aware?" he asked them.

"They told us on the road," Harlow responded. "How are we supposed to make a crust with all these levies?" Complaining was part of the Armenite tradition.

"Tell someone who cares," the guard said, looking around their cart for anything of worth that he could confiscate. They'd disguised Alban with sores on his legs and mud through his coat, so the guards would see a horse who was more trouble than he was worth. It worked. The guard looked up at Titan, and Harlow saw his stare falter. She tensed.

"What happened to him then?" The guard nodded to the bloodied rag over his face.

"Pub brawl. Glass in the eye. Gruesome," Harlow said. "We'll have to see a healer."

The guard looked at her with suspicion. "Let's see it then."

As Harlow raised the cloth, she poured the vial she'd been holding down over Titan's forehead, and by the time the cloth was up, his eyes had swelled shut and were oozing a red and white pus-like substance, which also stunk horrendously like rot.

The guard screwed up his nose. "Gods." He fanned the air in front of his face. "Go on then," he growled. "And for pity's sake, wash yourselves."

He stepped aside and Harlow lifted the reins. Alban pulled the creaking cart forward, moving with a limp that he'd been trained to use on cue.

They didn't speak at all as Harlow navigated them through Dolma's shadowy slums. It was a city of inequality in that way and many others; the nobility lived up near the sun and the poor languished in the darkness of below. She found the house and they rumbled into the dilapidated interior, out of sight from the street. There they stood on a secret platform that wound all the way up to a high apartment above, with no other entry. Once the floor was locked down, Harlow allowed a sigh of relief. Titan lifted off his blindfold and she quickly doused his face with an anti-serum, the swelling subduing immediately, leaving him with red rims and bloodshot eyes.

"Not bad. For a man who's never wiped his own arse," she said.

He took the insulting compliment without retort, no longer taking her bait. She led Alban into the next room, which had been converted into stalls for the horses. The placid draft horse nudged her gratefully as she poured out oats for him to eat while she untethered him. Titan helped her with the straps, removing them swiftly and skillfully. She could feel his eyes on her as she washed down Alban's coat and checked his hooves.

"What is it?" she asked when the feeling continued beyond comfort.

"I don't know of many ladies who would tend to their horse's needs before their own," he said.

"Then you're clearly not keeping the right company," Harlow replied, and saw him taking exception before he could stop himself. "I know many ladies who not only delay their own needs, but completely forgo them for the sake of their children and companion beasts."

A thought came to her mind of one of the Draul mining camps they had liberated. The people were starving and the women had been cutting bits off their own bodies to keep their children alive. They say time heals all, but she'd come to understand that that was just a lie.

"What are you thinking of?" Titan asked, his voice very still.

"Things I wish to forget," she replied honestly.

They left Alban to rest and walked out into the main apartment space, where Harlow started to warm water in a long tub and metal in a pot. As she did, Titan moved around the room, looking at her maps and scrolls, studying them closely.

"Your strategy is unique," he finally said.

"I'm a different race," she replied.

He nodded. "Farnortherner. When did you come here?"

"As a child."

"Why did you leave the Farnorth?"

"I don't remember. Actually, that's not completely true. I remember a lot of screaming."

Titan's eyes darkened. "Farnortherners used to travel here on occasion. I never saw one with my own eyes, but I knew they could sometimes be found near the Cys where they anchored their ships, but then they stopped coming and there hasn't been a one in many years. Perhaps something happened to your people?"

She remembered the Almighty telling her that her land had been overrun and all her people killed, that she could never go back. For all she knew, she was the last of her kind. It was a very lonely and confusing sort of feeling.

A long low horn blast echoed across the city and Titan went to the window. Harlow saw his back tense.

"The periphery army is marching out," he said, his voice hard. "The centers will follow and then the courts."

Harlow remained silent. She knew what he was thinking.

"I need to refill your wound," she said. He watched the soldiers marching out the front gate for a while longer before coming to her. He was holding his jaw tight and she saw his eyes drift toward the floor where the platform was locked.

"You should be in Ironeye. I know," she said. "But if you try, you'll be in your grave instead. And then what? Take off the tunic. Lie down on the table."

Titan did as she said and Harlow inspected the prime again before pouring metal into it. He didn't even grimace this time.

"Now to get rid of this stink and all the clay," she said. "Immersion is out of custom, I fully understand, but you're going to have to get into the tub or the smell will linger forever."

"What about you?" he asked, eyeing the warmed waters inside the tub.

"Me on this end, you on the other. Both keeping our hands to ourselves, just in case you think I'm trying to seduce you again."

Titan raised his chin and gave her a look. "As I've already mentioned, I spoke without full context."

"What are you saying now," Harlow asked, dragging off her tunic. "You want me to seduce you?"

She realized she was being tiresome and using the Corinthian language in a way that irritated him greatly, but he didn't flare, he just looked at her in a very similar way to how the Almighty had before him, with a silent contemplative patience.

She started unwrapping her undergarments and he said, "I'll turn around?"

"I look the same as every other woman naked," she replied. "And I know you've seen plenty, so no need. Unless there's risk of you being overcome by my great beauty," she added dryly.

She left only the metal yoke around her neck, which she never took off, and stepped into the long tub, sinking beneath the waters, welcoming the warmth. She started washing her face and breaking off the clay parts while Titan undressed and stepped in opposite her.

"Shall I turn my back?" she asked, just to be further infuriating.

He snorted and said, "Not unless there's risk of you being overcome by my great beauty."

That made her laugh.

He lowered himself very uncomfortably into the water and sat there looking like he was sitting on sharp spikes.

"The quicker you wash yourself, the quicker you can get out," Harlow told him, throwing over a bar of soap. Then she realized he may have been feeling uncomfortable from memories of Ravana's water attack and she gave a less smug response. "I can help you if you wish."

"It's been two years since I've been anywhere near a naked woman," Titan said. "It's best if I wash myself."

Harlow laughed again, and felt his eyes fixed on her face again. She glanced at him. He had paints running down all over his skin.

"You are – entirely singular," he said with caution.

"Are you trying to boost my wounded ego?" Harlow responded, scrubbing at her own face.

"No, I just wish for that to be heard."

"It's heard," Harlow confirmed. "However as you said yourself, you haven't been with a woman in two years, I think whomever was sitting here naked and within arm's reach would seem entirely singular."

"Then you'd be wrong," he said firmly.

"Here," she said, throwing him a dissolving tonic. "Your make-up is running."

He caught it and gave a grunted *Ivar*. It was a word the Almighty had favored as well.

She felt his eyes on her as she continued washing herself.

"Once I saw a person turn a herd of wild horses stampeding toward a cliff. Was that you?" he finally asked.

Harlow remembered the day well, but hadn't realized anyone had seen it.

"Could have been," she said, and he nodded, as though she'd confirmed it.

"Did you ever try to tell the King Sirion the truth of you after you were released from the iron?"

He tried to ask mildly, but she could tell it was a question of great import to him.

"Yes." Harlow looked into her memory, then quickly away.

"He didn't accept?" Titan was studying her carefully.

She shook her head.

"I don't want to lie," she said, being honest with him in a way she'd sworn never to do again after the cave. "But I know people are not ready for me to be a woman. I count you among the most progressive and intelligent in the halos and you were horrified. You, more than anyone, know what I'm capable of and that still wasn't enough."

He swallowed slowly contemplating the words, then said, "We're taught that men fight and women care for the children, by both genders. So it's how we believe. And there is reason behind that. You are an exception, do you understand, you are a singular exception. Women in general ..." he chose his words very carefully, "should not have to be exposed to the violence a warrior is exposed to."

"But they are," Harlow said. "The amount of times we've ridden into a town or a camp and found carnage. The men have been taken or gone to fight and the women are left there, and when they're attacked, they're left begging for mercy and screaming without any skills or weapons to defend themselves or their children because – they shouldn't be exposed to violence." She realized she'd raised her voice and lowered it. "*Should be* means absolutely nothing to me. The truth as I see it, Lord Liege, is that the main reason why women are not permitted to fight is man's fear of change beyond their control, not their gallantry. To have children and not have any way to defend them from torture or death." She shook her head. "Do you understand what that must feel like?"

Titan's face had gone very still again and she could see that he was listening intently to her words.

"I don't know what that must feel like," he admitted.

"It seems that if you accept having children, you have to accept that your own heart will rip from your chest and go walking about, away from you, finding its own path,"

Harlow said. "And I don't fear death at all – I don't think you do either – but the sound of a mother crying over the body of her child – it follows me everywhere. It haunts my every breath and it drives me to the brink of insanity!"

Her words hung between them until Titan broke the silence with his quiet response. "Fathers cry too." The words struck Harlow hard.

"Yes they do," she said after some time. "Forgive my rage. It's all too easy to blame."

She stood and stepped out of the bath, going to the cupboard, trying to compose herself. The conversation had hit upon all her weaknesses. She heard Titan stepping out of the water and walking over to her. She opened up the space behind the cupboard, revealing disguises and various armor.

"Armenite armor," she said. "It'll get us through the city and into the pipes."

She handed him a tunic, cintus and subs, which he wrapped around himself, then she started fastening the armor around him. She was touching too much skin for comfort but it couldn't be avoided. She worked in silence until Titan said, "Do you believe I incited this?"

"No," she admitted. She'd spoken the words when she'd been burning from his rebuke, but she hadn't meant it.

"You don't believe that?"

"She's a *Samyaza* – that's not your doing."

"I've read every scroll and book available to me and I've never seen the word."

"It's from the Book of Sighs," Harlow said. "And you don't have a copy because your great great grandfather had them all destroyed."

She bent low to fasten his boots.

"It didn't say much of them, only that Manah, the original demon of *Mĕthmalay*, was born to an angel mother called Ulex and a demon father called Belphanganor. Manah was the first of his kind, and when Ulex brought him into the heavens before the gods, he was sentenced to die. As he was struck down, his mother started crying and could not stop, flooding the lands with the salt of her tears, and in these stricken waters Manah was reborn in the image of his father, and he himself became father to many monstrous things."

She looked up and saw Titan watching her keenly. She knew they shared a passion for mythology.

"It sounds like myth," he said.

"Yes, but it's also true," Harlow told him. "There are demons in the waters of *Mĕthmalay*, and somewhere in her life Ravana has encountered one, who has filled her with the powers of Manah – in exchange for what, we don't know. There's great strength to it, you saw what she can do, but she's forfeited her life. She serves Manah now, and sooner or later he'll drag her into the sea and she will try to take you with her."

"Why?" he asked.

"Because she loves you."

"*Nea*. She doesn't love me!" He rejected the notion.

"She feels she does, and so she does."

A realization showed behind his eyes at the words and he lowered his head. "In my garden, I felt myself drowning in her, but I also felt something inside me fighting back. What was this thing?"

"Your power."

"My power from who? Another demon?" The struggle to say the words was clear on his face.

"No," Harlow told him. "It's from your ancestors. From our bloodline. It's not from evil. The same scroll talked about your forefathers being Watchers, protectors of the people from evil things. My race as well. We all started off quite similar before Hydria split in two."

"Are you saying you're also – different?" Titan asked.

"I don't know what I am," she admitted. "But I definitely feel something when you tap into your power."

"What?" he asked, studying her with those strange, beautiful eyes.

"I'm not sure. I do know that fire doesn't burn me."

"It doesn't? Not at all?"

She shook her head. "I was cast in iron and I have no scars and no burns at all."

He looked her up and down, realizing the truth of her words.

"Back at the cave," he said. "When I said there was nothing unnatural in this world, you said, 'What about you and the Lord King Apollo before you?' What did you mean? Did you know the Almighty?"

"Everyone knew of him." Harlow sidestepped the question.

Another horn blast echoed out across the city and Titan turned toward the window. It was a welcome distraction.

Chapter 25
Eli

HYDRIA

FARNORTHERN HALOS (BLED)

Eli threw off his dress and rechecked the implements he had tied to his arms and knees, then went back to the drain, lowering himself into it and clamoring downward. After some time, he looked back up and saw a small circle of light where he'd begun. His heart rate kicked up and a sudden panic to get back to the light hit him. He wasn't particularly claustrophobic, but this pipe was snug – very snug. He struggled to restrain himself, focusing on the feeling of Nelly's little claws digging into his wing, and forced himself to keep moving, finally finding a place where the pipe continued down but also split off to the side. He climbed into the side pipe, sliding along in slimy substances that he tried hard to ignore.

It was too dark to see anything at all, and that was probably a blessing. As he slid, Eli dragged his hand across the top of the pipe above him until he came to an upward facing pipe, then continued on, counting another seven of the same. He stopped at eight and squeezed himself upward into the pipe, which by his calculations should take him into King Apollo's cell.

Using his magnets he climbed up the pipe, his hopes rising as he finally spotted dim light above him. He moved a little faster, the light growing larger as he went, until he came to a grid above him. With almost unbearably cautious movement, careful not to make any noise, he pushed up the grid. Eli lifted himself and peeped out, and his heart leapt into his throat.

Just in front of him stood King Apollo, his arms stretched out on either side of him by chains attached to the walls, and his legs locked onto the ground. He still wore the mask and his head was hanging to his chest. As Eli struggled up out of the pipe, Apollo stirred and lifted his head. As his eyes met the king's Eli broke down and ran to him, throwing his arms around him and crying into his bare chest. His skin was humming from his electromagnate power and it faded all Eli's pain and sadness. It was exactly what he needed at that moment to help him keep going.

In the absence of pain he could gather his thoughts. He looked up into the king's unfathomably dark eyes and said, "King Apollo, I'm not sorry – I mean – *I am* sorry. I am so sorry for crying all over you. I just ..." He held back more tears and wiped his nose. "I'm Eli – Anklebiter. I'm not a king. We need your help. The Indemeus X, he's just about to take our world, and there was a foreseer who told a Dray captain, Shah-Jahan RaAhura, that he could stop the X, but we have no idea how except she said your name before she died, and we found your map pieces in our world with the enchant, and we were attacked again by the Ripper and Silho became a portal and I came here – and I got hit in the face – twice – and there's a girl – I think I'm in love – the darkness has started in Scorpia, it's the beginning of the end." He had to slap a hand over his mouth to stop his ranting.

There was movement from behind the cell door and Eli leapt into the shadows. After a few long moments of waiting and watching, he came back out to stand in front of the king.

He breathed deeply, then said in Corinthian, "I'm sorry."

Apollo's eyes flickered. It was his own language and Eli wondered how long it had been since he'd heard it.

"I'm here to get you out," Eli said. He undid Apollo's heavy mask and lifted it away, revealing his face which, although it was as scarred as his body and half concealed by his bushy beard, was still undeniably regal. Eli reached for Apollo's manacles, but the sound of the king's voice reverberating through the cell stopped him.

"You must not."

Eli saw it then, the triptwitch wrapped around and embedded into Apollo's upper thigh. It was a very cruel, dark magical device, a trap that could be tripped by external triggers. It would also self-destruct and kill the person wearing it if anyone tried to remove it without having the key and solving its puzzle. Eli had never seen one in real life, but he'd read about them in Ev'r's old journal.

"It's a triptwitch," Eli told the king. "I can get it off but I need the key. It wouldn't look so much like a key as a small metal rod with little notches running down the sides. It's actually called a splint. Have you seen it?"

It wouldn't be something Mordan could keep on him, as cursed objects like that tended to have aversive effects if carried around, but he would certainly be keeping it safe. Eli's mind returned to Mordan's chamber – surely it had to be there.

"I have given my word that I will remain here," Apollo spoke again. "It is my word." Eli heard the finality in his voice. "Mordan-Grieg approaches. Replace the mask. Go back to your cell. Go quickly!"

Mordan. Terror struck Eli hard and he pushed the mask back over Apollo's face and ran for the drain. He leapt in and scurried downward and through the pipes as rapidly as he could. By the time he reached his cell pipe, his heart was a fleshy pulsating mess blocking his throat. As he clamored upward, he heard a distinctive *ech ech* from the pipes below, which only served to propel him faster. He flew out of the pipe, kicked back the grid and ran to his desk, dragging on his dress and throwing the papers around to look as though he'd been working. The lock to his cell sprung and the demon king himself stepped in with energy, as though he was surprising a friend. He was wearing a purple suit and actually looked quite sharp. The chemical odor from Mordan's body stung Eli's eyes and he did his best to look hard at work.

Mordan carried a plate of green slop to the desk and sat it down.

"Don't look so scared," he said. "It's just seaweed."

For some reason, he had the chair Eli had carved in his other hand and he sat down on it, saying, "It's actually quite comfy."

Eli stared at him, wondering why he was there so soon. They'd only just spoken. Did he know about Apollo?

"So ..." Mordan said. "How's it going?"

Eli gulped. "It's coming along."

"Along where?" Mordan's eyes flashed.

"It's progressing – forward – toward completion. I haven't really had a very long chance."

"I know. But I get sick of waiting," the demon king said almost apologetically. He crossed his legs and sighed, thinking for a moment before saying, "Why did you ask for what you asked for? You could have had so many other things – why that?" Mordan looked up and his eyes burned into Eli's face.

Eli considered the question, and chose his words very carefully. "What they did to the mother. It struck me as very cruel."

Mordan stared at him, searching. "Yes it is. It is cruel," he finally said, sounding almost robotic. He stood up abruptly and took the chair with him to the door. There he turned back and said to Eli, "I let them go. I actually just let them go. I just told the Almighty."

He smiled and made a snorting sound as though he couldn't believe it himself. "Now I'm going to handle a few executions and then I'll be back. Keep working."

"I will," Eli told him.

"Good. You're a smart boy. Not too smart I hope. Don't be too smart, will you?" Mordan shook his head and Eli nodded and then shook, unsure which response he was supposed to be giving.

Mordan smiled at him and left.

Going to handle a few executions. That meant he wouldn't be in his chambers. It was Eli's chance to search for the splint – he had to take it. He stood up from the chair and immediately fell to the ground. His body was exhausted and his mind shattered, but he had to keep pushing. It was their only hope.

Chapter 26
Ramses

HYDRIA

KIRITH-JEROM (TAOR)

As rain pelted down on metal rooftops of ramshackle buildings, Ramses and the brothers rode through the mud streets of Taor. It was lively and crowded for such a tiny place and on such a stormy night, perhaps because it stood as one of those strange border towns on the edge of four kingdoms all at once, or perhaps because it was offering a two for one special at the local brothel, which Aron pointed out and Vitali pretended not to notice. Drunks lurched about with their arms around each other's shoulders, traders walked up and down calling out their wares and someone almost pissed on their heads from a balcony above. They had to physically restrain Vitali from going after him.

They found the inn without needing directions. It was the largest and noisiest place there. And with their hoods drawn down over their faces, they left the horses with the stalls master and headed in. Grayweather had nipped Ramses, trying to stop him from leaving, and Ramses had comforted the geld and settled him before limping after the brothers, leaning heavily on his stick.

The inn, by the name of the Warhorse, was not silently majestic, powerful or even sturdy like its namesake. A sign featuring a dancing pig swung on one hinge, a general drunken ruckus spewed from within and a man and his purchased woman were doing the deed noisily at the entrance.

"One has to appreciate a proper welcome," Aron said drolly.

They entered and Vitali walked up to the bar, rapping on it with one fist. He spoke in broken Kirithi.

"Give us a room with no fleas, bedbugs or piss stains, and throw in supper for free."

Ramses looked around them. Judging from the state of the reception, Vitali may have just asked for the impossible. And indeed, the proprietor, whose enormous chin was only outdone by his spectacularly huge nose, looked Vitali up and down as though he was crazy. He barked something back, initiating a long argument over price and conditions that ended in what sounded like a competition for who could produce the most mocking bark of laughter.

Finally the elder Storon and the owner reached an agreement, though neither of them looked in any way pleased with it. The proprietor clicked his fingers at a skinny hunched woman wearing a bonnet, strands of gray hair wisping out around her face. She led them to a set of rickety stairs that groaned and trembled beneath their bootsteps. Aron helped Ramses up to a long, narrow corridor, which took them past a dozen or more rooms, the sounds of snoring, eating, arguing and sex drifting out beneath closed doors. The woman stopped at the end of the hall and unlocked the last door. She gestured in with a surly expression, then dumped the big metal key in Vitali's hand. He eyed it as though she'd just handed him a piece of fetid goat dung and hastily slipped it into a pouch on his belt. Before entering the room, he made a square warding hand-sign then kissed his thumb. He did it another three times. It was Anacharasi superstition and once Ramses may have mocked him for it, but not now, not after what they'd seen.

Ramses looked around the room and felt pleasantly surprised. He'd been expecting to see a place where the least discerning fleas may choose to make their home and good food goes to die, but it was actually respectable, with three small but neatly made beds, a nicely crackling fire, some comfortable looking chairs and a table with colorful flowers in a pot. Their floral smell mingled with the warm, sweet smell of the burning wood. Ramses let the warmth from the fire wash over him.

Vitali closed the door in the woman's frowning face and pushed a chair underneath the door handle, while Aron dumped his bag beside one of the beds and went to stand in front of the fire, warming his hands. Ramses dropped his pack as well and limped over to the window to peer beyond the shutters down to the main street of Taor below. With the drumming of the rain on the rooftop, the flickering flame torches lighting the streets and the people walking and riding through the semi-mist, it looked almost like a dream.

"Will you open the shutters for a moment?" Aron asked.

Ramses did so and Morrison fluttered in immediately, swooping down onto Aron's shoulder. Ramses tensed, waiting for any sound, but mercifully the bird kept his beak shut for once. Ramses closed the window and turned back to see Aron and Vitali dragging dry clothes out of their packs. Vitali tried to take a swig from his flask, but nothing came out. He peered into the flask in annoyance.

"No more cough medicine?" Aron teased his brother. "Must be a miracle cure, I haven't heard you cough in years."

Vitali threw him a dark look.

Aron put a tunic down on the one unclaimed bed and motioned for Ramses to take it. He moved toward them with difficulty and lowered himself onto the bed, finding it surprisingly soft. The smells of soup and bread wafting up from the common rooms below made his stomach growl savagely. He pulled off his wet tunic and, looking down, saw he was leaner than he'd ever been, his heavy muscles eroded and his ribs showing. He caught sight of his leg and shivered. The thought that he would be better off dead niggled in his mind constantly, the only thing that chased it away was his drive to find Titan.

"It's a pleasant room," he said to the brothers, trying to distract himself.

Aron snorted with laughter. "Yes, it's the grand palace. You can address me as Lord King from now on —"

He realized what he'd said and who he'd said it to, and his face reddened.

Vitali sat down on his bed and kicked off his wet boots, saying, "Never mind my brother, he learned his manners from a rabid mountain baboon."

"Don't put yourself down like that, brother, you taught me well," Aron returned bitterly.

"Oh I'll teach you alright!" Vitali warned, and Aron's face darkened dangerously, the scar over his eye tightening.

"Supper smells appealing," Ramses said, trying to prevent them brawling again.

Vitali turned his glare on him before yanking on fresh socks and his boots and storming out of the room. He slammed the door behind him and Aron cursed.

"*Abram*." He boiled for a moment before glancing at Ramses. "I'm sorry for before."

Ramses shook his head. He gripped his arm where the lion had bitten him, the wounds had started to throb.

Aron leaned over for a look and clicked his tongue. Morrison made a clicking sound as well.

"We're getting low on supplies. I'll cover it, but we'll have to get one of the women here to dress it properly tonight and I'll stock up tomorrow." He started dragging things out of his pack and a crumpled painted picture fell out, drifting to land beside Ramses' foot. He bent down to pick it up, but Aron swooped in and snatched it away. He stuffed the parchment back into his bag.

"Did you paint that?" Ramses asked.

"Me? Do I look like a man who paints to you?" Aron glared, showing a striking resemblance to his brother.

"I've painted, I quite enjoy the pastime," Ramses said, sensing he had hit a sore spot but not knowing why.

Aron's face softened again. "Well, it's not as accepted in Anacharasis as it is now in Corinthia."

Ramses nodded and let the matter go, not wanting to push the point. Aron found a bandage in his pack and Ramses held out his arm while he wrapped it around the oozing wounds. He noticed Aron was careful not to make the binds either too tight or too loose.

"Why are you helping me?" he asked for the first time.

Aron looked up at him. "By Darro's orders." Ramses understood it was the simple answer to a complex question.

"Why is he helping us?"

"All those who walk the righteous path are one – all those who walk the righteous path —"

"Are brothers," Ramses finished. "I noticed you both favor Corinthian over your own tongue."

Aron hesitated for a moment, then said, "Our mother was Corinthian. She died when I was a boy though."

"So that's why Vitali speaks it with less accent – he's older."

"By fifteen years," Aron told him.

"I didn't realize it was that much," Ramses said.

"That's because of my being wise beyond my age, isn't it?" Aron said with a grin. He dragged off his drenched tunic and laid it over the chair near the fire. As he turned back to grab his spare, Ramses noticed he had a deep scar etched into his chest, across his heart. It was a name – Sabella.

"Your girl?" Ramses asked, and Aron looked taken aback. He pulled the fresh tunic on without responding. Ramses realized he'd again hit a raw nerve and wondered why Aron didn't make a stronger attempt at hiding his emotional afflictions. But as he thought about it, he knew, this was what happened when a warrior only kept company with those he has known his whole life. They knew what not to notice, what not to say. His mind turned to the Companions. With his leg, he would not be permitted to continue as a Companion, nor a warrior rider. Lost in these dark thoughts, he stood without his crutch and fell flat on his face on the boards.

"Easy now!" Aron cried out and helped him back up to the bed. Ramses groaned. He had shooting pain all through the leg that was gone and could do nothing to soothe it.

"How is it possible?" he asked Aron with a strained voice.

"I'm no physician," Aron said. "But Darro has all manner of scrolls in Oas. Hopefully we will find answers there."

They sat in silence while Ramses collected himself.

"Is there a woman you left behind in Corinth City?" Aron eventually asked.

"Yes. About seven thousand of them," Ramses replied, making Aron snort with laughter.

"Like father, like son," he said, and then a moment later realized what he'd said and his face reddened again. It appeared neither of them could stop stomping on each other's wounds.

"You. In Anacharasis?" Ramses said.

Aron looked down.

"Did she – pass?" Ramses asked.

"My love," Aron pointed to his chest. "She lives, well and happy, a mother, a wife – just not mine." He gave a quick and unconvincing smile.

"I'm sorry," Ramses offered.

"No matter, it only hurts when I think of her and I only think of her every moment of every day." Aron gave a sad laugh and it reminded Ramses acutely of his father. His stomach growled and Aron said, "Come – let's eat."

"I prefer to eat here," Ramses said, feeling in no way fit to attend the dining room.

"As would I, but if you ask for door service, without a doubt they'll use your bowl as a spittoon," Aron told him. "It's good for us to get out and see what rumors are about anyway. We'll be back. Keep watch from the window," he said to Morrison, who fluttered up onto the beams above their heads.

The dining room was in full swing when they descended the stairs. A banjo band was playing music, commoners were jigging about, laughing, singing, drinking, eating. Some were playing games, knife throwing, and the Theselonian game of quadro with wooden cards. An overwhelming smell of hot food mingled with an undertone of body odor. A few rough-looking commoners threw glances their way, and they eyeballed Ramses' leg with suspicion, but Aron walked with enough confidence to put off any unwanted attention.

They kept their hoods up and sat down at a spare table in one corner of the crowded room. As they sat, Ramses noticed Vitali was already there at another table, holding bread in one hand and spooning in stew with the other. He was hunched over his bowl and eating fast, pausing only for a moment to scull down his beer. He glanced over and saw them, then looked away again. Aron signaled to a serving girl to bring two. Beside them, a gathering of commoners were discussing Harlow Darro, everyone eager to have their say.

"I heard he's rallying forces on the border. He'll take the throne, mark my words," one woman said.

"He has over two hundred thousand warriors already, and the number is growing by the day," another knowing soul put in.

"He has his sights set on Corinth, he wants to unite all the kingdoms into one. Mark me. I said it before it happened," a wizened man predicted.

Aron leaned over to them and said, "I hear that for breakfast Darro eats twenty-five eggs, ten loaves of bread and a full side of venison, all by himself, but no one has ever seen him use the latrine – ever."

This revelation was met by mystified stares, superstitious hand-signs and murmurs of *The Unbreakable*.

"He's no ordinary man, you know," an old woman croaked with shining eyes.

"You can say that again," Aron murmured. He shot a glance at Ramses.

The serving girl brought them two bowls of steaming white bean stew with fresh bread, and another woman put two pints of beer and two shots of some kind of liquor down with the food.

Ramses looked up to say thank you and the girl caught sight of his face. She gave him a warm smile, her eyes lingering on his, before the older woman bustled her away.

"Good gods man," Aron said. "You've half reached the blessed plains looking all but a beggar, and the women still want you. To have half your luck." He smiled, but there was strain to it.

Ramses stared down into his bowl, so agonizingly hungry, but scared to eat in case it made him sick.

"Slowly, you'll be fine," Aron encouraged him. He took a bite of bread and shot a glance toward his brother, who was gulping down another pint. There were five empty cups on his table. A scruffy bearded commoner beside Vitali coughed and snorted, and the elder Storon covered his food, eying him savagely.

Aron smiled. "If there's anything Vitali hates it's being breathed on, coughed on or sneezed on. If you do all three he'll likely kill you where you stand."

"There's a few things Vitali hates, isn't there?" Ramses commented.

"A few, oh yes," Aron laughed wickedly. "Cheers," he said, holding up his cup to Ramses. Ramses tipped it with his and they drank. He felt the strong ale putting some fire back in his blood.

Another serving woman passed by their table and picked up Aron's empty cup. Her other hand, Ramses noticed, was black and withered. Aron saw as well and said, "Excuse me good lady, can I trouble you to clear my brother's table over there?" He tucked a coin into her pocket.

She gave a nod and headed over to Vitali. He glanced up from his stew and saw her hand and startled back, spilling beans all over himself.

Aron turned away and sniggered into his arm. Vitali looked over and saw him. He scowled, shoved back from the table and staggered drunkenly out of the inn.

"It looks like he's enjoyed one drink too many. Will he fare alright out there on his own?" Ramses asked. With the hunt on their trails, they didn't need the attention. He truly needed to sleep in a bed for at least one night.

"He'll be fine. He'll find the largest woman in town and get inside her, and then he'll be fine." Aron gulped back the shot and grimaced.

"The *largest* woman?" Ramses asked.

"Vitali likes his women big, and I don't mean big," he held his hands out in front of his chest, "I mean big." He held them out to his sides.

Ramses gave a nod. "Yourself?"

Aron shrugged. "They're all the same to me."

"And to me as well," Ramses agreed. He lowered his spoon to the table. Both his bowl and Aron's were scraped clean.

"I'm still ravenous but it may be folly for either of us to continue on," Aron added. "Come, let's walk it off, and find Vitali, then perhaps return for more."

Aron purchased them each a cigar and helped Ramses outside into the soggy streets. They headed down the road, keeping under the eaves and out of the rain. Ramses looked around, taking in everyone who passed them, alert for signs of soldiers. At the side of one dangerously tilted building he noticed what appeared to be bars right down low, and behind them he spotted the faces of children looking out.

"Are they trapped?" he asked Aron, nodding toward the bars.

When Aron looked the children quickly vanished from sight. "Yes and no," the younger Storon said.

Ramses wiped a drop of rain off his neck. "What do you mean?"

"It's because of the vendettas. They follow old law here, even in the lower mountain regions like this. When there's blood feuds between family clans, they don't stop until every male of the household is killed – one vengeance killing after another. So the boys need to stay in hiding, in cellars and attics."

"Until when?" Ramses asked.

"Until forever," Aron replied. "The mountain has a long memory."

"I am sure the Almighty would have outlawed this practice," Ramses said.

"Indeed he did," Aron confirmed. "But it's closing in on thirty years since the Almighty rode this land. They don't fear his justice anymore, only Darro's, and Darro is but one person."

Ramses took in these words and said, "The Lord King Osiris and Lord Liege have also accomplished much."

"Very true," Aron agreed quickly. "But Apollo of Ironeye was always on the move, you remember – no one knew where he would show up."

The silence hung between them for a time before Ramses said, "Do you think the Lord Liege lives?" He felt his heart filling with dread. "Those claws ..."

"He's alive," Aron said without allowing any doubt. "I'm assuming they don't call him the Titan as flattery."

"No," Ramses said. He had earned the name.

"And let me assure you that they don't call Darro 'The Unbreakable' for nothing either. He's riding with the best."

"Have you ridden as Darro's companion for long?" Ramses asked.

Aron laughed. "Oh yes."

"Your laugh sounds like a lifetime."

"True," Aron said. "We grew up together. Grew up, grew old." For a moment Aron's eyes lost their sparkle and he just looked tired. "I took him for granted, pushed him away, felt jealous, hated him, wished him dead, wished myself dead, wished I was him, wished he was me, wished I could take everything back ... He's forgiving. Always been so."

It sounded like they'd ridden through the highs and lows, there and back, and it reminded Ramses of himself and Titan. It made him feel better.

"How did you first meet – you and Darro?" he asked.

"I was no more than seven when Vitali brought him to our grandmother's house on The Rise ... and Harlow was even younger, but being cast in metal, there was no way to know exactly how young."

"It's true?" Ramses turned to him with surprise.

"Oh yes." He laughed ruefully again. "It was just after the Almighty failed to return. Vitali was a soldier in King Sirion's army and his legion was ordered to the border, where word said a band of Drauls were tormenting a bunch of commoners. Vitali tells it that he stumbled over something and found it was a metal form on the ground, and he'd thought it a statue until it started to make sounds. He realized what he was seeing, but couldn't believe his eyes. His commander ordered him to put the child out of its misery but the trouble was, Vitali couldn't fit his sword through the eyeholes in the metal." He paused to puff on his cigar.

"What happened then?" Ramses prompted.

"Nothing happened. Vitali couldn't kill him – the only way he could have done it was to drop Harlow in water and ..." Aron shook his head to say that wasn't an option and Ramses' skin started crawling. "So his commander said to just leave him, but Vitali thought that any boy strong enough to survive being cast in metal deserved something better. So he managed to get him to our grandmother's place, hoping she could get the child to take in something that would kill him faster than starvation, but when she went to mix the poison, they found Harlow's mouth was free enough of metal and he could eat and drink, and it went from there. Each day his strength grew until he was able to move, and we were shocked, but he did it – he lived. Not long after that his horse Naro showed up alive."

A commotion down the street took their attention.

"Here we go," Aron said darkly and helped Ramses to move faster toward the sounds of a brawl. They found Vitali being set upon by a group of townsmen. Aron immediately jumped into the fight, quickly dispensing the men while Vitali stumbled around, struggling not to topple over.

"This one put his filthy hot hands on my lady!" an outraged man standing back from the fight shouted at Aron, gesturing to a plump woman beside him. Ramses noticed she was looking slightly guilty, suggesting that Vitali's filthy hot hands had not been entirely unwelcome.

"Well, what's she doing standing on the corner like a bed maid?" Aron demanded.

"You look like a bed maid, you bog swine," the man spat back, pointing at Aron's face. Vitali snarled and tried to rush him but Aron held his brother back, laughing off the grave insult. He looked up from under his hood and met the man's eyes. "Be gone. I'll end you."

The tone of his voice alone made the crowd disperse rather hastily. When it was just them again, Vitali shoved Aron back, slurring.

"Did I call you to help me, boy? I had everything in hand."

"The only thing you had in hand, brother, were the enormous tits of another man's wife," Aron threw back. "Why does it always have to be the married ones?"

"Why? Why? It's not your place to question me!" Vitali reeled, bumping into Ramses and glaring at him. The smell of his breath reminded Ramses of August.

"Not my place? I stand your equal, I'll question you as I like," Aron said.

"Equal!" Vitali laughed uproariously with exaggerated volume.

Aron shook his head and turned to leave, but Vitali grabbed his arm and said, "No, you began this and now you'll hear everything I have to say. You think I don't know? That I don't see you sitting up at night when you think me asleep, crying over old love letters like a woman, painting your little pictures of where you would have lived with her."

He threw his hands all over the place, imitating a crazy person.

"After everything I've carried you through, you still take yourself down the same dark path over and again. After everything I've sacrificed! She. Never. Loved. You. She was only using you. The whole time."

"She was forced to marry! Her father gave her no choice."

Ramses looked around them nervously. This was clearly a long running family argument that he'd been dropped into the middle of, and he wouldn't have begrudged them the necessary airing of their grievances if others weren't watching them as well.

"Rubbish," Vitali said. "You know it as well as I."

Aron glared at his brother and said, "You stand in judgment, riding high and mighty. Still trying to live up to your father's expectations. Still failing."

Vitali took a swing then, which Aron sidestepped.

"Admit it," Aron said as the two brothers circled each other. "Your disdain for me has nothing to do with her. It's because of this." He pointed to his face. "These eyes. I'm the son of another man. We both know it."

"Don't you dare breathe those words or I'll break your teeth," Vitali said. "My mother was a lady of virtue."

"A lady who was stolen from her homeland and forced into serving *him*. I still remember enough. She wasn't just our mother, she was a person too."

Vitali growled and lunged at Aron, tackling him. They went rolling through the mud, throwing punches.

Ramses hobbled after them, trying to break it up.

"Get up!" he ordered. "You're making a scene. People are watching!"

It was enough to get them back on their feet and apart.

"Honest to the gods you two can fight!" Ramses said. "I'd give up my life to bring my sister back for just one moment."

The words tumbled from his mouth before he even knew what he was saying. Both brothers looked at him in silence. He felt a pit open up inside him.

"Get back to the inn," Vitali muttered and stumbled off, leaving the two of them to follow. By the time they reached the room exhaustion was riding heavy on their shoulders. Morrison greeted them with blessed silence as they entered. Aron and Ramses collapsed immediately into their beds, while Vitali completed an elaborate sleep routine of tucking and untucking the sheets, performing warding signs, walking around the bed a certain number of times and moving the bed around until it was a particular distance from the walls. Finally he lay down, but then immediately leapt back up, thrashing all over the place and throwing a leaf up high into the air as though it was a scorpion.

"*Abram!*" he snarled at Aron and Ramses saw Aron, pretending to sleep, smile a fraction. Vitali had to start his routine again and when he was finally finished, he extinguished the lantern and the room fell to silence briefly before the snoring started.

Ramses lay still, staring upward. His arm was pulsating and his missing leg itched and burned. The sheer exhaustion drifted him halfway to sleep and then he woke, very cold and shivering. He felt August's hand on his shoulder in the darkness.

"Tato?" Ramses whispered.

"I'm here," his father said and patted Ramses' shoulder. "Sleep. I'm with you."

Ramses closed his eyes and from a great distance heard Aron's voice calling him.

"Ramses, Wake up! Wake up!"

Chapter 27
Eli

HYDRIA

FARNORTHERN HALOS (BLED)

The doors to Mordan's chamber were open and unguarded. Eli was suspicious of this at first, but on second thought, it really wasn't that surprising. Who would be foolish enough to break into the demon king's office? Eli gulped and stepped over the threshold. *Enter the fool*, he thought. He paused there for a moment, wringing his hands, then he forced himself to move.

Where would Mordan keep the splint? It was of great importance. King Apollo had been essential to Mordan's plan, but there was also a personal history there – Apollo had been Mordan's prisoner for decades and he had come to him straight away to tell him about the mother and child. Eli knew that meant something. The commander would have known exactly what that something was, but Eli just knew the relationship was significant to Mordan – so he would be keeping the splint in a significant place. He searched the table where Mordan kept the Indemeus X's blueprint, but found nothing. He turned in a circle, searching the walls and gadgets and books. The partial wall of books caught his eye. Mordan had been speaking with the Indemeus behind there – maybe that was his inner sanctum, so to speak. Eli headed for it, walking around the wall, then stopped dead in his tracks. Mordan stood there, leaning forward over a table, studying something.

Eli stumbled back, almost crashed into a chair and then scurried beneath another table, pressing himself into the shadows and putting a hand over his mouth. Mordan straightened up. He looked over his shoulder with a wary expression, scanning the room, then went back to his work. Nelly wound around Eli's neck and started gnawing on his dress with terror. If Mordan caught them it would be over, and Aquais and everyone in it would be lost. The pressure Eli felt was immense. He clutched his sapphire blade and random thoughts and memories started darting through his mind, as though his life was trying to flash before his eyes. He forced them to stop, settling over one memory, a conversation he'd overheard between his grandparents. It was just after he'd dropped out of school with aspirations of becoming the world's greatest inventor. His gran'ma had been crying, saying, *I wanted better for him, I wanted so much for him,* and Grampy said, *He's finally happy, what could be better than happy?*

The air beside Mordan sparked and flared and the smoke pillar form of the Indemeus X appeared, its body and face obscured and shifting. Mordan fell to his knees.

"Do you have it?" the Indemeus asked, his voice coming through distorted.

Mordan breathed out heavily. "The thing is. I need a bit more time."

"Your time is up."

"I know, master, but I've found someone. He's the answer. I know he is. I beg you. I will have the answer. I will get it. Don't do anything to her. Please. I will have it to you. I just need a fraction more time." His voice was so desperate and frightened, Eli felt confused.

Indemeus considered the request and then responded, "One more day."

Mordan almost collapsed from relief. He bowed to the ground, saying *thank you* over and over. Indemeus' form faded out. Once it had, Mordan's shoulders started shaking as though he was sobbing. Eli stared in disbelief, jolting back as Mordan leapt to his feet and swept all the things off his desk in rage. Then Eli watched him pick up an object off the ground and hug it to his chest. He whispered to it and placed it gently on a high shelf.

Loud slapping footsteps sounded in the chamber behind and Mordan gave a deep sigh of irritation.

"What is it?" he bellowed.

A ratha stuck his head around the corner and said, "We just received message from the North. The Almighty's grandson, Tarrus, is being hunted by a witch."

Mordan seemed to be so distracted by other thoughts that he barely heard what his demon said. "What?" he asked.

"A witch. *Samyaza.*"

"So get rid of her," Mordan replied.

"Yes, majesty."

Mordan's face changed. "Actually wait. Still get rid of her, but then bring him in. Yes. Bring him in. Quickly. Right now. Yesterday. I need to give the Almighty some motivation."

Mordan's eyes took on a fevered look. "With the two of them together, we might make it. It'll be alright." He looked back at the object on the shelf. "Everything will be alright."

"Majesty. Should I tell the executioner that you're not coming?" the demon ventured.

"No, I'm still coming," Mordan snapped. "Must maintain order. No one else will."

The demon wisely kept quiet and the pair of them left together.

Eli realized he'd been holding his breath and exhaled in a rush. He crept out from under the table, checking around before standing up. His eyes went to the object on the shelf. He had to get it down. Eli tried to move Mordan's table to stand on, but it was bolted down. He stacked up a pile of books, but couldn't make them high enough to reach without toppling over. He tried several other ideas before collapsing on the ground in exhaustion, expecting to hear Mordan returning any moment. If he had his wings he would have just flown up there. He reached around and touched the place where his wing should have been, feeling utterly defeated. And then he felt soft fur, and Nelly popped back out of his dress.

"Nelly!" he said. "See that box?" He held her up. "Go get it for me. Knock it down."

He put her on the wall and she scurried upward and along the shelf, then nosed the box over the edge. Eli caught it deftly and knelt down. He couldn't see any tricks or tracks on the lid – Ev'r had given him a few lessons on that – so very gingerly he flipped it open. It was one of those old music boxes with the creepy twangy music and dancing figure, but this one didn't make any sound, and the dancer didn't spin. It had stopped. Eli grinned. He reached into the box and pulled out the splint.

"Thank you," he whispered to the Khaiti god, and to Nelly as she leapt back onto his shoulder. Eli jumped up on shaky legs, tried to put things back as close as he could to the way he'd found them, leaving the box on the ground under the shelf on its side, looking as though it had fallen, then he ran from the chamber.

On his way back to the cells, he took a wrong turn and somehow ended up in a spooky looking demon kitchen that was in a filthy state and stunk of rotting death. He guessed there was no such thing as health inspectors in the demon world. He walked around a bench and came upon a cage full of horribly cramped birds, which rested on top of a cage of cute porcupine creatures that looked like they were smiling even though they were clearly terrified. He started backing away. He couldn't get involved. He had to go. He bumped into something behind him, spilling out a bucket of bird heads. He almost gagged, but managed to hold it in.

"No. I can't leave them," he said, running to the cages. The least he could do was open the cages and give the animals a chance to escape. He flung open the doors and the birds burst out. The porcupine creatures also leapt up and started climbing the walls to the dirt ceiling, then started burrowing quickly, cutting a path upward with the birds following them out. Eli smiled despite himself, then ducked down as a lesser demon sharpening cleavers and wearing a blood-splattered apron walked in. He spotted the cages and stopped short and Eli realized he had to move first, he had to take him out before he alerted anyone.

Grabbing a large metal plate, Eli leapt up and ran screaming at the demon chef. He smashed the plate into his face and the chef fell over backward. He started to get up so Eli hit him again, knocking him out, then dragged him into a cupboard and locked it, wedging a heavy utensil between the handles. As Eli stood panting from the effort, he heard a low growl coming from the shadows behind him. He turned slowly and saw a gigantic bear sitting in a cage. His fur was matted with blood and his face scarred. His eyes called to Eli, vicious but lost.

"Hello, friend," Eli whispered, edging toward the bars. Nelly nipped his back, telling him not to be crazy, but he kept going. "Look up there," he said to the bear. "Go up there. See?" He carefully opened the door and stood behind it, trying to shield himself. The bear limped out, cast him a look, then climbed up onto the bench and pushed up into the tunnel, digging and widening it significantly.

With shaking hands Eli ran out of the kitchen from hell and stood there, turning one way and then the next. He was completely lost. Suddenly from inside his dress the glow worm he'd taken and forgotten all about, who had since transitioned to firefly, took off. Eli watched it fly then realized it might be going back to its own kind, and they lived right near his cell. He ran after it, his heart lifting higher and higher as he started to recognize landmarks. He was on the right track. He passed the fireflies and was on the final stretch when the spectral-breed, Octavia, stepped right into his path. He cried out and almost fell over, but then he looked into her face and saw she wasn't angry. She looked in pain and desperate. His eyes went to the binding band around her neck.

"I'll take that off you and then you can get Sanfrass out?"

Carefully he reached for the band and jimmied the lock open. Octavia gasped as he removed it. The deep indent suggested she'd been wearing it for a long time. She turned swiftly and vanished into the wall and Eli kept running. Ahead, he saw King Apollo's cell door. He was almost there.

Chapter 28
Ev'r

HYDRIA

FARNORTHERN HALOS (ESZAK)

Ev'r blinked. For a moment she'd imagined she was a Ravien again, staring at Golmaria, the city where all the Ravien gathered. A city where life had neither slowly evolved nor violently erupted, but simply ended. Changed. One bite and it all changed. She lowered her head, her jaws felt enormous, but when she looked up again the city was not Golmaria but another place where life had stopped. This city was huge and sprawling, built into the side of a steep cliff, all its buildings and streets now reclaimed by nature. Thick vines wrapped around crumbling pillars and gigantic beheaded statues. Ismail stood beside her, looking around.

"Getting anything?" she asked him.

"The same. On and off. No rhythm to it. Strong bursts and then nothing at all. It feels like the augmentor really doesn't know what they're doing."

"Speaking of people who really don't know what they're doing." Ev'r looked down at the trackers and Christy Shawe. Kane had called a break, they'd been walking for an eternity and everyone was tired and hungry and the water had run out. They'd followed the sound of a waterfall to this fallen place.

Ev'r left Ismail wrapping plaster around his blistering toes and went down to the pool to fill up their flasks. She kept her eyes on the dark shadows circling far below as she bent over the water. Straightening up, she caught sight of Silho standing inside one of the ruined buildings, staring up at a chipped and faded tile mural on the wall.

Ev'r had never seen this type of art before, and she had been treasure hunting for a long while. She walked into the building, looking up at the picture. It was of a woman, and she could have been Silho's twin.

"Does it feel like home?" she asked Brabel.

"Why should it?" Silho replied without turning around.

"It's your mother's land isn't it? Can't imagine why she wanted to leave the place," she said dryly.

"Oren was a princess here," Silho told her. "Given to the Omarian prince, Lecivion, when the Omarians stopped the ratha demons taking over the land."

Ev'r looked around. "I'd be asking for my money back."

"She left him and he took his revenge."

"Love can drive you crazy," Ev'r murmured.

"My father was an Omarian diplomat, stationed here."

"So you're starting to get a picture of where they both came from," Ev'r said.

"Doesn't mean I know them any better," Silho said.

"Do you know what's worse than not knowing your parents?" Ev'r asked.

Brabel glanced over her shoulder.

"Knowing them."

She turned to leave and Silho said, "You can tell Ismail to stop feeling guilty about Hammersmith. I already know."

That stopped Ev'r in her tracks. "Is that so?"

"I can touch the ground and see the past. People seem to forget that."

"Ismail thinks of you as *consan*, you know," Ev'r said. "I think you're an arrogant little gadfly."

"I think you're jealous," Silho shot back.

"I think you're right," Ev'r admitted. "We can call a truce if you like."

"Truces are for people who think they're going to lose."

Ev'r smiled. "I'm liking you more and more every day, Silho Brabel."

She turned again and picked her way out of the ruined building. Ismail would be relieved to hear what Silho had told her. She glanced back at Brabel and saw Kane was now talking to her. Ev'r doubled back, wanting to hear the conversation, wanting to hear Kane try to explain himself.

"Can you see anything?" he was asking Silho.

"Nothing much, nothing clear."

Silence hung between them until he said, "When you sided with him it became clear to me that you're not committed to our relationship. Not in the way I need. He wanted to tear us apart, he's been trying from the beginning, and you still defended him – against me. You finding what he's done forgivable means you don't care enough about us. If I would live and die and give up anything for you then I expect the same, and if you don't feel as much for me as I do for you, then I don't want to be with you."

His delivery was blunt as hell, but Ev'r at least partially agreed with what he was saying. Who wanted to be in an uneven relationship, throwing everything into it while the other person held onto their other options? Then again, he was the one who just banged his ex-girlfriend in full view of everyone, which kind of undermined his zeal.

"I have lived and died for you," Silho said, sounding tired. "I've done everything you've said – everything your way. If you think that me not wanting to see Jude dead means I love him or that I don't love you enough, then there's really nothing I can say. Apparently I have stunted emotional intelligence, whatever that means."

By the way Kane was looking at her, it was clear he was trying to read her, and was finding it frustrating without his skill.

"I think it's best we end it now," he said.

Silho didn't respond, though Ev'r saw her shoulders drop a fraction.

Kane turned and left, passing the place where Ev'r stood.

"Nicely done," she said sarcastically.

He gave her a warning look but then turned, catching the sense of something. His forehead furrowed and Ev'r followed his gaze back to Silho. Jude was standing there now.

"Girl's trying to have a moment and everyone wants a piece," Ev'r murmured, and Kane signaled for her to shut it. She only did because she wanted to hear what his majesty had to say for himself.

"I'm really sorry Silho," Jude started.

Silho shook her head.

"I do love you."

"At least somebody knows how to say it," Ev'r muttered. Kane's body couldn't have been any more tense.

"As friends," he added. "I know you don't want anything more. I accept that. And I wanted to say maybe you can still fix things with him. I know he loves you. We are under extreme circumstances and no one's perfect." His voice sounded strained. "Plus, we may not have very long. I can understand why he was insulted. You're not always clear with your emotions."

Ev'r gritted her teeth. Was he really trying to say this was Silho's fault?

"I never asked you or him to be with me," Silho said. "You can both trutt off as far as I'm concerned. Together."

Good girl. Stand strong, Ev'r thought.

Jude blinked. "I'm so sorry, Silho, I didn't mean to insinuate anything. I just think maybe you should try to see things from all sides. And Diega can be – convincing."

Ev'r stifled an angry laugh.

Silho snorted out smoke and Jude took the gigantic hint, moving his thoughts on quickly.

"Everything aside, I guess it leaves a space for you to make your own mistakes."

"I already did – trusting him. Trusting anybody." Silho stood up and walked away.

Jude lowered his head. His grand gesture hadn't really gone down as he'd hoped. Guess he should have stopped blaming the victim.

Ev'r turned to say something sharp to Kane but saw he was already walking away, his footsteps silent. She followed him back up to the top, where the others were waiting. Diega was trying to get her transflyer to morph from the coin and Shawe had his back to her. Ev'r went to Ismail and threw her arms around him, kissing him deeply. This wonderful man. He looked surprised but happy.

Once everyone had gathered on the ledge, Kane said, "We can't fight the ratha, so it has to be stealth, and we stand a better chance moving as separate teams. One team falls, the others continue. So pair off."

Everyone looked around, figuring out who they hated least.

Silho went to stand with Christy Shawe. Fairy girl with Kane. *Surprise, surprise.* Jude was left standing alone.

"Alone again, how sad," Ev'r said to him and he gave her a look down his straight nose.

"Jude with us," Copernicus said, surprising everyone, especially Jude. He walked over to them and Kane said, "We continue due north in parallel, one klick apart. Move out!"

As Silho and Shawe went to leave, Diega said, "Shawe, wait."

He ignored her.

"So it's like that?" she said.

"Give up, Sunshine," Shawe said, glancing back. "Honestly, don't trouble yourself, love." He nodded to Kane. "Me and him, we've been through everything. In the end you women don't mean a thing."

"Is that how you really feel?" fairy girl asked.

Shawe laughed at her. "I feel like I need to drop a gigantic bog, but there's not a single toilet to be seen. That's how I really feel."

Ismail snorted and Silho suddenly knelt down, her fingers disappearing into the rock.

"It's Eli," she said, then looked up at them. "He's in trouble."

Chapter 29
Titan

HYDRIA

ARMEN (DOLMA)

Dolma didn't have the sophisticated aqueducts and sewerage systems the Almighty had designed for Corinth, but it did have long well structures where people could pump water up and throw waste down, and the wells led to tunnels beneath the city. These were aged and cracked and prone to caving in and blocking up the wells. Titan held the flame torch up to the roof above them and examined it with mistrust as they rode Alban deep below the Armenite royal city.

He'd wanted to take the reins, but Harlow had told him to ride behind her – she knew the way, and it was easier for her to direct the big workhorse than to give him directions. At least, that was what she said. Titan suspected she was just used to being in command. But so was he. And that wasn't the only issue. The closeness of their bodies, now that they'd discarded the heavy Armenite armor, and the friction between them from the horse's movements, and the feel of her hair against his arms, and the smell of her skin, was making him harder than he'd been in a long time. She felt it, and cast him a look that was difficult to read, but he was sure she was more amused than anything.

"I told you I needed to ride in the front," he said, trying to shuffle back from her. "I can't help this. It's physiological."

She snorted. "That truly sounds like a personal problem in which I'm entirely disinterested."

"Really? Then why is your skin so hot?" he said, pushing away from her again as he slid back in.

"It's called friction, Titan. I believe you wrote a book on it."

"Not on this kind of friction, I didn't," he said.

He tried to focus his mind away from her onto the truth of war that was unfolding all around him, outside of his control. He could feel the poison of Belphanganor's Prime radiating through his body, even as Harlow's serums muted the pain. He had now accepted that he had to rid himself of the mark, as Harlow had been saying. Then nothing would hold him back from returning to Ironeye – before war broke, he hoped. But his fear that there may be no way to get free of the mark lingered. He saw images of Ravana dragging him below the surface, he felt the coldness of the water and the claws on his face.

An elbow to the ribs brought him back to sharp focus. He found he'd wrapped his arms around Harlow and was holding her very closely. His body was tingling with an urgency, a thirst almost beyond his control. It was too much.

"Stop now," he ordered, the sound of his voice making Alban pull up. "We're swapping!"

He jumped down and Darro slid back with some reluctance. He could see she was concealing her smile.

"This is not amusing," he told her.

"And I am not amused."

He jumped up in front of her and took the reins, immediately feeling more in control of himself and his body. Out of nowhere, Ravana's shrieking face rushed in at him and he jolted back, smashing heads with Harlow. She had her sword drawn while he was still scrambling. The image vanished, leaving them in the darkness.

"What was it?" Harlow asked.

"I saw Ravana." His throat felt dry.

Harlow held the light close and checked the mark from over his shoulder. It was weeping already, much sooner than last time, saltwater running down his chest.

"Alban, go!" Harlow said in a low voice. She clicked her tongue and the workhorse broke into a heavy gallop.

They ran on, coming out onto a ledge with a drop on one side into a deep ravine. Titan felt something, a vibration, beneath them, and Harlow put her hand on the reins, diverting Alban into a small space in the wall. She extinguished their torch and they sat in darkness while the vibrations increased until Titan heard the rhythmic pounding steps of an army marching toward them. Both he and Harlow peered over the edge, down into the ravine. An army appeared. Titan did not recognize their armor, their colors or even the look of their faces.

"Cytisians," Harlow whispered and Titan's skin prickled. The swamp dwellers had always been considered enemies of the Halos, and here they were, being driven forward against Corinthia under the lash of the Halos kings. He could see by the way they moved, the way they carried their weapons and their own bodies that they were not marching by choice. And he saw the red mist hanging around the faces of their commanders. Harlow clicked to Alban and the horse backed up through the tight space until they found an opening on the other side. They kept riding, not slowing until their path ran down into water, where a small boat awaited them.

"I know," Harlow said, when Titan gave her a look. "But it's the fastest way there."

She jumped down and he followed her, and they led Alban aboard. The workhorse seemed perfectly at ease, but Titan's nerves were spiking. The way the boat rocked made his legs unsteady and he saw how dark the water was beneath them, the torch flames reflecting in ripples all around. Harlow pulled up the anchor with expert speed and the current caught them, sweeping them away. Titan sat down solidly and remained there as Harlow steered with an oar.

"All the water beneath the Halos runs to one place," Harlow told him. "A cavern in Cy Lasea that leads out into *Mĕthmalay*. I've tested it many times. Look beneath where you sit."

Titan dragged out a chest from beneath his legs and opened it to find more armor.

"Throw me mine and fasten your own. I have a feeling we may meet trouble ahead."

The words made Titan's skin prickle and he swiftly separated the armor out. Harlow fastened her helm on last. Both their helms had a full metal zivas covering their faces.

In a sudden move, Harlow jammed the oar against one wall, bringing them to a stop that threw Titan forward almost onto his knees. The former Kí gestured silence to Titan and he looked past her to where the ghastly forms of Ravana's glooms were walking over the water ahead of them.

They were walking in a circle as though they were waiting for something. Harlow carefully lowered the anchor then stepped back, grabbing Alban's reins and indicating that Titan should jump out onto the narrow dirt ledge beside them. He did, then helped the workhorse over. He noticed how quietly the big horse was stepping. The three of them moved back the way they'd come until they reached a rocky place in the wall, where Harlow opened up a hidden door. She led them through, then crouched down and took out a map, spreading it over the ground. Again, Titan was struck by the skill of Harlow's design.

"We're here," she whispered, her voice sounding different behind her zivas, more warrior than woman. "This is Oas Havre, where we must go. The straightest path is blocked, so we must detour through here. It is an underground refuge for mine survivors. We can't let them see who you are. We can't trust anybody at this stage."

Titan nodded, following the direction of the path Harlow was tracing on the map. They walked Alban until the tunnel widened enough for them to ride, and then they took off, with Harlow collapsing the tunnels behind them as they went to stop anyone from following. Titan kept their path in his mind, and as they came close to where Harlow had indicated the refuge to be, he heard a murmur of voices and smelled the faint smoke of cooking foods.

Harlow brought Alban to a trot as they approached a doorway lit by torches, where two men stood guard. They were obviously not expecting any visitors from the way they jumped up and fell over themselves trying to find their weapons.

"Calm yourselves," Harlow called to them.

They squinted through the shadows, then one of them said with shock, "It's Darro himself."

The other one just stared with an open mouth until his companion punched his arm, urging him to help open up the doors. Alban rode through and Titan heard them saying with reverence, "the Unbreakable" in the same way people said "the Almighty". It gave him a very strange feeling.

They rode on until the tunnel opened into a large cavern where many rows of survivors were sitting down to eat. There was a warmth to the space, a laughter and amity that Titan could sense all around him. Then the first person spotted them, and silence rippled through the room as they all turned to look, saw and stood. Harlow dismounted with Titan and they walked Alban through. Titan looked from one face to the next and saw emotion brimming and overflowing. A woman stepped forward and held up a young child with burn scars on his face and arms.

"You saved my son!" she cried out.

"My son!" came another voice from the crowd.

"My children!"

"My wife!"

And then the whole cavern erupted into sound as everyone desperately shouted out their story to the person to whom they owed their lives. They wanted to touch Harlow's armor and as they pressed close, Titan heard the names of the mines that Harlow had shut down being called out as well – Shemal, Mukesh, Ainmire. When someone called out Morcvara Harlow paused and looked back. A young man stood there, horribly deformed from old injuries. He held up a hand to Harlow and she gave him a nod.

"You got us free seventeen years ago," a woman said, stepping into their path. "He was just a baby – now look at him." Her son stood beside her, wide-eyed and nervous, staring at Harlow.

"Chris," Harlow said, and the woman's eyes filled with tears. "You remember us."

They pressed through to the doorway on the opposite side of the chamber and continued on, the voices still calling out behind them.

They rode through the rest of the refuge. It had clearly been there for a while, with lives being established and lived out beneath the earth. Titan had never had any idea that places such as these even existed. It was indeed well hidden. They came to more doors, which were opened for them, and they rode out to the tunnels beyond. When they started to head uphill Harlow slowed their pace to give Alban a rest. The big horse had done them well and was slick with sweat, their combined weight enough to buckle most horses' backs.

"We'll need to ride overland to the sentinels where Anakis is waiting. Oas is right there," Harlow said.

Titan's mind moved through what he had just witnessed.

"You were closing mines seventeen years ago?"

Harlow nodded. "It didn't take Petacula long after the Almighty left. He knew your Lord Father would be well occupied with putting Corinthia back together."

"You must not have been very old?"

"I don't know exactly," Harlow admitted. "I don't know how old I am."

At least seventeen years of active subversion against Petacula and those like him, Titan thought to himself. All those years of saving lives and ending them, no wonder Harlow had looked down on him at the cave. He realized he must appear very green to her, maybe very arrogant as well. These thoughts brought him shame.

"Those people – they love you like people loved the Almighty."

"They're poor desperate souls," Harlow said. "Clinging to any hope. It's not anything to do with me."

"Please do not disrespect your sacrifice," Titan said. "I wish to be the warrior you are, the warrior my grandfather was, but I have not succeeded in this respect." It aggrieved him to speak the words aloud.

"How have you not succeeded?" Harlow asked him. "On the night before the King's Hearing you were bringing justice to that skin trader and mercy to his victims. And to many others before that. Do not forget that the Almighty was the king and he answered to himself and himself only. You are the liege and you answer to your Lord Father, what latitude have you had to ride anywhere other than where he ordered?"

Titan held his silence. It was the truth, but he did not know how to respond to it.

"Maybe that's why you chose to use the mask and cloak. You felt the call and could not act on it as yourself?"

"What you said in the cave, that there must be something truly broken inside for a person to only feel like themselves when they were pretending to be someone else?"

"Truly, Titan, if I am to put aside the words you said to me, you must do the same," Harlow said.

"And I will, but I wish to know if you believe them."

"Of myself, yes – I know I am broken. I accept that. But I don't believe you're broken. I believe you're holding back your power because you're afraid of being unnatural, and I can understand why, but I think once you accept the truth of yourself, that you are unnatural but that this is a gift, then you will find a trust in yourself that will be unshakeable. And then the great things you will do will change this world around you."

Titan's heart skipped a beat at her words and he felt heat spread through him – it was high praise from a person he respected first from a distance and now for the person she really was. It silenced fears that had tormented him with increasing ferocity since he'd discovered what he could do. In ways, he'd terrified himself, and hated himself.

"Can I tell you a truth?" Harlow said, and he could hear the caution in her voice.

"Of course."

"I did know the Almighty, as much as a small child can know a king, and he was the same as you – gifted. He said once that the world was not ready for it, but that one day they would be."

The revelation shook Titan to his core and left him speechless. *The same as you – gifted.*

"May I speak another truth? I have held it for many years, and now that we know each other, it feels less like holding and more like keeping from you. And I don't wish to do that."

Titan held his breath, wondering if Harlow was about to tell him of the Almighty's fate.

"I know you tried to save your brother's life."

Titan blinked. "My brother?" He thought she must be speaking of Ramses.

"He was born – with strange appearance."

A feeling dropped heavily through Titan.

"The Lord King ordered him to Cytisus and he was taken there, but you went and got him."

Titan could feel his hands start to shake and a tightness all across his chest. No one knew this. He had defied his father in an unforgiveable way. If anyone had known, he would have been put to death. He still would be.

"You gave the baby to an old cordager out in the swamp who said he would care for him. You paid."

Titan tried to swallow, but his throat was too dry.

"That cordager was the Almighty."

Titan's breath stopped and he felt as though he may fall from Alban's back. Harlow reached back to steady him.

"What happened to him?" he managed to utter.

"I don't know, but he wasn't killed or left to die. I was holding him and wouldn't give him back and the Almighty said that no harm was intended for him. He never lied."

"No he did not," Titan said. "He must have been greatly disappointed in me." A pain seared through him.

"He didn't seem disappointed at all," Harlow told him. "He seemed to know you would come. He seemed to be depending on it, as far as I could tell anyway." No one could truly know the mind of the king.

"I would have done the same as you," Harlow whispered, finding his hand and clasping it.

They rode in silence from there, Titan lost in thoughts and questions, until they broke out on the border of Anacharasis, Armen and Kirith-Jerom, under big pillars of rock known as the Sentinels. They heard a whinny and Anakis walked out with Naro and Winta and the rest of his horses. He and Darro greeted each other warmly, but then the sound of clashing swords and shouting reached their ears from deeper within the forest.

"It's the brothers. And Ramses," Harlow said. She leapt onto Naro.

"Ride! Go!"

Chapter 30
Ramses

HYDRIA

THESELON (TAOR)

The face that Ramses woke to made him startle back in shock. It was a sleeping woman with a hairy wart on her chin bigger than her nose. He struggled up in bed, breathing heavily and clutching the blankets under his chin like a virginal maid on her wedding night. His eyes felt like they were on fire. The woman, dozing in a chair beside Ramses, gave a snorting snore, flashing a glimpse of brown teeth. A thin line of drool dribbled from the corner of her mouth, sliding down to saggy breasts, one of them hanging out of her dress. It had four dark nipples, like four eyes staring at him. He stared back, mesmerized, until a strong smell of lavender and mint drew his attention to a basket beside the woman's chair. It was full of herbs and jars and fabrics, the wares of a provincial healer.

Ramses felt a sweat break out on his forehead and the room started rocking slightly. He suddenly felt unbearably hot. He shifted on the bed and it groaned and creaked in protest. The healer woke with a snort, a mucusy cough and loud blast of gas. She saw Ramses staring at her and spoke in a common Theselonian dialect.

"Ow, well look at you now. As pale as death, when I came in, but look at you, awake and all, told ya companions didn't I, lad," she said. "Told em Helga was as good a healer as any of them well-to-do physicians in them palaces – attending to their king's arse warts and nose hairs and what have ya."

Ramses inwardly cringed at the disrespect as the woman continued.

"Told em didn't I, lad – yes indeed. Best in all the lands be I. At remedies – and other things," she cackled, making a crude gesture. "And a fine strapping boy ya be."

She grinned at him, raising her eyebrows.

"If you don't have coin to pay, I'll accept other forms of payment, if you understand me." She raised her eyebrows again and leaned forward to twist Ramses' nipple. He was completely lost for words. Someone's tiddly backwater grandmother was trying to seduce him.

The door to the room opened and a girl entered, carrying a tray. Ramses recognized her as the serving girl from the night before. She was wearing a plain country dress, overly tight around the bodice. She smiled shyly at Ramses as she set the trays down beside the bed, giving him a full look down her top. Ramses felt movement from beneath his blankets. Despite everything. He guessed he'd have to be fully dead before his cock would stop ruling his life.

"I'll sit with him and feed him, grandmother," the girl said.

"If you wish, youngling," Helga agreed. "I have to go empty my bowels anyway."

She took to her feet with effort, picked up her basket and made for the door with a heavy sideways waddle.

Ramses and the girl watched her go, and as soon as the door clicked shut the girl pounced on top of him, kissing him on the mouth. He tried to hold her back but she clawed at him, dragging their faces together.

"I'm not in the best state," he tried to explain between her kisses. "I can't right now."

He tried to sit up but she shoved him back down and straddled him, whispering in his ear.

"You just lay there and leave all the work to me."

She sat back and ripped open her top, exposing large soft breasts. She grabbed his hand and pushed it against them, and before he could put forth any further complaint, she was bare naked, his tunic was up around his chest and she was riding him like they were going to battle. Ramses felt extremely unwell, but she was screaming out with pleasure.

Suddenly the Storon brothers burst through the door. Morrison, on Aron's shoulder, was sounding an urgent alarm.

"Good gods, man," Aron said, seeing the girl.

"Up, wench." Vitali grabbed her off Ramses and shoved her naked and protesting out the door. Then he dragged the two other beds over and wedged them up against the door. Ramses heard many heavy boots stomping up the stairs as Aron heaved him up out of the bed and half carried him to the window. Vitali was already half out. Ramses could hear Grayweather whinnying to him from the street below.

"The packs," he said.

"No time," Aron told him.

Vitali leapt and after a moment they heard him call out, "Throw down the cripple."

"Uncalled for," Aron muttered to Ramses, swiftly helping him up to the sill. Ramses maneuvered around and Aron gripped his wrists, lowering him down. Fists started pounding on the door, shaking the beds.

"Let him drop," Vitali called, and Ramses panicked. He'd end up breaking his other leg as well. He tried to grip onto Aron, but he'd already released his grasp and Ramses fell. Vitali caught him solidly from the back of his stallion. Grayweather pushed in beside them and Ramses started to climb onto him, but Vitali yanked him back.

"Behind me! We're leaving the gray!"

"No!" Ramses shouted at him with such force that the elder Storon didn't argue. Ramses grabbed the geld's reins and managed to climb into the saddle. Aron dropped down and Vitali shouted, "Run!"

The horses took off and Ramses glanced back to see faces poking out from their window.

The Storons' stallions were breeds of speed and distance, but Grayweather bravely held his own as they belted down the back forest tracks. They could hear the thunder of the soldiers' horses not far behind.

"Woah!" Vitali suddenly shouted, and Ramses had to pull up hard to stop Grayweather smashing into Aron's stallion. Ramses directed the geld to one side to prevent the collision. He looked up and saw they were completely surrounded by ambush soldiers with crossbows aimed at them. The pursuers on horseback thundered in as well and the captain, one of Gideon's men, wearing the head of a jaguar as a hat, gave a smug smile. Ramses kept his head down in case they didn't already know who he was.

"Harlow Darro's men," the captain announced proudly. "The Storon brothers, correct? Aron and Vladimir."

"Vladimir!" Vitali shouted. "Who in Acheron is Vladimir?"

"That's right. Aron and Vladimir Storon," Aron laughed.

"Why does no one remember my name?" Vitali said. "It's easy, even for illiterate imbeciles like these." He nodded to the captain, whose grin soured.

"We're taking you to the king," he said. "And then we'll see."

"Go back to the arsehole that shat you out and crawl back in," Vitali spat at him. "We ain't going anywhere."

Ramses dared a glance up to judge their chances. The odds weren't good. Grayweather was rolling his eyes, his ears pressed back hard against his head.

A guy with huge legs and long dreadlocked hair in the Armenite fashion noticed Ramses looking and said, "What are you staring at, pretty boy?"

Ramses blinked and replied in their tongue, "The same thing everyone else is staring at – that bog swine's ball sack you call a face."

Aron laughed out loud again, despite their dire situation.

"When we're done you'll be sucking this, pretty boy," the Armenite said, pulling his cock out the side of his subs.

"So you say," Ramses replied. "But just so you know, I have teeth like a lion."

"We'll have to knock them out then."

"You can surely try, if you wish to meet Methusael this day," Ramses threatened while his mind worked fast, trying to think how they were going to get out of this. He felt ill enough to drop without anyone hitting him at all.

As he looked around, his eyes made forms and shapes of the soldiers, of their horses, of the trees and the boulders.

He saw that the tree branch above his antagonizer was loose, and that bringing it down on his head would make his horse shy back, producing a ripple effect among the others that may buy them some time. He glanced at Aron and saw that the younger brother was still laughing, but his eyes were on Ramses and they were dangerous.

"Attack!" Ramses shouted.

He lunged forward and Grayweather reared up. Ramses knocked the branch free and it crashed down on the Armenite with the big mouth. Before he fell, he got a shot off with his crossbow and it nicked Ramses' shoulder. It knocked him off balance and he tumbled off Grayweather's back, hitting the ground hard. He rolled over, trying to get up, but the Armenite was on him. He smashed a fist into Ramses' face, jarring his neck back and knocking him half senseless.

He couldn't fight back, all the strength gone from him. All he could do was try to block the blows while the clashing of steel and yelling voices rung out all around him. The Armenite grabbed a rock and lifted it above his head, smashing it down on Ramses. He raised it again, but then a look of confusion crossed his face. Someone had appeared right beside them. A warrior in shining armor.

"Let me assist you with that," Darro said to the Armenite and shoved the rock back into his face, knocking him out.

"Rams!" Titan dropped down beside him and Ramses stared up with blood streaming down his face, unable to believe it was really him. The world started rocking and spinning and he closed his eyes against the sickness swelling inside him.

Chapter 31
Titan

HYDRIA

ANACHARASIS (OAS HAVRE)

"*D'osto?*" Titan asked Ramses, a word that in High Corinthian meant *Are you alright?* and literally, *You look close to death, can you keep riding?* They'd carried Ramses like a dead man through the underground tunnels to Harlow's hideout and spent the whole day and night treating his wounds. Harlow had alternated between attending to Ramses and searching her vast library of scrolls and books for a way to remove Belphanganor's Prime, without yet finding the passage she remembered reading. She was keeping her feelings behind her face, but Titan knew from the way she kept checking the mark that she was worried. They'd poured more iron into it, but the weeping and pain was returning faster each time, and he could taste the tang of saltwater on his lips.

With word that Ramses was now waking, Harlow had returned to the room, her face covered by her helm, the Storon brothers and Anakis with her. Titan stood beside Ramses' bed, looking down at him. His brother hadn't just lost half his leg, but also more than half his body weight. He was so bloodied, bruised and emaciated that Titan could barely look at him for the pain he felt inside, but he made himself look Ramses in the eye.

"*D'osto?*" he asked again. Ramses licked cracked lips and said, his voice hoarse, "Yes. *D'osto*, Lord Liege?"

Titan gave a measured nod.

"You took fair injury, Ramses of Ohai." Darro stepped forward to examine him. "Your leg on the fall, your arm with a lion, your shoulder and head with Gideon's men. Is anything left unsaid?"

"Well, I have an itchy arse and chafe between my legs, if you'd like to weigh that in as well," Ramses answered with thinly veiled anger at Harlow for pointing out his weaknesses.

"Too bad no one's cut out your tongue," Vitali barked at him.

Harlow continued inspecting Ramses' injuries. "The infection is gone at least – the fever too. We'll need to keep it that way. Your arm needs more ointment."

"I'll get it," Aron said, and left the room with his alarm bird on his shoulder.

"We'll go as well," Harlow said, and Titan gave a nod.

Once they had left the room Titan leaned down and embraced Ramses firmly. He had already been through more than any man could bear, and now this.

"Look at the strength of you," Titan said, and saw the surprise in Ramses' face.

"I'm not strong anymore," he murmured.

"You're stronger than ever,' Titan reassured him.

Aron returned with the paste and while he was spreading it over the wound, Ramses' eyes closed again and he fell back into rest. His face looked so peaceful that Titan's chest tightened in fear and he leaned down to check his breathing. Life was not peaceful.

"Lord Liege, you should take some rest now too," Aron said.

"I'm fine," Titan replied, though the pain from the prime had grown almost unbearable. He saw Aron glance at his chest and Titan looked down to see a growing patch of wetness.

"Harlow's chamber is down this tunnel," Aron said. "You should go find her. I'll stay with Ramses."

The disquiet of his voice prompted Titan to concede.

"I'll return," he said.

Titan left the room and started through the tunnels, soon discovering that Harlow's true hideout was a reflection of the person she was – intriguing, frustrating, almost impossible to navigate and full of hidden places and dead ends. He followed a feeling inside him until a light appeared up ahead, and he found himself at the door to Harlow's chamber. She was not present, but from the maps, designs and strategies, he knew the room was hers.

He stepped inside and moved to her planning table in the center of the room. The map she had laid out was of the entire Northern Halos, including Cytisus, and it stood as the most detailed and complete map of the Halos that he had ever seen, it had clearly been a long work in progress. It was well beyond even his knowledge. The insight into Harlow's mind left him feeling almost light-headed, but there were other immediate feelings too, doubt that it was accurate, doubt that she had completed it herself, and this made him think. He had never doubted the maps of hers that he'd collected when he'd believed her a man, but now he doubted on instinct, even though she kept proving her skill over and over. He felt ashamed that he had such deeply ingrained beliefs, that he had assumed a woman could not possibly be as skilled and intelligent as a man. The words kept replaying in his mind – *women are not warriors, women are not warriors ...*

Some of the writing on the map was in a language or code that he didn't immediately recognize. The writing was so tiny. He picked the parchment up to bring it close to his face, and as he did he noticed that one side of the map was thicker than the other. He turned it over to inspect. It looked the same, but he had definitely picked up a variation. Very carefully, so as to not damage the map, he felt over the parchment, feeling for an edge, until his fingernail snagged on something. He used the fine point of the pinion on Harlow's table to peel the paper back. Between the two pieces of parchment he found another. It was written in the same unfamiliar language as the map, but as Titan looked at the words, they formed meaning in his mind.

I don't know what to say, only that I need to say something. Maybe it's foolish writing a letter that will never be read, but I need to get it out of my head and these words can never be spoken. I wouldn't even know how. I don't know where to begin, there's no beginning that I see ... What the leaders used to say about me ... they wanted me to be punished for my ways – it was improper, they felt, for a small girl to be the companion of a king. You gave them no response. You had a way with silence. You made it say everything for you. I heard them saying they'd never seen a more disobedient and unworthy child. And it cut deeply. I didn't see myself this way, but their rebukes made me even more furious. Even at you. I was so scared you'd send me away that I fought you, but you

*saw through everything. Kings didn't hug. But you did. Kings
didn't let defiant, furious, screaming, damaged children keep
them company. But you did. Your compassion saved me. You
lived by the law, and you transformed it ... I pretended you
were my grandfather. I refused to call you Lord King. In truth,
I knew you weren't my grandfather, I just wanted you to be.
I was so confused. My heart was broken and I didn't know
how to talk about why. I didn't have the words to say that I
ached to go home, to my mother. I couldn't comprehend that
she was gone forever, so all I could do was cry and scream
and say no to everything. And scream at you when I loved you
so much. Even at that age I would have walked into Acheron
for you. The Almighty. When I asked you why they called you
that, you got that look in your eyes, like you were smiling on
the inside. You weren't allowed to smile on the outside.*

*You said, "Almighty? A man could look into that word and
get lost forever in his own greatness." You didn't see yourself
as Almighty. You saw yourself as the king, and the entire
world as your responsibility – every person in it, no matter
how lowly or rejected, diseased, deformed or forgotten, as
worthy of your mercy, and every walking horror, every evil,
every black heart as deserving of your punishment.*

*I miss you. I love you. I wish I'd said it when you were still
alive. I wish I'd known how.*

*If you were here, the world would be a different place. The
monsters would still be hiding in fear. But maybe you would
look at me now with disappointment, because I haven't grown
into the lady that you said I would ... I'm a monster too.*

Titan heard footsteps behind him as he finished the letter.
He turned and saw Harlow standing in the doorway, her
face covered by her zivas. Titan felt an understanding form

inside him. She had been taught by the Almighty as a child. Harlow entered the room and spread a scroll out over her map, then she saw him holding the letter.

He broke the heavy silence. "Please remove your helm so that we may talk face to face."

Harlow didn't respond, so he started to repeat himself.

"I said —"

"You do not command me." The hardness of her voice made Titan pause.

"No," he agreed. "I do not." He understood he had encroached on her true self, and that it was too much for her.

"You're not a monster," he said.

She held her silence and he went to put a hand on Harlow's shoulder, but she lashed out, shoving him away. She swung and Titan blocked, but the impact made him stumble. Harlow struck again and he tried to sidestep the blow, but she was fast and he was forced to engage and swing back. They fought hand to hand and he could see it now, the Almighty's training behind her every move. The armor gave her advantage, and his height gave him advantage and he realized one of them would have to be seriously injured before the fight ended. He had no desire to hurt her, and he didn't believe she wanted him down either. He took a chance and stopped, dropping his hands by his sides and standing straight. He saw Harlow's strike coming for him, felt the instinct to duck, but didn't. Her hand stopped just in front of his face and he stared at the blank eyeholes of her zivas.

Harlow retracted and stood straight before him. He started removing his clothes.

"What are you doing?" she asked.

"Undressing."

"Why?"

"I see the truth. I threaten your sense of control, when that is all you've had to hold onto, but in the bathing water you spoke to me as yourself, I believe. Perhaps undressed I am less threatening."

He took off his clothes, throwing everything aside and sitting down naked on one of Harlow's chairs. She watched him for a second and then unlocked her helm and zivas, lifting them off her head and placing them down. Her eyes were wary, frustrated, but also slightly amused.

"Now we can sit. As equals." He indicated the chair in front of him.

She sat, but said, "Have you considered that we may not be equals, but that I am your superior?"

"Don't push your fortune," he said, and saw a smile at the corners of her mouth.

After more silence she said, "Are we talking or just staring at each other?"

"I'm waiting for you to talk," he said.

"I haven't come before you. You asked me to sit – so what do you want to talk about?" she said.

Titan studied her face as she spoke. He believed he was starting to understand. Harlow used words as her weapon to keep him back. If he was angry and frustrated, he would be too distracted to examine Harlow and her feelings too closely.

"Where is he?"

Immediately the iron left her eyes and she looked down to the floor. "My memories are ruined," she admitted. "I just remember pieces and I'm not even sure if I remember them truly or if they've been warped."

He nodded. It happened when people were tortured, especially children.

"I don't remember the actual day he left. I've tried – many times," her voice caught. "Sometimes I think I see something, but it vanishes like smoke. I know I don't believe he's dead. I feel that."

The words sparked emotion inside him and he swallowed slowly, waiting until he was in control before speaking the words he knew he must as the Lord Liege.

"You love him," Titan said. "But the great king has ridden from this world into the Blessed Plains, otherwise he would have returned to his people."

"Unless something has kept him," Harlow said.

"Do you really believe any man could have kept Apollo the Almighty for all these years?"

"A man, no," Harlow said. "But maybe something else."

Titan's eyes narrowed slightly.

"You've seen it yourself, Titan," Harlow said. "Other things exist on this earth."

Titan resisted the urge to touch the prime. He wanted to reply but the words he knew he should say were different to the words he wanted to say, and the two warred in his mind.

They sat in silence until Harlow started to unlock the metal yoke around her neck with a particular combination of moves. She slid the yoke off and opened it up on her lap, lifting out a chain with a ring on it.

Titan felt as though his whole body dropped through itself and onto the floor in a rush. It was one the Almighty's rings.

Harlow held it out to him and it was a struggle to raise his hand to take it. It sat in his palm, shimmering and warm. In his mind, he saw the ring on his grandfather's finger and it made him remember so many things he'd forgotten. He could even smell the Almighty's scent and hear his voice so much more clearly. He noticed there was an inscription inside the ring that hadn't been there before and he recognized the Almighty's hand: *Harlow Darro.* He had given it to Harlow and signed it hers. Titan released a shaky breath.

"How did you keep it safe all these years?" he asked.

Harlow showed him a long scar on her forearm beneath her armor.

"I hid it there when the Drauls took us all into the camp." Her voice sounded flat. "I didn't do it by myself – one of the women helped me before she was taken. An older woman who used to tend the Lord King." She focused on the ground as she continued. "I just wanted to say ... I couldn't let it go. I wanted you to have it – for a long time, but I couldn't be without it." She looked up and met his gaze. "It was selfish and I am truly sorry."

Tears glistened in her eyes for a moment before sinking back into their green sadness, and Titan heard the truth in her words.

"Do not be sorry," he told her. "The Lord King gave this to you because he meant it for you. It was the correct thing for you to keep it." He tried to hand it back to her, even though everything inside him was crying out to keep it.

"He did give it me," Harlow said. "And now I'm giving it to you."

She nodded and Titan retracted his hand, holding the ring close to his chest.

"Why?" he asked her.

She looked around the room in thought. "If someone had something that belonged to my family – *anything* – and they kept it even if they loved them too, it would kill me. If I did the same to you what sort of person would that make me?"

Titan nodded, understanding that everything inside her was screaming to keep it as well.

"Do you remember when he gave it to you?"

She flashed a quick smile then, her voice recovering some of its color. "Yes. I had a way with moving quietly and listening in to conversations I shouldn't. I listened into a meeting between the Almighty and King Sirion, way back then, and got caught, and Sirion wanted me punished. And I thought I would be. What I did was a serious offense, as well you know."

Titan nodded. It was extremely serious.

"I hid."

"The Almighty found you?"

She sat back in her chair and thought for a moment. "He wasn't angry at all. He said I had a gift and that if I could sneak up on him and his *ata-ajua* without them knowing, he would give me a piece of his jewelry – anything I wanted."

Titan smiled, but his heart also sank, he knew something was coming.

"I tried many times, and I finally did it, and I was so very pleased with myself that I didn't think for even a second that maybe he had allowed me to, because something was wrong."

Titan nodded.

"And I was so busy demanding what I wanted that I didn't comprehend what he had written on the parchment in front of him, but I see it clearly now – *Time is gone.*"

Titan's stomach clenched at the words. He lowered his head. *Time is gone …*

"I wonder …" Harlow started, then stopped herself.

"What do you wonder?" Titan prompted.

"A woman can't be a warrior, we both know that. Just can't – here and now. But why did he teach me how to fight and ride and plan and everything if he didn't intend for me to use it?"

Titan let her words sink in. He couldn't answer, neither of them could. It was branded into their minds – one could never fathom the mind of the king. They weren't even allowed to try. But he silently did, and the answer came back to him, but he couldn't say it. *He did intend you to use it.*

Someone cleared their voice at the door of the chamber and both Titan and Harlow looked sharply toward it.

Aron stood there with his bird, both of them looking awkwardly between Titan's nakedness and Harlow.

"Apologies," he said, his eyebrows flickering. "Ramses of Ohai requested that I leave him alone, but I really don't think he should be alone." The darkness that came into Aron's eyes was alarming. "I can't help him."

"Go," Harlow said to Titan with an urgency that spurred him immediately to his feet. He grabbed his tunic and ran back down the halls.

Chapter 32
Eli

HYDRIA

FARNORTHERN HALOS (BLED)

King Apollo raised his head, looking through his veil of long gray hair as Eli clicked the cell door shut behind him.

"I've got it!" He ran toward the King, fell flat on his face, staggered up and kept running. "I also released a bear and a spectral breed and imprisoned a demon chef. So we're going to have to really move."

He unstrapped the king's mask and was met by eyes that spoke unflinching refusal. With close to three decades as a prisoner and his word of honor standing between them, Eli knew he'd have to pull out the big guns. He remembered how Apollo's eyes had shifted when he'd spoken in Corinthian, so he tried again.

"Mordan was there, in his chamber, and he was talking to the Indemeus X."

The king watched him, listening.

"And then he was talking to one of his demons and he said your grandson Tarrus is being hunted by a witch."

Eli saw the words registering in the king's eyes, and his skin started to heat up.

"Mordan sent them to stop her, but he said to bring your grandson in, as motivation. Indemeus has given him one more day to do whatever it is that we're supposed to be doing with the plan. Trust me, he's as desperate as anyone can get."

The king lifted his head and straightened his back, rattling the chains that held his arms out on either side of him. "This is not part of the pact." His voice vibrated in the walls. "Just me – that was the deal."

"He's not sticking to the pact, King Apollo," Eli said. "It's over. The universe is falling apart. Please believe me. I saw their master plan in Mordan's chamber – the Indemeus X is attacking in waves and Hydria is in the seventh wave of worlds. He'll take your world too, just like he's taking Aquais right now!"

Eli expected a reaction, an outburst, a furious rage, but instead an utter stillness settled over the king's face, and he was instantly more frightening than all the angry and murderous people Eli had ever seen, put together. Eli took that as a yes.

He knelt down in front of the king and held the splint up to the triptwitch. His hand started shaking. One wrong move, one minute twist or bump in any direction other than exactness and he'd kill the king – and the universe. There was pressure, and then there was this. Every muscle, even ones he never knew existed, clenched. A faint started to take him and he counted aloud through gritted teeth, determined that his body wouldn't fail him now. Nelly crept up from his wing and curled around his neck.

"Okay." He breathed out the words, then cast a glance up at the king.

"I have – I mean *I haven't* – ever done this before. Ever – and it's impossible." As he said the words, his arms flopped down by his sides.

The king studied his face and said in Corinthian, "You have come here from another world. You have drawn mercy from a king who cannot be merciful, and influenced another king who cannot be influenced. How many times must you defeat the impossible before you start to believe in yourself?"

At the king's words, Eli began to cry – not a dignified, single-tear-running-down-a-stoic-cheek cry, but a face-screwed-up, red-eyed, snot-streaming, making-sounds-like-a-hungry-baby-donkey cry. *Don't forget to fly …*

Eli fought to compose himself and when he did, his hands weren't shaky anymore. He felt incredibly tired, but also like someone had lifted a heavy weight from his back. His blinked to clear his eyes, then set his mind to the task. *Just do the job.*

He slid the splint into the triptwitch's lock and studied the pattern of the puzzle, eyes flitting from one wire to the next. He saw it – the solution. With nerve-shivering care, he started twisting the splint, extracting the wires one by one so that the central loom would hold. When the last wire was out, he turned the splint all the way around and then withdrew it.

For a moment nothing happened, and Eli could heard the individual beads of sweat dripping off his face, making sounds like very small piglets as they fell. He had no idea why, maybe he had concentrated so hard that he'd caused himself an aneurism. Then the triptwitch popped. It gave off the burnt tar stench of dark magics and the steel band of the trap ripped out from the flesh of Apollo's upper thigh and fell, bloody, at his feet.

Without making a sound, though Eli himself was cringing at the agony he knew the king must be feeling, Apollo dug his fingers into the wound and found the trip, then started pulling it out from where it was coiled through his body. It came out squirming and fighting, sometimes looking like a worm and sometimes like a chain. Eli recovered from his initial horror and leapt in to help. He grabbed the nasty sucker and joined the ripping. It came out like a clown's neverending scarf until finally the end appeared, with little hooks that kept embedding themselves back into Apollo's flesh.

Eli's hands moved faster and faster, until they were a whir and the trip could not keep up. He wrenched it loose and fell back with it covering his face before leaping up and flinging it away. It hit the wall and popped, vanishing. After a moment of stunned silence, Eli went for Apollo's manacles. The king had his eyes closed, and his skin was very pale with a greenish tinge. A triptwitch was a death sentence, whether it stayed on or came off, but he had survived. Eli looked frantically at the door, knowing they had already taken too long.

"King Apollo," he said, quickly tearing his dress and using the fabric to bind the king's wound. The king stirred. "You're an electromagnate. You can break these chains faster than I can pick them."

He'd said the word "electromagnate" in Urigin. Apollo narrowed his eyes, then shook his head. "I cannot."

Eli wondered for a moment if he meant he would not, but did not pause to discuss it. He just started picking the locks until Apollo's arms and legs were free. How the king remained upright Eli could not even comprehend. And gangsters thought *they* were tough.

Eli put a hand around King Apollo's back as though to help him forward, realizing as he did so that it was completely ridiculous. Even emaciated, Apollo weighed probably fifty times what he did. But he set his jaw and said, "We'll go back to the kitchen and up through the tunnel the animals made."

Apollo shuffled forward and Eli grimaced, expecting him to go down like a ton of bricks, but he kept his feet and as they moved toward the door he seemed to be gaining strength with every step.

They made it out into the tunnels and then it was a fight against themselves to keep going. With every step Eli thought, *I can't take one more step*, and then he did. They found themselves halfway to the kitchen before they hit a road block. Right ahead Octavia was fighting against Gibbit and a group of other slavers. Sanfrass lay unmoving on the ground in front of them.

Eli stopped in full sight and King Apollo dragged him into the shadows. Octavia fought on savagely but uselessly against the slave master. Eli couldn't understand why she wasn't using cos magics or the host of other inborn skills of a spectral-breed. In arm-to-arm combat they were about as effective as soft spaghetti.

"King Apollo, I'm going to distract them," Eli said, pushing a metal blade into Apollo's hand and drawing the sapphire one for himself. "You keep going straight. It's all straight from here."

He broke away quickly before he lost his nerve, and found himself running full-barrel toward Gibbit. He leapt, ballet style, over the top of the slave master, who was wrestling Octavia to the ground, and yelled out, "Hey Gibbit, you stink."

He had no idea why he said that, it was just what came out. And then he was running, with Gibbit and his slavers thundering behind him.

"Stop, you little maggot!" Gibbit snarled. Eli had never been less motivated to stop in his life, or more motivated to run, and he became even more so still as he heard a distant *ech ech* echo out behind them.

He sprinted, searching desperately for somewhere to hide, but there was really nowhere, the endless tunnels providing no relief or hope. And then they hit a dead end, a solid rock wall with nowhere to go.

Eli put his back to the wall and clenched the blade in his hand just as the slavers broke around the corner. Gibbit was at the head of the pack, holding his bloodied whip. The others had swords and cleavers that made Eli's weapon look like a splinter.

He gulped but held his position as they crowded around him, glaring. Gibbit sneered, slapping his whip into his hand with anticipation. It sparked a sudden rage in Eli and he shouted, "You think you're such big men, don't you? But you're not, you're just weak, pathetic lunatics." He spat at their feet.

Eli had never been a big spitter, but if spitting was what it took to get the message across, so be it, and in this case it was more than effective. Gibbit's expression twisted from shock to fury to murderous in under a second, and then they were all closing in, big sweaty white muscles bearing down on him, with a rock wall at his back and a less than effective blade in his hand. He realized he hadn't thought this rescue through as well as he should have.

The commander always said you have to have not just the start of a plan but the end as well, and contingencies for everything that could go wrong. But he didn't have time to even gulp. He thrust the sapphire blade out in front of him. The slavers saw it and stopped, exploding in a roar of laughter. Eli took the opportunity to strike first. He lunged forward and stabbed the blade into the closest slaver, who gasped and reeled back. Eli almost vomited but held it in, attacking again and again while the slavers tried to figure out what was happening.

"Get him!" Gibbit snarled, and they all attacked at once, eight against one. They were bad odds but Eli fought hard, his speed working to his advantage. Gibbit couldn't get the whip up fast enough. Eli stabbed several more of them before they overcame him and threw him to the ground, pinning him. Gibbit stomped on his hand, forcing him to release the blade.

"Hold him," he said to the others and they stretched out his arms and legs. Eli cast a frantic look around. Gibbit punched him across the face, knocking a tooth loose and almost blacking him out. The slave master dropped down hard on Eli's chest with one knee. Eli gasped and Gibbit smirked. He leaned low into Eli's face and whispered, with breath that smelled like off milk, "You're going to hurt. And you're going to love it."

"Why would I love it, you trutting psycho?" Eli yelled. He used his tongue to break off his cracked tooth and spat it right into Gibbit's eye.

The slaver roared and reeled back, clutching at his face. He crashed over several of the other slavers, making them loosen their grip on Eli. He immediately took advantage and struggled free, then scrambled to his feet. One of the slavers grabbed his shoulder, dragging him back down, but Nelly shot out of his collar and bit into the slaver's hand.

"A rat bit me! A rat!" he screamed.

Eli crawled toward the sapphire blade and managed to grab it then spun, ready for round two. If they thought he was going down easily, they were so wrong.

Gibbit lumbered forward, blinking, unfurling his cruel whip. He cracked it at Eli, who rolled out of the way. He heard it whistling up again and knew he wasn't going to be able to dodge this time. He looked up, saw Gibbit bearing down on him and braced for pain. But before he struck, Gibbit's face took on a pensive expression, as though he was experiencing a moment of clarity, maybe a change of heart or an epiphany, then half his head dislodged from the other half and slid onto the ground with a wet thump. Eli only had time to exhale before the slave master's body dropped as well, revealing the person standing behind him.

King Apollo.

The other slavers turned, appeared to collectively soil their undergarments, then tried to run, pushing each other out of the way. Apollo finished them before they'd even started. Eli almost smiled, breaking the first rule of escape – don't celebrate until you're actually out.

A shadow moved behind them, amassing shape and form as it neared. A strong chemical odor filled the air and Mordan appeared. Apollo moved back in line with Eli, the two standing side by side. Mordan looked from Apollo's freed leg to Eli, his eyes brimming with sadness.

"You betrayed me," he said. "You. Betrayed. Me."

Despite everything, Eli actually felt guilty. "I'm sorry," he whispered.

"You're dead," Mordan said, giving him a nod.

The king stepped in front of Eli and Mordan said, "We have a pact, Almighty, and you are a man of your word."

"You have broken the pact. My grandson. My world."

Mordan shivered, his eyes rolling, as he momentarily lost control, realizing the truth was out.

"My daughter. *My world*," he growled. "I guess we both have everything to lose."

Eli's skin prickled all over at the words. He didn't know demons cared about their children – or anything, for that matter.

The two kings lunged for each other, fighting hard, Mordan using every ratha weapon he had and Apollo countering with speed and strength. Mordan's skin was ripping in places as they hit each other over and again. His wings broke free at the back, huge black vulturous things, and his horns erupted out through his head.

Eli clambered around the walls, looking for a way he could somehow intervene in Apollo's favor. Mordan darted out his poisonous tongue and managed to wrap it around Apollo's neck before the king could cut it off. The toxins made Apollo drop his blade. Mordan grinned his creepy clown grin, then began reeling Apollo toward him.

Eli ran in to help and Mordan swished him back as though he was a feather on the breeze. He struck the wall and hit the ground holding his chest. The sound came much closer – *ech ech*. A chill swept through Eli and then an idea formed in his mind. He heard Ev'r asking, *Is it a good idea?* in the way she did every time he came up with a cunning plan, and he said, "It's the worst."

He leapt up and started shouting, "Hey, Ripper! Hey! I'm here. It's me. I'm here!" He tore off his dress and started flapping his remaining wing, with poor Nelly clinging on for dear life. "Come and get it!"

Mordan cast him a suspicious glance, his vile tongue still dragging Apollo in.

Eli expected to hear the *ech ech* coming progressively closer, to have some warning, but the silence was broken by *ech ech* blaring right in his face as the Ripper suddenly appeared, no face, just claws.

Only Eli's speed saved him. He launched himself headlong toward Mordan's feet. The demon king tried to stomp on him, but he rolled again and then the Ripper hit Mordan, dividing the demon king's attentions as he was forced to fight for his life as the Ripper went after his gigantic wings. He released Apollo and Eli grabbed hold of the king, trying to help him. Apollo picked Eli up like a child and took off running.

Eli looked back over the king's shoulder and saw Mordan battling the Ripper. Every wound he inflicted on the creature appeared on his own body as well and then the Ripper regenerated. He saw Mordan realize and stop, grabbing one of his own horns and cracking it off his head. He gave a long yowl of pain as he did so, but the Ripper screamed out in agony. The reaction made Eli think the horns must be something very serious. Both the Ripper and Mordan were still staggering around as Apollo turned the corner, almost crashing into Octavia, who was struggling with all her might to lift Sanfrass. The king scooped them both up as he charged past and Eli found himself with the spectral-breed on his lap and Sanfrass on hers.

"Hi," Eli said as Octavia looked back at him in shock.

Apollo crashed through the kitchen door, kicking the chef, who had managed to free himself, in the chest and sending him flying out of the room. And then the king was climbing upward. Eli clung on, dirt pelting down all around them as the king proved once again why he was called the Almighty. They broke through in the middle of the flat plains behind Bled. Eli blinked into the sun, which had seemed so dim when he'd first arrived but now felt blazing.

Apollo put him down and Eli turned in circles trying to get his bearings. They appeared to be standing on a dried up ocean bed littered with huge ships and even huger bones of gigantic sea creatures. Up ahead, he spotted the wall he had seen in the distance when the slavers were taking him up to the skull city.

"We must cross *Mĕthmalay*," the king said, but Eli didn't know what he was talking about.

Behind them the ground erupted and Mordan dragged himself up, his horn only partially regenerated. He saw them, raised a glowing red sword in the air and bellowed. The air around them shivered and the sky above burst to life as Mordan's summons brought every demon crashing toward them.

Eli watched them coming like a tidal wave. There was no way they could outrun or outfight them. There was no way out.

Chapter 33
Ev'r

HYDRIA

FARNORTHERN HALOS (HOLLOWLAKE)

It appeared that Snacksize had somehow managed to draw the attention of every single demon in the world and simultaneously infuriate them. Below the hilltop where they stood, he was running as fast as his short legs would take him, which really was pathetically slow, across a desert scattered with shipwrecks and bones. The demons were closing fast behind him.

"Talk about a slow-moving target," Ev'r said. "Where is he even running to?" She glanced at Ismail and the darkness of his eyes said things were about to get bad – for Eli, and for them if they tried to intervene. Beside Ev'r, Silho raised her hands and drew in a massive blast of strength from the demon masses, exhaling a fireball from her mouth. It opened the gap between them and Snacksize and even brought some of the lesser demons crashing from the sky.

"Hit them again!" Kane commanded.

"Keeps cutting out!" she said.

"Keep trying. Keep hitting them!"

"I'm getting stronger waves too," Ismail said. "There's a change."

"Waves," Kane said, running his eyes over the ground as though his senses were twitching. "There's a breakwall on the other side of the desert." He pointed into the blurry distance. "They've dammed the place."

"We flood it?" Shawe said, surprisingly managing to put two and two together.

Kane nodded. "Can you morph the *Ory*?" he asked Diega.

"I can try." She grabbed the coin from her weapon belt and threw it up, shouting, "*Xpel!*"

It was all very dramatic but the coin just flopped to the ground.

"Nicely done," Ev'r said, and fairy girl swore at her in Fenlen.

Silho gasped, drawing in another rush of lightform, but it wasn't going to be enough to stop them.

"Ismail, can you carry Shawe and Jude over to smash the wall?" Kane asked.

"He's not going anywhere without me," Ev'r said.

"He can't carry three."

"So he leaves one of them behind."

She locked eyes with Kane and he saw she wasn't budging.

"Shawe and Keets?" Kane asked Ismail.

He gave a military nod, looking like the soldier he once was. There was a snapping sound as he broke his wings out through his back.

"Stand on my feet, grab my shoulders," he said to Ev'r and Shawe, and once they had, he took off.

"Trutt you're heavy," he grunted, struggling with the weight of the rhinoceros-blood gangster.

"Quit crying and fly," Shawe said.

"How about he drops you on your head?" Ev'r snarled as they soared above the desert toward Snacksize. A flying demon suddenly swooped in at them from above and made a grab for Ismail's neck. Shawe swung a punch, sending it ricocheting away.

He gave Ev'r his cocky smile and said, "Feel free to lend a hand at any time, Keets, if it's not too much trouble."

Ev'r drew the Morsus Ictus, and as another demon dove down on them she cut it down mid-air.

"Good enough for you?"

"Good enough for a girl." Shawe clobbered the next one and it fell like a stone.

Ev'r laughed in anger. "You're so lucky we're otherwise occupied, podsucking gadfly."

"Heads up," Ismail said as they hit the main group of flighted lesser demons. Ev'r clenched her blade and Shawe clenched his fist, then Ismail hit them with a wave of telepathic energy that sent the entire flock haywire, repelling them as Ismail flew through. They swooped low over Snacksize and he caught sight of them, jumping up and down with joy as he did, waving both arms.

"Keep running!" Ev'r shouted at him. He had a few others with him, a gray-haired man with a ripped body, a spectral-breed and something else with wings. Typical Snacksize, picking up strays wherever he went.

"Get to a ship – water's coming!" she shouted, looking back over Ismail's shoulder.

Eli paused for a moment, understood, then started tearing for the closest wreck.

"Let's hope he picks one without a hole," she said to Ismail. He circled above the breakwall, giving them a glimpse of the massive crashing waves held back behind the dam. A shark, monstrous beyond belief, leapt out of the water as they flew down to the wall. She heard Shawe curse.

"Too much for you, Christy?" she said.

They landed on top of the wall and Shawe rammed his fist down into the structure. It tremored and started splitting, even though it was incredibly thick and towering high. She felt it begin to shake beneath their boots.

"A few more like that and you'll have it," Ismail said.

"Just get ready to fly. I don't want to eaten by that trutting thing." Shawe nodded down to the circling shark. He struck the wall again and the shaking increased. Ev'r looked back toward Eli and saw he had reached a ship, but the demons were right on him.

"Speed it up!" she said to Shawe. He put his full force behind a series of powerful blows, once, twice and a third time, and the fracture opened wide and water started spraying through. The breakwall was quaking in a way that said rupture was imminent.

"Hold on again!" Ismail instructed. He leapt, lifting them into the air as the whole thing broke open, stone bricks tumbling and the water exploding inward. They were almost caught up in the furious wave, but Ismail managed to carry them higher just in time. Shawe was staring down as other frightening creatures of the deep washed through, a gigantic octopus, more sharks, a crab the size of a building.

"Hell no," Shawe breathed, his face growing pale.

"Remember that time you called us filthy scullion scum?" Ev'r threatened Shawe.

"I can't remember calling you anything else," he returned defiantly, and Ev'r had to admit he had balls.

"You're my enemy's enemy," she said. "For now."

"For now," he agreed with equal bitterness.

They flew over the top of Eli's ship, which had been picked up by the blast of water and was rushing backward, away from the wall. Ismail swooped down and they landed on the deck as the ship lurched from side to side and the wind whipped their faces. Eli flew into Ev'r arms and she only had a second to glance at the gray-haired man, feeling a strange calm sweep through her, before Shawe shouted above the roar of the waves.

"They're in trouble." He nodded back to where Silho, Kane, the Fen and Jude stood on the hilltop, which was rapidly looking smaller and smaller.

"I'll go for them!" Ismail said, and Ev'r grabbed his arm. She felt a trickle of her magics, maybe enough – maybe. "I'll go, you won't make it."

"Then take me with you!"

Ev'r gave a nod. She concentrated, reaching for the magics more deeply than she'd ever had to, even when she was a beginner. She found the murk and struggled to sink them through. They moved out toward the others, but her steps were sluggish, even in the drift. She could hear Ismail grunting in pain and see his hazy outline. She cut out of the murk and they dropped down beside Silho with the tidal wave roaring toward them. She and Ismail grabbed the others and Ev'r strained.

"I can't get back in!" she shouted, starting to panic.

She stared at Ismail. They had to go, but they could only carry one extra. He tried to grab Silho but she ripped out of his grasp.

"*Claude animus meus.*" Kane spoke an illusionist enchant to Ev'r. "Say it. Close your mind to everything but the magics."

Under any other circumstance she would have told him to jump, but right now she did exactly as he said. She closed her eyes and repeated the enchant aloud. She felt herself dropping a level of consciousness closer to sleeping than awake, and in that place she could see the magics flowing around her. She reached her hands out to the others and jumped in. When they cut back in they were on the deck of the ship. Ev'r didn't remember getting them there. Ismail hugged her, kissing her fiercely.

"Trouble," they heard Shawe say.

"What trutting now?" Ev'r shouted, and he nodded to the waters. Bubbles were rising all around them. Evidently these demons could swim.

"Arm up!" Kane commanded them, and Ev'r drew the Morsus Ictus.

Ismail's eyes scanned over the deck and he spotted some thick shipping ropes.

"I have a plan," he said.

"Is this a good plan?" she shouted.

"Not particularly!" he said. "Kane, two lassos with judas knots big enough for a transflyer head. Jude, Shawe, be ready to throw them."

The other men ran for the rope and Ismail went to the side of the ship, leaning over, his fingers skimming the water as it lurched from side to side. Ev'r held onto his back and felt the energy run through him. He was concentrating so hard it looked like all the veins in his forehead were about to burst. Beside them, two of the monster sharks breached the surface as Ismail used his shark bloodline to call them in.

"Throw!" he shouted, as his connection was severed by the augmentor.

Shawe threw the rope but missed. Jude threw and missed also. Ratha demon heads were breaking the surface.

Out of nowhere, two more ropes sailed over the top of all of them, finding their marks around the sharks' heads. Ev'r turned. The gray-haired man was tying the ropes to the thick mast, fastening them just as the sharks took off, dragging the ship behind them. Their velocity threw everyone off their feet. Ev'r rolled across the deck as they flew through the waters, barely skimming the surface. She managed to sit up and saw the land they'd come from fast shrinking to nothing behind them. Ismail sat up beside her and then Eli's grinning face appeared right in front of them. He was so smashed up it made even her wince.

"I have good news and bad news," she said.

Snacksize's grin widened. He was missing a tooth.

"The good news – we've left the ratha back there. The bad news – you're not beautiful anymore. What were you thinking, taking on an entire demon army?" She slapped him across the back of his head.

He laughed and hugged them both. "I knew you'd come."

"Head count!" she heard Kane call out.

"Diega," fairy girl said, and they each called out until everyone was accounted for, except for the three strangers Eli had brought along for the ride. Ev'r gazed up at graybeard behind them. He was giving off some strong electromagnet pulses and the longer Ev'r stared at him, the more she wanted to run to him – inexplicably. She'd never felt anything quite like it.

"King Apollo of Corinthia," Eli said, introducing the man, and everyone fell silent, the wind howling around them. Snacksize had actually found him. The king. Apollo was gazing up at the sun and the sky, like a man who hadn't seen it for some time.

"Is he the augmentor?" she asked Eli, tearing her eyes away from the king.

"The augmentor?"

"All our skills are out."

A realization came into his eyes. "No, I don't think so. I don't think he can actively use his skills either."

"We can't jump until the augmentor stops blocking us," she said.

"Well, let's hope he's on this side of the ocean and not back there," Eli said, pointing behind them.

Ev'r noticed the other two strangers moving beside them. One was the creepiest-looking thing she'd ever seen in her life, and the other a spectral-breed who wasn't going to win any beauty pageants either.

"Who's the freak?" she asked Eli.

He grinned. "The girl I'm going to marry."

He looked over at her with affection in his eyes.

"That thing is going to rip your heart in half – literally. And then probably eat it!"

The girl saw Eli staring at her and he waved. She spat in his direction and the spectral had to hold her back from charging at them.

"I think she's warming to me." Eli's eyes were shimmering with hope.

Ev'r returned her attention to the king and saw he was looking behind them, to where a darkness was gathering, and she felt the truth.

The fight wasn't over.

Chapter 34
Ramses

HYDRIA

ANACHARASIS (OAS HAVRE)

Ramses awoke to find Aron sitting beside him, scratching a picture on a small, torn piece of parchment. He felt Ramses looking and immediately started scrunching it up, then stopped himself. He held out the paper and Ramses took it, looking down at the image of a house on a hill. Using only charcoal, Aron had made the house feel alive.

"Our house on the Rise," Aron said. "When it still stood."

"I want to say you're truly talented, but I don't wish to offend you," Ramses said, his throat sore and voice worn. Morrison hopped from one foot to the other on Aron's shoulder.

"And I want to say thank you, but I have to be offended," Aron replied, flashing his smile. "How do you feel?"

"Crazy," Ramses gave the first response that came to him.

"Aren't we all?" Aron said quietly. "On the bright side, you're now as broken on the outside as you feel on the inside."

"That's not bright," Ramses said. "Not one bit."

"You're right, it's not."

They both gave a laugh that didn't quite make it.

"How is Grayweather?"

"He's fine. He's in the stables below with the other horses."

"Below?" It troubled Ramses that they would be stuck there should things turn bad – it was why Corinthians had open stables.

"Harlow has triggers to release them if – if need be." He glanced at Ramses, his expression darkening.

Ramses nodded, feeling a heavy exhaustion descending on him again, bringing with it a dread that seemed to fill every part of him.

"Would you mind," he said to Aron, "if I had a moment to myself?"

"Of course." Aron stood and Ramses looked up at him. Aron had been good to him. It was something that needed to be acknowledged.

"Thank you, Aron of the Rise. It's been an honor." Ramses extended his hand.

Aron took it, smiling, but as his eyes met Ramses' his smile faded.

"My honor, Ramses of Ohai," he said. He started to back away but then paused.

"Are you sure you don't want me to stay?"

"I'm sure," Ramses said. Aron gave a nod, hesitated, then left the room, Morrison looking back over his shoulder with knowing eyes, and eyebrows drawn inward.

Ramses lay still for a moment in the silence, then struggled to sit up. There was a mirror on the other side of the room and he was drawn to it. He wanted to see himself. The way he trembled and grunted as he tried to maneuver out of bed brought him feelings of shame. He finally managed it, and used the chair Aron had been sitting on as a crutch. Halfway across the room he had to lower himself down to rest, his heart was beating so fast.

When he made it to the mirror the sight that met his eyes was of another man. He was not mighty. He was broken and hollow-faced. Ramses ran a hand down his rough face and exhaled a shaky breath. He lowered his eyes, unable to look at himself any longer.

When he looked back up his reflection was gone and he was looking into a room as though he stood at the doorway, and he could see August inside, hanging, dead. Tears rushed to his eyes and he tried to run into the room as he had on the day he'd found his father, but he crashed into the mirror instead, shattering it and falling backwards. Blood ran hot from his head. He looked up at the broken mirror and saw her in the shards. His little sister.

He reached out and touched her face and her reflection vanished. He closed his eyes. His mother laughed there behind his memories. She was a truly beautiful woman. Mesmerizing, people said. To Ramses she had been a stranger who merely pretended to care for him and his sister when someone was looking. She belittled August. She shamed him and enjoyed his pain. And yet, he kept trying to make her happy.

She'd wanted to leave him for another warrior, but August had convinced the other man to be honorable, and he'd taken another woman as his wife. His mother had taken Ramses and his sister to Cy Cyrene, stood on the cliff looking down at *Mĕthmalay* and jumped, dragging them down with her. Ramses shuddered, feeling the cold water hitting him. He could taste the salt filling his throat. They'd died, but he'd somehow found the surface. And then August had left as well.

He put his head in his hands and cried. Warriors never cried, but he was not a warrior anymore. He was nothing. A chill ran over his skin and he looked up at August. His father knelt in front of him, a light in his eyes even though they were despairing and full of grief at seeing him so wounded.

"Why?" Ramses sobbed, clinging to the front of his father's tunic. "Why did you leave me?"

August wiped away Ramses' tears, and when he spoke his words were a struggle and his voice was very soft.

"My boy." He stroked Ramses' face. "I knew you'd be better off without me."

Ramses shook his head, not understanding what he was saying. "Why would you ever think that?"

"I just knew I had to go, and take the pain with me."

"But you didn't take it with you," Ramses said. "You left it with me!"

August's own eyes filled with tears and he stared at Ramses, wordless, aghast.

"I'm sorry." August grabbed him close and rocked him from side to side. "I'm sorry, my boy, my boy, I'm so sorry ..."

Ramses' head nodded down and when he lifted it he found himself sitting alone, holding himself. He stared at his fractured reflection. He suddenly understood August's pain. It hurt too much. The past was a lie, the future was blackness. There was nothing ahead but more pain. He just wanted it to stop.

His hands found a piece of broken mirror. It had a sharp edge – it would be quick enough, and final. He held it up and saw his eyes reflected back. He hesitated. The door burst open and Titan lunged at him, knocking the glass out of his hand and grabbing hold of him as he tumbled sideways.

"Let me go!" he shouted.

But his cousin only clutched him tighter, and with Titan's touch, he felt the pain draining away until he was numb.

"Why did she do it?" Ramses whispered.

"Rams, I don't know. I wish I did, *cursil ios*," Titan said quietly, talking as a man and not the lord liege.

Ramses closed his eyes and tried to tie together the torn fragments of his control. When he felt strong enough, he looked up and Titan let him go, keeping a hand on his shoulder.

"Why did you choose me as your Companion when you knew I was broken? Was it pity?" Ramses asked him after some time.

"No," Titan said firmly.

"I see my father. I talk to him like I'm talking to you," Ramses admitted in a sudden rush of words.

Titan's expression didn't change or even flicker. He just nodded, listening.

"Is it really him?" Ramses uttered.

"I thought I knew everything and now I realize I know nothing. I don't have an answer, brother," Titan said.

"Everyone loved him." A smile came to Ramses' lips, despite everything. "That laugh. He brightened the darkest days."

"Except his own," Titan said.

"Except his own," Ramses murmured in agreement. "I don't know what to do."

"We're prepared for life. Nothing prepares us for death," Titan said.

"There's no future for me. I don't want to live like this."

"There is a future," Titan told him. "You can't see it right now but it's there, and one day you will feel differently.

Just because you think you need to end it now doesn't mean you have to. It's just a thought. It's just one option."

"What are the other options?"

"Live. Keep fighting, one more day at a time. In honor of your father, for the man he was. I'll help you. August never let anyone see his pain. We're taught to suffer in silence and pretend the pain doesn't exist, but how are we supposed to fight an enemy that doesn't exist?"

"There's no way," Ramses murmured.

"So we talk about it. We make it real and fight it."

They looked at each other and Titan said, "Service to the Lord King, Honor in Battle, Sacrifice in Brotherhood, Sanctity in the Afterlife."

Ramses nodded. The words brought him comfort, but then he looked down and saw his leg.

"The Lord King will retire me. I can't be a warrior rider."

"You have a way with matter, my brother," Titan said. "You'll fashion yourself a replacement leg to move as you need to."

"I'll be unnatural."

Titan raised an eyebrow. He extended his hand to Ramses' bed, where a shield hung on the wall as decoration. The shield sprung off the wall and shot into Titan's grasp.

"If you are unnatural, what does that make me?" Titan asked.

Ramses was utterly speechless.

"That person in the city, attacking the skin traders – that wasn't Darro."

Ramses snorted, looking for falter in Titan's face, but there wasn't any. He was being truthful.

It took Ramses a moment, but then he said, "Are you trying to outdo me now?" A smile crept onto his face and he gave Titan a light shove, feeling some of himself returning from the darkness.

"Trying?" Titan's tone was playful. "That's never taken any effort at all."

They sensed movement at the door and looked over to see Aron standing there, looking at them and the broken glass, his composure shaken. He opened his mouth, but then Morrison started flapping his wings wildly and screaming, "Flee! Flee! Flee!"

Titan gasped and a jet of water burst from the mark on his chest, smashing away the metal covering it. Ramses fell backward, shocked, and Aron lunged over, trying to press a hand against the water, but it was too strong. Water rose up all around them, along the walls and over the ceiling, trapping them inside the room.

A form took shape from the flood.

Ravana.

Chapter 35
Titan

HYDRIA

ANACHARASIS (OAS HAVRE)

Princess Ravana Nazar paced around him, lovely. Her lace gown trailed behind her and her fingers traced the scars on Titan's back. Her hair brushed soft against him as she leaned down and kissed his lips. The rotten taste of her breath made his stomach turn. His first instinct was to pull away sharply, but he tempered his movements, not wanting to make the same mistake twice. The water was still running from his wound, less but continuous. It pulsated in his chest and his limbs felt weak. Ravana straightened up, smiling at first, but then the smile soured into a snarl.

"There's another woman," she said.

"No," he assured her. He cast a quick glance toward Ramses and Aron, sitting sprawled against the wall. Water had wrapped around them like ropes, as it had around Titan, binding their arms to their sides. Ramses' face was deathly white and he was staring in horror. Aron was alternating between almost smiling and looking completely savage.

A cluster of Ravana's glooms stood over them, looking less like women now and more like the monsters they'd become.

"No," he repeated to Ravana. "There's no one."

Dark forms moved behind the water. Titan avoided looking at them, hoping with his every fiber that it was Harlow, and that she would know how to breach the walls and deliver them from this.

Ravana leaned in close again and Titan held his breath, staring her solidly in the eyes. She searched his face for answers. Her lips twitched.

"You're lying to me," she snarled.

"I'm not," he said. "There's no other woman."

"I. Don't. Believe. You," she said, tapping his chin, and then knocked his chair over backward. She grabbed him by the balls so tightly that he almost blacked out.

"There's no one!" he shouted.

She maintained her grip, hovering her other hand in front of his face and whispering, her voice splitting and distorting. "Speak the truth."

Titan felt a prickling sensation sweeping through him, but he gritted his teeth and drove it away, resisting whatever sorcery she was trying to use. Ravana's eyes widened in surprise at his resistance.

"Get away from him you ravenous harpy!" Ramses bellowed.

"I still don't believe you," she whispered to Titan, "but I don't want to hurt your body. I need that."

She released him and turned on the others, looking between them. "You!" she said to Aron.

"Did you have to antagonize the insane and possessed?" he said to Ramses.

Ravana motioned to her glooms and they forced Aron down onto his back. Titan watched as Ravana's hand started shaking and huge, elongated black claws broke out of her skin, her fingers stretching horribly. She advanced on Aron and he started thrashing around, trying to get free from their grasp. Titan thought he heard Aron's alarm bird screeching from beyond the water. Ravana fell on Aron and he started screaming, a terrible, agonized sound.

Titan fought the water binds, the beast inside him snarling, rising up, but he couldn't break their unnatural hold. The thought made him remember what Harlow had said about his power, about accepting the truth of it. He whipped his head to the other side and saw the sword the glooms had taken from him and thrown into the corner. He stared at the weapon and willed it to move.

At first it gave him nothing, as Aron continued to cry out, but then it suddenly flipped up into the air. He imagined it going through Ravana and the sword flew through the air toward the princess. Just before it hit her, her head turned with eerie speed. She screamed as the blade pierced her head and she exploded into water. Her glooms vanished with her, along with the water binds, though the water trapping them inside the room remained. Titan kicked the chair away from him and leapt up. He and Ramses reached Aron at the same time. The younger Storon lay on his side, gasping, a pool of blood spreading beneath him. He looked down and saw all the blood and started hyperventilating.

"She's cut my balls off!" he gasped.

"No," Titan told him. "It's just a cut."

"Only a cut," Aron said, his voice high with hysteria. "That's okay then!"

Titan placed a hand on Aron's shoulder and he immediately calmed, the pain and fear easing as his composure returned to him. Ramses was rapidly binding the wound to stem the blood flow. Titan didn't think she'd hit an artery, but there was still a lot of blood. Aron lay on his back, staring at the water flowing above them.

"I guess no life is ever perfect, is it? There's always regrets," he said.

The words made Titan even more uneasy than he already felt. They sounded like acceptance.

"This is not a time for reflection," Titan said to him. "Now is a time to fight."

"It feels like time," he murmured.

"It's not your time, Aron of the Rise," Ramses said, giving him a shove.

"It feels like time," Aron repeated.

"It's not," Ramses insisted.

"You were going to go, so why not me too? Why do I have to stay in this godsforsaken nightmare?" He put a hand to his head and held it wearily.

"Well I'm staying now, and so are you," Ramses told him. He grabbed Aron and dragged him up to sitting. "Do you understand?" Ramses asked him.

Aron hung his head but then nodded.

"Are you steady?" Titan asked him.

"I am," he confirmed.

Titan took his hand away and Aron collapsed, crying out. Titan went to grab him again but felt his own head go light, and he slumped over to one side. He heard chanting, and the pain of the prime exploded. It felt as though he was being dragged down into the ground. He grasped for Ramses as the water poured from his chest. His cousin held onto him.

"She's dragging me down," he said to Ramses. "She'll take me to *Měthmalay*. I can't fight it."

"No!" Ramses said, giving him a violent shake. "Use everything you have!"

A blast of red-orange light ripped through one of the water walls, opening up a hole. Vitali vaulted through, with Anakis behind him. Vitali spotted Aron covered in blood and bellowed, "What have you done to yourself?"

He grabbed his brother up and Anakis lifted Titan and Ramses, one over each shoulder, with an ease that made Titan feel weightless. Anakis leapt back through the fire and Titan flinched as the flames licked his skin.

They crashed out on the other side and the giant put them down. The fire blazed up and then leapt out of the wall, the water sealing over behind it. A light flashed from the flames and then they extinguished suddenly, leaving Harlow standing before them unscathed. Her eyes met Titan's and she said, "Quick! To the library!"

He nodded and the group moved swiftly down toward the scroll room, Titan supporting Ramses, and Anakis supporting them both. As they ran, Harlow collapsed the tunnels behind them using her inbuilt triggers. Water began dripping down on their heads. They burst into the library and Harlow locked it down, extra thick walls with metal plates sliding down over the existing walls and door. An ordinary intruder would have been completely blocked, but Ravana Nazar was not ordinary, and the walls began quaking. Harlow finished reinforcing them with every trigger she had, then turned to Titan.

"I need you to tap into your power again."

"That's how she found us!" He hadn't thought just showing Ramses a momentary glimpse of what he could do would cause them to be found.

"She's here now," Harlow said. "And if you tap your power, I can use mine too. I've been noticing something. I can touch a wall or the ground and see into the past to find what was happening there. I may be able to find the scroll."

Titan looked around. There must have been thousands of books and scrolls stacked up around them.

"Darro," Vitali said, his voice grim. He nodded to one wall and they saw water had started streaming in. Harlow looked back to Titan and he breathed.

"Okay." He concentrated and saw Aron's paths opening up before him, many paths leading to death and only a few to life.

Harlow dropped to her knees and put a hand to the ground. Her eyes swiveled as she saw something no one else could. She sprung to her feet and started ripping into her scrolls, tossing them aside and burrowing deep until she came back with one in her hand. She spread it out in front of them and everyone crouched down, holding the edges flat. Titan could see Harlow had made attempts to translate the words, which were written in an ancient language he hadn't been taught but still understood. Harlow ran her fingers over the translation, struggling to read the faded and smudged words.

Titan saw familiar words, and read aloud, "The Curse of Manah."

"Yes!" Harlow said. "Can you read it out?"

Titan leaned in and read, "Belphanganor's Prime is inflicted—"

"No, go to broken – how is it broken?"

Titan skimmed through and found the words.

"The encroached partakes in the sacrament of matrimony – oldstyle." He squinted, trying to read the faded letter. "Oldstyle," he confirmed.

"Oldstyle?" Vitali repeated.

"Are they talking about a sex position?" Aron asked in all seriousness.

"It's not a sexual act, you *abrams*!" Harlow shouted at them. "It means by blood."

'What by blood?" Ramses asked.

"Matrimony through blood." She held up her hand and acted out an incision. "That's the old way."

"So he has to get married? That's it? That's all?" Aron asked.

"Yes, and I should have thought of it myself. I read—" She gestured back to the rubble of her scrolls. "Marriage started to protect against witches."

The walls shivered and they heard a groaning, crashing noise.

"That's the exterior walls giving way," Harlow said. The water was now coursing into the room.

"Anak – trigger the release for the horses," she said, and the giant nodded and headed to the wall.

"Congratulations!" Aron said, drawing Harlow's knife from her calteus.

"What?" She stared at him.

"He needs to get married and you're the only female present. I like your odds!"

"This is not a joke," Vitali snarled at him.

"And I'm not joking," Aron said. "These walls are going too, any moment."

Titan looked at Harlow's face and he thought, *Yes – she is the one.* She was strong, her heart was a refuge for the forgotten and her mind was a force to be reckoned with.

Harlow was the person he had been looking for, not just for two years but for his entire life. He loved her.

"No!" Harlow said, taking Titan by surprise. "We're not going to be forced to marry because of a witch."

"You have some better offer do you?" Aron said. "Some other ruler of the entire world that wishes to take you as his wife – or even some other way to get us out?"

The walls were quaking and water lapped at their feet.

"Harlow," Titan said. "I'm not being forced. I want to."

"*Nea*," she said in Corinthian, rejecting the notion.

He looked into her eyes and said, "You don't fool me at all, and you're stuck with me now – regardless."

He leaned in and kissed her. It was entirely against custom, but at that moment he didn't care who was watching. A massive spike of pain drove him to the ground, water flooding out of him. He couldn't lift his head, and the water started filling his mouth and nose. He felt someone grab his hand and there was a sting in his skin, then he heard Ramses say, "Witnessed before warriors, witnessed before the gods. Man and wife."

And then the pain stopped. It receded like a tide until it was no more. He sat up and checked his chest. Belphanganor's Prime shrank and faded away to nothing. The walls stopped shaking and the water cut off. They stared at each other, breathing heavily. Titan realized he was clutching Harlow's hand in his.

The wall beside them suddenly collapsed, the metal denting and warping inward. Ravana appeared and screamed, "I love you!"

A monstrous beast burst out from the ground beside her and flung her across the room, where she exploded in water.

"Woah!" Vitali shouted as the beast charged them.

Harlow reacted first, leaping to her feet, sword in hand, driving the monster back and countering its attacks. Anakis joined her and then so did the others, Vitali throwing Titan a sword. The monster was unlike any enemy he had faced. It had a red sword and fought savagely, using the sword and other parts of its body that were fashioned as weapons. And every one of their strikes that found its mark healed immediately.

The monster huffed a noxious green cloud in Aron's face and he collapsed, but then Anakis hit it with his axe, massive strikes over and over, driving it backward. Its sword started glowing and making a humming sound, then the monster leapt back into the hole it had made and vanished. Vitali started performing all kinds of wards but then he noticed Aron lying on the ground and he fell down beside him, shaking him and shouting out his name.

Harlow grabbed a vial from her tunic and poured what looked like sludge down Aron's throat. Titan imagined it must be the ooze of some gelatinous slug or similar. Aron started to stir. Ramses helped him up and Vitali punched Aron right in the face, shouting, "*Abram!*"

While Ramses tried to restrain the brothers, Titan noticed Harlow had walked to the edge of the crater in the ground and was looking down. He saw her legs bend and realized she was about to jump. Both he and Anakis lunged at her at the same time, grabbing her out of mid-air.

"What are you doing?" Titan demanded.

"I remember ... those creatures were the ones who took the Almighty. I saw a tunnel open up in the Sinani Desert and they took him under."

Titan stared at her as the sound and scent of flowing water reached them from the tunnel below.

"There's a river down there?" he asked.

Harlow nodded.

"Where does it lead?"

"*Mĕthmalay*. Cy Lasea," she said.

"You were going to swim after it?"

"I have boats below," she said. "The current flows fast. I have to go after it." Her eyes were set.

He nodded. "I'm coming with you."

"As am I," Ramses said, struggling up, using his sword as his crutch.

"No more water," Vitali spat, and Aron vomited solidly on the ground beside him.

"The two of you collect the horses and ride for Cy Lasea," Harlow told them. "If we don't return and you don't see sign of us there, go straight to King Osiris and tell him everything."

They both gave confirmation, and Harlow looked at Titan.

"Are you ready?"

PART 3

Chapter 36
Eli

HYDRIA

FARNORTHERN HALOS (ADRIA SEA)

He slept for micromoments at a time, during blinks between waking, when even his boundless energy reached absolute depletion. They'd all gathered. They'd all agreed on tasks to keep the ship moving and prepare for attack. And then they'd dispersed across the decks, but before long everyone had gravitated close again, drawn toward the king. He was magnetic. And not just because he was an electromagnate, but because his presence threw a circle of supersensory warmth around him and everyone wanted to stand in his light.

As a general rule of thumb, Eli refrained from staring at people, strangers in particular, no matter how fascinating they were. For imp-breeds, staring was quite literally a pastime, but over the year-cycles Eli had come to realize that innocent gazing was easily misconstrued by those outside his race as creepy goggling, it made women uncomfortable and men want to punch him in the face, so he normally restrained himself. But every time he tried to look away from Apollo he found himself dragged back again.

With the scary-wild beard and long, tangled hair, the king bore some resemblance to the homeless man who used to trash dive outside of the old headquarters, a poor unfortunate who had spent many a long hour locked in impassioned argument with himself, when he wasn't cackling at the rain or accosting passersby with manic gibberish. But that man's eyes had been glazed and vacant, tired, whereas the king's eyes were extraordinary, even more so now they were out in the light. He had two irises in each eye, a rich chocolate brown with lines of gold. They were like the calm center of a storm, a direct view into the sharpest of minds, and when they looked at you, something happened. As Eli had thought in Bled, it felt like home. Even for people who had never had one.

The way the king sat watching over them now reminded Eli of the many times Grampy had sat beside him throughout the night, ready to comfort him when he woke screaming from nightmares. Gran'ma had a rule – no sleeping in their bed, even when Eli was completely and utterly positive there was a clown-faced monster lurking in his closet that would devour him horribly as soon as he closed his eyes, so Grampy had volunteered to sit with Eli, even though Gran'ma thought it was the most ridiculous thing he'd ever done.

"There's nothing there!" she'd hissed, and Grampy had responded, "That's not the point."

As Eli had wriggled down in his blankets, which Gran'ma tucked in straight-jacket tight, he'd looked over and been comforted by the sight of Grampy sitting beside his bed, with his small moustache, which he always managed to shave crooked, and his walking stick resting across his legs. He'd seemed so formidable. Looking back Eli knew he had been frail and ill even then, but to a young Eli it'd seemed like nothing could ever get past him, that those arms would hold him forever …

Eli lowered his head, taking in a deep breath of the salty sea air. He'd been given strict instructions by the commander to rest, but he just couldn't stop jittering, or thinking. He knew what was behind them, and it really didn't feel like the time to sleep. Eli stood carefully and looked around at the others. King Apollo and Ismail were at the bow of the ship, beside the wheel. The king had redrawn his map and had given Ismail directions on where to steer the sharks. Ismail could speak their language, and was communicating with them using very low frequencies that the rest of the group struggled to hear, even as his telepathic skills to control the sharks' minds came and went. The king had said they were headed for the place where all the tides of the ocean came together – he'd called it Cy Lasea. Apollo told them there was a sword there, beneath the waves on the seabed, which would defeat Mordan-Grieg. That was why the king had written the map and split it into five, giving the pieces to his bodyguards to take out into the world, looking for someone to free Hydria.

Ev'r sat close to Ismail, doing a weapons inventory with the boss, sharpening blades and making new weapons out of objects they'd found on the ship. Silho was getting all the ropes in order, re-twisting and mending them. Diega was using her morpher skills where she could, and a hammer in between, to mend leaks and cover holes in the ship, trying to reinforce it as much as possible, while Jude stood preparing some food from the emergency rations they kept on their weapon belts and what Christy had caught with the bow and arrow they'd found aboard. He had tied rope to the arrows and was shooting flying fish as they breached the surface. He was preparing them for Jude to cook on the kiln-like structure near the wheel. Eli could see little Nelly standing beside Shawe's boots, gobbling up pieces of fish he was dropping down for her. She shot Eli a look over her shoulder.

"Traitor," Eli whispered, but he couldn't help smiling at her mucky little face chomping away. He glanced behind him for the thousandth time, peering over the railing down into a slightly recessed section in the middle of the boat. It was partially covered by a tarpaulin, and Sanfrass and Octavia were sitting beneath it. Sanfrass was hunched up in one corner with her head on her knees and Octavia had an arm around her. They hadn't moved at all for quite a while, and Eli had let them be. Sanfrass' mahogany hair sparkled in the sunlight, even thought the sun was so faint and distant. He could imagine that she'd shine under the Aquaian suns.

The thought made him wonder if Aquais was still there. Bad feelings ran through his chest. He turned back and saw Jude coming toward him, holding some food. He gave Eli a warm smile and offered him a board with no fish, then lowered the other board down into the recess for Octavia and Sanfrass.

"Thanks," Eli said.

He met Jude's glowing blue eyes. They looked at each other for a few moments, then hugged fiercely.

"Eli, I'm so sorry," Jude said.

"I'm sorry too!"

"You're my best friend and I've been lost without you." Jude squeezed him tightly with his metal prosthetics.

A shadow fell over them and they pulled away to see Shawe standing there, holding a board with fish on it. He looked down at them with utter disgust, a cigarette dangling from his lips.

"Harden up you two sissies," he said around it. "Take some fish, insect," he said, using the nickname he'd given Eli when they were kids.

"No thanks," Eli said.

"Why not? What's wrong with you?"

"I don't eat meat."

"No meat?" Shawe's brow furrowed. "Why not?"

"Because I love animals."

"I love them too – on my plate, beside my mashed potato and carrots."

"Well, I love them alive."

Shawe screwed up his face. "So you'd rather starve to death than eat an animal."

"If I was starving to death, it would be different, but I'm not – I have plenty here."

"Yeah, looks real tasty," Shawe said dismissively. "That's why everyone thinks you're a girl, you know – no meat on your plate, no meat on your guns." He flexed his bulbous muscles.

"That's not the reason," Eli said.

"Keep telling yourself that." Shawe turned to go.

Eli's eyes moved over the group. Everyone was working hard, but the divide was obvious. Silho wasn't looking at Copernicus at all. Copernicus wasn't looking at her either, and Shawe was ignoring Diega in every obvious way possible.

"What's happened?" he asked. Jude sighed deeply, rubbing the Androt barcode on his neck.

He recounted to Eli the events of their journey through the Farnorth of Hydria, and Eli shook his head.

"I didn't mean for her to get hurt. I never wanted that," Jude said, looking over at Silho.

"I know you didn't," Eli said. "Everything will be okay."

Jude gave half a smile and patted Eli on the back. "I'll get the rest of the food handed out." He walked back across the deck and Eli wandered over to Diega.

She looked up and smiled her dazzling smile, her star bloodline marks sparkling up and down her arms.

"How's the face?" she asked.

"Bit tender." He felt around the different patches of pain. "How are you?"

"Fine," she said but her eyes didn't look fine, and he knew she was thinking about Alejan.

"He'll be okay," Eli reassured her, with no idea if that was actually true.

"What if it's already been taken when we finally get a portal open? What if there's nothing left? What if he's not there?"

"Then we go into the Indemeus X's realm and get him back," Eli said firmly, and Diega snorted. "You weren't in Omar. You don't know what it was like. It was so hot and everything was sinking ..."

"He's with Luther," Eli said.

"That's not comforting, Eli," Diega said with force. "He's a trutting Midnight Man."

"Yes and no. He's got the bloodline but he's not dangerous. Not to us, anyway, and certainly not to a baby. If I was forced to leave my baby with anyone during a crisis I'd want it to be him. He can dissipate, throw all kinds of magics and generally frighten anyone away, but then he also cries over butterflies and rainbows."

"Alejan gets upset when I have to leave him to come into work and now ..." Her voice faltered and she glanced over at Shawe. "He doesn't even care."

"He calls him Christy Junior – what does that say to you?"

"Shawe loves himself, that's what it says."

"He's angry," Eli said. "Do you blame him?" It wasn't at all like Eli to be so direct, but all the tiptoeing and sugar-coating had been drained out of him in Bled. "I thought you liked Shawe?"

"I trutting hate him. He's a pisshead thug." But her reaction was so extreme and angry that it completely undermined her words.

After a few moments of sadness-laden silence, Eli said, "Maybe you can sell it to him like this – he slept with the boss's girlfriend, and now you've slept with the boss – so now they're even. I know he'd appreciate that logic."

"I don't have to sell him anything," Diega said.

"Or maybe you could tell him sorry for breaking his heart?"

"Are you concussed, Eli?" Diega stared at him. "Breaking his heart?"

"You love him and he loves you. You told me yourself – he saved you and Alejan in Omar."

"Well, things have changed, haven't they?"

"And Silho?"

"What about her? She should have backed the commander." Diega shifted where she sat. "You just have to accept it, if we don't die here or back home, the trackers are finished. It all started going downhill when Silho latched onto us."

The words hurt Eli's heart. He'd thought Diega has started to move past her dislike of Silho.

"Just do me a favor and stop self-destructing," Eli said, and Diega's eyebrows flickered with surprise at the hardness of his tone. "If someone else is attacking you, I'll fight them to the death, but you're attacking yourself and it's killing me!"

Footsteps sounded behind them and Jude appeared with two boards of food.

"Would you mind taking Silho's to her?" Jude asked Eli. "The last time I spoke with her, it didn't go so well." He dropped his gaze.

"I'll take it," Eli said. "If you and Diega make up." He stared at them sternly until they gave each other slightly amused looks and clasped hands, military style.

Well, that was two fixed. Now to get Silho on board. Eli headed over to where she was fixing some nets. He put the food beside her and sat down.

"Weren't you supposed to be resting?" Silho asked him lightly.

"Can't," he said, looking over the edge to sharks gliding through the water beside the boat. They were following the sharks who were at the front pulling the boat forward, all drawn in by Ismail's commands. The sharks were beautiful and terrifying creatures. It was surprising Christy Shawe hadn't tried to put them on his plate beside his carrots and potatoes. Eli looked back to Silho, noticing her Pyron bloodline marks of flames had faded, whereas the emerald green of her Omarian firebird dragon was bolder than ever and the little pictures across her neck and chest were standing out against her pale skin.

"I was just talking to Diega," Eli launched in. "She's worried about Alejan."

"Clearly," Silho muttered.

"You know, I'm not an expert on relationships. I've never really had one except for being accidentally married to Flintlock, but I think the boss feels more comfortable when everything is wrong. I can see how that might lead him to sabotage a good relationship without meaning to," Eli said, pointedly.

"I understand that," Silho said. "But he said it's over."

"Maybe he just said that because he was upset?"

"When does he ever say things he doesn't mean?"

That was true enough. Suddenly Eli's good intentions hit a wall. He clasped Silho's hand and said, "Anything you need, I'm here, okay? Until some crazed demon wipes me off the face of the universe, I'm here for you."

He looked back to the commander. He wasn't the kind of person who would ever be jumping up and down with happiness, but since being with Silho he had seemed less unhappy than ever before. Why just end it like that? He wanted to talk to him, but he knew Copernicus wouldn't talk.

"Diamond's gone, isn't she?" Eli said suddenly.

Silho's expression softened.

"I'm really sorry, Eli," she said.

"*Lai Lai,*" he whispered, trying to hold his tears back. "Can't be."

Silho's eyes flashed to the front and Eli saw that the king had stood up. There was a splash behind them, and a scream. Eli whipped around. Octavia was standing on the edge of the ship crying out and he knew – Sanfrass had jumped overboard.

He sprinted across the deck and vaulted straight over the edge and into the water, landing a short distance from her. He swam for her, trying to hold her above the waves, but she fought him away. Then he heard a swoosh as a net closed around them, and they were yanked into the air, pursued by a gigantic shark who had been rising beneath them. The shark followed them up and up until they were too high, then it crashed back into the water. Eli looked down and saw that King Apollo had hold of the rope. He lowered them back onto the deck, where Octavia hugged Sanfrass, crying, and Ev'r slapped Eli across the back of his head again, shouting, "Are you trutting crazy?"

As the net was lifted off them, Sanfrass leapt up, her red feather wings dripping wet, and tried again to get over the edge. Eli grabbed hold of her and she smashed him away.

"Let her jump, ungrateful gadfly!" Ev'r said, but King Apollo stepped in and took hold of Sanfrass' arm, and she could do little to resist. He sat her down and crouched in front of her.

"You don't belong in the darkness and it doesn't belong in you. You were born in the light. You're free from that place."

She stared up at his face with her striking silver eyes, crying tears red like blood.

"Land ahoy!" Christy called out.

Eli stood and looked ahead to see forms in the gray distance. He turned to Apollo, but he was looking behind them instead, to where the storm at their backs had blown up and out, racing faster than before. Mordan was coming.

"Prepare for battle," the king said.

"Arm up!" the commander ordered. Everyone ran for the weapons, knowing how little use they'd be against the demons and their king.

Chapter 37
Ev'r

HYDRIA

NORTHERN HALOS (ADRIA SEA)

Ev'r held onto Ismail's back while he hung over the side of the ship, concentrating all his psychic energy, filtering through the augmentor, into urging the sharks to swim faster. She looked toward the land ahead, and then at the black cloud behind them.

"We're not going to make it," she said to Ismail. He glanced back at her, his face wet from the sea spray and eyes bloodshot from effort.

"We need to leave. This won't end well," she said.

"Leave to where, Zara?" he said. "Truthfully, where can we go that the Indemeus X won't eventually take? There isn't any place. That's why all the foreseers are ending themselves and taking their families with them."

Ev'r stared at him. They'd both known this as fact, but neither had said it aloud.

"We've found the king, it's a chance to stop the X. We have to keep fighting until there's no hope, and then we fly," Ismail said.

"Usually when there's no hope, it's because someone is dead," Ev'r told him. "And then it's too late."

"I'm not going to leave you, I promise," he said. "Just stay beside me – in case I need rescuing." He gave his wolfish grin and Ev'r had to smile back.

He turned back to concentrate on the sharks and something struck the boat from the side with incredible force. They were propelled out of the water and catapulted through the sky so fast Ev'r thought they were going to collide with the cliffs, but they fell short and came down catastrophically hard on some rocks just before the shoreline. The ship exploded and Ev'r felt Ismail's arms closing around her as they were thrown, skimming like stones across the water before plummeting into the depths with the waves crashing over their heads.

Ev'r broke the surface gasping, but ducked again immediately as a flying piece of debris almost beheaded her. Lightning sliced the sky and thunder roared inside the demon storm. Everywhere around her she saw gleaming eyes closing in on them.

Feeling a flash of her magics returning to her, she summoned an annihilator curse and threw it at them, driving the demons back as Ismail beat his wings and dragged them out of the water. Ev'r looked down and got a brief aerial view of the disaster.

The king and Diega had found their way to the circle of rocks jutting up from the water, but everyone else was still swimming toward it. A flying lesser demon burst out from grayness and Ev'r slashed the Morsus Ictus, bringing it down.

Another figure rose up beside them and Ev'r saw it was Eli's new friends – the bird woman with big red wings, carrying her spectral friend. The spectral cried out, pointing into the water, and they saw Eli being dragged under. Ismail plunged down, skimming over the surface, and Ev'r grabbed Eli up, cutting off the hands that held him.

They landed on the rocks as the others were dragging themselves up. A demon grabbed hold of Kane's leg and he spat venom into its eyes. Another two went for Silho and she shifted to lightform and drained them both to dust, using the surge of power to smash another away from the group. They all crowded close together, watching the water around the rocks.

"The sword sunk close to here," the king said above the roar of the waves and storm.

"You're an electromagnate, raise it!" Ev'r said.

"He's being augmented," Eli reminded her. "Just like the rest of us. Jude, what about the magnetic function on your arm?"

"I broke it trying to fix SevenM," Jude replied, smashing a lesser sea demon back as it leapt at him.

A massive ratha demon with a glowing red sword and skin hanging off its scales slammed down onto the rocks beside them.

"Mordan-Grieg!" Eli screamed.

The demon king shot its tongue out toward Apollo. Kane reacted, slashing upward with his blade and cutting it off. The ratha ran at them and King Apollo blocked the attack with his sword. They fought, matching each other blow for blow, balancing precariously on the rocks with the waves breaking over them. Christy, Jude, Diega and Eli's two strays ran in to help him, Shawe beating down demons with his bare fists and laughing like a madman. The new spectral was surprisingly skilled, sinking into surfaces and rising up unexpectedly. She melted into a ratha and exploded him from the inside, then became another ratha and turned him against the other demons. Every time the augmentation fluctuated she was booted out of the body and had to try again.

Ev'r felt an increase in her own magics and was throwing curses and enchants, trying to stop Apollo from being overwhelmed, but the ratha kept clawing back up onto the rocks. There were so many of them, and the only advantage was that the rocks were so small only a certain amount could get on at one time.

Silho dropped to her knees on the rock and said, "I may be able to see where the sword fell." She tried to concentrate, then shook her head. "It's so broken. I can't focus!"

Kane put a hand on her shoulder and crouched down with her. They looked at each other for a moment and Silho's breathing steadied. Her fingers sunk through the surface. And then she leapt up suddenly, diving into the demon-infested water.

"Silho!" Kane shouted. He jumped in after her and Ev'r knew they weren't going to make it. Managing to shift into the murk, she sunk down and saw the sword shining up ahead, a magical object inside the drift. Ev'r sped to it and grabbed it up then made for the surface, cutting out there and seeing Kane dragging Silho's limp body back onto the rocks.

A demon smashed down onto Ev'r's head, almost breaking her neck. She lost her grip on the sword and it sank again. Ismail snarled, leaping at the ratha from the rocks. It gored him with one of its poisonous horns and Ismail crashed into the water. Ev'r just managed to grab him as he sank, struggling to keep his head above the surface. The demon came at them again. Ev'r threw a curse that wasn't strong enough to work, but then Eli's winged girlfriend tackled the monster from the side, driving it away.

Ev'r cradled Ismail's head, seeing the scene before her as though in slow motion. The ratha were tightening their circle around the king. Jude was down, Silho was down, fairy girl was down and Eli was hanging on by a thread. Kane and Shawe were fighting back to back, but losing ground. The fight was all but over.

Ev'r knew they should have gone while they had the chance. Now it was too late.

Chapter 38
Ramses

HYDRIA

NORTHERN HALOS (ADRIA SEA)

As the boat crashed out through the mouth of the cavern into *Měthmalay* the sight that met Ramses' eyes was pure madness. There were hideous monsters of the sort that had attacked them in Oas, and other unnatural forms, everywhere – on the rocks, in the water and in the storm-stricken sky. He saw people there too, in the distance, fighting the creatures back. Ramses clung to the side of the boat, shaking as though he was freezing. He couldn't stop it. The fear was overwhelming and beyond his control. The sea surged around them, throwing the boat left to right, savage winds driving them back toward the jagged rocks of the cliff. Anakis leaned his great weight ahead of them, steering them forward.

"Titan!" Ramses heard Harlow shout. "It's him!"

Him. Ramses fought to turn his head and see.

"*Lord King!*" Titan yelled. One of the distant figures paused mid-swing to look their way, and then a monster smashed him down to the ground.

"No!" Harlow leapt overboard and Titan tried to follow her. Anakis grabbed him and threw him back to Ramses, who released his stranglehold on the ropes to grasp onto his cousin. Anakis leapt in after Darro.

"Rams, it's him!" Titan tried to pull out of his grip.

"I know, but you can't swim!" Ramses held onto him tightly. "What about your – powers?"

Titan blinked and breathed to steady himself, a measure of rationality returning to his eyes. He straightened and Ramses struggled up as well, even more frightened of Titan jumping overboard than he was of the water. They saw Harlow had already covered a wide space very quickly, a powerful swimmer even in her armor. Anakis wasn't far behind. Harlow burst up onto the rocks, driving back a mass of creatures. Ramses heard a word screamed out above the howl of the wind. *Draigar!*

The monsters started leaping off the rocks and vanishing beneath the waves, others flying away as fast as they could, leaving just the creatures who had attacked them. Harlow hit the beasts like a whirlwind, but Ramses could see they were healing as rapidly as the first had. She couldn't get to the Almighty, who was fighting from his knees, a huge monster bearing down on him with a jagged red sword and others pressing in all around.

Ramses felt Titan shudder, then a bolt of lightning surged from the sky and struck a group of the beasts, and then another, and another. The wind swept up behind them, hurtling them toward the rocks. From one side Ravana rose up, standing on top of a wave. She lunged across the boat, dragging Titan over and into the water. Ramses shouted out, staring at the spot where Titan had vanished under the surface. He couldn't go after him – he couldn't swim, couldn't even walk now, without his leg. He cast his eyes around frantically and saw a paddle. He snapped it shorter and tied it to what remained of his leg with ropes he cut from the side.

Then he leapt in and sunk. The terror and the memories rushed over him and the cold water closed all around him. He fought for the surface, kicking, propelling himself upward. He broke into the air, gasping. He couldn't see Titan in all the confusion, waves kept smashing him in the face. A mournful cry sounded above him and Ramses saw a big white bird circling above the surface ahead of him. Ramses thrashed his arms and legs and propelled over to where the white peacock flew. He dived under and squinted through the water, seeing Titan's form beneath him struggling with Ravana. He kicked toward them with speed, using the paddle to drive him, and smashed into Ravana from behind. He grabbed her around the neck and wrenched her backward.

Armored figures exploded through the water all around him – Argos, Afton, Ruan, Herra and Sention. The *ata-ajua* had found them. They ripped Titan out of Ravana's claws and started dragging him upward. Ravana tried to follow but Ramses tightened his grip around her neck, holding firm even as the hands of her glooms tore at him from all sides. As they sank through the water Ravana managed to get around to face him, and he could see her face quite clearly as it changed – she was a poor, frightened girl, she was a demented monster, she was a thousand different lovers, she was his sister, she was his mother dragging him down with her, forcing him to pay for her mistakes when he and his sister were just innocent kids. He fought savagely then.

"You're not taking me!" he shouted through the water. "This is my life! You do not own this life! You will not take it!"

He could feel Ravana's water binds trying to wrap around him, and heard the chanting of her glooms, but it kept fading out and Ravana started screaming. Something was blocking her power.

Ramses saw the rocks beneath them, saw their angle and moving shapes. One boulder was balanced precariously. He saw he could push it free. He propelled down to it, ripping the paddle off his leg as they fell. As they reached the rock, he lifted the sharp end of the paddle and drove it through Ravana's chest with force, pinning her to the boulder, then he shoved it off from where it was balanced and it dropped, spinning down and down.

Ramses kicked and grasped toward the surface, but his body was fatigued and they had fallen far down into the salty depths. He couldn't hold his breath any longer. Just as it felt like his chest was crushing in, a heavy rope dropped down through the water and struck him on the head. He seized it.

Ramses was propelled upward, finally breaking the surface, unable to draw air for a few moments, until suddenly his lungs gasped it in. He saw ahead of him to where the *ata-ajua* were dragging Titan out onto rocks. He was fighting them, trying to get back to Ramses. Aron was standing beside them, Vitali lying on the ground at his feet. Aron held the rope that Ramses was clinging to.

Morrison swooped over Ramses, screaming. With a quick smile, Aron hauled him toward the rocks. Ramses rose up on one wave, and as he dropped down he came even with a woman and a man trapped in a sea current, being dragged back toward the cliff. He grabbed onto the woman's shoulder and she almost stabbed him with a black machete, only stopping herself at the last second. She had short hair like a man, and pale green eyes the color of the storm sky above them. She took hold of the rope, dragging the man with her, who was bleeding from the head and starting to stir.

Aron reeled them in until their outstretched hands grasped the rocks, and then he and Titan and the *ata-ajua* dragged them up. From the clifftops above, they heard horses screaming. Ramses looked up to see the forms of Darro's horses, plus his own Arah and Titan's Farahman galloping along the edge, and at the back of them was Grayweather. Ramses' heart lurched – he thought they were about to jump over the cliff, but Titan released a long whistle that meant *stop and stay.*

Ramses turned, searching across the waves to where the Lord King Apollo was still fighting, Darro was still trying to beat the monsters back from him, but they kept coming, kept swelling. Other strangers stood with her, fighting too. He heard Aron curse and whipped back around, fearing the horses had leapt. Ravana had risen up on top of the waves with another of her glooms.

"Trutting sea witch!" Ramses heard the woman they'd dragged in say, speaking an old trade language. Aron hurled his sword at Ravana's form but this time it just passed straight through, as though she was made of water. She started running at them, screaming. The *ata-ajua* crushed in around Titan to protect him.

"We need fire!" the woman yelled.

Ramses remembered how Darro's flames had ripped through Ravana's wall of water. He grabbed at Vitali's pocket as he lay prone and dragged out his "cough medicine" flask.

"Alcohol!" he said. The woman grabbed it and took something from a bag on her back. She took a swig from the flask and then, as Ravana was almost on them, she spat out the alcohol and lit it with her device. The spout of fire struck Ravana's face, driving her back for a moment, but then she was flying toward them again, burning. A streak of lightning drove down from the sky and struck her, first from one side and then another, then a final one exploded her into a giant spout of water that splattered down on them. Ramses heard the woman whispering some words that made Ravana's glooms dissolve. He watched them all vanish down into the water, free from the witch's curse.

"I think we've found our augmentor," the woman said looking at Titan, and nudging her companion, who had managed to sit up. Vitali was stirring as well. Titan stood, staring back toward the Almighty and his grim battle.

"He's humming." Ramses heard the woman speak again. "He's an electromagnate as well." She tried to get closer but Argos blocked her. "There's a sword under the water. It's the only thing that will kill the demon king," she said to Titan, looking over to the huge beast fighting the Almighty. "You can draw it up."

Titan nodded. He held his hands over the waves and Ramses felt the prickling from his cousin's skin surge. All manner of metal started flying up out of the water until a magnificent, gleaming warrior's sword leapt into his hand.

"Harlow!" Titan yelled out and threw the sword, propelling it toward Darro. "Cut him down!"

Harlow caught it and leapt up onto the backs of the other beasts, lunging toward their king. She took off one of his arms, but it grew straight back, and Darro almost tumbled into the water. Anakis grabbed her just in time. The Almighty fended off a blow from the demon king that had been aimed at the giant's neck.

The woman's brow furrowed. "How?" she whispered.

Another voice rang out and they saw a boy jumping up and down on rocks not far from where they stood. "The horns!" he screamed out. "It's his horns!"

"Cut off the horns!" Titan yelled to Darro. The beast had two very long horns on top of his head.

Darro heard. Anakis launched her upward and she dropped down onto the demon king. With a hard swing she chopped off his horns. He released an earth-splitting scream and then Darro took his head. She turned on the other monsters around them, cutting them all down, until those remaining melted backward into the water and retreated. The storm receded.

Chapter 39
Harlow

HYDRIA

ARMEN (CY LASEA)

She found herself back at the beginning, kneeling on the rocks beneath the cliffs of Cy Lasea. Returned, but changed. The sunshine warmed her back and the water lapped at her fingertips. In one hand she clenched a sword and it caught the light, reflecting up toward the heavens. A white bird circled high above, crying out a victory call.

A name etched into the handle of the sword caught Harlow's eye – *Saeed Akeem Arafat Melchoir*. The words rang true in her heart, and she remembered him, the warrior who had paid for her life with his own.

A shadow fell over her and she looked up. The man before her appeared to be the ghost of a person she had once known, but then her eyes found his and she was a child again staring up at a mighty king. He took her arm and helped her to stand, and she was aware of her armor and of everything she was that she shouldn't be.

The Almighty pulled her into his arms, and her fears faded into joy. He lived.

"It's been so dark without you," she whispered.

Chapter 40
Titan

HYDRIA

ARMEN (CY LASEA)

As Harlow delivered the final blow, Titan was already diving into the water and swimming toward her. He'd never been taught, but it felt like a return to something he'd always known. The *ata-ajua* swam around him, Argos at his side. As his hands touched the rocks, someone seized his arm and dragged him up from the water, and he found himself eye to eye with the Almighty. They stared at each other with the same eyes, yet Titan doubted the truth before him. Words formed on his lips but failed, and he started to embrace his grandfather, then stopped and tried to kneel instead, his movements confused, disoriented. The Almighty grabbed him up in his arms, squeezing him so tightly that Titan caught his breath. The Lord King pulled back, holding Titan by his shoulders and giving him a shake, as though to test his strength, as he had when Titan was young.

"Is it you?" Titan heard himself say, his voice rough.

"*Se*," The Almighty confirmed. He touched a hand to Titan's face and said, "My eyes expected to find a boy, but you stand a grown man instead. I never thought I would look upon your face again."

Titan struggled with his emotions, fighting to stay composed. He saw Harlow and Anakis standing behind the Almighty. His eyes met Harlow's.

"Your father?" the Almighty asked him. "He lives?"

"He's well, Lord King," Titan managed.

He saw his grandfather's eyes flash relief, then they looked behind him to where the Storons were helping Ramses climb to them over the rocks. When they stood before the Almighty, Ramses bowed his head, unable to look up in shame over his injury and current state.

Titan moved to his cousin's side and said, "Lord King, Ramses has fought every kind of unnatural for me."

"I saw," the Almighty said. "You have your grandfather's strength. How is Aramasas?"

Ramses swallowed slowly and said, "Forgive me, Lord King, but he has ridden to the blessed plains."

Titan saw another flicker in the Almighty's unwavering stare.

"How?" he asked.

Ramses wiped a hand over his face, and Titan saw he was trembling.

"He died defending ..." His cousin started and then stopped. Around them the ocean hushed and whispered, it crashed against itself, against the rocks, against the sand. The peacock cried out a long, thin note. Titan could taste the drying salt on his lips, mixed with the iron of blood.

"Speak, Ramses," the Almighty prompted him.

"He passed away in a harem house. His heart stopped," Ramses said, then released a shaky breath. "I've been telling a different story for a long time. He deserved better."

The Almighty silently took in the words before asking, "And your father?"

Titan saw Ramses faltering. If Aron Storon wasn't propping him up on one side, he may have fallen.

"Lord King," Titan stepped in. "Warrior Augustus took his own life."

"*Ivar*," the Almighty said, his face hardening. "This is bitter news." He reached out and took Ramses by the arm, helping him to shuffle nearer. He leaned down and spoke close to his face. "After all this loss you're still standing, and you're still fighting. I saw you throw yourself into this sea without hesitation, for your cousin. Ramses of Ohai," he called him, and Ramses lifted his eyes. "*Dobrus*."

It meant literally *good*, but it was the Lord King's blessing, and who the Lord King blessed no man could question.

Ramses exhaled another shaky breath and tears slipped down his face. "Lord King," he whispered.

The Almighty put a heavy hand on his shoulder and his eyes moved to Aron and Vitali standing behind Ramses.

Harlow spoke up to introduce them, "My men. Vitali and Aron Storon, and this is Anakis of Abigar."

The Almighty nodded to each of them and they bowed their heads. Vitali was pale and swaying on his feet.

"He saw you fighting here and jumped right off the cliff into *Mĕthmalay*," Aron said to Harlow.

"You jumped off the cliff?" Harlow asked.

Vitali shrugged and looked away. "Someone had to," he said gruffly.

"He can't swim one bit," Aron added, his smile twitching. "He sank like a rock."

Titan noticed then that the others, who had fought the demons with them, had gathered around. They were strangers – strange strangers, all with an appearance he had never seen nor imagined before, all ragged and bleeding. They had fought hard and had the wounds to prove it.

Titan saw Harlow was staring at one of the strangers, a woman with green eyes remarkably like Harlow's own. Ramses was looking at another of the party, a man with a silver tinge to his skin and eyes bright blue, and, more interestingly, metal arms and legs.

"King Jude of Scorpia," the Almighty said, nodding to the man, and Titan noticed the foreign king's wounds were oozing white blood and healing faster than should be possible.

"King Jude," he greeted him, trying to keep the apprehension out of his voice.

"They are warriors from another world," the Almighty told him. "It is under attack."

The words jarred Titan's memory.

"Lord King. Corinthia is also under attack. All but Theselon have united against us, and Vitor-Petacula has formed an army of Cytisians. All together, we face eight hundred thousand at least," he told his grandfather.

The Almighty's eyes sharpened at the news.

A boy, the stranger who had warned them about the demon king's horns, stepped forward.

"King Apollo, we have to go to Aquais. You're our only hope of finding how to stop the Indemeus X."

The King regarded him. "First we ride for my city. I must see to my people. Then I will tell you everything. The truth of Shah-Jahan."

"How far away is your city?" the boy asked.

"Two sevens from here," the Almighty said, looking up to the cliffs where the horses had gathered.

"Two sevens – as in two weeks?" the boy said. "I don't think we have that long." He glanced back at his group.

"If he stops augmenting, we can fly there," the woman who had fought Ravana with them said, nodding at Titan. "He's blocking our skills. If he stops, we have a craft. We'll get there in hours, not weeks."

The Almighty turned to Titan and he could feel his face heating up.

"I don't know what they mean, Lord King," he said. "I don't know what to stop, or how."

"I will tell you everything," the Lord King reassured him. "For now, we need speed." He placed a hand on Titan's neck, and Titan understood he was going to put him out.

He gave a nod and felt the Almighty squeeze his neck and then he felt himself falling. Harlow's hand clasped his and he heard a word echo out that sounded like *expel*. There was a crack of sound and a flash of light and then he was gone.

Chapter 41
Eli

HYDRIA

CORINTHIA (IRONEYE)

Diega had brought the *Ory-6* down on the plains behind the city of Corinth, out of sight of the hordes gathered at the city gates and the people within. King Apollo had said too much too soon was too much too soon – an aircraft in a place where they hadn't yet discovered one-piece underpants would have blown too many minds.

Apollo himself seemed completely at ease in the *Ory* – looking over the control boards and even taking the steering yoke when Diega offered it. He was a man way ahead of his time. His grandson, Titan, had stayed unconscious until they touched down and then the king had woken him, and his augmentation had cut everyone off again. He was so powerful, but had absolutely no clue how to control himself.

They'd all ridden in from behind the city. The looks on the faces of King Apollo's soldiers and his son, the current king, when they had arrived was something Eli would never forget in all his days – however many he had left. The king there welcomed home not just his father, who had been missing for close to thirty year-cycles, but also his son, who had been feared dead. It was emotional to say the least. The Corinthians were hardened men who didn't show much emotion on the outside, but Eli had muffled-sobbed enough for everyone involved.

Then King Apollo had put on armor and ridden out with his soldiers, greatly outnumbered. But just the sight of him and the sound of his voice, so loud it seemed to shake the air and mountains all around the plains, had sent their enemies into chaos. There was mass retreat, mass rebellion, confusion and terror. They'd turned on each other, and their ranks and ferocity had crumbled.

Eli looked now out across the royal city and the land beyond. It was a beautiful place really, sweeping, majestic, wild and pure, not processed to death like Aquais had been over the eras. Eli was completely unused to seeing a sky that wasn't full of speeding transflyers, and there was a peace to the undisturbed blue. But the place was most definitely barbaric in ways, even in the most civilized areas.

It was a survival-of-the-fittest culture, which was where Shah-Jahan came into it. King Apollo kept his word – as soon as the enemy had been driven back, before he'd even taken off his armor, he told them that Shah-Jahan was not a Dray, he was a Corinthian, the second son of Apollo's son, the current king, Osiris. He'd been born strange, so he'd been taken to the swamp beyond the mountain ranges and left there to die. But Apollo had gone to get him, knowing the baby was not so much deformed as special.

Apollo had already held some knowledge of the possibility of other worlds, other races, and of portals. He'd taken the baby to a woman he knew, a Dray woman, the foreseer, who he'd given refuge at one time, and she'd promised to take him back through to Kullra Fornax and give him sanctuary there. Shah-Jahan had grown up as a Dray, his skill such that he not only blended in but became captain. Eli wasn't sure what that would make him, he could be some kind of shape shifter or mimic or even something else entirely.

And now the Almighty was back. The truth was out, and it was time to go.

But they hadn't been able to leave immediately. Even with Titan knocked out, Silho hadn't been able to raise a portal. She'd burned herself badly during the fight and needed some time to get her strength back. Every day felt endless, but it couldn't be helped. They just had to wait.

Eli watched as a swarm of butterflies flittered past his window, looking like petals floating on the wind.

"It's actually not called a swarm," Eli told Nelly, who was sitting beside him on the window ledge. "It's a kaleidoscope, did you know that?"

She gave a deep, irritated sigh and dropped her head onto her paws. She did not share his fascination with insects and plants.

Eli grinned to himself and looked back out at all the beautiful butterflies. In a way it worried him that he was feeling better than he should, not just because it might mean his brain was quietly plotting a delayed but colossal nervous breakdown, but also because maybe it wasn't. In the past weeks, he'd witnessed and suffered unspeakable horrors, and yet here he was, gazing absently out his window and enjoying the breeze caressing his face.

He should have been a wreck, a sobbing, sitting-in-the-corner-rocking, shaking mess, but he was somehow holding everything together. Even when horrible memories replayed in his mind, they didn't break him like they should. Instead, it felt like they were propelling him, fortifying him – and that just wasn't like him. It was scary to think he was changing in ways that may never be unchanged.

He held out his hand and one butterfly sat on the tip of his finger, flexing stunning sparkling pink wings. He thought of Diamond and her shimmering eyes and glitter bombs and that tutu that left nothing to the imagination, and all her made-up songs, her unstoppable mind and unshakeable love.

"Diamond," he murmured, tears prickling behind his eyes. He wished it weren't true. The butterfly left him and fluttered into the sky. He watched it, until it vanished into the kaleidoscope.

Someone knocked on his door and Eli jumped down from the windowsill to answer it. He found one of Titan's messengers there.

"The Lord Liege wishes to see you."

Chapter 42
Ramses

HYDRIA

CORINTHIA (IRONEYE)

The great city of Ironeye took form from the mists of dawn, beams of light reflecting from the towers to the streets below and out to the Barbarian Plains beyond, now a temporary home for a multitude of liberated Cytisian soldiers. They would be processed and either returned to their lands or taken in, and Ramses could not have been happier that he would not be the one judging who should go where.

A stunning turquoise and orange Dawn Bird landed on the rooftop behind him and sent out its haunting cry into the sky above. From his balcony, Ramses watched as the camps beyond the city started to stir, fires being lit, people stretching out their night's sleep. For many of the Cytisian captives this was the first freedom they'd ever tasted, their first days without pain, degradation or fear, their first hope that they'd be reunited with their loved ones. The Cytisians had always been thought of as mortal enemies of the Halos, but as Ramses studied them now, they looked very much just like Corinthians. They were just men.

He grunted and raised the weighted bar above his head. Not long ago, if someone had suggested he'd be exercising before dawn, he would have laughed, heartily. But here he was. He lowered the bar, paused a moment to dull the burning of his muscles, and then pushed up again. As Titan had said, strength would not return to him as a matter of right, he would have to fight savagely to reclaim it; to battle against the injury of both his body and his mind as though it meant to take his life – and it almost had. If it hadn't been for Aron and Titan ...

The thought disturbed him greatly, but he could not change the past. Titan had told him he needed to accept that he had seen the darkest places of his mind and that he had returned different, in many ways. Titan had said it wasn't an end but another beginning, starting from a place of wisdom and experience that many warriors never attained, and although Ramses still didn't trust himself, he trusted Titan completely. And so he was fighting to win his strength back – and he was talking. As uncomfortable and unnatural as it felt, he, Titan and the other Companions were talking about everything, without censoring anything, and the more they talked, the more they said. It was never easy, but over the past few sevens it had felt like a weight was lifting from his shoulders. Except for now, when he was lifting actual weights from his shoulders. He grunted again and pushed the heavy bar upward.

"Come on!" Chey spoke behind him, stepping out onto the balcony. "I could have done a hundred by now."

Ramses lowered the bar and picked up his crutches, shuffling around to face his cousin, who stood with his arms crossed over his chest and a cocky smile on his face.

"Go on then!" Ramses said. "Stand on one leg and do a hundred. No, actually – starve yourself, drain most of the blood from your body, and *then* stand on one leg and do a hundred. I would bet you couldn't even do one!"

"Is that so?" Chey said.

"It is," Ramses returned.

The two men regarded each other for a moment then they both laughed. Chey came forward and embraced Ramses, thudding him on the back.

"Since when have you risen before dawn?" Chey asked as he pulled back.

"Since I stopped sleeping at all," Ramses said, and Chey clicked his tongue. "Give it some time, brother."

The curtains behind them stirred as Mohan stepped out.

"*Cursil ios,*" Mohan said, embracing Ramses firmly. His eyes went to Ramses' missing leg and then darted away. He kept his head down, hiding his emotion. As expected, Mohan had taken their absence and Ramses' injury the hardest, and he was still suffering. Many times he'd told Ramses that if he could give him his leg he would, and Ramses believed it.

"How's your pain?" Mohan asked him quietly.

"It's not bad at all, brother. Don't be concerned," Ramses assured him, even though it was quite often excruciating. He nodded toward Chey. "He's more painful than the leg."

Mohan gave a shaky laugh and Chey shook his head, grinning. "Sounds like your balls are black now."

"My legs gone but nothing else. Trust me, I'm not going without. Have I told you about the girl at the inn?" Ramses responded.

"What girl at what inn?" Chey asked, already laughing. Ramses took in a breath, ready to tell a greatly elaborated version of the story, but stopped as Hammer, newly shaven, pushed out through the curtain and joined them on the balcony. Prayers started rising from the temples of Ironeye around them, and Hammer's hard eyes dared any of them to mention his face – as though there was really any chance that they wouldn't.

"*Cursil ios*," he said, clasping Ramses' forearm.

Ramses laughed, both at the uncharacteristic courtesy and at Hammer's face. "Either you've finally taken a woman or I still look like death."

Hammer lifted his chin and said, "My business, not yours."

"You missed a spot," Ramses teased him.

Mohan sniffed and wiped his eye and Hammer's brow furrowed. He started to say something but stopped himself, and Ramses saw the ire on his face melt back into something less severe as he regarded his brother.

A clatter of armor sounded behind them and Titan's periphery guard and his *ata-ajua* filed out onto the balcony, with Titan himself stepping out into the open air. The Companions dropped to their knees, with Ramses making it almost a quarter of the way down before Titan said, "Rise, brothers."

He came over, Argos and the *ata-ajua* around him, and announced, "I'm officially married."

They responded with cheers and congratulations.

"What about the wedding?" Chey asked him.

Titan clicked his tongue and said, "The way things stand at the moment, a full ceremony would not be prudent. The Lord King has given his blessing and we've given our oaths. We are married and it is enough."

"The princess is agreeable to this?" Mohan asked.

Titan smiled and said, "She dislikes attention."

Ramses could hear the affection in his voice and it gave him a warm feeling in his chest. Harlow Darro made an extremely unlikely princess, particularly as the whole of the Halos was just now waking up to the fact that she was a woman instead of a man, but Ramses could feel the strength of the bond between her and Titan, and the strength of Darro herself.

"She'll have to move past that," Chey said. "You stand at the center of the Halos and she stands beside you now, as do we."

"*Ivar*," Titan said, in a way that meant he had something more to say and was preparing it. It gave Ramses an uneasy feeling.

"Brothers. I have decided that I will ask the Lord Kings Apollo and Osiris if I may return with the travelers back to their land to fight the demon that threatens us all."

The Companions fell to silence, staring at Titan. Leave when they had just returned home? Go to another world? Just the thought that there was another world was still entirely foreign and unbelievable.

"I do not assume that you will accompany me. If I go, I feel it is unlikely that I will return." His words hit each of them hard, leaving Ramses light-headed. "But I cannot stay here and wait for someone else to fight for us. It is not the warrior way. It is not the righteous path. The Almighty put his life down for me – for all of us. He gave himself up as prisoner so that we would be spared, but things have now changed. The Almighty has confirmed the threat. This demon is real, and it is only a matter of time before he targets Hydria, unless he is stopped. So I must petition the Lord Kings to allow me to go."

"I'm coming with you," Ramses said immediately. "Wherever you go."

To say he wasn't silently terrified and beyond would have been a gigantic lie, but if Titan was going, so was he.

"And I," Hammer said.

"Us as well," Chey answered for himself and Mohan.

Titan looked them over and said, "Thank you, my brothers. I've asked the traveler named Eli to come here to discuss the possibility of us going. I wanted to speak with you first, but there's no point taking it to the kings if it's not physically possible. I'll admit, I do not know how this – change – works."

Titan turned to his Captain of Periphery Guard. "Has he arrived?"

"He's here, Lord Liege."

"Send him in," Titan gave the order and the Captain left the balcony, returning a moment later with Eli, the traveler who had freed the Almighty. He was the only one of the travelers who spoke Corinthian, and what he lacked in pronunciation, he made up with enthusiasm. The others of Eli's group seemed like closed books, soldiers who had seen enough to treat everyone with great mistrust, and Ramses could understand that, but Eli seemed different. He'd met them with an open heart and an open mind, and Ramses had quite taken to him.

"Eli, thank you for coming here," Titan said. Eli appeared surprised to be thanked, and responded, "No, thank you, for asking me. I'm glad to be here, really."

"I want to ask you something."

Eli paused and clasped his hands behind his back.

"Myself, my Companions and my *ata-ajua* – we wish to return to your world with you when you go."

The short soldier's eyes swiveled as he took in the words.

"Is it physically possible? Do you have to be of your race to go through?" Titan asked.

"Yes – I mean no – *no*. You don't have to be of any particular race," Eli said. "I'd have to talk to the boss, but I don't see any reason why he wouldn't agree."

"I have not spoken to your Commander of my wishes yet, however as you know, he has been instructing me on how to control my strength with —"

"With the illusionist enchant," Eli finished. "He said you're making fast progress."

"He's a strong teacher," Titan said graciously. "So it's decided, I will speak with the Lord Kings and with their permission we will accompany you back to your land."

"If it's still there," Eli said, and Ramses saw a heaviness fall on the short man's shoulders.

"If it still stands," Titan agreed. "Is there any change to Silho's condition?"

"I saw her last night. She's making progress too. She's the only one who can really know when she's ready to try. She said maybe a few more days, maybe less. She's trying her best, but she can't control her healing."

"I understand," Titan said.

"Speaking of healing, how are you feeling?" Eli asked Ramses in a direct manner that would normally be considered disrespectful, but coming from Eli it caused him no offense.

"Still some pains," Ramses answered with caution, knowing Mohan was listening.

"I'll take a look," Eli said, coming forward and crouching down beside Ramses' leg without waiting for Ramses to agree to it. "Just hold your skirt up," Eli said, using the feminine version of the word and making Ramses snort with laughter. Hammer looked outraged, but Titan gave the gesture for leniency.

The traveler examined Ramses' leg, touching it without reserve or ill-ease. Ramses knew many of the warriors avoided looking at his leg or touching him for fear of the bad luck it would bring, and though startling at first, it actually felt comforting that Eli did not share this concern.

"It's healing nicely," Eli confirmed. "You know, if you come back to Scorpia, if it's still there, I can fit you with a prosthetic or a graft, or even grow your leg back, if I can get enough movement from your nerves."

"This is truly possible?" Titan asked, watching Eli carefully.

The short soldier stood up and said, "Definitely. Jude's arms and legs are all prosthetics."

Ramses nodded. He had witnessed the strength of the silver-skinned man's unnatural limbs.

"All Ar Antarians have prosthetics. It's part of their culture. And grafting and regrowth is very common. It's not difficult, except for brains ... and wings." Eli dipped his eyes for a moment, then added, "If Scorpia's there, then it won't be a problem."

Ramses felt a ragged, torn and thin sort of hope form inside him. Was this truly possible?

"We shall see." Titan brought the conversation to a close. "Now I must speak with the kings."

"And I'll go talk to the Commander," Eli told them. He hurried away without being properly dismissed, leaving Hammer with more furrows in his brow than he'd ever had before.

Ramses saw Titan giving the slightest of smiles. He went for the door and the *ata-ajua*, the Companions and periphery guards fell into step – a significantly slower step, to allow Ramses to navigate the staircase with his crutches, but he did it, with a hundred thousand thoughts running through his mind. Halfway down the staircase, Ramses felt a chill on his back and looked over his shoulder. He saw August standing at the top of the steps. His father gave a smile, then vanished into all the rays of light that streamed in through the window.

Chapter 43
Titan

HYDRIA

CORINTHIA (IRONEYE)

Every person could have countless paths in life, each decision taking them down a slightly or very different road. Titan could see where these roads would lead for almost everybody, but not for himself. He could not see his own pathways, so had always walked in darkness, but now he felt as though he had a light to follow, to look to, wherever he went. He saw her standing at the doors to the king's chamber, with Anakis and the Storon brother at her side. Harlow. She was his light. The Almighty had said that so much of life was spent stumbling in the darkness of uncertainty, but that when he was despised by hateful men he knew he was walking the righteous path. But for Titan, being loved and wanted by a person like this made him sure he was facing the right way, stumbling still, but looking right. He had told Harlow this the night before, and the words had taken her by surprise. She hadn't really known how to respond. For once. The thought brought a smile to his heart, but he kept a straight face as he ascended the steps with the Companions and his *ata-ajua*. They stopped in front of Harlow.

"My wife," Titan greeted her. She was wearing partial armor, her calteus and a short green tunic, which suited her well, but he could see from the suppressed laughter in Aron Storon's eyes and the irritation on Anakis' face that the brothers had been mocking her for it. He'd had to accept that their friendship far predated his relationship with Harlow, and would allow some leniency for that, but not too much.

"You look beautiful," he assured her. Aron stifled a snort, and the bird on his shoulder copied the sound. The Companions all looked uncomfortable at his display of affection, suddenly finding the sky and everything around them of great interest.

"*Ivar*," Titan said to them. "If you can't express emotion to your own wife who can you express it to?"

"Forgive us, Lord Liege," Mohan said.

"We've never heard you call any woman beautiful before," Chey added.

"Is that so?" Titan said. "What a shame I've held so many words in for so long."

On impulse he leaned forward and kissed Harlow on the lips, not too lingering a kiss, just a kiss, but it sent the discomfort of the group shooting skyward. Vitali looked like he'd just been kicked in the back, Hammer seemed frozen to the spot. Ramses grinned and Anakis gave Titan a look, as if to say he hadn't forgotten the past and that when it came to Harlow Darro, Titan should tread carefully from now until eternity. Harlow herself was as composed as ever. She put a hand on his shoulder and said in that way she had, that at first he'd loathed and now had come to appreciate, "If your goal was to create the most awkward meeting of all time, you've succeeded."

"My goal was to show my affection for my wife," he said.

"Why? What have you done?"

Titan smiled at her suspicion but then sobered. "We're here for a reason."

"I assumed that," Harlow said, wary. "No one comes before the Lord King without a reason."

"Quite true." Titan paused a moment to compose his words. "I will petition the Lord Kings to accompany the travelers back to their land."

He watched her face as he said the words, but she gave away very little.

"And us as well?" she asked, an edge coming into her eyes that made Titan see there was only one answer to the question.

"I wanted to leave the decision to you, but I knew you, of all people, would understand my reasoning."

A battle raged across Harlow's face. They had just been reunited with the Almighty after all these long years. To leave now seemed like madness.

After a while she lowered her head and said softly, "I do understand. The war's not won."

Titan nodded. That was exactly as he felt.

The great doors to the Lord King's chamber opened and Quintus appeared.

"Lord Liege. Companions. Princess and companions. You may enter," he said.

Titan took Harlow's arm and they followed Quintus in, walking down the red carpet past the armor of all the fallen kings of Titan's line. The empty space where the Almighty's armor should have been but had never stood was now closed in, because he yet lived. Titan could feel everyone noticing and it gave him a tingling feeling across his skin.

Quintus announced them and they filed into the Lord King's private meeting chamber. Titan was surprised to see only his father, Lord King Osiris and his *ata-ajua* there. The Almighty was absent, as were the Lord King's Companions and advisors.

Osiris beckoned them forward.

"Speak," he said to Titan, and by the way the word sounded, Titan sensed his father already knew what he intended to ask.

"Lord King, it appears that soon the travelers will return to their land." He paused, feeling the ferocity of his father's eyes burning into his face. "And I would ask, Lord King, humbled before your great wisdom, to send me, my companions and the princess to fight the demon." Titan could hear everyone breathing heavily around him. He kept his eyes on his father, with his powerful arms resting on the backs of his marble stallions.

Osiris gave a nod. "You have my blessing to go. You must seek the Lord King Apollo's blessing as well. Go and do so now."

"Yes, Lord King," Titan said, a mix of emotions sweeping through him. He wanted to say more to his father. He wanted his father to say more to him, but as the silence dragged on, he realized neither of them were able to say anything. He felt Harlow's hand on his arm, and let her guide him around and up to the doors of the chamber, where he stopped to look back. The Lord King was sitting, looking ahead of him, contemplative. He didn't see them leave.

* * * * *

Titan knew where to find the Almighty. They had always shared a favored place – the garden. The original garden atop his quarters had been completely destroyed by Ravana, but it had been rebuilt. Truthfully, it did not have the same feeling, but Titan imagined that one day it would be just as beautiful, maybe more so – many bad memories had been washed away. As he and Harlow reached the top of the staircase and moved out into the garden, Farahman, Winta and Naro trotted over to greet them. The horses were whickering in a certain insistent way and walking close enough to be their shadows. Titan knew they sensed that a change was about to happen, and they didn't want to be separated again. Titan patted Farahman's neck, he had no intention of leaving him behind this time. They walked together to the center of the garden until they saw the Almighty up ahead, looking up into a quercus tree, where the white peacock was perched among the pink and red flowers. Apollo's wounds were starting to heal. He was still favoring one leg, but every day brought further healing. Titan felt Harlow's hand squeezing his arm. The Lord King sensed them coming and turned. They bowed before him and he said, "Rise."

He looked them over, then put a hand on Harlow's cheek.

"This color suits you well," he said. "As does your armor."

"I said the same, Lord King, and it made everyone profoundly uncomfortable," Titan told him.

The Almighty gave a nod and said, "You said it. That is what matters."

Harlow lowered her eyes and Apollo's face hardened.

"Your path is leading you both to a new land?"

"With your permission," Titan said, hardly surprised he already knew as well.

"You have it," Apollo said without pause.

"We don't want to go," Harlow looked up. She took hold of the Almighty's hand and he held hers tightly.

"I know you do not," the Lord King replied. "And I do not wish to see you go."

"There's little choice," Titan said.

"There is always a choice," Apollo responded. "And you are both choosing bravery and sacrifice. The warrior's choice. Even when you were the littlest of girls," he said to Harlow, "I knew you would grow up to be strong, to fight battles and save lives. I saw it in your path so I taught you all I could in the time we had."

"Everything I know of any worth came from you," Harlow said.

"You honor me," Apollo said. "You both do."

Apollo put a hand on Titan's shoulder. "I belong here. Your father belongs here. But Tarrus, you belong to a much different place. What you can do is more than I – more than any king of our line or any person of this world. Find your brother. Keep us all from being dragged to Acheron."

Titan felt the heaviness of his grandfather's words setting solid in his chest.

"And while you are gone, we will be riding across the Halos to bring justice to Gideon, Petacula, Gorse and Maneam Nazar." The Almighty looked down at Harlow. "Your maps will serve us well to dig them out. They have escaped nothing. And then when you have fought, and you have won, find your way back here. I will be waiting, and so will your father."

Titan felt a stinging behind his eyes. "I wanted to say much to him, but I said nothing."

"He knows," the Almighty said. "And he's not disappointed. The world is not what we thought it was and

444

change comes difficult for men like us, made of iron." He hugged them both closely against him. "Take care of each other. I'll tell you a last truth. Before I was taken, I had intended to return Harlow to Corinth. I intended you two to be betrothed early, married later, and from all the madness that became of that dream, you found each other, and now you are together. Don't let anything tear you apart."

Chapter 44
Eli

HYDRIA

CORINTHIA (IRONEYE)

The commander had agreed to the Titan, Harlow and a select group of their people coming when they jumped over to Scorpia, or at least attempted to. Eli found himself continually, almost obsessively, reminding himself and others that there was no certainty in what they would find. It was meant to keep his hopes and expectations down.

"Not that it's helping with that one little bit," he said to Nelly as he hurried along another marble hallway, trying not to look as completely lost as he felt. A messenger had come to tell him that Silho needed to see him, and he'd said he would take himself to her room, that he knew exactly where to go. And now his ill-deserved confidence had gotten him lost somewhere in this luxurious maze of stone, tapestry and gold that all looked confusingly similar. He stopped and looked one way and then the other, sure but not certain that he'd already run down this hall several minutes ago. He decided to keep going anyway. As he reached the end of the corridor, a face pressed out from the marble and Octavia pushed out of the wall and into his path. Her body and face held the stone effect for a moment longer before shifting back to her usual appearance. Sanfrass stepped around the corner and Eli felt butterflies in his stomach, a whole kaleidoscope of them. He thought for a second of saying something about that, maybe trying to make a joke, but so far every attempt at humor with Sanfrass had ended with her punching him in the face, so he decided against it.

Sanfrass' beautiful silver eyes locked onto his face, wary still, but not as angry anymore.

"We heard the Corinthians are coming back to your world," Octavia said in her whispery voice. "We're coming as well." Eli heard, but it took him a moment to register. He thought it had already been decided that they would stay in Corinth. He wanted Sanfrass with him, he wanted to stay together, but he wanted more for her to stay safe. And the same went for Octavia.

"We can fight," Sanfrass said with her heavy accent, seeing his reluctance.

"I know, but we don't know what we'll be facing, or if Aquais is even still there."

"We don't belong here," Octavia said. "We belong with you."

Her words gave him a warm buzz inside and he realized it had to be their choice. He had to give them that, just like with Ismail after he had been a prisoner for so long. No matter what, it had to be their decision.

"It's your call," he told them.

"Then we're coming," Sanfrass said.

Eli saw they were all reflected in the shiny marble wall beside them. The way they were standing made it look like Sanfrass' wings were his own, stretching out on either side of him, making him look whole again. It felt like a good sign, either that or misplaced false hope that would eventually lead to disappointment and probably death. Eli chose to believe it was a good sign.

They turned at movement behind them and saw Ev'r and Ismail heading down the corridor. Their bruises were turning yellow and their stitched cuts closing up.

"Snacksize! We've been following you all over the place!" Ev'r called out to him. "Where are you even going?"

"I've been trying to find Silho's room, but I may have gotten lost."

"May have?" Ev'r said, coming to stand beside him. "Her room is way over the other side."

"Ah," Eli said. Ev'r shook her head and gave him a very light shove. It was meant to be playful, or as playful as Ev'r got anyway, but Octavia and Sanfrass bristled. Octavia's eyes glowed and Sanfrass shook out her wings loudly. Ev'r eyed Sanfrass, who eyed her back. Ismail looked like a wolf who had detected an unpleasant scent. Eli quickly intervened.

"Why were you following me?" he asked Ev'r.

"It's time to fly," she said. "Silho's ready."

A feeling ran through Eli like a long cold eel slithering through his stomach.

"Well," he said, and turned in a circle three times before he could stop himself. "I think everything I'm taking is already on me."

He felt down his Corinthian-style tunic and touched Nelly in one pocket and his sapphire blade from Bled in the other, along with various other odds and ends.

"Let's go then," Ev'r prompted him. "Everyone's meeting now."

"Sanfrass and Octavia are coming with us," Eli told them.

Ev'r glanced at the pair again and said flatly, "Great."

"Do you need to pack your things?" Eli asked the two women.

"Belongings are meaningless," Sanfrass told him.

"Okay," Eli said. "Good for traveling light, I guess."

Ismail make a very canine sound in his throat.

Despite the divide between them, they walked together through the palace of Ironeye and out into a central courtyard, where they found the rest of the group. Diega stood beside Jude, looking keyed up and more than ready to make the jump back to Alejan. Jude had SevenM in a bag on his back. His face was composed but there was a sheen of sweat across his forehead. He exchanged a glance with Eli and nodded. The boss stood with Christy Shawe.

The commander had made some movement toward conversation with Silho over the last while. She'd been in pretty rough shape, which had seemed to soften the commander up, to a certain extent. It was the complete opposite to Shawe, who had taken to farting loudly every time Diega tried to talk to him. And while the ability to fart on cue deserved some appreciation, it really wasn't helping their relationship.

Silho was the last to enter behind Eli. Her eyes were very serious and her face looked drawn and pale.

"Glad you could finally make it," Diega snapped at her.

Silho exhaled a blast of fire, making Diega lunge to one side.

"Are you trutting crazy?" Diega shouted, leaping back to her feet.

"Yes," Silho said. "I am. Keep your comments to yourself and fall in line."

Eli saw Ev'r was smiling. Diega managed to stay quiet and everybody else obeyed, including Sanfrass and Octavia.

"She's really not crazy," Eli said to them, giving a little laugh. "She's a very sweet person."

They looked at him as though he was the crazy one.

"Are you well enough for this?" the commander asked Silho as they moved up the stairs to the main meeting hall of the palace.

"I have to be," she said. "Time's running out – maybe it's already too late."

They walked out into a lavish waiting area with a vaulted glass ceiling looking up into the skies of Corinthia. One of the king's men was waiting there, and he headed through a pair of doors to announce them in one by one.

Warrior Eli Anklebiter of Ufftown sounded so very ridiculous in such a serious setting that Eli almost started laughing as he entered the grand hall, but the sight of Apollo the Almighty stopped him. Under Apollo's stare Eli no longer felt ridiculous, he felt bigger and taller than he ever had, and he remembered everything they'd survived together. He walked down the steps to where the others were gathered beside Titan and his men, and Harlow with her men. They all had their horses with them. Ramses had two – a brown and a gray. The commander had explained to them that no one really traveled via horse in Scorpia, and Titan had explained back that it wasn't about travel. They had a bond with their animals that meant separation was not an option.

Speaking of bonds, Harlow's giant bodyguard had become very fond of Nelly, and Eli had become very fond of him. He'd told Anakis about all the different sorts of gargantuan-breeds in Aquais. He wasn't going to be alone anymore – depending on what was left when they got back. Anakis looked at Eli, and Eli patted his pocket to assure him that Nelly was riding along. Together they all stood before Kings Apollo and Osiris and a large gathering of Corinthian warriors and guards, waiting for Apollo to speak.

"Everything remains the same and everything has changed." All eyes were fixed on the Almighty. "We now face an enemy beyond any we have ever faced. Not just Hydria, but the entire universe and all its worlds stand at war. These warriors before us came from another place, to which they must return. They are strangers to us, and us to them, but all who walk the righteous path are one, all who walk the righteous path are brothers." The whole room joined in with his last sentence.

"And our light goes with them, our beloved sons and the pride of our hearts." His eyes went to Titan and there was silence for several moments. "Our fate rests with you. Go now with our blessing."

He nodded to Titan, who turned to Copernicus.

"Repeat the words," the boss told him. "Take control."

Titan lowered his head, concentrating, as Silho walked away from the group, all the way down the hall to where there was a large clear space. She stood in the center of it, closed her eyes and whispered the words to open the portal back to Aquais.

"In my mother's house are many mansions."

The portal light blazed up and Silho vanished through herself. Eli saw the boss's control momentarily falter and emotion cross his face. To their credit, none of the gathered warriors even flinched, despite portal jumping being way outside of their belief system. He did hear Harlow, right beside him, catch her breath as Silho disappeared. He'd found Silho's cousin to be entirely formidable, but she also seemed to have a gentler side, just like Silho. The two women, believing for so long that they were the last of their kind, had started to form a cautious friendship.

The long moments stretched on, with all of them staring at the place where Silho had stood. Eli felt like he could hear time passing, the slowest it ever had. His stomach gave a long, low flatulent blast that echoed up into the lofty regal height of the hall through the agonizing silence.

The light blazed back and the air ripped open, and Silho jumped through.

"It's there," she said.

Eli almost collapsed. Jude hugged him from the side. Scorpia was still standing. There was still time to find Shah-Jahan, still time to stop the Indemeus X. The relief in the air was tangible, magical even.

With a final glance toward the kings, Titan led the group over to Silho. Apollo and all the warriors stood to honor their departure.

"Ready?" Ev'r whispered to Eli.

"Not in the least," he replied, and she smiled.

The portal lights flared and Eli felt himself soaring, as though he was flying.

Acknowledgments

Thank you Joel Naoum. Thank you for giving me and my stories a chance. I'll feel forever grateful to have worked with such a brilliant publisher. A million thanks also to all the team at Momentum, especially the wonderful Patrick Lenton.

Enormous gratitude to my fantastic editor, Vanessa Lanaway. Thank you also to my agent Jo Butler for your ongoing support.

To all my incredible friends and family for your love and reassurance, and to the whole crew of Momentum writers, most especially Amanda Bridgeman and Nathan M. Farrugia.

To the loves of my life, Joey and Danny.

To my brother, for always being there and my wonderful mum, my rock through everything.

And finally thank you to everyone who has read my books. This is for you.

www.ingramcontent.com/pod-product-compliance
Lightning Source LLC
Chambersburg PA
CBHW030755260626
47169CB00001B/67